Secret of the Snow Leopard

John C. Robinson

LOST
COAST
PRESS
Fort Bragg, California

Secret of the Snow Leopard
Copyright © 1999 by John C. Robinson

For information, or to order additional copies, contact:

Lost Coast Press
155 Cypress Street
Fort Bragg, CA 95437

Phone: (707) 964-9520
Fax: (707) 964-7531

Library of Congress Catalog Card Number: 98-067918

ISBN Number: 1-882897-29-3

Book production by Cypress House
Cover art by Ken Michaelsen
Cover design by Colored Horse Studios
Printed in the United States of America

First edition

2 4 6 8 9 7 5 3 1

SECRET OF THE SNOW LEOPARD

Acknowledgments

I wish to thank my mother, whose encouragement throughout the years was a limitless source of motivation. I also wish to thank R. A. Leacock for his initial vision, Nancy Cunningham for her view of the world, and Karen Raftery for her insightful review of this manuscript.

Contents

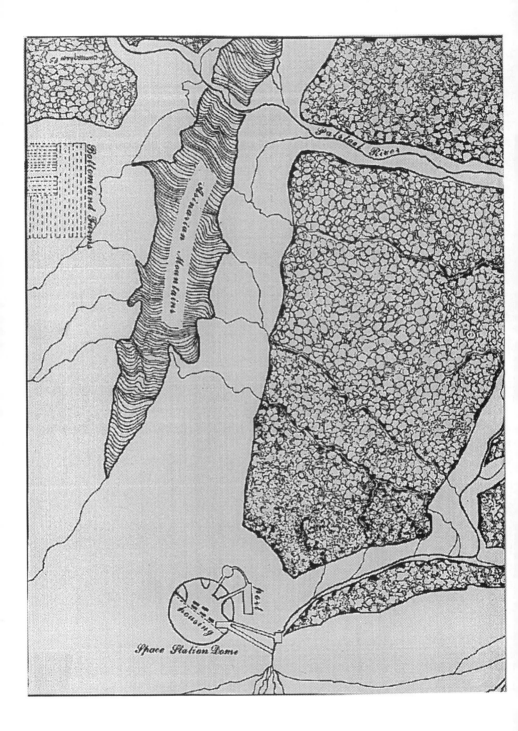

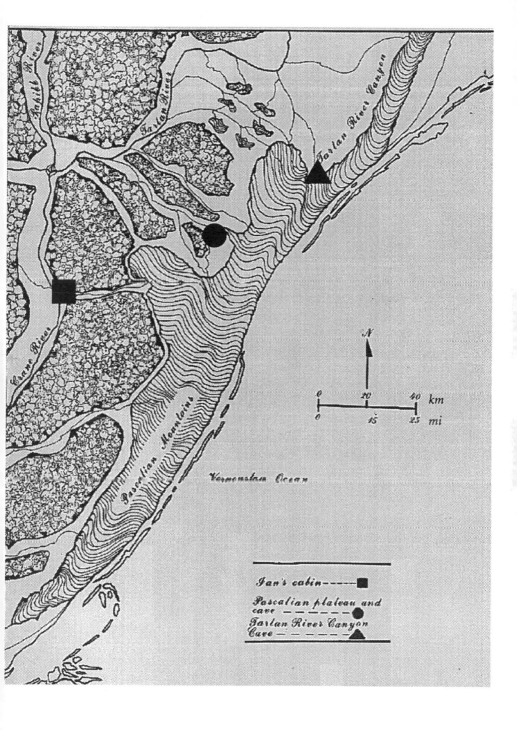

N

| 0 | 20 | 40 | km |
| 0 | 15 | 25 | mi |

Zahtl River

Jartan River

Jartan River Canyon

Cave River

Pascalian Mountains

Vermonslan Ocean

Jan's cabin — — — ■

Pascalian plateau and
cave — — — — ●

Jartan River Canyon
Cave — — — — ▲

Cast of Characters

■■■■■■■■■■■■■■■■■■■■■■
■■■■■■■■■■■■■■■■■■■■■■

EARTH CHARACTERS

Gregory Torrden, 2022–2117. Founder of Torrden Enterprises Inc.

Carl Torrden, 2058–2102. Son of Gregory Torrden; he and his wife died in a mysterious trans-car accident in 2102.

Paul Torrden, 2094–2178. Grandson of Gregory Torrden and current C.E.O. of Torrden Enterprises Inc.

Sam Gray, 2042–. Vice President and Primary Assistant in charge of operations at Torrden Enterprises Inc.

Julie Torrden, 2096–2178. Paul Torrden's wife.

Michael Torrden, 2134–2178. Son of Paul and Julie Torrden. Born on the *Stranahan,* he eventually becomes a member of the ship's crew.

Sammy Lassiter, 2096–2184. A camera-man.

Annah Striton, 2100–2178. Chief T.E.I. animal behaviorist. She later marries Sammy Lassiter.

Faye Lassiter, 2136–2182. Daughter of Sammy Lassiter and Annah Striton. She marries Michael Torrden.

Ian Torrden, 2169–. Son of Michael Torrden and Faye Lassiter. He is born on the *Stranahan* and becomes a colonist on Refander.

Brevin Johnson, 2100–2186. Chief medic officer on the T.E.I. staff, in charge of administering veterinary care to the snow leopards.

Laura Teltor, 2098–2182. A doctor aboard the *Stranahan.* She marries Brevin Johnson.

Jase Johnson, 2136–. Son of Brevin Johnson and Laura Teltor. He continues his father's work aboard the *Stranahan,* but later expands his profession as a medical doctor after becoming a colonist on Refander.

Liraah, 2170–. Daughter of Jase Johnson. She is born on the *Stranahan* and eventually becomes a colonist on Refander.

Sorian, 2092–2183. A guard aboard the *Stranahan*. He eventually becomes a Refander colonist.

REFANDER CHARACTERS

Josef Riverst. Commander in chief of the Refander colony world.

Lieutenant Richard Rielick. Second in command of the Refander colony world.

Baronhart Dietrich. Head of Security and Weapons on Refander.

Paula Witkor. A sociologist serving as the Economics and Public Relations Advisor on Refander under Josef Riverst.

Jakob Nicholiason. A farmer in the lower farmlands of Refander.

Lieutenant Sherry Kowlper. A young staff officer.

Captain Derek Gloid. Leader of Refander's combat shuttle fleet.

LORTAN CHARACTERS

Lon-Kyle. Vahrsta-Hd of the Whertos Warrior Force.

Leor-Kli. A member of the Vahrsta council on Whertos.

Ri-Torn. A member of the Vahrsta council on Whertos.

Si-Worln. A member of the Vahrsta council on Whertos.

Ten-Shun. A member of the Vahrsta council on Whertos.

Sren-Sol. A Lortan guard.

Lar-Modi. A Lortan guard.

Lorn-Tator. A famed Lortan warrior.

Brin-Loki. Deceased Lortan scientist. Inventor of the Brin-Loki Instrument.

MANDAR CHARACTERS

Brisb. Foremost leading scientist on Ekelon.

Elda. Daughter of Brisb.

Forj. A Mandar guard.

Stahl. A Mandar guard.

Prologue

The Sixteenth New World Launch had taken off from Earth several years ago. Aboard the large star ship there were nearly 900 crew and passengers. As this huge vessel neared the outer reaches of the solar system, it prepared for its first Hyper Leap, which would propel it towards its ultimate destination — a new star system that would perhaps take as many as 50 years to reach. In that time, many aboard the space ship would probably die, but many more would also be born; and the new planet to which they were en route would, theoretically, provide yet another new beginning-the sixteenth new beginning, in fact — for the human race. However, this one Launch would be different from all those that had preceded it, and from all those that would follow it...

It had been the star charters who noticed it first — a relatively stationary object of unknown origin and mass. Initially, it had been considered an asteroid, but as they drew nearer, they were able to confirm that the object was not of natural origin. The Captain asked questions, and he got answers: only seventy-two hours outside of the projected flight path, the star charters had said — a chance of a life time!

Nearly 48 hours later, the scientists aboard the Sixteenth confirmed that the object they were approaching was indeed what would probably be called a space ship — except, this was no ship that any human had ever built. Its position had not changed since it had first been discovered and the Captain, now hopeful that the inspection of the object would perhaps be uneventful, approved a closer approach. On the third day, they drew alongside of the alien craft. The vessel's most striking feature was its color: a rich ebony, that seemed almost to glisten all along its surface. It was roughly cylindrical in shape, with the apparent distal end being somewhat wider than the "front" of the craft.

For nearly an entire day, they studied this alien artifact, noting in exquisite detail the geometry of its design. The engineers aboard the Sixteenth speculated how the strange vessel was powered, and whence it had come. Many photographs were taken. However, in time, the novelty of the discovery began to wear off. When the midnight patrol shift finally came on, the scientists who had spent nearly 20 hours studying the mysterious craft feverishly discussed their theories about space travel and other life forms before retiring to their quarters for some much needed sleep.

It was all a dream.

A blinding flash of light. Round, and around. A pit of nothingness — no motion. Silent. They were all silent. I miss them but, who are they? Ceasing to think, ceasing to think. Now, there is the star ship, our star ship, the Sixteenth New World Star Ship. It's big! A woman, and a man — smaller ones. Who are they?

It was all a dream.

The first sign that something spectacular had happened came near the end of the midnight shift, when the Captain was wakened from his dream by his senior staff. The scientists had resumed their inspection of the alien craft and wanted more time to study it. When the Captain asked why, his crew told him about the dream he'd had — *his* dream. Dozens of people were reporting the same dream. It had to be an attempt at communication!

The ship's officers were put on a state of heightened alert. The Captain agreed to give the scientists another day to study the alien vessel. At first, time seemed to pass quickly. More sketches and drawings were made of the strange ship. Conversations fed on rumors as more and more crew and passengers gathered at the portal windows of the Sixteenth New World Launch to gawk at the alien craft.

Another dream.

A blinding flash of light. Round, and around. A pit of nothingness — no motion. Silent. The gray beings were humanoid in shape — they talked to one another, but never spoke. Loneliness. Ceasing to think, ceasing to think. This is…death? Now, there is the star ship, my star ship, the Sixteenth New World Star Ship. It's big! Alongside the gray being is a woman, and a man — smaller ones. Who are you? Leaving… Ceasing to think, ceasing to think… Who are you?

It was all another dream. When the Captain came to, he was still sitting in his chair, next to the helmsman's station. Had he just been dreaming? Looking around at the other crew members, he saw nothing out of the ordinary. Could he have been the only one dreaming — a waking dream? Was that why he felt so tired...and afraid?

Hours suddenly seemed like days to the Captain. When his drowsiness grew too strong for him to ignore any longer, he brought the investigation to an abrupt end. Then, before returning to his quarters, he ordered his staff to interview all of those crew and passengers who could remember their dreams. This report, along with a summary of the entire encounter with the alien ship, was transmitted back to Earth as the Sixteenth New World Launch began to increase its velocity en route to a rendezvous with its original flight path.

The crew was still spreading rumors about the Captain's highly unusual decision to sleep during the middle of his watch when the first medical alarm went off...

The epitome of an endless effort is itself without end.
— *Gregory Torrden (2022-2117)*

Chapter 1

■■■■■■■■■■■■■■■■■■■■■■
■■■■■■■■■■■■■■■■■■■■■■

Interview

Part 1. (15 October 2124)

Sammy Lassiter, a cameraman, trained his eyes on the three men seated at the long metal table. At the junction of the optic nerve axon and retina in each of his eyes, tiny micro electrodes sent the image impulses received from the special retinal receptors to the neural electro-sensor, a small plate which had also been surgically embedded into the depths of his cranium. From the sensor, by way of delicate wires interwoven along his left arm, the now interpreted impulses travelled to a socket in the palm of his left hand. In that same hand he also carried the camera-man's best friend: the Camera Pack, a device no larger than the average hand calculator. It, too, was plugged into the socket in his left hand. With its built in microphone, microelectronic memory chips, powerful aerial transmitter, and its direct link to the optic nerves of its carrier, the Camera Pack was able to simultaneously telecast and record a virtually endless array of news breaking events.

It took guts to be a camera-man, what with surgeons tampering with the optic regions of your brain and everything. Sammy had the guts. It took great peripheral vision to even qualify for the job. Sammy had about the best peripheral sight to be found. He was also exceptionally tall.

Drawing closer, Sammy peered over the heads of the other reporters who had been fortunate enough to get in front of him when the meeting had begun only minutes before. His thick, dark hair reflected the lights from the ceiling lamps and drew attention to his long, narrow face. The pale, unmarked walls of the small room seemed to accent the tension that was present at a subconscious level but gaining strength with each passing minute.

Paul Torrden, noticing Sammy's eagle-like stare, gestured at him, saying, "Why do they have to be here? Who let them in?"

Jerul Scalos waved it off. "They're only recording — nothing's being televised at the moment. Don't worry, you'll get your twenty-four hours worth of privacy. But, why do you even care? The people will hear all about it anyway. What makes you think we can schedule a space for you on any of the next four flights at this late date, Mr. Torrden?"

Paul glanced at the reporters again. Those eyes...the eyes of the camera-men: they seemed to catch his every move.

Paul's medium frame was upstaged by his clean-shaven, bald head and piercing, steel blue eyes. These features made him an instantly recognized figure wherever he went. And as the current head of Torrden Enterprises Incorporated, he knew that he was frequently featured in the news. He grimaced, then turned back to Scalos. "Sir, I know how you feel about T.E.I., what with all the trouble in the past, but this is more of a moralistic issue than a political one. I think things will be clearer if looked at in that way."

"Hey, Torrden, I don't feel this is a political or a moralistic issue. I think this whole thing is a piece of garbage; and that's with a capital 'G'. The planets to which we are sending our citizens probably already have native animals. Why do you want to take existing Earth species there? Hopefully, not to gain admission by way of a special cargo shipment.

"Why don't you apply just like everyone else? If you're qualified, we'll let you go."

Paul shook his head. "In other words, Mr. Scalos, you're saying the people will have everything they want on these new worlds? Hasn't it ever occurred to you that such a thing — a utopian atmosphere — has not, and never will, occur?"

Scalos leaned forward in response to Paul's pointed question. Several of the veteran reporters caught that movement and made a mental note of it — it was not often that Jerul Scalos appeared frightened by another man's words.

"But never mind that," Paul continued. "I and my colleagues at T.E.I. have been working hard on this project — an endeavor which is now three-quarters of a century old. I can personally tell you that, although we've branched out and expanded our scope of studies and operations, what my grandfather started is not yet complete. We must not be forced to stop in the middle. That's why we need a new place, preferably a new and virtually uninhabited world, where we'll be able to explore the potential of this particular study and follow all of the leads we've discovered so far to their rightful conclusions."

"And what's stopping you from completing it here? Are you aware that you'll most likely be long dead by the time any ship that leaves in the near future, even this day, for that matter, reaches its destination? You're sticking your neck out for people of the future, people who may not wish to support your experiments."

"There you go again," Paul retorted, visibly disturbed. "When will you ignore your Utopian dreams? What the hell do you think we're shipping people out to new worlds for, anyway? It'll still be another five to ten years before the first Tech Crews get to their destination and start the preparations for the later arrivals! Hell, the people we're sending out now won't even know if a planet will be ready for them until they or their descendants arrive. Now, I ask you, Mr. Scalos, why all the risks? We both know the answer."

Unnoticed, the reporters efficiently made a mental note to emphasize that last statement in their reports.

"In other words, Mr. Torrden, after you have plagued the government here for so many years, and thinking that your fun may soon come to an end, you have elected to hop to some other world and begin again...no, I can't have that."

Paul leaned forward. "Your biased opinions are beginning to —"

"Yes? Continue." Scalos allowed himself a fat, pompous smile.

At that moment Monte Demarest, the second government official, intervened, breaking the silence which he had kept throughout the meeting.

"Ah, Mr. Torrden, I do not pretend to be an expert on biologic speciation, but what makes you think that any Earth species you take to a new planet will survive? You have no records or data of the ecology for any planets outside of our own solar system. You won't even know what kind of environment to which you'll be sending these...what are they, snow leopards? You'll have only the vaguest idea of where the ship will land; and you can only hope that the planet will be ready when you arrive. Also, I might add, my limited knowledge of these matters reminds me that introduction of animals to new and different habitats has often been a failure even here on Earth."

To Paul, Monte Demarest, whose rugged and pockmarked face was enhanced under the focus of the ceiling lamps, appeared older than Scalos. Yet, Paul could sense the calm intelligence in this man.

"It has often succeeded, too," Paul replied, folding his hands. "But that is not the point. We do not intend to introduce Earth species to the planet's natural environment. On the contrary, all of our experiments would continue to be done with captive animals. And what everyone seems to be overlooking here are the conservation issues that have spawned one crisis after another in Earth's environment. Our abuse of the land, and the Uprisings that now threaten the political stability of the Pan-government, have resulted in the development of many species recovery plans that are not unlike the one we at T.E.I. have managed for the snow leopard. In fact, T.E.I. was originally founded to achieve this most basic objective: the maintenance of a captive population of leopards which perhaps could someday be used to repopulate the former range of this species in the mountainous areas of central Asia, once those ecosystems have been restored to their natural conditions.

"All I can say is this: T.E.I. employees are extremely dedicated and feel just as strongly about this research as I do. We have a sort of belief, an interpretation of Lamaism, if you will. Our love for our work is in our blood, and I'm sure future generations of the T.E.I. staff will wish to carry on this project to make it a success."

Scalos scarcely waited for Torrden to finish before taking up the attack again. "Now it's Buddhist religions, Torrden? You try every card, don't you? But you're not going anywhere. It's not —"

"The man's entitled to his say, Mr. Scalos." Demarest got a surprised stare from Scalos. Both officials glared at one another for several moments. Scalos' blockish face bestowed a dark shadow about his presence — a shadow that was felt more than it was seen. Sammy Lassiter and his counterparts made an effort to get a candid shot of the scene.

Then Demarest continued: "Mr. Torrden, I can't guarantee you a date in the near future; that is, within the next three or four months. However, in, say, eight months? I think we may be able to reserve a space for you — that is, if the amount of space you request is reasonable." He paused, then added, "Now, how much do you need?"

Paul raised an eyebrow and a quick calculation later said, "I would estimate around...seventy-thousand cubic meters. We'll supply most of the necessary support equipment ourselves."

"Seventy-thou —. Why, that's practically an entire level!" Scalos blurted.

After a shaky silence, Demarest slowly said, "Mr. Torrden, I may be risking more than I need, but I shall consider it. You will, of course, have to submit a report describing the exact amount and kind of equipment you propose to bring aboard as well as an itemized listing of materials you shall need."

Again, Demarest got a quick stare from Scalos. Again, Lassiter and friends directed the image to their Camera Packs; but most of the reporters, except for Sammy and a few of the other veterans, did not expect Paul's next remark.

"Is that all I'll get? A consideration...a promise of thoughts?"

"It's all I can give you right now," Demarest replied. "Sorry. Though I can see your moralistic viewpoint, your request seems somewhat trivial to me. May your day be good."

Paul knew there was nothing more he could do. Hoping that what he had said would carry his weight in determination, he quickly gathered his papers, rose from the table, and nodded a smiling salute to the two officials. He was bombarded by questions as the line of men and women reluctantly opened a pathway to the door for him.

"Have you given up, Mr. Torrden?"

"Is it true, what they say, that you don't have the magical ability to manipulate the government like your grandfather?"

"Will you make another request, Mr. Torrden? Or are you giving up for good?"

He reached the door and jerked it open. Then he paused, and slowly glanced over his shoulders. A sudden hush came over the reporters who had been following him. Paul stared into the eyes of the nearest individuals and saw the frenzied expectation that set these surgically altered story hounds apart from the rest of the population. For a moment, he contemplated how and whether he might use these reporters to his advantage. However, he quickly dismissed the idea and darted through the doorway, slamming the door shut behind him. Some of the reporters refused to believe this part of the story was dead and lunged toward the door. The other camera-men, meanwhile, returned to the original group, which was now encircling the two government officials of the Interplanetary Space Flight Commission. Sammy Lassiter was in the front row, having taken advantage of the ruckus caused by Paul Torrden's egress. He could see the faces of Scalos and Demarest quite clearly. Scalos' angry visage needed little interpretation.

Demarest, obviously noting his partner's distress, cautiously said, "The guy deserves it. After all, it's not really him that we're against; it's his grandfather, and Gregory Torrden has been dead for almost eight years. I think we should let that matter rest and look at this issue by looking only at Paul Torrden."

"I still think —" Scalos began. Then he stopped, and slowly gazed around at the circle of blank stares that coated the faces of the men and women who surrounded the table. "Well, jackals," he blurted, "you got your daily bread, so get the hell out of here! Whatever we decide, you'll learn about it soon enough."

Scalos had a reputation. The reporters knew it and were not about to see it in action. Though Sammy was not frightened, he somehow managed to be the first one out of the room. He had it all...even the ability to know when a story has been milked dry long before any other reporter could even begin to suspect that such a situation had occurred. Besides, he had another interest to pursue ...

When the room was clear Scalos began again. "I still think he's just doing this whole thing only to spite the Pan-government."

"Maybe, maybe not." Demarest rose from the table. "In either case, it's interesting to think that only a few things will be left to the descendants of the Earth when they reach whatever new planet that will be waiting for them. A few books, or whatever books will have become by then, and several gigagrams of metal. Maybe it would be nice to have a truly living memory from Earth. It is from that perspective that I have chosen to consider this issue. May your day be good."

Demarest headed for the door before Scalos could reply. There was a brief flurry of distant questions as the reporters pounced on him, like vultures on a carcass, and then the door was shut again.

Scalos sat alone at the table now, and he let his temper boil coarsely through his veins. Slowly, the oppressiveness of the small room began to lessen. Then, he stared down at the docket in front of him, grinning widely as his ink pen scratched through Paul Torrden's name a half dozen times.

After Paul had left the room and plowed through the reporters who had not been fortunate enough to attend the meeting, he strode quickly to the elevator and watched the doors close just as a frantically groping hand tried to wedge its way towards him. The doors opened again on the lobby of the ground floor, and the first movement his eyes caught was, at last, not a reporter, but that of a woman rising from a plush vinyl chair near the Information Desk.

"Did you get it, Paul?"

He shrugged his shoulders. "You know how they work it, Julie. One guy uses authority to scare you into making a mistake and another guy tries to be Mr. Nice and hopes you feel you owe him a favor." He paused, and shrugged again. "I don't know. Demarest sounded at least half honest. At any rate, nothing will happen for T.E.I. for several months, yet."

She took his arm. "Scalos was the authoritarian, huh?"

Nodding, he led her to the door. They both left the Government Building, stepping into the cool, crisp October evening. They boarded the deck of one of the down escalators which, after Julie pushed one of the control buttons, quickly whisked them downward to the trans-rail station at street level. After they stepped off the escalator, Julie pushed the "CALL" button that was located on the station's pedestrian control panel. Then she turned toward Paul.

"What are we going to do if they decide not to let us go?"

"In that case, we'll go," he replied bluntly. "When one strategy doesn't work, you try another. We just have to be careful not to lose sight of what we're fighting for, okay?"

"Do you think we're fighting for too much?"

"No...and yet, I hate to even think it, Julie, but, in a way, we may not know what we're fighting for at all."

"You mean the new planet and everything, right?"

As he nodded his agreement, the trans-car arrived. Julie was ahead of Paul and he idly watched her figure as she took a seat in the vehicle. She had never had the striking features that most men looked for in a woman; but then, he had married Julie more for the inner beauty of her personality than for anything else. Still, he had to admit he had always been attracted to her shiny, black hair, which gave her a cool morning look — like she was ready both for love and intellectual pursuits at the same time.

"Sam won't be too glad to hear about this."

Julie's voice brought him out of his reverie.

"No...but he should hear about it as soon as possible. Then we'll be able to think about our next move."

"Want to go P.C., then? I can call ahead and let Sam know we're coming." When she saw Paul's quick stare, Julie hastily added, "No, really. We'll get through the Uprisings quicker that way."

Paul hesitated again before climbing into the trans-car. Priority Clearance speed always reminded him of that awful accident with his parents. However, as Julie said, it would allow them to quickly pass through all of the fighting in the Mid-West Region. His eyes still on Julie, he activated the microphone on the dash of the trans-car.

"Trans-rail operator, this is Paul Torrden, Key Card code blue, requesting Priority Clearance using maximum speed. One additional passenger: Julie Torrden."

Paul glanced down at the dash where three sets of alpha-numeric keyboards were displayed. Within seconds, the dome light behind the blue keyboard flashed on and he responded by entering in his license number and destination sector. After a pause, a crisp, synthetic male voice returned, "Paul Torrden, your records are clear. Priority Clearance granted. Car in use registers as operable. Make sure you and your passenger implement the protective suits. The compartment is now unlocked. Please remember that these suits must be properly returned to the compartment; otherwise, an appropriate charge will be made to your account. This trans-rail company assumes no liabilities for injuries to you or your passenger. You may begin when ready. May your day be good."

Julie was already taking the suits out of the compartment in the rear of the car. The suits were made of a puncture/fire retardant material and were designed to fit comfortably over the outer garments of any passenger. Extra padding was provided around the head, neck, and trunk areas. Passengers also had the option of plugging an air line from the suit into the dash of the trans-car. Air tanks from the trans-car could then automatically inflate air sacks within the suit in the event of a catastrophic collision.

Two minutes later, when they were both inside the protective garments, Julie threw an inquiring glance toward Paul. Paul nodded and they quickly secured their restraining seat straps.

Paul hurriedly composed himself as Julie reached for the red lever that would put the car in motion. His stomach left him for a second, and he could feel the blood draining from his face even as he was pushed backwards against the seat. Objects approached at an alarming rate of speed, only to career past his eyes and out of his peripheral vision in a blurred micro-second of suspenseful action. He tried to calm himself by thinking about the myriad of things he still had left to do today.

Soon his sense of time became distorted. He could feel the stale warmth of his breath on his upper lip inside the helmet of the protective suit. An impending urge to flee the missile-like vehicle unexpectedly surged up within him, and his mind furiously contemplated all of the methods by which he could attempt an escape. His nerve endings were pummeled by this onslaught of thoughts and feelings but, to his amazement, he remained motionless in the chair. A quick glance at Julie found her to be experiencing minimal difficulty; he wondered how she did it.

Then the windows of the car suddenly were covered with an opaque screen, and micro-vision film clips were flashed before his eyes. Though the films were there to help pass the time, they were of no use to Paul. His mind repeatedly conjured up visions of fighting police and protesting citizens — scenes that were all too common these days.

Eventually, he shut his eyes, but the problems of the Pan-government persisted. The Triship of Covington, Wein, and Danks had not done a bit of good for the Earth so far, he thought, and they were sure to lose their bid for reappointment. The only thing wrong with that was that the new candidates for the Triship — MacAllister, Burton, and Syutsen — had given indications that, if appointed, they would reshuffle some of the lower Commission leaders; and if they dismissed Demarest from the Interplanetary Space Flight Commission, which was quite likely, T.E.I.'s chances for a flight in the near future would be practically smothered by the simple swaying of a pen on paper.

In time, his stomach told him when they had reached the mountains; and he was not even aware that he had begun talking aloud to himself. His eyes were hurting from the strain of keeping them shut for so long when he noticed the car was decelerating. Ten minutes later, he was sure that it had come to a complete stop. He fumbled with his seat belt and protective garment, and had gotten partially free of the restraints when he realized that his vision was blurred. He clumsily removed the helmet. Momentarily, the sensation of dizziness overwhelmed him.

As his circulation improved, however, his vision began to clear. He then heard a voice outside the trans-car.

"It's over." That voice was inside the car — Julie's.

Then he heard the click of the door as it was pulled open. Cold air swam in. Two old, yet lithe, arms reached in and deftly helped him out of the safety suit.

"And you want to go flying off into space?" A kind-hearted laugh. "Now tell me, it's obvious you used P.C. to get back here, so you must have important news, eh? But which is it, good or bad?"

Paul stepped out of the car and looked into Sam Gray's green eyes. Though Sam was over 80 years old, he still carried an impressive, fairly tall stature; and his surprisingly youthful-like qualities more than spoke for themselves. Paul realized then that both Sam and Julie were staring closely at him...and he knew why.

He gently twisted out of the old man's grasp. "I'll be all right, don't worry about me. It's probably just a psychological barrier. I'll be over it by the time we get our flight. And if I'm not, I'm going anyway."

"*If* we get our flight," Julie added as she began to put the protective suits back in the rear compartment.

Paul glanced at her, then turned back to Sam. "Scalos is throwing his weight around again, Sam. He talks about T.E.I. as if we are responsible for the political failures of the past five decades. I think he believes the Earth can still attain the society everyone was hoping for some fifty odd years ago."

Sam nodded his understanding. "That's because of Gregory, Paul, although you already know that. Scalos never had a good word to say about him. What about the other one, Demarest is it?"

"That's the good news. He appears to like our proposal, even though he knows the other government officials aren't too partial to us. He handles himself well in front of the press, though; so if he is for us, I don't think he's going to let someone like Scalos change his mind."

"Jerul Scalos still needs to be watched," Sam cautioned.

A quick *whirr* signalled the departure of the trans-car as it responded to a call by some other citizen in need. It rotated 180 degrees on its axis and quickly slid eastward along the rails, gathering speed as it went.

Julie approached Paul and took her husband's arm. "Let's go inside, I'm cold."

Sam shrugged agreeably and led the way.

Part 2. (15 July 2124)

My research on the Torrden family has proven most fruitful and entertaining. Indeed, it is quite likely that this will probably be the only account of this acclaimed family which shall not be written for profit. I have been greatly impressed by the quantity and quality of the many events that have surrounded Torrden Enterprises Incorporated (T.E.I.) since its controversial creation in 2051. But the whole story itself started ten years before that, with a young man named Gregory Torrden ...

Possessing a high degree of capability and intelligence, Gregory Torrden surprised everyone who knew him by choosing not to pursue a doctorate after attaining a Bachelor of Science degree at the age of 19. Instead, he initiated a long-term wildlife behavior research study and became a prominent member of the Earth Wildlife Alliance (E.W.A.), an organization just beginning at that time. In light of what occurred only five years later, many people have accused him of joining the E.W.A. only to use his membership as a defense against the protestations that were eventually raised by that organization when it learned of his intentions to expand the scope of his research.

While this conclusion by the masses appears to be the most logical one, I suspect that this accusation is not totally correct. My belief stems from the fact that all my records show Gregory Torrden to have been an extremely intelligent man, as I have already mentioned; and intelligent people have been known to fool the public.

My investigations have shown that sometime in 2046, Gregory Torrden was seeking funding for the construction of the buildings and the now infamous dome which make up the facilities at Torrden Enterprises Incorporated. The purpose of the dome, once revealed, shocked many of the financiers who were approached by Gregory Torrden. A four-year expedition to the southern Himalayas would be launched, Gregory said, to capture several snow leopards and to protect the species from eventual extinction by breeding them in a controlled environment. It was stated that, under such conditions, beneficial research could also be performed upon the leopards. He received violent objections from the general public and, more importantly, from the E.W.A. Indeed, his proposal was in no way novel: international programs already were in existence that included successful captive breeding programs and had as their objective the continued survival and conservation of the species.

It should be noted that, typically, snow leopards occupy vast ranges and occur in low numbers. Torrden obviously knew that a frequent byproduct of any kind of breeding program, especially one within the limited confines that characterizes a controlled environment complex, is the sacrifice of the naturally occurring integrity of the species in question. He also must have known that the size and the complexities of the facilities and structures required to ensure successful implementation of the project would be cost-prohibitive. It is therefore commendable that this man was still able to contact the right sources and the right supporters to pull it all off. The T.E.I. facility, complete with research laboratories, training classrooms, and a captive population of snow leopards was established by 2051.

The remodeling of the facilities at T.E.I. just four years later, in 2055, drew additional public outrage and government inquiries. It was then that T.E.I. expanded its scope of research to include other animal species and a variety of cognitive behavior studies. The E.W.A. rejoined the growing tirade against T.E.I. about 15 years later, when it became known that the leopards would soon be included in some of the behavioral studies.

By then, many people began asking what Gregory Torrden's true intentions really were. I think he expected the protests on the part of the public, but not on the part of the E.W.A. (the latter group flatly rejected his applications for research funds). What motivated Gregory Torrden to continue in spite of such overwhelming opposition? The people were against him; even the most respected ecological organization, the E.W.A., was against him. What was so important to Torrden that made him take such huge risks?

My theory is that he initially joined the Alliance so that he, a young man known then only for his intellectual pursuits, would have a source of appropriations to finance his proposed trip to the Himalayas. Later, he must have observed something that sparked an even greater interest in his inquisitive mind. What could this have been? As T.E.I. continued to develop, the upward spiraling costs of its programs only added fuel to the growing opposition in the public and the Pan-government. Throughout all of this he must have had a reason for his actions, an objective which he has apparently never revealed to the general public.

Over the years, researchers at T.E.I. have published many landmark articles concerning the role of macromolecules and nerve cell activity in learning and memory storage. However, my experience and instincts tell me that there is more to T.E.I. than meets the eye. To answer all of my questions, I shall have to continue my research.

Part 3. (15 October 2124)

The large, man-made cave was huge and decorated with ridged slopes, sharp stones, and projecting ledges. A minute part of an elaborate domed enclosure, it was dimly illuminated by artificial lighting which was augmented by the reflected sunlight that streamed in through the dome.

The cold could be felt by Sam and Paul as they stood in one of the several elevated observation portals set off from the spacious hallway that surrounded the controlled environment complex. From where they stood, they could see the snow gathered at the entrance of Cave One, its whiteness spreading outward in all directions. Though most of what was present was artificially produced, the hinged roof would be opened in the winter to allow natural precipitation to fall within the complex.

A single snow leopard lay with its back against the rocky, cold floor within the cave, a look of silent contentment emanating from its creamy-gray, cat-like face. The tips of its long, furred tail moved randomly. The lightweight radio collar — a device that allowed T.E.I. technicians to follow the movements of individuals — that all of the leopards wore was barely visible beneath its thick fur.

Without warning, another snow leopard stealthily loped into the cave. He was large but somehow controlled the grace and beauty of his form. The rings, or rosettes, along his gray-white coat had begun to fade with age. He carried his tail behind him in an artistic, swaying motion, the darker spots accenting its otherwise creamy-gray color. Almost with an air of dignity, he lithely moved towards the single snow leopard.

Paul idly watched as the two leopards began to slowly groom themselves. He sometimes felt he could actually feel that deep attachment, a diagnostic feature of the pair bond in the snow leopard.

"Colonel looks like he's ready," Paul stated, admiring the large leopard. Colonel had always been his favorite, maybe because of the animal's size: he was larger than any of the other 44 leopards, with a body length of almost 130 centimeters. His tail was nearly an additional 100 centimeters in length, and he weighed nearly sixty-five kilograms. All slightly above average for a snow leopard.

The huge paws provided ample support for the large, agile cat. Colonel looked directly at the portal as if he knew that the humans were there, and something in Paul's mind never doubted that the leopard did indeed know that they were there, watching him from behind the one-way mirrored glass.

Sam agreed. "Yes, he's proven himself to be quite capable of learning. I'm just glad these animals usually have cubs every other year. He and Phanta had a litter just last year, and she's due to come into estrus soon. It should make things a little easier, though, if we test him in the very near future. When do you want to start?"

"Soon, probably within two weeks. How long has it been since we've had an animal that's possessed so many skills?"

"Fifteen years ago, I guess. That was the third time around, but just another number compared to all of the failures we've had since then. To be truthful, Colonel is actually the first leopard since that time that appears to have all the signs of being capable of scoring highly on the tests."

Paul nodded thoughtfully. Then: "Everything is all set, I take it — at the school, I mean?"

"Yes, I left word. All those who qualified should be there by now. Know what you're going to say, Paul?"

Paul nodded silently. The two men watched the snow leopards for several more moments before resuming their walk along the hallway which connected the research facilities with the small, private university at T.E.I.

"Pretty much. I'll improvise as I go along. I just hope it's what they want to hear. We have too many new personnel and not enough older, more experienced individuals; and though I hope a lot of the new ones decide to go, I just hope they make the right decision in their own minds. They won't be of any help to us out there in space if they don't."

They had reached the hallway leading to the main auditorium. Paul halted and turned to the older man. "Tell Julie I'll see her in a couple hours."

"Fine," Sam replied.

As he approached the podium, Paul noticed that the almost ethereal hubbub of voices suddenly ceased, like the last tick of a clock. The variety of faces in the lecture hall proved to be an interesting contrast to the snow leopards he had observed earlier.

He waited several long moments, for effect, before speaking. "I probably don't have to tell you why you're here, but I'm going to anyway. No doubt, you have heard it a thousand times before, and you will probably hear it a thousand times more.

"To date, there have been eighteen New World Launches. With luck, T.E.I. will be on the twenty-sixth. You are here right now because you believe in the continued survival of the snow leopard as a viable species. And while this has always been T.E.I.'s primary objective, the fact that we now plan to take some of these snow leopards to another world does not infer that we are deviating from the course we set out on so many years ago. In fact, by continuing our research on these animals in a less limited environment, we stand to increase the chances of ensuring the survival of this species on Earth. That said, let me be the first to remind you that you're here right now because your applications showed that you have the qualifications necessary to make such a trip possible.

"Now, don't get me wrong — we're not expecting you to serve a well-oiled machine one hundred percent of the time. For those of you who wish to pursue additional interests or take a friend or a lover along, no one's going to stop you. Just remember, this trip is not a freebie to feed your ego. You will be able to drop out any time along the way; that is, prior to leaving. After that, we don't know what we will do with those who can't decide on anything."

Paul paused and allowed the slight laughter to dissipate.

"We will be giving you every possible chance over the next seven or eight months to make sure this is what you really want to do. Also, your electro-mail accounts will constantly be updated when appropriate information comes to light. So, if there are any fence straddlers out there right now, I don't want to see you in eight months if you have not prettied your picture, okay?

"Another thing you should know: you will be living out the rest of your lives on a metal contraption, a spaceship with a destination we only hope will be ready when we get there. You probably won't even see pictures of the planet to which we will be headed. No one is forcing you to go. No one is expecting you to go. Only you can decide if this is for you.

"I'll stop here, mostly because anything else I might say would just be superfluous to what you have heard or read prior to this meeting. The primary purpose of this gathering is to address any concerns you may have, so let's get right at it. Are there any questions?"

Everyone hesitantly looked at one another during the traditional pause that followed. Then someone in the middle of the crowd piped out: "What happens if we don't go, Mr. Torrden?"

"Whatever happens, the Earth is yours," Paul said.

After another brief round of laughter, Paul added, "It might be wise to base your questions around what would happen *should* you go."

A young woman in the front row rose quickly and faced Paul. "Mr. Torrden, you stated that it might be eight months before we will know if T.E.I. has been granted a reservation on a New World Flight. I think it should be noted that the Thirty-five will have chosen the members of the new Triship well before that time. What political ramifications, if any, will that have, and have you made any plans to take it into consideration?"

Paul smiled to himself. This was the kind of insight he was looking for. And she had a good point, too.

"I have considered it, yes. And to tell you the truth, I am worried about the intentions of the new candidates." He debated whether he should have revealed that much, decided it was the right thing, and went on. "But there's not much we can do. Our alliance with the government is pretty thin, and the last thing we need to do is ruin it by applying too much pressure."

The young woman, apparently satisfied with Paul's answer, seated herself.

"What guarantees are there that T.E.I.'s original objective will ever be met if we do this?" came another question, from near the back row. Paul was now beginning to experience the rush of enthusiasm and guarded optimism that had captured the crowd.

"Almost sixty years ago," Paul began, "the nations of our world attempted to unite under one unifying code of laws and civilization. That experiment — destined to fail for many reasons, if not just for the amount of freedom it took from individuals — was the last nail in the coffin that buried successful conservation efforts at a global scale. In the time since the beginning of the Pan-government, we have seen more species go extinct, more habitat lost, and more degradation of the environment than at any other time in modern history. The Uprisings — our current form of uncivil disobedience, will have one of two immediate outcomes: more oppression of the citizen; or more anarchy in the society. Either way, it will be some time before the long term effect of this revolt will be known. At one time, one could reasonably argue that conservationists such as ourselves would one day win this battle — that efforts to reintroduce the snow leopard to its former range would be possible in our lifetimes. Now, however, those possibilities are dwindling, and our bid to move our efforts to a new arena, so to speak, is a natural outgrowth of T.E.I.'s efforts to continue succeeding where other conservation organizations have failed. The technology exists to get us home again; but if home is no longer here — we will at least be able to take with us one of the most prized jewels of this planet."

Several more questions were voiced, and Paul responded to each one. He quickly found himself developing a rhythm to his answers, and he was surprised that none of the questions caught him off guard. After a half hour, the number of questions began to wane and he eventually dismissed the group for the evening.

As the crowd began to shuffle towards the rear exits, the emptiness of the room began to echo back and forth between the walls. No longer the center of attraction, Paul was left to his own thoughts. Yes, MacAllister, Burton, and Syutsen. They were beginning to worry him as much as Scalos did, if not more.

He absent-mindedly leaned against the podium as his body sought relief from the adrenalin flow it had just experienced during the question and answer session. He watched the few remaining students leaving the auditorium, unaware of footsteps approaching him from behind. He would have been startled had he not naturally recognized the soft touch of that person's hand on his shoulder. Turning, Paul reached out his hand as if to touch Julie's breast. She evaded him, the way she always did, but the usual smile was not there this time.

"Sorry. What's wrong?"

"We just got a call from one of the central trans-rail operators. He said they received a request five minutes after we left the interview with the Flight Commission from someone who wanted to know exactly where we were going."

"And?" Paul decided to let her go on. What she had said by itself did not justify the worried look on her face.

"He said they were 'bout ready to let it go at that — you know, 'cause it's something that happens a lot with code blue Key Card users — but then they discovered that the identification number the person was using expired several years ago."

Yet another problem, Paul thought; it was as if Mother and Father Problem had copulated and had produced a lot of little children — all to be dumped upon his already troubled consciousness. He kicked that idea from his mind and said, "Don't worry, Jul, it's probably just a false alarm or something."

Paul knew it was a weak lie, and to cover up for it he began walking toward the main hall. He had not gone more than two steps when Julie stopped him.

"Paul, you know that's not true." She came over to him and he could see the hurt, understanding, and perception in her eyes. *Not too many people could express all of those features at once,* he found himself thinking.

"Besides," she added, "they think that whoever it was switched to a different trans-car somewhere out in the Mid-West Region, and the operators couldn't follow him after that."

"You've lost me, Julie. What does this have to do with T.E.I.?"

"Don't you see? Because of the Uprisings in the Mid-West, unless you request Priority Clearance, you have to use manual control for some two or three hundred miles. All our mystery guy had to do was transfer to another car and he'd be able to come all the way out here, untraced."

Paul began walking again. He knew that Julie was well aware he had already come to that same conclusion.

"I know there's not much we can do, but I wanted you to know." She was beside him, again.

Paul shook his head. "I could have the trans-rail operators consult us before granting anyone admission to our sub-sector, but unless we get more incidents like this one, I don't think I can rightfully do that. There's the general public to consider, you know. Anyway, I don't want to get paranoid, at least not yet. Come on."

"One more thing, Paul." She took his arm, stopping him once more. "You know I love you, don't you?"

"I know that, Jul. I haven't forgotten it."

She paused, appearing to weigh the depth of his answer. "I know you've been involved in a lot of work, but..."

"And that does not mean a thing. You know you're sensitive enough to feel it if I stopped loving you. And I'm willing to bet that you don't feel that way now, right?"

Julie answered his question with a troubled smile. Her hands ran down Paul's arm until they found his hand. She looked up into his eyes and, after a slight hesitation, leaned her head on his shoulder. Moments later, when they reached the hallway, they were accosted by one of the T.E.I. security men.

"Mr. Torrden, Sam Gray wants to see you immediately. He said it has something to do with the Thirty-five holding an emergency conference."

Paul suddenly felt helpless as he tried to settle the frustration mounting within himself. "That means either a full fledged citizen revolt is in progress, or they're planning to change the Triship two months in advance. Damn!" He paused, then asked, "And that's all he said?"

"Yes, sir."

"Okay," Paul nodded to the security officer. He watched the guard scurry back to his post, and then muttered, "Good ol' Mom and Dad...they did it again."

Noticing Julie's questioning stare, he added, "Don't worry, they're just a couple of parents I made up. Let's go see Sam."

Julie slowly shook her head as she accompanied Paul down the hallway.

Chapter 2

Colonel

Part 1. (10 November 2124)

Paul looked at Colonel, somewhat surprised that he could still be held in awe by the beauty of the large cat. Behind him, he could feel the curious eyes of the 70 students and staff members who had finally been chosen to represent T.E.I. in the New World program. They were clustered behind him in the large, elevated observation portal directly at the rear of the leopard's cave.

Paul wondered if the students were as nervous as he was, and could only guess that such was the case. Now, as he looked at Colonel, he wondered if the snow leopard also knew that 75 years of hard work at T.E.I. had come down to this one test. If only the leopard could speak!

The last time so much optimism had been openly expressed at T.E.I. over one of the conditioning tests, as Sam had reminded him, had been just 15 years ago, when he had been in his mid-teens. He had been in this same hallway, looking in through the observation portal with his grandfather, who had stood where he was standing right now. Though that test had failed, it had indicated that T.E.I. was apparently on the right track. Or at least that is what Gregory had said afterwards. And that, Paul thought, was where the mystery still lay: he was almost 30 now, and he could still not state, with any definite surety within himself, what his grandfather's *true* intentions had been all along. The program was almost totally based on calculated suppositions which, in turn, owed their origins to brief and carefully worded conversations between himself and Gregory Torrden. Paul clearly remembered one of the last things his grandfather had told him, only seven years ago: not to apply for a New World Flight until T.E.I.'s desired results were proven to exist.

Paul shook his head. Even if Colonel failed today's test, assuming one could list the criteria for failure, they would still have to do everything in their power to obtain a reservation on a New World Launch as soon as possible, especially in light of what Monte Demarest had told him this morning. The words of the I.S.F.C. official still hung clearly in Paul's mind.

Demarest was being ousted by the new Triship. He had read over Paul's report, and one of his last undertakings had been to approve the request and to schedule T.E.I. for one of the next two flights. It had been a surprise move, and was obviously riddled with risks. Demarest had said that his seniority over Scalos would be the only factor that could possibly prevent his approval from being vetoed by the Thirty-Five Consulting Members, being that the entire matter was in their hands until the Triship appointed a new I.S.F.C. official.

Paul had thanked Demarest. However, he had felt slightly guilty afterwards, feeling that Demarest might have kept his position longer had it not been for the controversy over T.E.I. And yet, Paul had to admit, Demarest had obviously sacrificed everything he had to get T.E.I. on the earliest flight possible; which was fortunate, considering the Uprisings were close to becoming a worldwide crisis.

He swore softly to himself. He'd read about what had taken place 60 years ago — when it was believed that a world government could provide better employment opportunities and a more stable standard of living, while eliminating poverty at the same time. He still found it hard to believe that the various nations had attempted such a thing; that decision had effectively declared a cold war upon the concept of free enterprise. In fact, the problems that T.E.I. faced today in many ways found their roots entangled in the very foundation of the Pan-government. It was common knowledge that Gregory Torrden had willingly joined the GAP (Group Against the Pan-government) movement in the 2170's. Paul even still had copies of the articles covering the now infamous decision by Gregory Torrden to keep the T.E.I. name, in spite of the government's repeated requests to change it. Those headlines, combined with the public's distrust over T.E.I.'s mission and the funding controversy that had erupted 30 years earlier, had produced a public relations nightmare that continued to exist to this day.

Through the portal's technologically attuned speakers, he could hear Colonel purring, a quiet puffing sound typical of snow leopards. It were as if the leopard seemed to understand the thoughts that were going on inside his head. Paul smiled to himself as he noticed the eternal, nonchalant expression in the animal's eyes. The relative lack of aggression among the majority of snow leopards never ceased to amaze him. *I wish I could be as calm as you, old boy,* he thought. *Then maybe I'd be able to start these tests on time.*

The thought of the test brought his retrospection back to his grandfather and the reality which T.E.I. represented. As he stared at the leopard, he had to come to terms with how far Colonel had been removed from his native environment. From an ethological standpoint, Colonel's behavior resembled that of his wild ancestors only in the most basic sense; everything above that, including the animal's innate fear of man, had been changed by his involvement with the T.E.I. program. The same was true for many of the other leopards currently held at the research facility. However, Colonel was only one of just two or three leopards that could truly be considered "tame" in any sense of the word.

Although his grandfather had initially founded a captive breeding program to replenish dwindling wild populations, during the last half-century some of the snow leopards had been included in the ongoing cognitive studies research at T.E.I. Each of these snow leopards was involved in a specific type of training program, the basic features of which varied in certain crucial areas from program to program. Colonel's training challenged the capability of the leopard to respond to certain high frequency sounds while navigating a predetermined route through the enclosure.

Paul knew only too well that the training had produced an animal that was no longer suitable for a return to its natural environment. Indeed, nearly a dozen of the leopards had been so affected by the training they had been subjected to. That reality both annoyed and perplexed Paul, and if it were not for the glimmers of truth and hope which continued to appear through all the confusion he would probably have lost faith in this project long ago.

He continued to stare at Colonel while unhooking the small communicator he wore on his belt. "On my mark." He spoke softly, as if it were important to not disturb anyone's concentration. T.E.I. technicians in the facility's central command center were standing by for his next signal. Behind him, he knew that the students and staff had already raised their binoculars to train their sights on the snow leopard. The test was ready.

Paul turned to face the crowd. "Okay, as you know, Colonel — the snow leopard you now see — has undergone an extensive battery of instrumental conditioning trials. By rewarding him at the appropriate times, we have trained — or conditioned — Colonel to search for and respond to a high frequency whistle. We usually refer to this sound as a 'seek signature,' and it can be electronically generated from any of the eight small transmitters we have stationed throughout the enclosure. The intensity of Colonel's training and conditioning has been such that, once we start the test, Colonel should abandon all other incoming stimuli during his pursuit of the seek signature's source.

"The objective of this test," Paul continued, "is to document Colonel's ability to respond to changes in the location of the seek signature's source while he crosses the entire 2.3 kilometer expanse of the domed enclosure. Additional novel stimuli will be provided during the test to analyze Colonel's absorption of his specific training program. These stimuli, most of which will require him to make instant — and hopefully correct — decisions have been installed as a part of many of the tests we give to the animals at T.E.I."

Paul turned to face the portal again. Behind him, he could hear members of the crowd begin to discuss the objective of the test amongst themselves. The time had come. He raised the communicator once again to his lips. "Okay," he spoke, "let's do it. Make me proud."

Paul's eyes never left the leopard. For a second, nothing about the scene in front of him changed. Then the animal suddenly became very erect, and the air around Paul appeared to take on a tense and crisp texture.

For a few moments, the leopard appeared agitated. Then, almost without warning, Colonel nimbly leaped sideways and began a half trot towards the cave entrance, his long tail weaving gracefully in the air. The fluidness of the leopard's movements prompted additional muffled conversation in the crowd that stood behind Paul.

He smiled to himself as Colonel left the cave. The test was officially underway. All of Colonel's reactions would later be carefully scrutinized by two of T.E.I.'s most prominent ethologists. Paul quickly returned the communicator to his belt. He glanced at the large overhead monitor on the wall above the portal and saw that Colonel had nearly finished descending the slightly sloping, snow-covered hillside that extended outward from the cave. At the base of the slope and directly in the leopard's path, a large metal wall was visible on the monitor screen. Colonel was approaching his first obstacle.

Paul turned again to face the crowd. "As Colonel approaches the wall, keep in mind that this leopard's conditioning has focused exclusively on ensuring that he obediently and constantly move in the direction of the seek signature. Until today, the source of the seek signature has always remained stationary, and there have never been any barriers to Colonel's movements. As part of this test, we will be changing the source of the seek signature periodically, and we will also be looking at how the leopard adapts to obstacles he has never before encountered. The first of these obstacles is the wall Colonel is now approaching.

"We have constructed this wall for the expressed purpose of this test. It is over 200 meters long, but it can be climbed if Colonel uses the boulders we have placed at several locations at the base of the wall. We wish to determine here whether this new artifact will make Colonel abandon his training."

As Paul fell silent, everyone's eyes returned to the monitor. Colonel had reached the base of the wall, and had come to a complete stop. It was clear he was somewhat perplexed by the foreign object. After a few moments, he began to pace back and forth. He approached the nearby group of large stones, and tested the stability of the boulders with his paw. Then he resumed pacing. He repeated these actions twice more before suddenly springing atop the boulders and leaping to the top of the metal barrier. Most other animals would have teetered there ungracefully, but the leopard maintained his balance as he looked out over the remaining expanse of the domed enclosure. Then, as had been expected, he leaped off the top of the wall. For an instant, he was lost from sight, but he immediately appeared in view again and the closed circuit cameras followed him across the flat stretch of the domed enclosure. The snow offered a cloaked contrast to the swiftly moving animal.

The leopard raced up the opposite slope, crossed several additional meters of ground, and then stopped. Paul continued his narration: "Colonel has now reached a new challenge. The seek signature has temporarily stopped, and in a moment will begin again, but not before the technicians release several grouse from a camouflaged cage about 50 meters in front of Colonel's present location."

As if on cue, two large, chunky, dark birds sprang forth from the earth near where Colonel stood. They flew for a very short distance before coming to a violently abrupt halt when they reached the end of the durable tethers by which they remained tied to the cage floor. They made several additional attempts to fly before coming to rest again on the surface of the snow.

However, the birds had done their job. Colonel, though still a good distance away, had been able to spot the movements quickly with his amazingly sharp vision. Paul held his breath, nonetheless, as he saw that Colonel was not moving. "We've restarted the seek signature, but it's source is now forty-five degrees east of Colonel's original direction. Colonel has to make a choice between continuing to respond to the signature or investigating the birds." Paul paused long enough to check on Colonel's progress. "Come on, boy, you can do it," he heard himself whisper.

Colonel remained locked in his stance, however, and appeared to be sniffing the air for additional clues. Paul groaned when, after an additional five seconds, Colonel began walking stealthily towards the grouse. The birds tugged at their tethers again in response to Colonel's approach, but the leopard had not taken more than four steps when it came to a stop once more. Paul felt as though he had been vindicated when he saw Colonel turn away from the grouse and begin on a path towards the new source of the signal.

The leopard's strides quickly grew longer as it raced up the hill toward the transmitter which continued to emit the seek signature's beckoning whistle. Over the next several minutes Paul continued to describe Colonel's movements for the benefit of the T.E.I. personnel. To Paul's amazement, the leopard's performance during this period was flawless. The direction of the seek signature was changed two more times, but Colonel responded immediately to these changes and seemed undaunted by the additional obstacles placed in his path.

As the end of the test neared, Paul gave the signal for the remaining 43 snow leopards to be released into the domed enclosure. "The other leopards have been confined to their individual quarters specifically for this test; but once they are released, it will be interesting to see if Colonel will be at all disturbed by the sudden presence of the other animals," he told the crowd. Paul continued to monitor Colonel's movements and, to his satisfaction, found that the leopard seemed almost unperturbed by the reintroduction of the other cats to the domed enclosure.

The apparent success of the test brought an admiring grin to Paul's face. However, as Colonel approached the very end of the preestablished test route, the T.E.I. security warning system siren interrupted Paul's narration. The siren was a loud, repetitive, ascending wail. Paul grasped the communicator from his belt and moved away from the other personnel in back of him. However, there was no way to avoid the sound of the siren. "Okay, guys, talk to me! What's happening?"

For a moment there was no reply, then: "Paul, we have a Priority 1 security breach. Repeat, Priority 1 security breach! Security Post 12 is not responding. Someone has accessed the enclosure through Post 12!"

Paul turned to the monitor. "Put it on the screen, now. And get someone over to Post 12 to secure that area!"

"We're on it, Paul."

As Paul and the others continued to watch the screen the scene changed from that of the leopards to a blank, snow-covered landscape. The camera angle panned back and forth for a few moments before coming to rest on the figure of a small girl walking fearlessly in the direction of a small group of leopards. Paul was momentarily relieved to discover that the intruder was unarmed, but he still found it hard to fathom how a small child could have accessed the enclosure.

As the camera angle drew back and continued to pan for a larger picture, Paul quickly spoke into his communicator. "Wait! Go back. There. Who is that standing outside Security Post 13?" The image of a man standing at the transparent observation portal on the far side of the enclosure was clearly visible. Paul knew that all of the observation portals were to have been secured before the test. Was this man somehow related to the child that had aimlessly wandered into the enclosure?

At length, the central command personnel responded. "We're not sure, Paul. Repeat, the subject's identity is unknown."

Paul's concern over this new development was quickly overshadowed as the camera angle returned to the snow-covered landscape. It immediately became obvious that the leopards, including Colonel, had already discovered the presence of the child. Paul knew that there was not enough time to send in a rescue team. As he helplessly looked on, Colonel approached the child. The leopard slowly circled the small girl, who by now had stopped walking. She reached out, as if to try to touch the leopard, but Colonel backed away.

Some of the other leopards approached the area, but only Colonel remained close to the child. Paul knew that inevitably one of the leopards would attack the girl, but he was helpless to do anything about it. Colonel cautiously approached the child again, as if trying to get her scent. He circled her several more times and then, without warning, he rushed upon her. The child fell to her knees, and Colonel towered over her.

Some of the people in the audience screamed, but the unspeakable did not happen. Instead of taking the girl's life, Colonel continued to stand over the child, looking at her from various angles as if she were a new-found toy. Other leopards approached, but Colonel did not let them come near the child. Some of these leopards, apparently losing interest, left the area, while the others looked on in a disinterested fashion.

The child was, to everyone's surprise, now petting the leopard. Paul knew that only the professional T.E.I. trainers had ever been able to approach the leopards so closely; and even then, they wore protective clothing and took other safety precautions. What this child was doing was unprecedented in his experience with the leopards. As he continued to look on, the other leopards suddenly rose and moved away from Colonel and the child, and as the camera angle withdrew even further, Paul could see that a rescue team was finally approaching the emergency scene in one of the T.E.I. 4-wheel drive medical vehicles. Colonel continued to stand over the child until all of the other leopards had left the area. The leopard stared at the approaching vehicle and watched it as it came to a complete stop less than 10 yards away. The child continued to caress the leopard's fur, obviously oblivious to the seriousness of her predicament and seemingly unaware that the men now approaching her were attempting her rescue.

Colonel stood his ground. The men had their stun guns drawn as they slowly approached the child. The lead marksmen carried a large rifle which, with one shot, would immediately kill the leopard; he had already taken aim on the leopard and had a clean shot — which Paul knew he would take at the first sign of trouble.

The men approached to within five yards of Colonel, who continued to stare at them, as if challenging the men to take the child that squirmed playfully below his belly. No one in the observational portal moved as the scene played out. The members of the rescue team were obviously discussing their next strategy, although their voices could not be heard in the observational portal.

Paul picked up the communicator again. "If necessary, you know what you have to do. Take no chances."

The central command center responded quickly to Paul's instructions. "We know that, Paul. We're exploring all the options."

The camera angle on the monitor closed in as one member of the rescue team raised his stun gun and took aim on the leopard. Paul knew that once the gun was fired, Colonel's reaction would dictate whether the lead marksmen would also have to take action. Several tense moments passed, and when it seemed that there was no time left, Colonel moved away from the child that had been the source of his attention and slowly backed away from the men.

Paul could hear the sighs of relief in the room behind him as Colonel continued to move nonchalantly away from the rescue team. Two members of the team cautiously approached the child and picked her up; she appeared unharmed. The ordeal was over.

Paul turned around, his communicator still in his hands. "Good work, fellas. Let's get the area secured. Give me a status report in one hour, pronto." Then, to the crowd in front of him: "*That*, needless to say, was not part of the test."

A wave of reserved, general laughter spread throughout the crowd of onlookers. As the mumbling continued, Paul noticed a disturbance in the rear of the crowd. Several people were quickly and forcibly making their way towards the front of the mob, and then the crowd drew back to allow Julie and Sam to approach Paul. The two had been stationed at the central command office during the test. Now, as they approached him, they looked like an old, noble king and his young princess, emerging victoriously from a hundred year battle.

Sam was the first to reach him. The old man was holding a digital stopwatch up for all to see, and as it twinkled in the light, it heavily accented the bright green eyes of his beaming face.

"I've waited many years for this, Paul: fourteen minutes and fifteen seconds, with only one minor error — and one very strange incident!"

Paul heard a cheer emanate from the crowd. Not only did the students know that the apparent success of the test practically guaranteed their positions on a New World Launch, but Paul also sensed that they shared his feeling that what had just happened represented a major contribution to what Gregory Torrden started over 70 years ago. Then a second surge of victory swept through Paul. In all the confusion, he had momentarily forgotten about the time factor; which was understandable since the time in which the tests were run had held little significance in the past, what with all the failures.

Julie reached him then, and as he put his arm around her shoulder he heard the crowd of students begin to chant a demand for a speech. Raising his other hand, he said:

"Okay, listen. We all deserve to be proud of ourselves today, right?" A cheer answered him. "Okay, but remember, a lot of the things we're doing now are going directly to the snow leopards; and they, in turn, determine how we feel, whether we're up or down, successful or not. Today we have apparently succeeded with only one snow leopard, but we still need to await the official word from our staff ethologists after they have analyzed all of the data. And it will also be a while before our next test will be ready. Which brings me to my important news.

"'This morning we received a call from Monte Demarest. If you haven't heard, the new Triship is removing him from his position as joint head of the Interplanetary Space Flight Commission. He was our only real hope, and his last move was to approve our application for a New World Launch.

"Now, hold on. That approval is only the word of one man; and, though I don't like saying it, it hasn't got much support from the other officials. But, if it does go through, we could be in on the mid-December Flight. That's six months earlier than what we expected, so I want all of you to take full advantage of all the facilities here at T.E.I. so that you will be in top condition — both physically and mentally — and ready to go on a moment's notice.

"Remember, we are not only serving ourselves, but we are serving our goal."

The assembled students and staff appeared to recognize the tone of finality in Paul's voice. As the crowd began to diminish, Paul began to wonder if he was being a trifle too strict with them. After all, he had —

"You did good," he heard Julie say softly into his ear, interrupting his thoughts. "The test, I mean." He looked down at her and could see that she had been just as happy as everyone else but had not yet had the chance to express it.

He shook his head. "That was mostly Colonel out there, Jul. All I did was give the command for the test to begin. He did everything else. Besides, we really need to wait to hear from our behavioral scientists — they have the final say on what really happened, what it means, and how significant it is."

"Yeah, but still, you supervised his training, remember?"

"That's true, Paul," Sam agreed. "You got to remember, anyone can bring a German shepherd — or any kind of dog or circus animal, for that matter — in here and train 'em for a week or so on the test course we've got set up and have 'em complete it in less than twelve or fifteen minutes with no mistakes.

"But, up until today, Colonel never saw that wall; nor had he ever seen any of the other obstacles we threw at him. This was even the first time we've shown him live birds. But he used his previous training to put little bits and pieces of information together, figure out what was expected of him, and put everything together in a logical sequence. And to do all that in fourteen minutes, covering over four kilometers, is utterly fantastic, Paul.

"True, Colonel did everything we wanted him to do, but you are the one who taught him to do those things."

Paul shrugged his shoulders. "Okay, you win, Sam. And while I'm defeated I may as well change the subject. Have our technicians gotten the child out of the enclosure yet?"

Sam leisurely nodded his agreement and Paul became embarrassingly aware that his question had been unnecessary. He remained quiet for a moment before saying, "You still have not told me if you are going or not."

"You know as well as I do that I won't be needed up there, Paul. Besides, I've been here longer than anyone else, and when you leave, someone's going to have to take over. You and Julie go 'head and find out what it's like to live and love in space — which is another thing against me, I can only find out what it's like to live up there."

That got a laugh out of Julie. "Sam, you know there's more to love than just a physical relationship."

Sam cocked his head sideways and raised an eyebrow. "Which is also true, and that's why I'm going to stay behind and make sure the snow leopards that don't go get all the love and care they deserve."

And that was that, Paul thought to himself. Sam was not going, no matter what they said to persuade him.

He could sense that Julie was preparing to continue the light-hearted argument when the hallway came to life with the voice of the P.A. system, informing Sam he had an incoming call.

"Sure that was not planned, Sam?" Julie chided as Sam began making his way down the hallway.

Paul called after him, "If it's anything important, I'll be by shortly."

The old man saluted his acknowledgement as he disappeared around the bend in the hall.

"I'm going to miss him, Paul."

"We all are. But he does have a point. He will probably do more good staying here than he will out in space. He knew my grandfather better than anyone else, including myself."

"What bothers me, though, is that, well, something's missing. Colonel did a great job today, true. But what did he *really* do?"

"You're not starting on that again, are you, Paul?"

"No, really, think it out, Jul," he persisted. "All these tests we've been running, and the training and experiments — they're in the program Gregory wrote up who knows how many years ago. I have gone over them a thousand times and, damn it, I keep asking just how much progress we've really made towards documenting how reasoning and insight work in animals. Our staff behaviorists are always a step or two ahead of me, but we're still in the theoretical stage. I'm sure a lot of people who have worked closely on this program over the years have come to the same conclusion at one time or another.

"What gets me is that there's something wrong. Gregory once told me that we would one day see his true intentions. It makes me wonder what he was after that would have made it so bad if he ever told us before we discover it on our own."

"And you do not think Colonel's performance today meant anything?"

"Oh, I do. But how do we go about proving it? What do I look for? It's like living a dual life. I really enjoy this work, but I'm so afraid it's going to come out wrong. I'm sure I can trust Sam to carry on things here when we're gone, but after him, who's left? And how am I going to be sure that the animals we take with us will give us the answer that we are looking for?"

"I don't know, Paul. Sometimes I've had those feelings, too. But something tells me that Gregory foresaw a lot, and I think that one day we're going to all of a sudden find out what it is that we've been searching for for so long."

The communicator's signal at Paul's belt interrupted their conversation. Grasping the device in his hands, Paul quickly responded. "This is Torrden."

It was central command again. "Paul, we sorted things out. A small group of animal rights activists were demonstrating at Security Post 12, when an altercation broke out between them and other tourists. Our officer there attempted to resolve the matter but in the process he was disarmed and the activists attempted to enter the enclosure through that Post. They were unsuccessful, however, because our officer from Post 13 arrived just in time. There was an exchange of fire, but no one was injured, and the activists eventually surrendered. Unfortunately, in the melee, the child somehow managed to crawl through the Post's access gate, which had been damaged by the activists. Her parents are relieved to get her back. By the way, they were not part of the disturbance."

"Any word on the mystery man at Post 13?"

"Negative, Paul. He was gone when our men arrived."

"Damn!" Paul reattached the communicator to his belt.

"What is it, Paul?"

"Someone was at Post 13. But why was he there, and what was he doing?"

"I was in central command when they counted all the students. No one was missing."

Paul looked at her sharply. "Are you sure?"

"Yes, who was it then?"

Paul shrugged his shoulders. "That's what I'd like to know, Jul. The only reason I'm worried is because whoever he was, he was out of uniform."

"You mean someone not working for T.E.I.? Could it have been someone else associated with the Launch, maybe?"

"I doubt it. Everyone was told to meet here at Portal One. These are the only one-way mirrors we have. If I could see that guy, so could Colonel. It's possible distractions like those that make evaluation of the test results that much more difficult."

She half smiled at him. "I think you're getting paranoid."

"I'm not the only one who should be. We're not the most loved people in the world, Jul, and if somebody found out they were getting cheated out of leaving this fucked up Earth because some 'liberal-minded official' decided to schedule a group of animal lovers and its pack of snow leopards, you'd think they'd be pretty mad, too, right? And most of our facilities are still open to the public: anyone can walk in here with a solid, well thought-out plan and do a hell of a lot of damage."

"Maybe we could still find him?"

Paul threw up his hands. "You know we get between five and seven hundred visitors each day. We just can't go searching everyone or asking them to leave."

They were silent for a moment. The footsteps of a guard echoed purposefully down a distant hall. The artificial lights glared down from above, illuminating the blue color of the old, but clean, walls of the T.E.I. hallway. Paul looked up at the ceiling and then back at Julie.

"And I love you, too."

"What?"

"I just wanted to tell you that before you accuse me of the opposite — I'm sorry I got mad."

"I'm sorry I ask stupid questions," Julie answered, putting her arms around Paul's neck.

"Your feelings still safe to bet on?"

"They'll always be."

He placed his hands around her waist and kissed her, letting his lips melt into hers.

"Someday someone's gonna be around."

"Well, until then..." and he playfully started moving his hands up toward her breasts.

She nimbly leaped out of his grasp. "Not in public, Paul," she mocked. Then she grew serious again. "Let's go see if Sam has anything for us."

As they continued walking towards the Housing Sector, Paul went over the security problem again in his mind. Until things died down, they could refuse to admit anyone; or they could strengthen the already existing security. Either way, it amounted to the same thing: the next two months were going to be two of T.E.I.'s toughest. The fact that they'd already had some minor public disturbances at the facility did not help matters any. Somehow, it seemed, T.E.I., Gregory Torrden's icon of nonconformism, always managed to get on the wrong side of people.

They soon stepped off the elevator onto the third floor of the Housing Sector. When they got to Sam's room, Paul could tell from the look on his face that the old man had good news.

"Come on in, Paul, Julie," he beckoned. "Have a seat, and before you do, here." He pulled out two already prepared drinks from the right hand drawer of his polished mahogany desk and extended them in the direction of the couple.

Paul and Julie took the drinks before sitting in the chairs that Sam had provided for them. Paul broke his smile long enough to say, "Whiskey? What's the occasion, Sam? I know we could not have been granted a space this early."

Sam smiled and pulled out an additional bottle and glass from his drawer of surprises. He unscrewed the top and poured the liquor into the glass until it was three-quarters full.

"Pineapple wine — never could get away from the stuff. But as for your question, Paul, no, we didn't get a space. Yet. That call I received was from a member of the Thirty-five. They want to see us in two days. They are interviewing everyone who has been recommended for the December fifteenth Flight. We still have a chance, Paul!"

The three of them brought their glasses together and sipped to Julie's jubilant toast of: "To the success of T.E.I."

"That is if we play our cards right, Sam," Paul warned. "The public knows of our interview, I take it? That's what I feared. You know we'll have to disclose practically everything related to our projects if we even hope to appeal to the Thirty-five?" Sam nodded again, but before he could reply, Paul went on: "And the attitude of Jerul Scalos is a pretty popular one down there. If we fail to impress the Thirty-five, not only do we have to suffer the inadequacies of remaining here on Earth, but we will have to face a pretty large number of people that will certainly want to resurrect many of the questions that have been asked about us in the past."

Sam took another sip of his wine and wistfully nodded his head. "But only because of their ignorance, Paul. No, I haven't forgotten that. I also haven't forgotten that I have waited more than a half century to see the final product of what your grandfather started. I know now that I'll never see that product, but the least we can do is make sure nothing stops the process necessary for its completion. Besides, we've been working so hard, we have practically cut ourselves off from the rest of what's happening outside."

"What are you getting at?" Julie queried.

"This. The Triship has not been able to do a damn thing to control the masses. Curfews, police reinforcement, nothing's working. If this trouble keeps up, the public's gonna turn on us sooner or later. To them, we are just another product of the last century that has not done a thing for the benefit of the people. Take the disturbance at the end of today's test, for example.

"And in addition to all that, the latest news line from the Sci-Tech Research boys over at the Eastern Shore has it that the Sixteenth New World Launch is returning to Earth."

Paul leaned forward. "Returning to Earth? Why?"

"Can't say for sure," Sam shrugged. "But you remember all the ruckus that was raised several years back, when we got those photographs of the alien ship that they found? Well, it seems not too long after that, they started documenting 'behavioral problems that jeopardized the success of the mission,' at least that's how they're reporting it on the news. You know, what they found was some pretty spooky stuff — I guess the confinement in space for such a long period of time began to wear down everyone. But all of this is just conjecture — everything's hidden behind a wall of bureaucracy, as usual."

"Will this delay the next Launch?" Julie asked.

"Can't say," Sam shrugged again. "Until they lift the news blackout, it will be difficult to guess what the Pan-government will do."

Paul took another sip of his drink. "Which brings us back to our original topic. What else did they say about the interview?"

Sam cleared his throat. "That's just it — nothing. They obviously did not want us asking questions about it. We can assume, of course, that they'll want to see our research reports and any important internal correspondence."

Paul nodded slowly. He and Julie finished their drinks and stayed to talk with Sam a little while longer before returning to their own room. And all through that time, something kept nagging at the back of his mind. Things were going well, and yet, it was as if some god were frantically throwing snowflakes of warning at him — and he just could not quite catch the entire snowball.

Part 2. (18 October 2124)

After many fruitless attempts to discover published works by Gregory Torrden, I am forced to draw the conclusion that, aside from scientific papers, no books that were written by Gregory Torrden have ever been made available to the general public. It is rumored that a private collection does exist; but that the volumes of said collection are the property of T.E.I.

Thus, my task looked hopeless until I visited the main branch of the Earth Wildlife Alliance, located just 300 kilometers south of T.E.I., three days ago. Upon recognition of my...societal status, the E.W.A. revealed, though reluctantly, certain portions of Gregory Torrden's original application for funds that was submitted to the organization. Of appropriate interest is the following quote that appeared in his résumé:

"...The so-called latent capabilities of animals may...never be recognized by man. Indeed, these intellectual capabilities may be in full bloom, in which case it is man who is then fooling himself when he fails to avoid or understand the anthropomorphic pitfall when dealing with animals ..."

This particular quote caught my attention in that it served as the thesis statement for the "Personal Beliefs and Attitudes" section of the E.W.A.'s application. Only time will tell whether or not it has any significance to T.E.I.'s research.

Although it has long been known that T.E.I.'s primary objective has been the conservation and continued survival of the snow leopard, it is peculiar how tightly the secret of Gregory Torrden's research motives have been withheld from the general laity. Of all the students that have attended the T.E.I. university, it has been said that only those who choose to become full-time T.E.I. employees are ever told what is actually taking place with respect to the major research endeavors; and this information is only divulged to members with three years or more of employment at T.E.I. Though there have been drop-outs, it is fascinating to note that no one has ever been able to accurately reveal the truth behind the myths!

Even Paul Torrden, who is presently the organization's C.E.O. (his father, Carl Torrden, was killed in a questionable trans-car accident in 2102), has been noted on several occasions to obviously refrain from exposing his grandfather's primary research intentions. Only three days ago, for example, in a meeting with the Interplanetary Space Flight Commission, Paul Torrden took care to collectively label T.E.I.'s 75 years worth of behavioral research as a "project" — an all too commonplace description for such a monumental secret.

Indeed, over the past 50 years, T.E.I. has received many attacks, in various accusatory forms, from the Pan-government, the E.W.A., and, of course, the public. An attempt was made to lessen these political assaults by opening T.E.I. to public visitation in 2105, but this action has done little to achieve its desired goal.

And now, given the present world situation, it would appear that T.E.I. may soon be forced to reveal its ace of spades.

Part 3. (11 November 2124)

The inevitable circumstance of which I spoke nearly a month ago is almost at hand; tomorrow, the I.S.F.C., in coordination with the Thirty-Five Consulting Members, will interview Paul Torrden and his associates to determine if T.E.I. will be granted 70,000 cubic meters of space aboard the Twentieth New World Launch. (Some critic, in a weak attempt at humor, suggested that all the fighting would stop for several hours because so many people would want to know the outcome of the T.E.I. predicament.)

However, of greater importance, is the fact that I was lucky enough to attain what I feel may have been an unprecedented view of the snow leopards yesterday. Allowing for the facts that I have never seen snow leopards in their natural habitat nor studied their characteristic behavior in captivity, I must confess that several of the leopards at T.E.I., for some reason that I can not identify, did not meet the expectations one would normally have for cat-like behavior. As a result, I am finding it harder and harder to completely ignore the quotation that I cited in my 18 October entry.

In light of what I have seen and read on this fascinating topic, I find that I am very eager to learn the result of tomorrow's meeting.

Tomorrow also marks the occurrence of another event that may affect T.E.I. — the return of the Sixteenth New World Launch, after only nine years in space. Initial reports of hysteria, paranoia, and other clinical symptoms of psychological afflictions among the crew and passengers of the Sixteenth surfaced as early as several years ago, but only very recently has the I.S.F.C. disclosed the news of this Launch's return to Earth. The secrecy and classified nature of tomorrow's landing have been more widely publicized by the Pan-government than the actual event itself. Although the actual touchdown site has not been announced, it is known that the entire crew will be placed under strict and unlimited quarantine. To what extent these actions foreshadow the discovery of heretofore unknown hazards affecting the New World Launch program (and therefore the date of the 20th New World Launch's departure) is not known.

Part 4. (12 November 2124)

So far the trip had been a complete disaster. As soon as they had left T.E.I., bad fortune began raining down upon them. Their guards had been able to do little to protect them as mobs of angry people tried to prevent them from reaching the trans-car. As a result, Paul and Julie were both somewhat scratched and bruised, mostly because they had tried to give Sam more protection than they allotted to themselves; and all the while the old man had complained about how durable he still was.

When they reached the trans-car, they had been automatically told by the trans-rail operator that P.C. clearance was no longer being granted due to the occurrence of a large number of uncontrollable derailments; and that if they still wished to ride, speeds in excess of 125 kph were considered unsafe and would not be covered by the trans-rail insurance system.

Fortunately, they had anticipated such complications and had planned for them by leaving earlier than necessary; but still they were delayed along the middle part of their journey by the most frenzied fighting to date in the Uprisings' riots. Four times they had been forced to stop — for periods of up to an hour — due to the occurrences of temporary electrical failures or gruesome accidents. That had been strange: emerging from the artificially induced tranquility of the travelling trans-car into a maelstrom of smoke and blood created by people who, more than anything else, resembled savages and did not care who you were, where you were from, or where you were going. The T.E.I. team had nearly become victims of the riots when they barely missed getting caught in the cross fire between the police and an anti-socialist group ...

...and it was not getting any better. A lot of pre-2070 alliances had been established again, and there had been rumors that P.O.W. camps and terrorist activities were being organized once more in some areas of the world.

"We're slowing down," Sam said, cutting into Paul's thoughts.

"Are there going to be more crowds?" Julie asked, her eyes closed.

None of them was looking at the micro-vision clips. Paul was beginning to think that the Economics and Transport Commission had wasted a pretty sum of money on the installation of that service in the vehicles.

"Probably, Jul. Just guard the documents. Make sure we don't lose anything."

He did not want to tell her that it was going to be worse than it had been at T.E.I.; besides, he felt sure she knew that already. Yet, he felt overly uneasy when, as the trans-car came to a stop, the apparent size of the crowd made itself known by way of the intensity and variety of incantations and shouts he could hear. The micro-vision film clips came to a stop and the screens rolled back. Julie stifled a scream as about 15 people charged up to the car and hastily peered in through the now transparent windows. They began to rock the vehicle back and forth, and several of them, equipped with sturdy metal instruments, had already partially jimmied open one of the doors when a meager amount of government police forced its way through the crowd and formed a half circle around the broken door. It had begun to snow, but still the people would not leave: in their attempt to escape anarchy they were unknowingly producing it themselves.

Aided by the poorly developed protection of the police, Julie followed Sam and Paul through the door. They then proceeded to make their way slowly to the steps of the Government Building, shielding their documents as best as possible from the wet snow, rocks, and whatever else had been borne into the air amidst the chaos.

Within seconds, the frenzied atmosphere was punctuated by tumultuous cries from the crowd. "Take 'em down, take 'em down!" came the yells, from several directions. Paul thought, for just a moment, that he saw a gun pointed in his direction. But then he was buffeted by the circle of officers as they tried to negotiate a path for him toward the Government Building.

The pushing and shoving suddenly became more violent, and Paul's fears of a firearm in the crowd was suddenly realized when a loud *pop* rang through the air. There was a half-second of silence, after which the intensity of the oppression around their protective guards resumed.

The policeman next to Paul abruptly halted. The guard's wide-eyed appearance and shortness of breath caught Paul by surprise.

"You can count me out of this, sir!" the policeman shouted at the guard in front of him, who was presumably his supervisor. "There's far too many of them, and not nearly enough of us. I signed up with this outfit to feed my wife and kids, not to be remembered by having my name engraved on some damn wall." The policeman's supervisor had no time to respond as the frightened officer quickly bolted into the crowd, seeking his own safe destiny.

A groping hand suddenly latched onto Paul's shoulder, and he could feel himself being pulled into the angry mob. A pain shot up his arm as another rebellious member of the crowd latched onto his wrist. However, just as quickly, the remaining police officers closed the gap that had been created by their frightened comrade and one officer used a club to beat the crowd away from Paul.

After a few more seconds, they began slowly moving forward again. It took ten minutes to reach the steps and an additional five to reach the doorway of the large hall. Paul found it hard to believe he was sweating profusely in the -4 degree Centigrade weather.

Once inside, several of the officers directed them to the elevator. "That's not the worst of it," one of the officers warned, "every one of those nuts out there has got himself a source in here. They usually know about what's going down before we do. Though, with people like you, I guess it really doesn't matter." A wry grin spread across the officer's bearded face.

"Just tell us where we have to go," Julie blurted.

That brought the officer to an abrupt halt. He stared at Julie for a couple moments and then smiled again. "Sure, lady. You just walk into that there 'vator, press a button with a three on it, and get off on the third floor, 'kay? Then you go to room three-fifty-six, pick a number and wait — they're running behind schedule. There it is, see, we *could* have taken you there, but you said 'tell us,' so we told you.

"Come on, they're not worth the trouble," he finished curtly, turning on his heel and leaving the other guards to more or less follow him; and all of them did, not doing too much to hide the grins on their faces.

Paul normally would have said something, but he kept quiet, as their small group was drastically outnumbered. One thing was for sure, though: T.E.I. was certainly nobody's favorite around here, and he knew he'd be surprised if he found anyone who would even be willing to listen to their arguments.

They rode the elevator up to the third floor, and when they got off, another policeman with a digital clipboard and tally instrument stopped and questioned them. When he'd heard enough, he directed them to room 356, which was nothing more than a small dusty side room that branched off from a huge auditorium. One man and two women were already ahead of them.

"It won't be long," the officer said. "Either you make it or you don't. It's that simple." With that he turned and headed back toward the elevators.

Sam had been unusually quiet, and Paul could tell by the grim look on his face that the old man's optimism of two days ago had almost dwindled to total pessimism. As they sat down in the corner of the room, near where they had entered, a door on the opposite side opened up and a man in a green flannel suit beckoned for the two women to follow him into the auditorium. Before the door closed, Paul estimated he saw more than 400 people. He guessed that almost half of them would be public visitors. Another hundred or so were sure to be reporters; and the remainder, of course, would be made up of the various government officials.

Julie sighed. "It looks so hopeless."

Sam looked at her, shaking his head. "We're gonna get it, Julie. I don't care if I have to sing and dance for them or tear all my hair out. If that's what it takes, then that's what I'll do."

Sam had no more than finished talking when the man on the other side of the room focused his attention on the T.E.I. staff. He had a thick but well trimmed, brown moustache and a smile that just would not quit. A nervous glint sparkled in his eyes.

"That's pro'bly what it's gonna take, if not more, old man," he blurted. "They've got three times the number of applicants than they can handle and they're not letting anyone — hey, aren't you Paul Torrden, from that leopard place?"

Paul nodded, reluctantly.

The other man's moustache seemed to quiver with anticipation, as if he were contemplating the significance of Paul's presence. "Well, gee, ain't that something. Listen, I hope you and your leopards make it, you know? It's a damn shame everyone's against you. Used to see pictures of them animals myself. Always loved them in a way, you know? I —"

He stopped as the man in the green suit opened the door and pointed at him.

"You're next."

The brown moustache gathered up his coat. As he left, he turned to Paul. "Good luck, and may your day be good. You just might make it, Mr. Torr —" and the door closed shut on his words and his smile.

Sam stood up. "I bet you he's practiced that grin for weeks; it never left his face."

Julie laughed. "Still, he's the only nice thing that has happened to us the whole day."

Sam agreed. "I could use some of my wine, too." He began pacing the room, his small shoes clicking dully on the streaked, tiled floor. Each member of the trio became lost in his/her own inner thoughts.

However, the long-practiced smile was apparently all the man with the brown moustache had going for him: five minutes later the green-suited officer opened the door once more.

Paul and Julie gathered up the data sheets and followed Sam into the auditorium. Paul could feel the eyes of everyone on them as they walked toward the two empty tables in the front of the auditorium which their green-suited chaperon had casually pointed out. The Thirty-five Council Members were seated in ranked chairs directly in front of these tables; while the floor was mostly populated with lower government officials and reporters. The public witnesses lined both sides of the auditorium and were separated from the officials and reporters by a long row of police personnel.

Paul could feel the tension in the air. As they made their way through the crowd he thought he recognized one of the camera-men. But he did not have much time to think about it, because his eyes fell on Jerul Scalos; and what he saw told him that this was the man who would be their last barrier to the December 15th flight. They had no sooner sat down than when R.L. Dennings, Spokesperson of the Thirty-five, addressed the trio.

"Paul Torrden, will you please rise. You are here to represent Torrden Enterprises Incorporated. Is that correct?"

"Yes, yes it is," Paul answered.

"Will you please inform the Council members and the public of the identities of your two colleagues," continued Dennings.

"The woman is my wife, Julie Torrden, and this is my head assistant at T.E.I., Sam Gray."

"Thank you, Mr. Torrden. As you know, yours is a special case, and we will appreciate your cooperation to the fullest extent. It is normal in these matters to let those parties who have expressed opposing viewpoints to present their cases first. In this instance, Commissioner Scalos of the Interplanetary Space Flight Commission has expressed a desire to present to the Council data which support his recommendation that your request be denied. You may be seated. Commissioner?"

Scalos stood up then, and his inauspicious expression turned into a wide but shallow smile as he shifted his gaze from the T.E.I. representative to Dennings. "Councilman Dennings, I thank you kindly. However, I feel that Torrden Enterprises has manifested its own opposition over the last seventy years, and so, in the interest of the public, I think we should start off not with learning what the public already knows, but with hearing the obviously audacious reasons as to why sixty or more people will have their applications ignored to make room for some wild animals. I therefore pass on my right as first speaker and offer the floor to Mr. Torrden."

Dennings thought the request over for a moment, his fingers running idly through his long, black hair. Though his appearance had shocked many over 15 years ago, when he had been appointed to his present position, his witty intellect and bold demeanor at hearings had gained him much respect. "Very well. If there are no objections, Mr. Torrden, will you please rise and present your arguments?"

Paul stood up again, silently cursing Scalos. The damned official had chosen his language perfectly. And every word had shouted one meaning: to turn the Thirty-five against T.E.I.

Paul walked around to the front of the table. "Councilman Dennings," he began, "my arguments are actually my grandfather's, and everything I tell you today will essentially be what he told me over ten years ago.

"This was Gregory Torrden's main line of reasoning: he noted that at the beginning of the last century there had been several important debates in the field of science, particularly in ethology and comparative psychology, as to whether or not animals actually think and reason as we do. The lay people who supported this idea did so mainly because they loved animals so much that they could not admit that animals could not think, as they blindly associated 'not thinking' with stupidity. And even those who felt sure that animals lower than primates could think and reason as humans do, *and* claimed they had evidence that this was indeed true, were never able to fully satisfy themselves that animals were capable of insight learning, which is the highest form of learning that we know of.

"Even the scientists who studied these matters disagreed amongst themselves. For over a century, some argued that the way in which animals set about to solve problems is nothing more than the culmination of trial and error learning, or instrumental conditioning; their line of reasoning was that if a certain behavior is followed by some reward or punishment, the frequency of that behavior will change as a result, thus representing a conditioned response. Yet, others argued that at least some species of mammals, and indeed most primates other than man, solved problems using learning processes that transcended mere instrumental conditioning. In the end, it could be said that the concept of intelligence, and the notion that humans have more of it than other animals, was never universally accepted by the entire scientific community. Indeed, when we look at how each species interacts with its own environment, it becomes difficult to discern any difference in what we would call intelligence between one nonhuman vertebrate and another."

Paul paused for a breath and as quickly regretted it. Scalos was still on his feet and quickly seized the opportunity to attack Paul's remarks.

"One minute, Mr. Torrden, are you saying that over sixty otherwise normal citizens will be turned down to make room for a program that has spent seventy years trying to prove animals can *think*?"

The crowd of public viewers suddenly came to life, and though Paul could not decipher any particular words, he could sense the general discontent.

"Councilman Dennings," he appealed, "I have yet to complete my statements."

Dennings looked at Scalos, then at Torrden, and finally at the aroused crowd. He allowed his cool stare to silence everyone before saying, "You elected to have Mr. Torrden present his evidence first, Commissioner Scalos. Please allow him to finish before beginning your rebuttal." Then, staring at Paul, he added, "Please continue."

"Thank you, Councilman Dennings." Paul could feel that very little sympathy towards him remained in the crowd of spectators, but he found the strength to go on. "To put this entire issue into the proper perspective, we all must remember that there has always been a great deal of confusion involving the meaning of terms used by scientists studying cognitive behavior. For this reason, defining intelligence and measuring it is very difficult in humans and becomes even more complicated when one begins to apply these concepts to animals.

"Of the two views I outlined several minutes ago, my grandfather, of course, chose the side that believed animals could think and reason, and one of his first goals was to verify that this was indeed true. In order to do this he made two assumptions, the first of which was that a purely instinctive mind is rigid and stereotyped, and thus not open to change. It is only a mind that is prepared to respond to certain, predetermined stimuli, resulting in completely functional behavior patterns that cannot be altered by the experiences associated with their performance. Thus, no matter how many times an animal performs the behavior, it is always the same behavior. These instinctive responses are, then, innate behavioral mechanisms, and are perhaps largely genetically determined.

"The second assumption that he made was that any system can be overloaded, especially an instinctive one. With these two assumptions, then, he set out to prove this generalization: an animal incapable of reasoning would not be able to react appropriately to a complex combination of stimuli designed to elicit an equally complex variety of responses."

Scalos was on his feet again. "And have you proven this generalization, Mr. Torrden?"

Paul could feel his confidence returning. "We feel we have, yes."

"Oh?" Scalos' reaction was one of surprise and suspicion.

Paul motioned to the documents on the table. "We brought with us records of all the major advancements we've made. They include the special protein diets our chemists have formulated for the project as well as the results each succeeding generation of animals, including the snow leopards, have given us. I might add that, due to the limited number of snow leopards available to us, we have essentially just observed the outward behavioral effects of our program in that species. However, we have approached the issue from a neuro-anatomical and physiological point of view in more numerous animals, such as dogs and rats."

Scalos' cunning face turned into his trademark pompous smile again as he turned from Paul to the Thirty-five. "Councilmen, I appeal to you. This man wishes to use seventy thousand cubic meters of space — that's an entire deck, gentlemen — to prove that animals can think. And all he offers as proof for his so-called advancements are graphs, tables, and meaningless words on paper that have had seventy years to become the lies and exaggerations which they probably are. Tell me, Councilmen, is this worth it?"

Paul was momentarily numbed into silence by the apparent turn in events. Scalos had turned the interview into a hopeless court hearing! The Thirty-five were sure to decline his application, especially if they allowed themselves to be influenced by the public visitors on whose faces a clear reflection of anger was beginning to show. And yet, deep down, he could feel the simple morality of the whole issue haunting him as much as Scalos' blind obstinacy. He barely heard Dennings ask him, "Is that all the proof you have, Mr. Torrden? Is there any other evidence you wish to present?"

Paul motioned to his documents. "That is all we have, Councilman Dennings. If you wish, the data we have here may be interpreted by an independent and impartial ethologist. We believe that all of our claims will be upheld."

Those words did not even have time to echo back and forth in the suddenly quiet room before Scalos abruptly straightened, appearing to grow several inches in his apparent victory. "Can anyone help this man?" he cried out, waving his arms dramatically. Then, turning to Dennings and the rest of the Thirty-five, he said, "Councilmen, I move that this organization's application be denied."

Dennings played his fingers through his hair once more. He glanced at Torrden but the T.E.I. official did not volunteer any additional information. "Very well. I will now ask the Thirty-five to vote on —"

"I can help this man!"

That produced an uproar in the crowd. Who was it? A camera-man, of all things!

That produced a momentary surprised look in the face of R.L. Dennings. No one interrupts the speech of a Council Member, especially a speech by R. L. Dennings!

That produced a look of recognition in Paul Torrden. It was the camera-man he had noticed when he had approached the table where he now stood; it had been the same camera-man who had been present at his first interview with the I.S.F.C.

Sammy Lassiter stepped forward, his tall figure commanding as much attention as his inappropriate exclamation had.

Dennings quickly regained his composure. "What is your name and purpose, camera-man?"

The crowd quieted down under Dennings' authoritative voice.

The camera-man approached the front of the auditorium. "I am Sammy Lassiter, and if I could have access to a closed circuit televisor, I think I can provide the evidence needed to validate Mr. Torrden's claims."

"Hold it," Scalos raged, "he doesn't even represent T.E.I.! How can —"

"You were the one who asked, 'Can anyone help this man?'" Dennings said coldly. "My tolerance of the disorderliness which has characterized this interview has about reached an end, Mr. Scalos. The legalities of this matter can not be ignored." He motioned to several of the guards as he continued: "We shall have the screen lowered and provide a closed circuit system, as the camera-man requests."

Sammy turned and winked an eye at Paul, which only served to deepen the mystery for the T.E.I. representative. The crowd continued to buzz, and law enforcement personnel and reporters were in constant motion as they sought the most advantageous positions from which to view the impending spectacle. Paul found himself glued to the floor in confusion. He glanced at Sam and Julie, but neither of them was able to offer any explanation for the aberrant behavior of the camera-man in the front of the auditorium. It was only moments later when a large white screen was lowered from the ceiling and positioned in place above and behind the ranked chairs of the 35 Council Members. Two women guards then entered through a side door, carrying the relay unit for the closed circuit system of the auditorium. One of them plugged the long cord into a special socket in the front wall while the other guard carried the unit up to the table in front of Sammy Lassiter. "It's hooked up to the televisor, sir," she said.

Sammy Lassiter nodded his thanks and then did something most reporters did not do in public: he unplugged the Camera Pack from his left hand. He then placed the prongs of the short wires into the relay unit and began switching several levers on the Camera Pack. Finally, looking up at Dennings, he said, "If someone could extinguish the lights?"

Dennings nodded and, somewhere, a guard hit the switch. The auditorium was bathed in blackness for a moment, and the only sounds were those of the 35 Council members as they turned in their chairs to face the screen.

And on that screen appeared the snow-covered landscape of the domed enclosure at T.E.I.! Paul's first reaction was naturally one of shock and amazement. When had this man been allowed —. It was then that Paul sensed the captivation that beheld the audience as it watched a close-up view of Colonel emerging from the cave.

A second wave of shock rolled over Paul. This camera-man had to be the person he had spotted on the day of Colonel's test. But why —.

"Tell 'em what's happening, damn it!" he heard Sam whisper behind him.

And he began to narrate the scene, to describe the meanings and intricacies of the test. He presented the cold facts of Colonel's training to the audience. That the snow leopard had never been exposed to a metal wall and yet had crossed it as if it were not even there produced a stir in the viewers.

Paul could feel the momentum begin to flow his way again. He grabbed the wave and rode along, whipping it to make it grow.

His voice took on a firmer note as he informed everyone that Colonel had to recognize the fluttering birds as meaningless objects; that the electronic signal still commanded primary attention in the animal's mind. Paul smiled to himself when he saw Scalos lean forward eagerly as Colonel began walking toward the grouse. *Had Torrden's leopard failed the test?* No! Paul cried to himself, and he could hear the muffled obscenities stumble out of Scalos' mouth as Colonel altered his path in pursuit of the signal's source.

As the image of Colonel advancing through each stage of the test played out on the screen, Paul graphically described the meaning of the leopard's actions and how they reflected the animal's ability to adapt to unforeseen obstacles placed in its path. Everyone in the auditorium appeared to radiate intense anticipation as they awaited Colonel's each move.

However, no one in the room was prepared for the scene that immediately followed the end of the test. When the leopard started off toward the child, Paul could hear several cries of anguish pass through the crowd. He also caught a glimpse of Scalos, whose head was turning nervously in the darkness. The sight provided more confidence to Paul. "At this point," he said, "the only logical explanation I can give is that Colonel attempted to protect the child from the other leopards. Note how he appeared to guard her from the other animals that try to approach." At this point, Paul fell silent and let the rest of the film tell its own story.

The rescue team arrived and weapons were drawn as the men approached the leopard. Not a sound in the auditorium could be heard as leopard and man stared at one another. Then the stalemate was over. The audience came to life with a roar of approval as the majestic cat made the correct choice and moved away from the T.E.I. personnel.

Paul felt himself become one with Colonel as he watched the leopard race back down the hillside. He waited for the audience's exclamations of appreciation to die down before adding: "The child was successfully removed from the enclosure and reunited with her parents." And he had to allow himself a well-earned smile when the room erupted into applause as Colonel returned to the mouth of the cave. Of course! It was the living beauty of nature, not the ease with which one could semanticize words, that could always tame a hostile audience.

Paul was momentarily lost in his rediscovered pride as Lassiter flicked a switch on his Camera Pack that sent the auditorium into darkness once more. The lights came on only seconds later, and Lassiter narrowly prevented Scalos from taking up the attack again by speaking quickly himself.

"Councilman Dennings, I just happened to be at Torrden Enterprises when this test was being run. I am, in no way, in collaboration with Mr. Torrden and I can assure you that Mr. Torrden and I have not met until now. It is on the basis of these facts and, of course, Mr. Torrden's brilliant narration, that I ask for this recording to be accepted as legitimate proof of Mr. Torrden's claims."

Scalos pounced on the table in front of him. "This is outrageous, Councilman —."

Dennings quickly silenced him with a narrow stare. "I am quickly growing tired of your outbursts, Mr. Scalos." Then he turned to Paul.

"You said your grandfather was trying to prove animals could think and reason. Why, then, do you base your need to be accepted on a New World Flight on the grounds that you need a new place to complete your research when it has just been shown that you *have* completed your studies?"

Paul saw Scalos raise an eyebrow; the Commissioner evidently liked the question. It was the kind of inquiry the I.S.F.C. official would probably have asked himself in due time.

"The answer, Councilman Dennings, is two-fold. First, T.E.I. continues to work with Earth Wildlife Alliance officials in the fight to restore world ecosystems. In the event that the functioning of ecosystems in central Asia can be restored to their natural range of variance, it is our hope that we can help reintroduce the snow leopard to its natural habitat in the high elevation mountains. This is, and always has been, the primary objective of T.E.I.'s existence. However, given the turmoil that exists today on the Earth, we feel it is only fitting that this species be given every right to survive in perpetuity. To that end, we would continue to maintain our captive population at T.E.I., and as a fail-safe measure, we would maintain a second one aboard the New World Flight, and eventually at the new planet which is our destination.

"However, perhaps the more important answer lies in the fact that Gregory Torrden felt man ascribed too many human characteristics to animals. Again, what we view as intelligence or intelligent behavior in humans may not always apply with other, nonhuman species. He further supposed that there was an...alternate order of learning, if you will, one which is found in all animals to some extent, and which we have yet to discover. It is very important that we show that data, or knowledge, if you will, is not merely stored in an animal's memory; that it is actually cognitively manipulated as a means for accomplishing purposive tasks — that is, that animals have insight into the relationship between means and ends. This was his last goal, and so far, it has yet to be proven. We feel this alternate order of learning may be very significant and are only requesting the use of a new testing area to pursue this last goal."

Paul watched the Councilman closely. What he had just said had been one of Gregory Torrden's most emphatic beliefs; and though he was positive that it somehow fit into the mystery of the whole program, he knew he'd never be able to explain it any further if asked to do so.

R. L. Dennings held up his hand. "Very well. This matter has taken up enough time. Commissioner Scalos has pointed out that Torrden Enterprises Incorporated has created its own opposition over the last seventy years. Mr. Torrden and, inadvertently so, Mr. Lassiter, have made claims and arguments to nullify this opposition. I will now ask the Thirty-five to vote on the issue."

When, several moments later, the panel in front of the Council members illuminated itself to reveal the numbers, "24 YES to 11 NO," Paul was surprised to see that almost half of the audience shouted its approval. That very audience had been totally against him only 40 minutes ago.

But he got his greatest pleasure out of watching Scalos reluctantly pounce into his chair, angered defeat plastered across his face.

R. L. Dennings raised a hand to silence the audience, an action that was immediately obeyed.

"Congratulations on your acceptance, Mr. Torrden," he spoke loudly. "We will contact you within a week to make final transportation arrangements. If you will follow the two guards in front of you, they will lead you to your escort. Thank you for your attendance and may your day be good."

Once they were out in the hallway, Paul turned to Sammy Lassiter. "You've got a helluva lot of explaining to do, but man, what you did was certainly fantastic!"

"Well, it was actually very simple," Sammy replied. "I went into T.E.I.

as a tourist. Then I became a camera-man. I was actually looking for a source of information for an account I've been doing on your family. I began talking to a guard near one of the portals, and let me tell you, Mr. Torrden, he was very good at his job. He did not give me one piece of useful information and would have proceeded to throw me out if he hadn't been called to assist in some trouble further up the hall. While he was gone, I decided to take some candid shots of your leopards, which is quite easy since the Camera Pack can magnify anything I can see. I guess I was simply curious about why the guard did not want me to look through the portals."

"That's probably what did it for us, too," Sam cut in. "Everyone really enjoyed the vividness of it." The pleasure in Sam's voice abounded in his every word.

Paul took Julie's hand as they followed the guards into the elevator. They stepped out again on the ground floor and Paul was relieved to see that a different group of police officers was there to escort them back to the trans-car. But the trip through the crowd was not any easier. These people had not seen Sammy's film, and they just could not understand why this man and his snow leopards were being granted a place on the Twentieth New World Launch.

When they finally got to the trans-car, Julie was the first one to enter the vehicle. She began pressing the coordinates for T.E.I., and as soon as everyone else had entered the trans-car, it began to slide forward. The crowd gave way as the trans-car gathered speed, and the four occupants soon found themselves a good distance away from the Government Building. The screens came down automatically, with their usual boring display of micro-vision flicks.

Julie turned to the camera-man. "And where do you want to go? I almost forgot?"

Sammy's face showed a little surprise. "Well," he began after a moment, "I'm no longer good for the firm — reporters are not supposed to illegally film anything, you know. That's why our Camera Packs are monitored daily. Nor can we show anything to the public without prior approval from our bosses. It's unethical. They would probably shoot me if I showed my face in the office again."

He paused, thought a little longer, and then continued. "So...I could go with you — if you could squeeze one more man in on the roster. But —," he trailed off.

Before he could continue, Paul said, "You definitely deserve it, Mr. Lassiter. After what you did back there and all."

The camera-man grinned. "Thanks. And call me Sammy."

Julie laughed. "We'll have to. This old timer here is Sam," she said, pointing at the grinning face of the green-eyed old man at her side.

"And if I didn't thank you before, I'm doing it now," Sam Gray replied, nodding toward the camera-man.

Paul leaned back and chuckled to himself. He idly watched the micro-vision film that played on the screen nearest him. It depicted a snowy winter land of some child's imaginative dream. Paul closed his eyes. His own dream had become reality. They were finally aboard the Twentieth New World Flight!

Chapter 3

■■■■■■■■■■■■■■■■■■■■

The
Stranahan

■■■■■■■■■■■■■■■■■■■■■

Part 1. (18 December 2124)

T hree shuttles lifted off from the Earth three days ago to carry the passengers to the orbit of the 20th New World Launch. The Launch itself began without incident but not without intense anxiety.

Immediately upon the return of the Sixteenth New World Launch shuttles to the Old Alaska Port, the Pan-government directed the I.S.F.C. to keep the entire crew of that Launch under strict quarantine. When pressed by the news media for specific answers, the Pan-government refused to divulge any information, although several leaks from top ranking sources among the newly-realigned I.S.F.C. allowed a cadre of reporters to put together pieces of the soon-to-be world-recognized puzzle.

It was almost five years ago when the I.S.F.C. received the Sixteenth's first distress call from space. This initial plea for help described a series of illnesses that had appeared on all levels of the ship as the outer limits of the solar system were being approached. With only a few exceptions, all of these illnesses were similar to one another, and each case involved severe mental trauma and symptoms paralleling schizophrenia. The I.S.F.C. and the crew of the Sixteenth arrived at a decision to have the Launch return to Earth prior to its first Hyper Leap, although it has only recently been revealed that certain crew members did not favor this path of action. They claimed that some virus or plague had somehow infected many of the crew and passengers following their encounter with the now infamous derelict alien ship that was discovered by the Sixteenth in an unexplored region of our solar system. Unfortunately, the medical teams aboard the Sixteenth had not been able to isolate any known, or unknown, contagion to support that theory.

After returning to Earth, however, it was only several days before speculation surfaced that the top quarantine port in the Flight Council network had been breached. Later, as communication lines with the Old Alaska Port began to dissolve, two elite camera-men did an exclusive documentary on these events that revealed that quarantine efforts at the Port had been completely ineffective. An excessively large number of guards and other administrative Port personnel had begun to develop the same symptoms encountered by the crew of the Sixteenth within hours after the surface to ship shuttles had landed. It was then that the world learned that the returning crew of the Sixteenth New World Launch included only about 60 individuals — all of the other nearly 900 crew and passengers had died during the return trip to Earth!

After several anarchistic riots, law and order within the Port facility had been partially reestablished by an alliance of crew members from the Sixteenth and Port administrative personnel who claimed to have been unaffected by what many people were now calling "the mental virus." Several of these individuals were interviewed by the camera-men and described a process by which men and women "appeared to suddenly become possessed," expressing multiple personalities and loss of free will before slowly slipping into a state of semi-insanity. In the end, death came to the severely sick while they slept. Within days, residents in nearby communities were beginning to exhibit many of the same symptoms already referenced above. Government aerial surveillance maneuvers were even suspended after several of the pilots inexplicably lost control of their hoverplanes.

The remaining scientists at the Port continued their work in spite of the deteriorating conditions, and by early December, they finally announced that the results of their initial autopsies revealed massive destruction of cells in that part of the brain which is known as the corpus callosum. As a result of the scientists' announcement, the new Triship and the Thirty-five were heavily petitioned to invoke the exigent defense clause, which would have allowed the Sci-Tech Research Commission to unite with the International World Police for the purpose of eradicating the Port and "neutralizing" the known affected area. These recommendations were surreptitiously shelved by those claiming that no significant action could be taken until additional data were collected.

By this time, however, the restored peace and order in the remaining areas of the Port had begun to crumble, forcing an abrupt end to the investigation by the two camera-men who had illegally crossed the inviolate quarantine zone. During the chaos and confusion that followed, it appears that only one of these two camera-men escaped from the Port alive. He was immediately seized by the Pan-government officials, but not before transmitting his story to a scrambled black market network. I was able to pick up several stray feeds from the black market signal as the ship I am on now propelled itself further and further into space. I have documented above all that I have learned. Strangely, I fear that our Launch will be the last to ever leave Earth.

Part 2. (15 March 2125)

The ship was named the *Stranahan*. It had other, more common, names as well. Such as 'Generation Starship' or 'Twentieth New World Mission.'

Aboard it, Paul relaxed in his small but comfortable room. Julie was off exploring the ship, as usual. The *Stranahan* both intrigued and frightened her. It was only natural for her to want to find out everything she could about it.

He put down the Information Booklet she had been asking him to read ever since they had left Earth two months ago...or had it been three months? According to what he had just read, it really did not matter. The *Stranahan* would not begin its first Hyper Leap until after it reached the orbit of Pluto — which was still more than seven and a half years away. A number of such Hyper Leaps would be needed before their final destination was reached.

Paul looked at the book once more. It was thick. He'd probably never get it done — most of his time so far had been spent with the snow leopards. They had brought 34 of the snow leopards at T.E.I. aboard the ship. Most of the animals had adjusted fairly well to the new environment, although five of them had been dangerously sick for a couple weeks immediately following the take-off. These leopards had refused to eat and had later slipped into a slight state of shock, but the other species T.E.I. had brought aboard had reacted in a similar manner to the abrupt change in environment.

Paul was still amazed at the way his grandfather had successfully bred and raised his first snow leopards in the middle part of the last century. Although captive breeding had been successful elsewhere, Gregory Torrden had been one of the first researchers to achieve maintenance of a relatively stable population structure via captive breeding alone. The key had been in the creation of habitat attributes and artificial illumination that produced conditions not unlike the leopard's native habitat in the mountainous alpine meadows and coniferous forests of central Asia. And now, he, Paul Torrden was doing the same sort of pioneering his grandfather had done years ago, except that now the frontier was a spaceship!

Paul had been pleased with the way he and the T.E.I. medic personnel had handled that first emergency following the take-off. Brevin Johnson, the head of the medical team, had impressed him more than anyone else, though. Not only had he been one of the few blacks to ever attend T.E.I., but he was also one of the few students to get such an important position aboard the ship. Now —.

A knock at the door interrupted his thoughts.

He pressed the control lever near the bed and the door slid open to reveal the tall figure of Sammy Lassiter.

"Come in, Sammy."

The ex-camera-man strode forward. In his left hand he still carried his Camera Pack, even though it barely received the amount of use it had in years past.

"It's been a while, Paul. Where do you keep running off to, anyway — your snow leopards?"

Paul nodded. "I've seen you down there a couple times myself, it's just that I didn't say anything."

"I guess I have taken an interest in the leopards, too. Every time I see them it makes me mad that I never got a chance to read up on snow leopards until almost a year ago."

"Well, if you ask me, it looks like you've been taking an interest in more than just snow leopards."

Sammy laughed. "If you are referring to Annah Striton, I guess I can't deny it."

"And if you decide on anything, you won't regret it. She's a good woman."

"And while we're at it, let's not draw any hasty conclusions, either. I just met her, you know."

Paul shrugged his shoulders. "Have it your way." Still, he thought, she would be a good choice for Sammy. Slightly on the heavy side, Annah,

like Johnson, was one of the top medic personnel they had brought from
T.E.I. She was also one of the sharpest animal behaviorists he'd ever seen;
and if Sammy wanted to learn hard, solid facts about the snow leopards,
she was the person from which to learn them. He straightened up in his
chair. "Okay, so you obviously didn't come here to talk about women,
right?"

"A fair assumption, though I probably would not mind returning to
that subject later on," Sammy answered, pulling up a chair from the opposite side of the room. "If you remember, I told you a while back that I
was writing an historical account of your family. I was wondering if I
could finish it while on the *Stranahan*. It would give me something to
do."

"Sounds okay to me, Sammy. You'll probably have to get most of your
information from me, though I guess you already knew that."

"Yes, but I didn't want to impose on any of your valuable time. So you
wouldn't mind, then? I mean — if there..."

"Of course not. Two years ago I would have, but we've got no reason
to hide anything now. Besides, like you said, it will give you something to
do. I got a feeling everyone's gonna get pretty bored before we even get
out past Pluto's orbit. Eight years is a long time, and that's only the beginning."

"That's getting to be a pretty common complaint around here," a third
voice said.

Both men looked up to see the Captain of the ship, Bill Enders, standing in the doorway. He was dressed in a two-piece maroon uniform.

Enders invited himself into the room, allowing his eyes a quick and
thorough survey of the articles along the walls and on the table. He made
a quizzical face at the enormous quantity of books Paul had stacked in
the far corner.

"We can put those in microprint for you — it'll save on space. You're
Paul Torrden, right? Thought so. I met you once before, at loading time,
but it's been awhile. Bill Enders' the name. I hope you've found everything to your liking here on the *Stranahan*, eh?"

Paul stood up and shook hands with Enders, eyeing the man carefully.
"I've been adapting to it, sir," he said. "It's an appreciable change — from
Earth, I mean."

Enders flashed what appeared to be a P.R. smile and quickly turned to
the taller of the two men.

"And I take it from that Pack of yours that you are Sammy Lassiter, right?"

Sammy stood up and repeated Paul's friendly gesture.

"Well, it's nice to know I've met two of my most celebrated passengers. That's the only reason why I know your names. I've spent the last two and a half months trying to meet the eight hundred and twelve people we've got on board, and I've still got over four hundred to go." He pulled out a pack of synthetic cigarettes. "Smoke? No? Mind if I do, then?"

"Not at all," Paul said, returning to his seat. "You said 'celebrated' — is that good or bad?"

Enders lit up. The nontoxic smoke momentarily enshrouded his red-bearded face, then spread out in a wavy motion that was almost in tune with the steady, quiet drone of the ship.

"That all depends, Mr. Torrden. More people probably know of you than anyone else on this ship. And from the people I've talked to, I've come up with a very wide range of responses to you and your snow leopards. If you want my advice, I'd watch your animals closely. There's a lot of people around here just waiting for that first mistake just so they can raise a little trouble."

"I didn't know it was that bad. I mean, I figured there would be some, but..."

Enders removed the cigarette from his mouth, and as he exhaled, he sent out another cloud of smoke that promptly began its rhythmic diffusion into the air.

"I don't think your publicity is the blame for all of it, if it makes you feel any better. I'm beginning to wonder if that Flight Commission knew what it was doing half the time. They gave us some real winners, if you know what I mean."

"I can guess. We'll probably have more of them before the trip's half over."

"And that's what I'm worried about," Enders warned. "There's not too many who can actually face the fact that we'll probably die without ever walking on solid ground again. They *think* they can face it — that's why everyone applied for these New World Missions. But once they get up here, it's a different story. We've already got two serious cases.

"And then there's this leopard business. Normally we would have close to nine hundred people on a ship like this — that's the quota, you know.

Now we've got some crazy pessimists who are worried that, because we had to provide space for your animals and whatever else you brought aboard, there won't be enough people to propagate the race on the next planet."

"Do they have a point?" Sammy asked.

"Hell, no," Enders answered, tossing the cigarette into the automatic trash chute in the wall; it disappeared immediately. "As soon as everyone realizes how lonely it can get up here, you'll see babies popping up all over. And then there's always the safety valve: we're following a pre-charted course that will take us to a binary system not too many light years away from the nearest occupied sector. And, if anything unforeseen should happen before the end of the trip, there'll always be the engineers and Tech Crews on the planet already. And if things still don't go as planned, Epsilon Eridani is just in the next sector; that was the star the Twelfth Launch went to, so they should already be settled in by the time we reach our own destination."

"Sure, if everything works out all right. What happens if we make a mistake in our calculations, or if the planet's uninhabitable?"

Enders flashed his P.R. smile again. "That, Mr. Lassiter, is another question that keeps popping up around here. It was those risks that almost killed this program before it got started fifty years ago. And it is those risks that appear on every page of the application. There's not a person aboard that doesn't know about it.

"But, you see, that's one of the best things that came out of the Pan-government. Deficits were minimal since, strictly speaking, there really wasn't a lot of high price trading going on. A lot of people wanted this program, and now that they've got it, they just can't chicken out at the last minute — though, I guess you really can't blame 'em if that's how they feel.

"Now, then again, it's not like you're going on a suicide ride, either. The risks aren't all as bad as they seem. The Tech Crews that went out fifty years ago to the binary system we're heading for now have got the skills and know-how to make most any suitable planet habitable. Of course, it stands to reason that if there's an atmospheric problem, which will most likely be the case if there's any problem at all, then we just can't go running around in our birthday suits, right?"

"That's all true," replied Sammy, "but what if there —"

"In that case, whatever your 'what if' is, read your Info Book," Enders snapped. "It's obvious you haven't, and you're not the only one — I've been meeting a lot who haven't.

"Which reminds me, I've still got a lot of people to introduce myself to, so they can feel secure in knowing who's running the ship." He turned to leave, then stopped at the doorway. "Oh, and Mr. Lassiter, in response to your unasked question, the life of this ship has a safety valve of twenty-five to forty-five years, so that's no problem. And if anything ever did happen to the crews that went out before us, we've got the materials and technology to make a life support system of our own.

"Furthermore, if you have to worry about something, I'd worry about the Hyper Leaps. They might be eight years in coming, but from what little experimental evidence we do have, it's pretty conclusive that travelling at such excessive speeds is pretty risky business. If we remain in Leap velocity for too long…well, there's no more *Stranahan*. And the really scary part about it is approaching the velocity to enter Leap itself. It's got to be done gradually, whether we're accelerating to go into Leap or decelerating to come out of it. That's what I'd worry about, Mr. Lassiter — everything that we're doing that's new and relatively untried. May your day be good"

Before either Sammy or Paul could reply, Enders slipped out of the room and disappeared down the hallway.

Paul let a few seconds go by before he allowed himself a small laugh. "Well, so much for the good news of the day."

"It's a wonder he brought us any news at all."

"What do you mean?"

Sammy sat back down. "Enders is on the Comm at least once every twenty-four hours, right? Have you noticed that we haven't heard anything from Earth for a whole month now? No matter who I ask, no one seems to know anything."

"And you think he's hiding something from us?"

"Don't you? I don't know, but let me ask you this: what was the gist of the last broadcast we received from Earth?"

Paul paused for a second, then realization spread across his face. "You're not referring to the quarantine failure at the Old Alaska Port?"

"Precisely, Paul. Communications with the I.S.F.C. were at best erratic in January and early February. I bet you haven't even gotten a personal tele-message from Sam or T.E.I. for a month or so, right?"

Paul leaned forward. "Okay, Sammy, I'm game. But before we go jumping to conclusions and doing something we don't want to do — like insulting the Captain or spreading panic — I think we should wait and see if Enders explains it in his own good time."

Sammy stood up and began walking to the door. "Okay. Then again, maybe it's me — I think I'm beginning to worry too much." He held up the Camera-Pack in his left hand. "Maybe it's because I haven't covered the news in a long time. One day I'll have to get rid of this thing. And I know it'll be hard. It becomes a part of you, if you know what I mean."

Paul waved at him. "What you need is some sleep. Come back in five hours or so and we can start working on that book you want to write."

Sammy's face turned into a sheepish grin. "Well, I would, but...there's someone I have to see."

"Well, if you see Annah, tell her I said, 'hi.'"

The tall man laughed his reply and left the room. Twenty seconds later, Paul could still hear Sammy's laughter echoing down the halls. But as soon as Sammy had gone, Paul's face had become deathly serious...the camera-man had not been the only one to notice the absence of news from Earth.

... And the endless seconds of space rolled by. Brevin Johnson and Annah Striton had key roles to play as they got a breeding program for the snow leopards underway. The younger-aged animals that had not yet reached sexual maturity were eventually split into similar-aged, monogamous pairs. Both Brevin and Annah knew enough to realize that the choosing of mates is the result of a long series of elaborate courtship interactions between the two sexes, and this strategy gave each of the prospective pair of leopards ample time to become accustomed to one another. Several of the older leopards had already developed pair bonds on Earth. Colonel and Phanta constituted one such pair; and many hoped that the next set of cubs born to these two would hold the key to the realization of Gregory Torrden's goal.

...And the seconds became days. Captain Bill Enders, with surprising subtlety, discontinued his P.R. rounds; too many people were asking about Earth. Sammy Lassiter took up his pen once again and began writing about that legendary day when he and Paul Torrden thwarted the misguided malice of Jerul Scalos and turned an all too certain defeat into a monumental victory.

...And the days became months. Sammy Lassiter's proposal to Annah Striton was accepted and their union marked the fifteenth of an ever increasing number of marriages. Five snow leopard cubs were born, thus stifling the fear that the ship's environment would be detrimental to their endogenous reproductive cycle.

...And the months became years. Everyone had long since accepted the fact that something terrible had happened to the Earth. Enders had probably expected a mutiny, but that had never come: everyone just...refused to talk about it — they ignored it with a passion. However, another of Enders' fears did come true: the number of mental traumas steadily rose. And it was not until the eighth year out from Earth that Paul Torrden discovered what really could happen if one of those 'winners' decided to take it out on the controversial leopards ...

He was reading over the latest reports from Brevin and Annah. The *Stranahan* would be starting the Hyper Leaps in a week and everyone was still undecided if they should let the breeding program continue. They had raised the number of snow leopards up to 40, but the problem lay in the fact that almost two-thirds of that number was comprised of cats that were at, or over, the critical nine years of age for captive members of this species; and they'd already had more than their share of deaths. Even Colonel, who had sired four males and two female cubs, gave indications he would die in a year.

Paul shook his head. They would have to continue the breeding.

Julie rose from the bed and came over to him. "It's almost time, Paul. Are you going, or not?"

"What?" He looked up at her, slightly upset that she had interrupted him.

"Don't tell me you forgot."

"Oh. Yeah. You go on," he answered, his eyes returning to the paper. "I'll be there as soon as I call Brevin." Paul now remembered that Enders had asked everyone to gather in the Commons on Level Three — probably another one of the Captain's so-called 'Family Meetings.'

His wife stood looking at him for a couple moments before turning and leaving the room. Now, that was not the Julie he knew. She always spoke her mind when she was angry. Paul dismissed it from his thoughts, however. Being on the ship was beginning to change a lot of people. The last eight years had practically drained him of all his energy. He worked just as hard as everyone else did, and oftentimes he was sure he worked even harder than most. Maybe that was because he had something to prove to everyone else: that T.E.I.'s animals were actually worth all the trouble he had gone through to get them here.

Paul impulsively shook his head and cleared several papers away from the room-to-room Comm panel on his desk. He punched in his access code and followed that with the target code for the Level One breeding area. It beeped five times before someone answered it. It was Brevin. Paul hardly expected it to be anyone else. Who else but Brevin and himself would work so close to a deadline established by the Captain of the *Stranahan*?

"That you, Paul? I was 'bout ready to call you."

"Why, what's wrong, Brevin?"

"You'd better get down here right soon. I've a feeling the main thermostat's broke or something. We're not getting enough juice to cool the place down, I guess. If it gets any hotter down here, we're gonna be in some fine trouble."

Well, Julie would be angry at him now, for sure. "I'll be there in two minutes, Brevin."

Paul knew that he could not treat Brevin's news lightly. Evidently something had gone wrong with the primary cooling units on Level One. Such circumstances were pretty serious because the snow leopards, unlike other species of leopards, were sensitive to extreme heat. What made matters worse was that Level Zero, which was right below the leopards, contained much of the ship's propulsion machinery. There was enough heat coming out of there to do irreparable damage, given adequate time.

On his way to the down elevator he got questionable looks from people he passed who were going in the opposite direction. *Damn,* he thought, *wasn't anybody allowed not to go to meetings anymore; or was this just paranoia, or perhaps the result of eight long years in space?* The white glare from the walls of the ship did not help matters any.

The elevator doors opened and closed and he let the calmness of the chamber cool his temper as he descended from Level Two to Level One. When the doors opened, they revealed Brevin Johnson. The medic man was wearing a somewhat soiled white smock — a symbol of his hard working dedication.

"Did you check the main circuits, yet?" Paul asked.

Brevin shook his head. "I was going to, but I decided to call you first. Besides, it wouldn't do much good. Jenkins and his crew know more about how this place is wired than I do, anyway; 'cept they all went to the meeting, of course."

"Well, let's check it out," Paul insisted. "If we can't find the problem we can always get Jenkins. It's probably just a fuse, anyway."

Brevin shook his head as they proceeded to the main conduit switch-board area for Level One.

"I don't know, Paul," he said, removing the white outer garment. "Jenkins once told me they got something like thirty of forty fuses and circuit breakers wired into this place — one fuse wouldn't cause it to be this hot, would it?"

Brevin was right. Paul was surprised he had not felt it before. As they walked past the leopards, he saw that the older ones lay waiting, almost as if they were confident that something would be done; while some of the younger ones impatiently paced back and forth inside the large cages.

They rounded a corner and proceeded down a narrow, dead-end hall-way. When they reached the switchboard area, Paul briefly noticed the door was already ajar. Brevin swung the door open further and began walking in. It was then that Paul found that he still possessed the quick reflexes of his youth.

As the knife came flying towards them, he fell back out of the door-way and onto the floor. He heard Brevin scream, and a half-second later he saw the medic man stumble back out of the room, pulling the knife from his left arm, where it had embedded itself.

"Who the hell's in there?" Paul shouted.

Brevin was breathing heavily. "I don't know, but I think this is all he had," and he held up the knife. The seriousness of his wound could not be disguised — a bright red stain was already spreading throughout the pale cloth over his left arm.

Paul edged forward and leaned slowly around the metal frame of the door. On the left side, he spotted the incoming cables and wires for the primary electrical support and cooling systems on Level One. The engineers had briefed him on the location of these cables when he first boarded the ship. He saw that many of these cables had been cut and now drooped uselessly against the panel.

He let his eyes play to the back of the room, and in the shadows they fell upon a grin.

"I see you, too," the grin said.

As Paul let his eyes become accustomed to the darkness, the grin took on a face, and he could see the crazed eyes of a middle-aged man. A man he had seen somewhere before, but he just could not quite match the face with the place.

Paul carefully motioned to Brevin to go for help, but the medic man had taken only two steps when the grin shouted, "Don't you dare let that boy go!"

Brevin turned and slowly knelt beside Paul, his wounded arm now dripping profusely. "Play up to him, Paul, see what he wants."

But Paul did not have to say anything, for the grin began talking again.

"Don't you know what I'm gonna do? Don't you want everyone to know?"

Paul quickly decided that he had to learn more about the man's intentions. He slowly slid his hand up the inside of the wall until it fell on the light control dial. He turned it on, slowly...and was dumbfounded by what he saw.

"Oh, no, please don't do it, man," he heard Brevin groan. The medic man did not have to be an electrician by trade to see that many of the cables for the emergency function systems on their Level had been redirected to the main panel; apparently all the intruder had to do to override the system was to open the emergency circuit again.

Sudden recognition came to Paul then as he saw the brown moustache the man wore. The I.S.F.C. had not denied his request, after all. But why ...?

Paul stood up slowly, followed by Johnson. "What are you trying to prove?" he asked. There was no telling what would happen if the main circuits were overloaded. He began walking slowly towards the man, his legs weakening in response to his sudden nervousness.

"Everything. Everything we need to know," cried the crazed man, and he grasped the circuit lever for the emergency systems. "I just want to end it all, now, before your blasphemous animals do. They're taking up too much damn energy, d-did you know? Energy that *we* need." His laugh turned into a high, halting giggle.

Paul stopped again. As he tried to decide what to do next he realized that he had no experience on which to draw. "You didn't feel that way when we first met," he offered. He was not sure if he could reach the man in time. And yet, he could not wait for more help — there was no telling how long the meeting Enders had called would last. Besides, more people might only make —.

"I told you not to let that damn nigger leave!"

Paul looked around and saw that Brevin had tried to edge out of sight to the right of the doorway. The medic man moved back into the center of the doorway once again, and Paul could see the loss of blood was beginning to drain the color from his face.

He turned around and began his slow approach once more, faltering slightly when the man began to speak again.

"Besides, I think *you're* the one, Mr. Torrden. The crowds go crazy, and they all laugh and giggle when they see you on the stage, because you're the one! And did you know, suns are nothing more than bursts of bright energy? If you fall into one, it won't kill you. So why are people so afraid of them? Why does everybody travel in the damned fucking dark, huh? Why don't we make a sun?"

The man was apparently reaching the peak of his suicide-driven craziness. Paul figured he'd have to try to stop him now or it would be too late. Brevin evidently sensed his decision, for he heard a voice behind him whisper: "Careful, Paul."

The stranger's eyes frenziedly glanced at Brevin again, in response to the medic man's whisper. That's when Paul reacted. He knew he should not have, but the man had taken his hand off the lever for just that one instant! It could have been a lure, a trap, but he did not have the time to further evaluate the situation. Paul rushed forward and leaped upon the older man. But even before he reached him, he saw the latter's hand quickly shoot back up and yank the lever down.

He closed his eyes automatically, but his body and ears viciously informed him of the electrical volcano that the tiny room had suddenly become. His momentum carried him into the other man's body, and a sudden fear gripped him when he lost control of his limbs and saw his arms flap violently in the air as if he were an electrocuted marionette.

In the next split second, as he began to lose consciousness, he heard the engines cease and felt himself thrown wickedly backward by the sudden loss of velocity. His ears relayed to him yet another ferocious discharge, and as the ship flickered into total blackness, he dimly saw Brevin Johnson race toward him with a motion that resembled a lost soldier in the middle of a shell-wrecked battlefield.

The minute, little creature ran around on the gray matter. It stopped, looked down, and found nothing but spindly arms and legs.

Who was this? Could it be him? No! It was too small. The creature became frightened and started running again. Its fear propelled the gangling legs, moving them faster and faster, until the tiny body was lifted off the gray matter and ejected into the void.

The creature gasped as it realized the uselessness of its limbs in the eternal blackness. It floated along, screaming a thousand cries, hoping someone would heed its pleas for help.

And just when it appeared that there was no hope in the universe to be found, a twinkling caught the creature's eye. It was a star, and the light of that distant orb, as it flickered and glowed, ebbed on and off, somehow told the creature that help was on its way.

Then, as if to give credence to its declaration, the star shattered and segmented, dividing itself into a dozen infantile sparks, each of which suddenly grew into a facsimile of the solar luminescence from which it had been born.

The creature grew happy as it watched the process repeat itself again and again, until the entire universe was littered with the lanterns of light. The tiny being reached out to touch one, but stopped, as the stars suddenly began to converse with one another, their lady-like voices descending into a high pitched buzz that moved in union with their pulsating bodies.

"The Creature wants to touch us!"

"It only seeks help from its loneliness."

"No! It will rape us once again. Kill it!"

Tumultuous cries spewed forth from the creature's mouth as each star suddenly began to elongate into a thin, narrow strip of piercing light. The creature floundered, wriggling its tiny limbs frantically in every direction until it finally gained control of itself. In a frenzy it began to flee from the stars.

Looking back, it saw that each star had dilated into a lengthy, but vicious, bolt of yellow-red lightning. The stars neared the confused little creature, traversing parsecs of space in a matter of seconds.

The creature had no more than turned back around to resume its escape when it collided with its native gray matter. The matter opened up and allowed the creature access despite its wicked return.

Turning once more, the tiny being saw the cruel bolts of lightning approach its haven with awesome velocities, their tips sparkling with malevolent spurts of blue-white electricity.

And then, as if they recognized the creature's helplessness, the stars abruptly halted their descent and began to converse once more, their sensual voices carrying notes of pity and understanding that joined to form a song of hope.

It was in that final moment of vindication that the creature suddenly realized who it was; and that realization brought fear to Paul Torrden as he struggled futilely in the quicksand that was the vast expanse of his mind. He was too close, he had to get away, but no one would open a door.

Then the sounds of the stars caught his attention once more, and as he looked back, he saw that they had returned to their pulsating roundness. Gently, the words of the songs they sang walked into his ears, telling him to 'open your eyes,' to 'open your eyes.'

He felt his body grow, his legs and arms returning to their original size.

With the light of the stars he was able to see a door submerged in the matter of his mind. He reached for it.

Paul opened his eyes and was met with white light and a lurking shadow. The lurking shadow slowly became Julie. He could see the tears in her eyes and could feel his own disorientation through her hands, which grasped his ever so tightly.

"Paul. I'm — we were so scared!"

Something was wrong. He tried to sit up but his body responded by racking him with acute anguish. From the far side of the room — this was his room — he heard a noise and seconds later the tall figure of Sammy Lassiter appeared beside Julie.

"Here."

Lassiter placed a glass of water to his lips and gently tilted it. As he began to slowly drink the soothing liquid, Paul realized with surprising quickness how dry his throat was.

"Welcome back," Lassiter grinned. "Don't worry; Brevin told us all about it. Quite an event, too." He removed the glass from Paul's lips and placed it on the table.

"How long —" Paul began, startled by the crackling sound in his voice.

"Two weeks. You were comatose most of the time," Julie said. She had already composed herself. "How much do you remember?"

"Those reports. I — I remember reading some reports." He paused, looking blankly at Julie and Sammy. Then, almost as an afterthought: "A meeting — there was a meeting we were going to."

"Nothing after that?" Sammy asked. "Boy, you do have a thick skull — but I guess that's what you need to perform heroics." Paul's questioning stare evoked laughter from the tall camera-man. "You really must be telling the truth. I'll get you another glass of water and let Julie bring you up to date."

Paul allowed his eyes to quickly refocus on his wife. He could tell by her reaction that she saw the fear in his face. She took the glass of water offered by Sammy and placed it in his hands.

"It's okay, Paul. You did something...we can all be proud of." She glanced uncertainly at Sammy, then continued. "They said you might not re-member everything. It all happened so fast. You're right about Captain Enders' get-together. You never made it there ..."

As Julie explained to Paul what had taken place, he found himself entering a strange world of déjà vu, a sort of half reality. He remembered seeing Brevin's face during a briefly chaotic period of time, and he did remember a maelstrom of light, but everything else Julie told him was foreign to his memory.

He was working on his third glass of water when Julie took his left hand and squeezed it between both of hers. In a lower voice, she contin-ued: "Annah told me to give you the message that she went ahead with the breeding program; she said she found your notes. And also she said to tell you...that we lost Colonel."

Paul closed his eyes. He had wanted to be there. Colonel had been his favorite snow leopard. He would miss being able to touch Colonel, to watch the magnificent cat gracefully move with that four-footed sure-ness he knew so well. He also knew that Julie had made the correct decision in telling him this now. When he opened his eyes again he saw that Sammy had returned to his side.

"The Captain wants to see you," he said. "He should be down any minute now — we told him you looked like you were coming around. Sure you're okay, now?"

"Yeah. Help me sit up."

Julie and Sammy slipped their arms underneath him and eased him up until his back was against the headrest of the bed. As he recovered from the physical discomfort of two weeks of semi-consciousness, a new voice stole into the room.

"Normally, you'd be in the Sick Ward, but your wife here didn't want you mixed around with all the loonies."

Paul looked up and saw Enders standing at the doorway, his P.R. smile — or, rather, what was left of it — still decorating his face. His reckless manner of speaking about the ship's problems had not changed, either.

Enders walked in and pressed the lever to close and lock the door behind him. As he approached the foot of the bed, he blurted, "If you haven't heard yet, no one's blaming you for what happened. I was the first one Johnson spoke to, and we've made sure no one else knew that Corelli — he was the man you found down there — had it in for the ship because of your animals."

"Thanks," Paul uttered, but Enders went on before he could say anything else.

"As for Johnson, the next time you see him you can thank him for saving your life. Corelli was nothing but a fried mess of skin and bones when we finally got to him.

"And another thing — you can thank yourself for saving the *Stranahan*. Corelli was evidently only half way done with whatever he was trying to do when you caught him. As it was, we only lost ninety-six hours."

"I take it we've already started the Hyper Leaps, then?" Paul asked, glancing at Julie and Sammy. He could only detect slight differences in the vibrations of the ship and the way it sounded.

Enders nodded. "We're on our way." He reached into his pocket and pulled out a cigarette. As he lit up, he asked, "How are your legs? At one time the doctors thought you might be paralyzed."

Paul tried moving his legs. Though they hurt, he found he still had control over them.

"I guess they're okay. But I feel like hell. I thought they still had a lot of room in the Ward."

"We did," Enders said, expiring a stream of smoke. "But that was before — didn't they tell you?"

"Not yet," Julie said.

"Tell me what?" Paul winced, trying to lean forward in the eagerness of his anxiety.

Enders took another puff before saying, "The day you bought all this with Corelli — remember, I had called an emergency family meeting? Well, we finally heard from Earth; and it wasn't a very pretty picture. I'm beginning to regret having replayed that transmission."

"Why? What did it say?" Paul found he was somehow ignoring the pain that was still racing through his body. He remembered when he and Sammy had talked about Earth almost eight years ago, and how he had waited desperately, like everyone else, for some news.

"It was awful," Sammy said. "You could barely understand what the guy was saying."

"Who was he?"

"One of Mr. Lassiter's long lost brothers, one of those synthetically wired news men. Claimed he was reporting from the site of the Old Alaska Port. We have some reason to believe that he may have been one of the guys that broke quarantine regulations as we were leaving Earth. At any rate, we were able to boost his signal, but it was Mr. Lassiter here that was able to de-scramble it.

"I'm gonna cut right to the chase, 'cos there's no other way of getting around it. Mr. Torrden, the transmission we received indicates that the presence of an alien life form has been discovered on Earth. This confirms what some of the crew members from the Sixteenth were trying so desperately to tell us."

Paul flashed a quick glance at Sammy and Julie. They both hesitantly nodded their heads before looking away. It had to be true, then! His eyes returned to Enders.

"I know it sounds unreal," the Captain continued, "but it's all we have to go on. And there's more. This guy, or at least what was left of him, had to be authentic. His reports indicate that the alien ship the Sixteenth encountered was not a derelict ship, after all, like we've been led to believe. Apparently, there was a life form aboard, and there were allegedly two instances of documented communication — between the vessel and the crew members of the Sixteenth. The Pan-government did an analysis of those communications, which they released shortly after we left. It seems that this alien was capable of mental telepathy — communicating with the crew of the Sixteenth while they dreamed. And based on the images that people aboard the Sixteenth described, some have now theorized that this thing was lost, and perhaps even sick or dying. The crew of the Sixteenth made an attempt to solicit additional communication, but when they were unsuccessful they resumed their original flight plans. As we now know, is was not too long afterwards when all the problems began.

"By the time the Sixteenth returned to Earth, the I.S.F.C. knew enough about the on-board problems to issue the quarantine, but by then it was too late. What we heard and saw while we were leaving Earth was only the tip of the iceberg. Our mystery friend confirms that first hundreds, then thousands, and then *billions* of people developed the same illness that killed all those poor souls on the Sixteenth. Basically, what they got on Earth was a worldwide pandemic the magnitude of which we can't even begin to describe. It's as if this thing went supernova."

Paul frowned. "Why were we never contacted about this before?"

"We've already discussed this with some of our Sci-Tech personnel aboard. General consensus is that this guy's suspicions are really what we need to be concentrating on — they would go a long way toward explaining the answer to your question.

"This guy, who sent us the message from Earth — he calls himself part of a secretive network of survivors. From what little evidence they have, they now believe that whatever was released on Earth, it wasn't released by accident. Even though the logs of the Sixteenth indicate that no actual contact was ever made with the alien vessel, *something* was nevertheless given to the crew of the Sixteenth. However it operates, it's nearly one hundred percent fatal — everyone that's apparently been exposed to this thing dies within three days; some live much longer, but they're nothing more than a living vegetable. Only about three to four percent of the population appears to be immune to this thing. Whether it's a virus or bacteria, we don't know, but it is perhaps the most contagious disease that has ever been encountered.

"At first, all of the survivors joined together — but then some of them went underground. They — and this camera-man is included among them — believe that the plague, or whatever it is, has about run its course.

Earth is now rebuilding itself. But this underground network is going one step further. They believe that this thing won't stop at Earth, and they're preparing for the next encounter. Their reasoning is that wherever this derelict ship came from, there must be more of them traveling through space. This camera-man knew he had to warn us — he even sent us a number of classified medical files that documented the spread of the plague, and everything that was done to control it. Apparently he used his Camera-Pack to transmit a scrambled message in our direction; it took him several years to get the up-link just right.

"We have to regard this warning as real. His transmission included some unique footage from the Old Alaska Port. The visual images corroborate everything he said. I only regret that we couldn't ask him questions." He paused for a second, then said, "We always wanted to know if there were other intelligences in the universe — I'm glad I wasn't there when that question was finally answered."

Paul continued to stare at the Captain, his face registering extreme disbelief. If all this were real, Sam was probably dead by now, and T.E.I., and most likely everything else, was just a thing of the past. All that was left of his grandfather's dreams was aboard this ship, and even then fate had almost dealt him a black ace two weeks ago in the form of an insane lunatic named Corelli. Abruptly, he cursed himself; he was being too self-centered. A lot of other people aboard the *Stranahan* had probably lost just as much as he had, if not more. There was Julie, for instance. She had loved Sam, too; but she had also enjoyed taking rides in the trans-cars to different parts of the Earth — to see new people and experience new things. And though the Uprisings had rudely forced those trips to become only memories, this new information had probably pushed those memories to a part of the past she would not want to look at anymore.

Enders nodded at him. "There's your answer to your question about the Ward. Everyone looked like you do now when they heard that message, and some of 'em haven't returned from the little worlds they've thrown themselves into. They were either scared shitless or they couldn't face the fact that everyone they knew had probably been killed or 'consumed' in less than a month's time. For some, it may have been both.

"At any rate, I'm glad you didn't stop Corelli from doing what he did."

"Why is that?" Paul asked slowly, still a little numb from everything that had been said to him over so short a period of time.

"Because as soon as I'd finished playing that transmission, and began feeling sick about doing it, Corelli must have done his little trick. I admit, it wasn't the best thing that could happen to a ship like this, but it sure got a lot of people to realizing that they didn't have to sit back and die without doing something about it. We'd probably have lost everything if it hadn't been for the cooperation we got.

"Well, I'll let your two friends here fill you in on anything else you want to know. I guess it goes without saying we took a popular vote on whether to continue with the mission or return to the Earth. Not too surprisingly, the general feeling was that we should not abandon the mission. We've got a long way to go, and there's still a million things I got to do. Besides, if you don't mind my saying so, you look pretty ragged. Two weeks of almost constant sleep really does a number on a man. But I think you'll be glad to know the doctors feel you haven't lost as much weight as they thought you would. I guess you're a real fighter."

Paul could not agree more. His whole body was an aching testimony to Enders' words. As the Captain left the room, Sammy went over to the table and picked up the half full glass of water. "Think you can handle this?"

Paul raised his arm. The pain began screaming at him, like a mother at her naughty boy, but he ignored it long enough to take the glass from Sammy Lassiter's hands. As he did so, he noticed something was missing.

"Where's your Camera Pack?"

Sammy grinned. "It's retired. Not thrown away, mind you, but just retired. Things were hitting a little too close to home. Maybe someday I'll have a good reason to use it again."

Paul finished the glass of water and handed it back to Sammy. The lanky figure returned it to the table before saying, "Meanwhile, I'll let you get some rest. Like Julie said, you really had us scared. I'm glad you're back. Besides, how could I finish my book without you?" He laughed and stepped out of the room.

Paul shook his head, then looked back at Julie. "I'm glad we brought him along. He makes life aboard this ship bearable sometimes."

Julie smiled. "Then let's hope he lives to a ripe old age. Enders said it would be another forty to forty-five years before we get to the new planet. And I want you to be alive, too, when we get there, so lie back down and get some sleep."

He did as he was told, knowing his condition was too poor to justify any objections he might have made. Still, he jokingly asked, "How much will the fee be when it's all over?"

Julie smiled, bent over, and kissed him. "You're a silly man sometimes, Paul Torrden," she said, "but I love you, anyway."

He closed his eyes, amazed at how tired he was. Thoughts of Earth entered his mind and he turned them over for a while before pushing them out again. He'd have more time to think about that later. Right now, his mind, as everyone else had pointed out, needed more sleep.

Paul recovered fairly quickly, surprising both himself and the medical personnel who had been assigned to him. He diligently performed a regular set of exercises to re-tone his muscles.

He was also pleased to receive a series of daily visits from Annah Striton, who briefed him on all progress being made with the leopards. Thus far, the first Hyper Leap had not produced any harmful effects, so she said, and he was encouraged to hear that she estimated there would be about 60 or 65 leopards by the time they reached the binary system.

Three days after he had heard the tragic news regarding Earth, Brevin Johnson came to see him. By his side was a woman Paul had not seen before. She had a well-rounded figure and looked to be in her middle or late 20's. Her long, blonde hair and radiant blue-gray eyes accented the youthful aspect of her face.

The two men shook hands. Paul could see that Brevin's arm had healed up pretty fast, though it still bore an ugly mark where the knife had done the most damage.

"Sorry I couldn't get by earlier, Paul," the medic man apologized, "but we've been swamped with work down there."

"So Annah has actually been telling the truth," Paul laughed. "No, really, you've been doing an excellent job, Brevin, and I wouldn't have cared if it took you a month and a half to come by. I'll always owe you one, you know."

"It was the least I could do under the circumstances, Paul. It should have been me who got messed up like that, but instead I had to wait and call you down." Then he grinned. "Guess I paid for it somehow with that knife. Oh, and this is Laura Teltor. She's the one who did such a good job on my arm, though she likes to be called 'Doc Teltor,' of course."

The woman eyed Brevin with a playful look that said, 'you'll pay for that later,' then said to Paul: "Glad to meet you, Mr. Torrden. Brevin's told me enough about you that I'm sure we would not want to miss out on having you and your wife at a party we're having on Level Four in two weeks."

"I think it would do you good, too," Brevin put in. "In all the time we've been here I don't think I've seen you up above Three more than five times. You spend too much time with the leopards, you're gonna become one yourself."

"Okay, okay," Paul conceded. "Julie's been telling me for years I should take it easy. And she says I should get out and meet new people, too. And to be honest, judging from how I feel right now, I know I'll be just fine by the time you guys start pouring drinks."

"I take it that's an affirmative answer, then?" Laura asked.

Paul grinned. "Wouldn't have it any other way."

As they continued talking, the conversation inexorably drifted back to the snow leopards, T.E.I. personnel, and related topics. Several hours later, after he had succeeded in convincing Brevin and Laura that he would be at the party, and they had gone off to do some other chores, Julie returned to the room.

Maybe it had been the way she had walked in. Or maybe it had been that he had worked so hard over the past eight years that he had forgotten what a woman could mean.

He didn't know which it was. He did not even know if it may have been something else altogether. But it really did not matter.

Getting slowly out of bed, he carefully walked over and pulled the lever to lock the door. Looking up at Julie, he read her expression and saw that she was still unaware of the feelings he had suddenly felt for her. They had been repeating that well known three-word epithet back and forth to each other for eight years now — in spite of the fact that each of them had felt something was dying between them. This would be one of the last things she would expect from him, this sudden flare of love and passion. He smiled, hoping that the thought, even by itself, would make her happy.

"Well?" he almost pleaded.

Sudden recognition crossed Julie's face. She came to him and took his hands.

"I — I don't know. How do you feel?"

"Well enough."

"It's been a long time, Paul."

"Too long."

Their hands separated and they slowly moved to the bed. Items of clothing found their way unhurriedly to the floor. His hands cupped her small breasts and caressed her body as they softly floated down to the bed. He kissed her deeply, running his fingers over her nipples and down her body to her thighs. Julie took him into her hands and he felt himself grow strong as he sensed the attraction of her womanhood flow into him.

When he entered her, he forgot at last about the snow leopards, about Colonel, and about the ship they were on. His mind rallied with the brilliance these forgotten emotions gave to it. His body marvelled that it could still move and feel this way after all he'd been through.

Together, he and Julie climbed plateau after ethereal plateau, and when they reached the top, they knew that the ecstasy of the moment was only a symbol for something much greater that they had found once more.

They made love the following night as well, and the act took on a regularity that, at first, surprised both of them. Though Paul continued to work diligently with the snow leopards, he found he no longer felt compelled to justify the T.E.I. project to everyone else aboard the *Stranahan*. Julie could sense this change in him, too, and he was glad to know that she had regained a certain level of contentedness once again. When the day of the party on Level Four arrived, Paul was sure that, if he had to live the rest of his life on the *Stranahan*, the pain of such a fate would definitely be nullified by what he had rediscovered.

Paul could not hold back the laughter when she asked him if he'd ever thought twice about applying for the New World Launch Program.

He did not know where Julie was, but he was sure she was enjoying herself as much as he was. He returned his attention to the woman with whom he had been talking for the past ten minutes. As soon as she had discovered who he was, she had asked a horde of questions concerning the snow leopards. Exactly what kind of animals are they? Are they nice and easy to handle? How big do they get? All were typical questions. He had heard them thousands of times before, back during the days on Earth when tourists came to T.E.I. He remembered those days well. Though he had not been required to interact directly with the public at all, he had done so nonetheless. Although those very public relations duties may have played a substantial role in the survival of T.E.I. as a 'successful' institution in the eyes of others, he recalled how quickly he had become disillusioned by that particular task. He knew there had been numerous occasions when just the sight of crowds of people had produced a violent revulsion within him. It was during those times that everyone appeared, at least in his eyes, to be a part of some large but secretive army. And what frightened him the most about that army was that he did not know what battle was being fought or even what the issues were.

The whole problem lay in the biology of it all — from a scientific viewpoint, not only did human behavior equate itself with the behavioral patterns of many other wild animals, but man had failed to acknowledge his behavioral flaws and to take necessary measures to correct them.

A philosopher, yeah, he could have been one; but who would listen to, or read about, someone who despised the fact that man had been gifted with the powers of insight learning, comprehension, and reasoning, and the ability to use or develop them all to a high degree?

But all that was for the past; and for the future, whenever his introspective mood would inevitably swing toward the downward side of the scale. Now, it was the present, and he was feeling great. That he could still intermingle with large numbers of people and enjoy himself pleased him.

"What was so funny about that?"

Paul almost laughed again, realizing that he had practically forgotten that he had been talking to someone. She was slightly smaller than him, with short, curled hair, a round face, and a somewhat plump and roundish body. She had asked him to make love to her once already, and he was sure the question would soon repeat itself. Yet, he was enjoying the whole process of it all, even though he knew he would never take her up on the proposal. Paul estimated she had looked more attractive at the beginning of the launch. But then, eight years of close quarters takes its toll on each individual person in a different fashion.

Shrugging his shoulders, Paul lifted the glass in his hand to his lips and sipped at the sweet artificial liquor before answering: "It's just that I've always thought of myself as keeping alive a dying tradition, you know, transporting several species of animals with the serious intention of ensuring their survival on a new and different planet. I mean, I've read that on the Tenth or Twelfth Launches they had some birds and several types of rodents, but I guess this is the first time anything of a large-scale type of endeavor has ever taken place."

"So?" She sipped at her own drink, looking Paul directly in the eye. He could see she was not really interested in the scientific aspects of his answers, but there was no way to avoid it. Besides, public relations was not his most skillful craft. He continued, nonetheless.

"Well, until you asked me if I ever regretted being here, I never fully realized that my main reason for doing all of this — that being the continued survival and further understanding of *Uncia uncia*, to be technical — is not a tradition at all, but a relatively unique happening, so to speak."

"And do you think it will work?"

"I have my hopes," Paul said reluctantly, realizing that he had somehow avoided that question for many months. Yet, he had to admit, it would be useless to be doubtful at this stage; and even if all the inevitable, unforeseen problems were suddenly unveiled, he would be a fool if he were to passively allow such expected predicaments to overcome him.

The woman smiled at him in a way that almost annoyed him and yet made him wary. "Don't you ever get lonely working with those cats all the time? I know I would. There's always so many other things to do around here."

Her loosely fitting clothes, which allowed more than the usual amount of breast and leg to come under public scrutiny, only served to enhance the meaning of her question.

"I enjoy it," Paul replied. "If a person's got to do a job, he should at least do something that will make him happy."

"Well, I still think you can get pretty lonely down there. Ever been up to Level Six?"

"Probably a couple times. I may have stopped off there several times with my wife on the way down from the Food Station or the Gym."

"Now, surely you don't —."

She stopped abruptly, glanced over his shoulder, and muttered to herself before suddenly leaving him. Paul dizzily smiled as he watched her move off to find some other apparently lonesome man.

The drinks were beginning to affect him somewhat, but he did not care. As he silently watched the noisily pulsating crowd, Paul was almost unaware of someone approaching him from the side until he heard the voice.

"I see you met one of our space harlots, Mr. Torrden."

Paul turned to face a medium-sized man with fiery eyes, jet black hair, and bushy sideburns of the same startling color. A wave of familiarity swept over him for a moment, then left as soon as it had come. He shrugged, "Everybody's got to have a niche in society, even if it's only a society of eight hundred and some odd people."

The stocky stranger laughed, the movement in his chest emphasizing his well developed muscles. "True, really. But I'm curious, how'd you manage to discourage her so quickly?"

Paul finished off his drink. "I mentioned I was married. That may have done the trick."

"Smart move, I must concede. And I hate to damage your ego. I mean, you probably had fun seeing through her act so quickly, but I'm one of Enders' roving guards. He's got about fifteen of us down here. Anyway, Virgie — that's the one you were just talking to — she knows I'm after her to keep her straight.

"Here, you ready for another refill? This is one of the few times we'll be able to drink and eat to our heart's content."

Paul nodded his approval and gestured for the guard to lead the way to the nearest bar. As they slowly made their way through the crowd, Paul suddenly remembered that he had seen the guard several times recently on Levels One and Nine. He mentioned this matter-of-factly.

"And you're wondering why I seem to be all over the ship all of a sudden, right? By the way, call me Sorian, it's an old nickname of mine."

"It had crossed my mind," Paul continued. "I can't say I pay that much attention to you guys, though, because I've not run into that much trouble recently, but..."

They had reached the bar. Sorian stopped and, so it seemed to Paul, was suddenly lost in pensive thought. Then, turning to Paul, he asked, "Mind if we go up to Ten, to the *Nightside*? We'll have to use our credit there, but I think you should know a couple things Enders has been holding back from the rest of us."

Paul laid his glass down on the bar. "If it sounds that important, no, I don't mind at all. Besides, I got a lot of good credit at the *Nightside* to burn — I'm not there too often."

"Well," Sorian replied, heading away from the bar, "let's see how much of your savings we can use."

Fifteen minutes later, after forcing their way once again through the crowd and riding up to Level Ten, the two men sat at a small table in the *Nightside*, the only facsimile of an Earth-like drinking establishment aboard the *Stranahan*. As they had expected, it was less crowded than usual as most of the regular patrons were on Level Four enjoying free food and beverages while they were available. Paul had purchased the first round of drinks.

"Okay, so what's the bad news, Sorian?" he asked.

The other man tasted the artificially refined liquid before saying, "Sorry I made it sound so ominous. It just came on the spur of the moment — the idea of telling you all this, I mean."

Sorian paused, and Paul patiently waited for him to continue, already realizing that the guard had his own elaborate way of making things clearly understood.

At length, Sorian said, "Have you ever wondered what's at the end of this flight for all of us? I know you have, and I know I have, too. Everyone on this ship must wonder that every day. The thing is, Mr. Torr , er, is it okay if I call you Paul? Okay. Ah, the thing is, we're all going through each day of this trip knowing that things *have* to be done and feeling secure that they will be done — by someone other than ourselves. I know we've got a lot of machinery here, and that we can produce 'X' or synthesize 'Y,' but we're going to be on this thing for at least forty more years."

He paused then, unknowingly allowing the dim lighting of the *Nightside* to color his words with a musky finality.

"Go on," Paul encouraged, deciding to let Sorian have full reign of the conversation, although he was already beginning to formulate some ideas of his own.

"Well, let me ask you this, then," the guard continued. "How many people do you think who started this trip at age twenty-five or older will see the end of it?"

"Probably not as many as we'd like."

"That's what I'm getting at — we need people to maneuver this baby we're on into a new solar system, to a new planet; we need people to continue to run and repair the production lines around here. In short, we're actually dependent on that next generation of ours for the survival of humanity as far as we're concerned. I guess what I mean to say is that

we, as individuals, are no longer important. If we don't unify, nothing's
going to come of this venture.

"Enders is always saying that we have the equipment to repair this or
fix that, and he's damned right, too. But who's to say that thirty or forty
years from now we'll have the know-how to use that equipment?"

Paul took a long swig on his drink and keyed in the code for a refill.
Ten seconds later he reached down into the space in the middle of the
table and grabbed his drink as it was delivered up the chute.

A computerized bartender — the irony of the situation suddenly took
on an unaccustomed seriousness.

He turned his thoughts over several times more before finally saying,
"Okay, I can see that you've done me a favor in telling me all this without
Enders knowing about it, but so far there's nothing you've said that I
wouldn't have realized myself sooner or later."

"Well, then I feel safe in knowing that I've at least alerted you to the
possibilities," Sorian replied, finishing off his own drink. Paul keyed in
the code for another one.

"You see, our main problem is motivation," Sorian began again, reaching in and taking his new drink from the chute. "We've got the Learning
Discs — there's no problem there. But I think you can see that the difficulty lies in getting students to listen to and *learn* from them.

"More than half of the people here are just that — people. A mob of
four hundred plus, all of them wanting just to go from this place to that.
You and your guys from T.E.I. make up almost one third of those that are
left. Then you got the crew and us guards — that's about two hundred
and forty people to run this whole monstrosity. In time, we're going to
need help from outside our ranks, from those four hundred plus who
think they're just getting a free ride.

"Which brings me to you, Paul. Your people are like a separate entity
around here. Sure, the aggressions that were once present when no one
knew what T.E.I. was doing with all those animals may have subsided, but
that's no guarantee that the dam will hold. As it stands now, by the end of
this trip we could be either a group of appreciably sane people or a pack
of half-mute illiterates. And if it happens to be the latter case, there's
going to be a lot of confusion and hell going on — I don't think it's too
hard for you to see what a nasty picture that would be."

Sorian paused again, long enough to gulp down half of his second
drink, before going on.

"The reason why I'm telling you all this is because whatever happens is going to directly affect your people on Level Two. You see, you've got it easy, relatively speaking; your people have an almost innate motivation to succeed in what you're doing. But if we don't get the people to run this ship some thirty or forty years from now, everyone is going to be without the facilities to succeed in doing anything.

"And when that comes about, someone's going to have to take the fall. I'm sure no one's going to blame the responsible party: him or herself; no, they're going to want to pin the blame on someone else."

"And the logical choice would be T.E.I.'s captive animals," Paul interjected.

"Precisely. 'If we only had more people and less leopards, this wouldn't have happened.' That's what they're going to say.

"I realize there's not much you or I can do about it. I mean, it's in the Regulations Manual: 'All personnel and their descendants are required to contribute their services to the extent that is necessary for the preservation of the life support systems of the ship.' You know the drill and all the buzz words, Paul. That's a rule that has to be enforced, but who's going to enforce it when the needs demand it? I'd hate to be part of the army of guards that has to convince five hundred or so people that if they don't revise their list of priorities, they and the *Stranahan* are going to slip off the face of history."

Sorian finished the last of his drink and placed the glass back down on the table. He stared at the empty container, apparently wondering if he had said too little or too much.

Paul keyed in for another drink, and the digital display promptly told him, in bright red letters, that he was entitled to one additional drink over the next 24 hours. He quickly drained his own glass and keyed in for the last shot. The two men sat in silence for a couple of minutes, letting the soft music of the *Nightside* accompany their personal thoughts.

"Again, I've got to admire you, Sorian," Paul said at length. The young guard had impressed him almost from the very minute he had met him. "I think a lot of us have come to the same conclusions you have. But like you said, everyone expects someone else to solve the problems that might crop up. However, I don't think our guys have it any easier than the rest. True, the research of the snow leopard is an attractive subject, but that's not all we do. Besides, there's a lot of biology, zoological anatomy, and physiology that one has to know before he can even begin to study any animal to an appreciable degree of understanding. We're just as vulnerable as all the rest.

"If you ask me, Enders knows about this whole mess. He's probably just trying to figure out some way to solve it. Anything can look good on paper; it's when you apply your principles to physical situations that complications arise."

Sorian nodded slowly. "That's why you'll probably see me all over the ship. I want to get to know the *Stranahan* like the back of my hand, you know, sort of like searching for all the possible problems and how to solve them. Machines like this are designed by geniuses, but less-than-genius people have to run 'em."

"And you think Enders should be doing more toward that same goal, right?"

"In a way. I mean, I'm not the one to tell him how to run everything, but it just seems logical that he should be doing more."

"And I think he will," Paul stated assuredly. "I would estimate that in another eight to ten years, he'll have a full-fledged training program underway. You already mentioned the Learning Discs; from what I hear, we've got a sizeable amount of younger people addicted to them so far. One of our problems there, though, is the environment of the *Stranahan* itself — it's too limited for the advancement of science. By the end, a lot of us will have experienced almost fifty years of near scientific stagnation."

"I have to agree with you there. I wish I could say I'm worrying too much, but I don't think I am."

"I just hope you keep worrying, Sorian," Paul said, standing up. "You've already got one person on your side. What we need is more like you."

"I don't know. It's hard to guess the actions of a mass of people. Maybe we'll all surprise ourselves somehow. Ready to head back?"

"Why not — for some reason I'm in the mood to meet people. That's rare for me."

"Well, let's go," Sorian chortled. He finished his last drink and began leading the way to the exit of the *Nightside*.

Over the next couple weeks, Paul reflected a great deal upon Sorian's words. Both men talked a couple more times, but Paul was most thankful for the fact that the guard had brought to light important points which most people would probably not think seriously about until it was too late. Still, it appeared that the critical point would not be reached for some time yet; which provided the ideal experimental stage to determine if Captain Enders was really a man deserving of his title.

In the meantime, Paul reread the Information Booklet and the Regulations Manual. He discovered there had been things that he had missed the first time around, when he had been so involved with the snow leopards. The wording of the manuals was typical of that found on Earth during the period of the New World Launches.

Yes, Earth, that place we all manage to actively avoid discussing in our everyday conversations.

Paul quickly tried to brush the irritating thought out of his mind; but at the same time, he slowly realized that he was a victim of his own induced paradox. *Yes, why not think of Earth? Isn't that where the problems began...?*

The manuals had given easy-to-follow guidelines, illustrating this, outlining that. The major pitfall there was that no one who had drawn up these plans had been in space for more than five years at a time, let alone 50. And once a New World Launch left Earth, it was never to be heard from again. Well, almost never.

Everything had been a big risk from the start. Like Enders had said, those risks had nearly killed the New World Launch Program before it even got off the ground. Paul smiled at his wry humor.

However, as he read on, he turned serious once again. No one knew just how good the technology was supposed to be. It had been estimated that the life span of the nuclear reactors would be maximized if the number of Hyper Leaps was held to a minimum; which was not so bad, considering that they had been able to shorten a trip that could have taken hundreds of thousands of years to one of about 50 years, as calculations went. Or was it as the crow flies?

"Come on, Paul, get with it," he muttered to himself.

Then came the question of how one was to tolerate 50 years of monotonous living, the quality of which was sure to deteriorate over time. So they provided medical facilities, placed a limit on the carrying capacity of a given ship, and instructed those that married to emphatically advise any children they had about the various positions to be filled in the ship, particularly the ones the parent held, if any.

And so far, things were not going too badly. However, like Sorian had pointed out, deviations do occur.

Electrical and medical technology had been emphasized in the Learning Discs, for those were man's two most delicate areas; without one or both, his numbers would decrease precipitously, a situation which, though tolerable on a world-wide basis, would spell disaster for the *Stranahan*. That was the disadvantage of being so damned specialized: a single mistake and you tumble like a king without a throne; a world without a sun.

Paul laid the books down. How many times had he done that lately; only to pick them up again? From all he could tell, there was not too much Captain Enders could do that was not already grossly outlined for him in the original plans. Still, there were possible modifications that could be made.

He sighed. Though he was glad Sorian had gotten him to think about all this, he was afraid he would let himself become overly obsessed with thinking of all the possible ramifications that went along with all of the possible problems.

And if that were not enough, he was beginning to worry about his own job. Even Julie had said many of the people in the T.E.I. crew were concerned about him.

Which was probably his own fault. When Colonel died, he had looked for anything to take his attention away from the leopards for a while. He swore at himself now, for it sure was not something someone with his experience should have done. But Sorian had happened along, and the opportunity had been too good to pass up.

Well, now he would have to pay for it. He was the one they all looked up to for guidance when it was needed. And why not? If it were not for his grandfather, they probably would not be here now. A failure on his part would mean a failure of the whole T.E.I. program. And after 80 years, that certainly was not the thing he was going to let happen. Although Gregory Torrden could not have foreseen the New World Launches in 2051, Paul felt sure that his grandfather would have supported his decision to apply for this Launch and to place the leopards on board.

Paul half smiled. Everything eventually returned to the basic problem Sorian had so boldly noted: motivation. Without motivation, the T.E.I. people would get nowhere. And he, Paul Torrden, was the motivative force.

Sorian had made the observation that Torrden Enterprises had been both a research station as well as a scientific institute, and that some of those who had taught classes on Earth were aboard the *Stranahan*. But everything did not always fit together like a recipe. You can not necessarily make a sandwich without bread; nor can you successfully conduct education programs without motivation.

At that moment his thoughts were interrupted as the door to the room slid open. Julie stood in the doorway for a second, then quickly entered the room. Though the years had told on her, like they had on everyone else, her rich, black hair intensified the inherent coolness of her face.

"I recognize that stare, Paul Torrden," she said, the door closing behind her.

"Oh? Is that good or bad?" he laughed, moving over on the bed so she could sit next to him.

"I always thought it had its moments."

"And what's that supposed to mean?"

"Oh, I don't know. I guess I'm just in a good mood."

"Meanwhile, my sexiest stare declines in the ratings."

"You know I was only kidding," she mocked.

"So where you've been, to see all your friends on Four?" Paul asked, getting up to replace the books on the shelf. Though the space his personal books and research papers had taken up had been empty for years, he felt a sudden longing for them. He liked the physical feel of turning worn pages when he was reading. The large-screen computer monitor that dominated the space along the room's rear wall was oftentimes more intimidating than it was user-friendly.

" — some personal matters to take care of today." He suddenly became aware that Julie was talking to him again.

"Anything important?" he idly replied, hoping Julie had not noticed his moment of inattentiveness.

"Probably." She paused for a moment, before asking, in a quieter voice: "Paul, what happens...what happens after us?"

And that was another question he had gone over thousands of times in his head. The suddenness of it left him speechless, nonetheless.

Julie, apparently noticing his uneasiness, came to him. "I'm sorry if I upset you, Paul..."

"I'm sorry it's gotten this far, Jul," he blurted. "I think you and I can both agree that something was missing between us for those ten years.

And then when we found it again, I felt so guilty. I almost felt it was too late, but I never knew how to...well, you know, I didn't know how to say it without hurting either of us."

"I know, I know," she soothed, taking his hands. "Every time we did it, I could see it in your eyes, and it meant something to me. Really. All that hope that was inside you, and how you felt you had to make it up to me."

"Hold it. You mean...?"

"Yes." She allowed herself a smile. "That's where I was today. It's for sure."

"What did they say?"

"That everything appeared okay and that I should be glad that I kept myself in good condition up to now."

"Would it make you even happier if I told you it doesn't make any difference if it is a boy or a girl?"

"It pleases me just to know that you care."

He kissed her, letting his hands slowly glide down to her waist.

"A token of my love. You know, it's funny, but I think we just started a tradition."

Julie smiled at him, her eyes lively and bright. "Maybe, but you never know what your parents would have done if they had lived to succeed Gregory."

"True," he conceded. "But you know as well as I do that Gregory always said that my father would have gone on to take his place when the time came. It's got to be in our blood — we're all snow leopard fanatics," he laughed.

"Okay, I surrender," Julie grinned. "Maybe we have started a tradition."

Paul kissed her again, then quietly said, "And I hope it's a tradition that never dies."

In the years that followed, Paul found that the monotony of travelling through space 24 hours a day (what was a day anymore?) never showed signs of diminishing. He was glad he had already resigned himself to the strong possibility that he might very well live out the rest of his life in the ethereal, eternal space that now surrounded him. He was also glad that he had the snow leopards to occupy his time when the boredom that was so familiar to the occupants of the *Stranahan* began to corrode the outer reaches of his consciousness. Paul realized now, as he had many times in the past, that the leopards had been his whole life. He was frequently visited by the magnificent Colonel in his dreams and hardly a day passed when he failed to think about that prized snow leopard of years past. Phanta, Colonel's mate, had not lived for more than a year after the Corelli incident. However, she had successfully given birth to six young in her time; and each of those cubs, now fully grown, possessed as much of the original spirit of their father as anyone could desire.

And, yes, he was glad of one more thing. Julie. Many lovers had found out that, on a trip such as the one the *Stranahan* was taking, you could not be as dependent upon your partner as you would like to be. However, he and Julie had never let one another down, and it was nice to know there was someone who cared about you when all your world consisted of was the repulsive familiarity of human faces, the hard but pleasing work that surrounded the current research initiatives, and the lifeless artificiality that emanated from tons of cold metal hurtling through space.

Julie...she was almost like a goddess, with that radiant black hair; but, no, he would never deify her like that.

Her pregnancy passed with startling rapidity. Without a sunrise or sunset, a new timetable had to be calibrated for everything one had done previously on Earth. It was fascinating: after being in space for nearly ten years, he was still in the process of getting used to it.

The child had been a boy. Julie had named him Michael. They had already decided that, if it had been a girl, Paul would have had to come up with a name. Paul had made a note of the child's birth year, 2134. Just for the record, he told himself; just in case anyone cares who knows how many years from now. Besides, what were Earth-years anymore? Answer: a convenient way to count the wrinkles on your skin and to estimate the fatigue in your body.

He and Julie were not the only couple to have a child, however. Brevin and Laura Teltor had married, and in 2136, Laura gave birth to a boy whom they named Jase. But it had been rough on them for a while. It would not have been so bad in a population of a million people, where there was more room for what others called "radicalism" and "deviance," but Paul could not quite believe that argument, either. It was not that Brevin was a close friend of his: from an objective viewpoint, he could see nothing wrong with the marriage. What mattered most, however, was that Brevin and Laura were happy together; and as long as that was true, anyone who ridiculed them had certainly deprived him or herself of the opportunity to observe what can happen when a man and a woman, through love, accept each other as people rather than objects and let the color and wisdom of their minds take care of everything else.

As if to get into the spirit of the year, 2136, Sammy Lassiter became the father of a girl whom he and Annah named Faye. Sammy had been practically in raptures over the arrival of his daughter, and when Paul had asked him why a few days later, Sammy had gotten out the old Camera Pack and said, "After years of feeling so artificial, knowing that I have all these wires and metal parts inside my body, it's great to know I can still have a child, that I'm still human enough to do so."

Then the blessed year of 2136 rolled to a close, doing it so slowly that it failed to warn anyone that the following years would be filled with the fear and danger of the unknown...and the unexpected.

As the months and years went by, Paul began to slowly take alarm at the way problems began to arise on Levels Nine and Ten. A lot of the machinery, especially in the Food Stores and Synthetic Productions sections, had begun to malfunction. Which was not all that unusual, except that the maintenance and repair efforts were continually delayed or ineffective.

Paul had not been the only one to notice, though. The queasy foreboding he felt steal through his body whenever he sensed a silent panic in the crowds aboard the *Stranahan* was not too comfortable, either. He knew that this was probably the most critical period for the *Stranahan*, as far as success was concerned; and if everyone did not begin to accept the responsibility of the trip as seriously as they should have years before...

He could not complete the thought, at least not consciously. But he had to give credit to Enders. The Captain had recognized Sorian as a possible driving force that could ignite the much needed determination and enthusiasm that was absent from the ship. He had appointed the fiery-eyed guard to head a committee that travelled throughout the *Stranahan* speaking to the passengers about what had to be done and what the consequences were if the buck kept getting passed on to the "other guy."

Then there were the Learning Discs — they had been only a minor success. While some students were able to quickly pick up the concepts and intricacies surrounding their own roles in the *Stranahan's* ultimate destination, and the responsibilities that were demanded of them, there were just not enough new, young students yet to compensate for those who, as Sorian had once noted, lacked the necessary motivation. Enders had provided his own punch by drawing up stricter penalties for those who failed to utilize the discs for the required length of time; but there was little that he could do as he was already on an unstable bridge in that he was always, at least potentially, the nonconformist as far as the Average Joe was concerned.

There were more problems, Paul knew. All one had to do was go out and look and he'd find them. They were all over, leaping out of the metal frames as prolifically as a colony of breeding *Drosophila melanogaster*. Eventually, one of those fruit flies struck home with a bluntness that made Paul wonder if, indeed, he was better off than most of the other people on the ship.

Julie had noticed it first, as she was the one who usually took Michael for his daily exercises at the gymnasium. After a three-day bout with the flu, Michael, who was now eight, had asked if he could resume his exercises. During the next couple days, however, he had tired quickly, and his recovery rate had been far too slow for Julie to completely ignore. She decided that a couple more days of rest were needed, but both she and Paul were still alarmed when Michael was suddenly stricken with violent and continuous periods of nausea.

They took Michael to the Sick Ward, but after an hour of waiting there were still no answers. Paul was already late for a meeting with the T.E.I. medic staff and, after Julie convinced him she'd keep him informed, he reluctantly left the Ward.

A half hour later, his thoughts still troubled by his son's condition, he found himself involved in a highly technical discussion with Annah and Brevin. Data outputs were spread throughout the room. Though they were in the middle of a Hyper Leap, both the behaviorist and the medic man had noticed something out of the ordinary in the way the leopards had been acting. The animals were becoming more short-tempered and Brevin had reported an alarming increase in the number of hostile encounters between T.E.I. personnel and the leopards. However, neither of the T.E.I. specialists could put a finger on what the problem was.

After they had examined all of the available information, Annah stood up and began scratching her head as she looked out over the piles of paper. "You know," she said broodingly, "some of these leopards are acting very similar to the ones we had problems with when we first brought them aboard the ship, from Earth. Paul, I'd like to get some special equipment together to do some neurological measurements on a couple of the leopards. It's a hunch I have."

"It's okay by me," Paul had conceded. "I've been around these leopards all my life — I don't need to tell you that. And I do remember the strange way these animals were acting when they were first brought on board. *That* does not bother me so much, since such a change in environment would affect any animal, even us. But what does bother me, is that I can sense something is wrong now, too, and whatever it is, it's got to be corrected."

Brevin nodded. "If it's any consolation to you, I don't think it's anything harmful, medically speaking."

"Somehow, I don't think it is either," Paul agreed, "but it is nice to have an expert opinion on such things. Keep me up-to-date on what you find."

"I'll get started on the tests as soon as possible, then, but I don't know how soon it'll be before I get results," Annah said, turning to leave the two men to ponder over the situation on their own.

Paul's eyes focused on the behaviorist. Over the years she had gained more weight and her fading brown hair always hung haphazardly about her stocky face. Yet, she was a likeable person and oftentimes appeared to be almost married to her work.

"Fine, it's no rush. And Brevin, I —."

"Paul?"

Somehow, the way his name had been said — in that tense, taut voice — made him feel as if someone had stuck an ice-cold finger into the small of his back. Turning, his eyes found Julie, and the chilling and unfamiliar look in her face made him forget that Brevin and Annah were still in the room.

Later, in their own room, Paul finally got the whole story.

"They kept running all these tests on him," Julie said. "Liver, urine, blood tests and all that. They said they had to be certain, because they weren't even too sure of what it was themselves."

She paused, and Paul solemnly nodded for her to continue. He was watching her, however, with concern, for she usually never had this much trouble saying anything.

"It's some kind of serious disease, they tried to explain it to me, but I...oh, I don't know. I-It's a disease...or syndrome or something like that which crops up after a viral infection, and they said that...it's sometimes fatal."

She stopped again, a pale look spreading across her face.

Paul took her hand. Those last few words had been little more than a whisper. "Are you okay, Jul?"

After a moment's hesitation she looked into his eyes, and then looked down again.

"I haven't let you down, have I?"

So that was it.

"Of course you haven't," Paul said, managing a half smile. "And what kind of question is that, coming from you?"

"He's your own son, Paul! *That's* what kind of question it is."

Paul could see tears in her eyes, for the first time in months. "I know he's my son, Jul," he began, making sure to keep a calm level in his voice. "And I do care about him. I love Michael just as much as you do. I only meant that, well, I hadn't expected this."

A knock on the cabin door prevented her from answering. She took a deep breath and nodded that it was all right.

Paul got up from the bed and pressed the lever to unlock and open the door. He was glad to see it was two people that he knew: Laura and the Captain.

"Sorry to disturb you, Mr. Torrden. Is it all right if we come in?"

Paul nodded, absent-mindedly watching them as they entered the room. Once they were inside, he closed the door again.

"I'm sorry about your son, Mr. Torrden. I came as soon as I was notified. Normally, I don't do this for everyone who gets sick, but it's just that there was little we could do, being that we have so few specialists for this particular illness. Hopefully, we —."

Yes, yes, Paul thought to himself, only half listening. Public relations all the way. In a manner of speaking, Enders was very good at that. But all Paul wanted from the Captain right now was to be left alone with Julie.

Slowly, like a fog rolling in, the shock of his son's illness began to sink in, chilling him with a numb, bleak feeling. He began to realize now why Julie had been so disturbed: she'd had more time to be exposed to it. Glancing over at her, he saw that Laura was talking softly to her. It had been a smart move on Enders' part to bring the doctor along.

He tuned back in to what the Captain was saying, more out of courtesy than curiosity.

" — promise is constant monitoring, I want you to know that our medical personnel will be doing everything possible to help him as much as they can and hopefully effect a recovery."

Which was like asking for miracles, Paul thought. A disease that was so exceptional that it had baffled a team of well-picked, highly qualified doctors probably did not have a cure. That, at least, sounded half logical.

"What's being done now?" he asked.

Enders threw a quick glance toward Laura, who stood up from where she had been sitting beside Julie. Her lengthy blonde hair swung several inches below the top of her shoulders as she turned to face the two men.

"We'll have to keep him under intensive care. That way we'll be able to run some more tests on his blood and liver. We'll also have to monitor his breathing and respiratory responses in case any difficulties arise in that area. Worst case, some exchange transfusions and what we call peritoneal dialysis treatments may be needed as well, if our suspicions pan out."

And don't forget to throw in a miracle, Paul thought as he and Julie gave their consent. After all the sympathetic formalities were exchanged, Paul pressed the lever to open the door. Enders and Laura had almost left when the Comm panel beeped an emergency signal pattern.

The Captain creased his eyebrows and quickly strolled over to Paul's desk. He punched in his access codes with deliberate jabs of his index finger.

"This is Enders. What you got?"

"Captain? Oh, thank God," came the voice. "There's an emerg — , ah, you're needed right 'way on the Navigation Bridge, sir."

None of the people in the small room missed the definite note of strained excitement that had been in the voice of the ship's officer. Paul was even further alerted when he saw Enders key off the Comm panel and move with determined quickness through the doorway and down the hall.

Laura was left standing for an indecisive couple moments before making an excuse about getting back to her work and following Enders.

Paul and Julie sat in uneasy silence for several minutes. At length, Paul said, "Let's have something to eat, and if you want, you can rest. Then we'll go up to see him, okay?"

Julie managed a half smile and nodded her head. "I'm sorry...for what happened."

"You mean for what we said?"

"Yes, I guess..."

"Don't worry about it. I just didn't really understand how you felt."

He kissed her softly and then rose to inspect the day's menu selection.

Twenty minutes later he wished he had not eaten at all. The emergency sirens began to blare again, and he realized with agonizing acuteness that they were due for reentry into normal space.

His first thought, strangely enough, was of the snow leopards, but he knew Brevin and Annah had not been as absent-minded as him and probably had everything under control.

He and Julie quickly went around the room, putting away all objects not anchored down. That done, they methodically slipped out of their regular duty body suits, replacing these with Launch-issue protective clothing. They then strapped themselves into the two large, multi-functional safety chairs located adjacent to the bed.

Standard. All standard. Everywhere on the *Stranahan*, people were doing the same thing, putting articles away and then strapping themselves in to await the change-over.

All standard.

And it was a good thing, too, because the reentry into normal space was not standard, not by any means. The first indication that something was wrong was the severity of the sickening feeling that accompanied deceleration. Paul realized, with a touch of nervousness, that it had never been this strong before.

That thought had no sooner crossed his mind when the room began to jerk haphazardly as if it possessed a life of its own. Paul felt something clench his arm and was surprised at how much strength Julie had in her hands. He thought he heard her say something, but amidst the sounds of laboring machinery and his own head slapping violently against the head-rest, he barely heard anything she said.

Then there were more sounds: muffled explosions, grinding and tear-ing metal, and the anguished cries of a few passengers who had evidently panicked and tried to escape the celestial earthquake by running along the finite corridors of the ship. Paul winced as he reluctantly pictured a human body thrown helplessly about the hallway, three to four bones snapping horribly with each merciless impact.

Suddenly, there was a horrendous tug that would have sent Paul and Julie flying into the opposite wall had it not been for their earlier precau-tions. It almost seemed that the *Stranahan* had been attached to a very long rope which had suddenly become taut. Visions of being stranded out in space, at the end of the line, came to Paul, and he almost cried at the irony in that thought.

After a few more minutes there was silence. Total. Everywhere. Paul looked at his wife and saw his own personal fear reflected in her eyes. Things were happening too fast.

Quiet, slow footsteps were the first sign of life. Low, distant voices soon became audible. Paul and Julie, recovered from the slight hysteria that had overcome them, both realized simultaneously that whatever ca-lamity had taken place was now apparently over.

He looked at her again and saw the obvious question in her eyes.

"I don't know," he said.

After several tense minutes, they hesitantly unfastened the straps. Paul knew the bruises and abrasions they had received were bound to be with them for quite some time.

Disobeying ship protocol, they doffed the cumbersome protective cloth-ing. Julie grabbed two robes and gave one to Paul. They then opened their door, cautiously walking out into the hallway. Four bodies were visible along the corridor, where they would stay until the medical teams came by. Paul turned to Julie before going on, but now it was her time to read his thoughts.

"It's all right. I'll be okay."

Other people began to come out of their rooms as they started slowly forward again. Then the ship's Comm came to life, Enders' voice crisp and rehearsed.

"Attention everyone, please follow emergency regulations and remain in your quarters until further notification is given. We encountered some technical trouble coming out of the Leap and until everything is worked out it is best that you remain stationary. Guards are posted at all elevator entrances, and anyone violating these orders will be subject to punishment accordingly. Please cooperate."

Paul took Julie's arm. "Come on, we'd better do as he says. Besides, I want to call Brevin down below and see what's happened to the leopards."

Julie shrugged her shoulders, taking a look at the four bodies and the rapidly filling hallway one last time before turning to go.

They had taken no more than a couple of steps before they were stopped by a voice that said, "I don't think you'll be able to do that, either."

Paul swung around. His eyes met those of Tom Saxter, one of the technical aides on his staff.

"What's that?"

Tom gestured nervously with his hands. "I don't really know. I was on the Comm with someone on Seven as soon as it seemed there were gonna be no more shocks. They said Enders was evacuating Levels Eight through Ten; something about extensive damage and several air leaks. Then I was cut off. I couldn't even call anyone on our Level. I think they jammed all non-essential communication."

"But what about the people in the Ward," Julie asked, and just as quickly the same chilling thought occurred to Paul.

Not waiting for the technician's answer, he began racing through the hallway toward the elevators. Several of the other people in the hallway barely had time to get out of his path. *Damn Enders' rules!* he repeated to himself. He silently prayed the thought of his son dying or lying dead on a cold mattress would not come true.

When he reached the elevators, he was stopped by a barricade of five guards.

"You heard what he said, Mr. Torrden. We can't let you through," said the foremost guard, a tall, burly man with a red moustache.

"I have to get up to Ten. My son could be dying up there."

"Hey, how'd you know about that?" The guard's eyes quickly squinted.

Paul felt something fall out from under him, and he had a dead sensation of suddenly feeling very small.

"It's true, then. God dammit, let me pass!" he drawled, at the same time starting forward.

But his bluff was met by the rock-hard, piercing stare of the guard.

"Look, Mr. Torrden, I don't know how you came by your information, and I don't know if your son is in any danger. All I know is that I don't want to have to report you, okay?"

Before Paul could reply, the elevator doors opened and Sorian stepped out. He must have seen the flash of hope that passed across Paul's face, for he immediately said, "Sorry, Paul, I can't let you or anyone else up there yet."

Paul debated, the speed of his thoughts making him slightly uncomfortable. There was definitely no way he was going to get past the guards and the frustration of that realization abruptly began to tear at his insides like a wild beast.

After that, things began to haze out. When Sorian volunteered to escort him back to his room, he vaguely sensed the relief that swept over the guards who had blocked his way.

As they began walking away from the elevator, Sorian said, in a loud, clear voice: "That was definitely out of line, Mr. Torrden. I really ought to report you to Captain Enders."

Paul stopped, eyeing Sorian with momentary unfamiliarity.

"Just keep walking," Sorian continued. "If you don't resist, I may hold off on that report."

With a cold start, Paul caught on to the game Sorian was playing. He quickly went along, and when they were out of earshot of the other officers, Paul said, "Okay, Sorian, what is it?"

Sorian took a deep breath. "I was up on Ten earlier, when Julie brought Michael up for his tests. I only remembered he was up there because people started talking about —."

"Sorian!"

"Okay, okay. He's alive, Paul, that's all I can say. As soon as it was safe to move about, I got on the first Evac team and he was the first one I got to."

They reached the main hallway and Paul could see Julie up ahead, coming towards him.

"What do you mean, 'he's alive?'" Paul winced at the demanding tone in his own voice.

"There's too many people here. Wait till we get back to your room," Sorian cautioned, stealing a glance along the hallway.

When they reached the privacy of the room, Paul hurriedly briefed Julie on everything Sorian had disclosed. Then they listened as Sorian continued to explain what had happened.

"As for your son," the guard uttered, "he was unconscious when I found him and I really don't know how bad off he is. Most of the patients were knocked around quite a bit. I guess I have to tell you, he wasn't breathing, but I gave him mouth to mouth to get him going again, and then I got him out of there."

Julie and Paul let the shock of that sink in for a while. They wanted to know more about their son — where he was, if he was okay — but everything that was possible to know had just been told to them.

Sorian appeared to sense that silent conclusion, for he went on: "What happened was, we stayed in Leap for too long. It began to tear the ship apart. As far as I can gather, with the dynamics of the ship and everything else considered, I think Nine and Ten are the weakest part of the *Stranahan*, and that's probably why those sections went first.

"We got her back into normal space, but just barely in time. Everything should have been all right, but the emergency seals didn't shut all the way. So, instead of just moving people from the damaged sections only, we had to get everybody off of Ten, Nine, and most of Eight.

"Most of that is hearsay, what with being on that Evac team and talking to the other guards on the way down here, but most of it's probably true."

Paul shook his head in wonder. "How'd it ever happen in the first place."

Sorian shrugged. "Don't know, really." The brevity of the guard's answer caught Paul by surprise. For a time, no one spoke, although the guard continued to stare into Paul's eyes.

Paul could sense there was more to Sorian's answer, and his suspicions were confirmed when the guard cautiously rose to open the door to the room. Sorian leisurely glanced up and down the hallway before closing the door again and returning to the chair in front of Paul.

"Actually, Paul, one guard I overheard said they had to change the original Leap destination at the last minute because...because a couple of the navigators claimed that their instruments had scanned the Fall-Out point and had returned signals not inconsistent with the readings that the Sixteenth originally documented when they discovered that alien ship. Guess it took too long to plot out a different course to a new Fall-Out point."

Paul swallowed nervously before asking, "Was our maneuver successful? Were we followed?"

Sorian glanced over at Julie and, apparently noticing she had not even been paying attention to what was being said, hastily replied, "Don't know that, either. Hey, listen, I'd better get back before those other guards get suspicious."

Paul stood up. "Hey, thanks for everything, Sorian. Our lips are sealed. And listen, if you find out about Michael before they let us out of here or allow us to call out, could you let us know?"

"Sure, sure. I'll go up right now. I'll get in touch with you as soon as I can."

After Sorian had left, Paul looked worriedly at Julie. The guard's visit had definitely upset her and he did not quite know how to approach her. He walked quietly out of the room a couple minutes later, having decided it would be best if he did not attempt to comfort her now. He knew they both needed time by themselves, and maybe this was as good a time as any to take it. Besides, he'd never been the one to smooth over a problem with flawless ease, and he knew that if he tried now, he would probably wind up making a fool out of himself or only worsening the situation.

When he got out in the hall, he leaned against the wall for a while. The medical personnel had finally arrived, and he passively watched as they loaded the four bodies onto stretchers and carried them back down the accessory hallway to the elevators.

The next thing he knew, his feet were following the medical team, and he felt an old, familiar, emotional...obsession. He recognized it immediately and just as abruptly, he stopped himself.

Should he not be with Julie, worrying about Michael just as much as she was? He felt a sudden giddiness, wondering if he did indeed love his son as much as he claimed. He knew he could not move until he answered that question, and when a voice from inside him said, 'yes,' he still hesitated before going on.

Somehow, someway, what he was doing was right; it had to be. If

Julie were mad at him later for walking out on her, well...that really was not the principle of the situation, and he knew that until he discovered what was, everything he did would be shadowed in his own personal doubt.

When he reached the elevators, he felt disjointed, out of place. Maybe this was what Julie was going through, he thought, realizing it was bound to get worse if his comparison were true. A strange fright ran through his body when he asked the guards if he could go one deck below to check in on the leopards. He had the distinct impression he was outside of his body, unlawfully observing everything he was doing, saying, and feeling.

He, the observer, and his body noticed that, while the red-moustached guard was still at the elevator door, two of the other four guards present had not been there 45 minutes earlier. Something inside himself was troubled by this and began tinkering with possible explanations, while something else was dully aware of the red-moustached guard saying to one of the new officers, "Take him down, Ron. And if anything happens, you don't have to worry. Just remember, I gave you the orders."

Two minutes later he found himself in front of Brevin, and two minutes after that he found himself downing a whole shot of some strong liquor.

"You all right, Paul?"

He felt a slow merging and grasped on tightly to the reality that was returning to him. He held out his glass for another drink, and as Brevin filled it, he managed a weak smile.

"Sorry. I got a lot of things on my mind, I guess."

Brevin managed a tense laugh. "Hey, you looked like you were in another galaxy there for a while. Something happen to Julie?"

"No...well, yeah, in a way, but we're mostly worried about Michael."

Paul downed the second shot, then gave the glass back to Brevin.

"That's just what you needed," the medic man said, laying the glass on a nearby counter. "Don't worry 'bout talking through it now — you can do that on your own time. I guess you're interested about the leopards, too, right?"

Paul nodded. "You read me too well, Brevin."

"Yeah, well, it's not the best news in the world, but it's not as bad as it could have been. Janey and her mother went. Then there was old Duncan and the two cubs Jackie just had. Other than that, we just got a lot of minor fractures and short tempers to deal with right now. We're still hanging tough around forty, and I think we can still make sixty-five by the end of this jaunt, if it ever comes."

"Sometimes...I wonder what it's like. Being taken away from your home and the environment for which you've been adapted. It's no problem for us — we wanted to go, but what about them?"

Brevin let his eyes roam over the rows of large cages filled with the silvery-colored leopards. Then he looked back at Paul. "I've felt that way, too, at times. And I'm sure the thought crossed your grandfather's mind many times. The sad thing is, I don't think anyone will ever come up with a moral justification. It's just something that we did, and now we owe these leopards everything we can give 'em."

"And more," Paul added. "They were meant to live and die by the laws of natural selection, not because of man's technological oversights."

As if to spite him, the Comm panel suddenly burst into life, the voice of Bill Enders ringing loud and clear.

"Attention, crew and passengers of the *Stranahan*. I apologize for the inconvenience of the disturbance and the delay we are now experiencing. I am sorry to report that Levels Eight, Nine, and Ten suffered extensive damage. Please follow Ship protocol and continue to report any serious injuries or other casualties through proper channels. We will get to you as soon as we can. A list of those persons receiving medical attention will be issued as soon as all information is final.

"You are now free to use the intra-ship Comm network and the elevators, the employment of which I restricted earlier to avoid unnecessary panic as we had to implement an evacuation operation on the upper levels. I still ask that you avoid Levels Nine and Ten as they are presently under repair. We are establishing temporary facilities on Level Eight, and we will notify the next of kin as to when it is advisable to go there.

"As for what happened..."

The Captain's words continued to flow on, explaining the reasons for the accident, and what had to be done as far as repairs were concerned. Sorian's sources had been pretty accurate. Which made sense, Paul figured. There was no reason for false rumors in space; hopefully, all that had been left behind on...*yes, you can say it: Earth. So long ago ...*

He felt Brevin's hand on his shoulder. "Get some rest, Paul. You're beginning to stare off into the next plane again."

Paul shrugged. "Yeah, I guess so. Thanks for that drink."

Brevin waved it off and turned to resume his efforts in restoring the containment facilities for the captive animals.

When Paul returned to his room five minutes later, Julie was still sitting where he'd left her. Then he saw the redness in her eyes. He sat down beside her.

"Hey, Jul, I'm sorry I left like that. I just did not know what to do."

She did not say anything for a few moments. Then, very softly: "That's okay, I understand. You've always been like that, you and I both know that."

She paused, and almost in a whisper, added, "Sorian just called."

He tensed, waiting for her to continue.

"He got there too late, Paul. They think that Michael may have gone without oxygen for too long and that he might have suffered some spinal or nerve damage during the accident."

She began crying again, and he put his arm around her, numbly amazed at the clearness in his mind.

Silently, they laid down next to each other on the bed and held one another for several hours. No words, no actions…just thoughts. They laid there until Sorian called again, this time from Level Eight.

They could see Michael if they wished.

When they arrived on Eight, Sorian met them and directed them through a maze of temporary work stations to the room in which Michael was located. Paul was beginning to wonder how he was ever going to repay Sorian for the latter's dedicated and loyal friendship. The guard reminded Paul of friends he used to have when he was a boy; friends who were always there to help, even when he got into trouble. He'd had trouble fighting back the tears then, knowing there was someone who cared about him and on whom he could depend. And Sorian had the same kind of love for him his childhood friends had possessed.

Paul's thoughts slowly dissipated as he followed Sorian and Julie into a room just off the accessory hallway. On the far side of the room Michael lay on a large bed, his head propped up against a fluffy pillow. His short, light-brown hair made him appear younger than he actually was. Laura was at the bedside, carefully adjusting the i.v. equipment. Paul noticed that Michael looked rather pale. He and Julie slowly approached Laura, inquisitive looks invading their faces.

"Hi, Paul, Julie," Laura said, turning to face the couple. She flicked a tiny half smile across her face and after it had disappeared, Paul wondered if he had indeed seen it all. "I'm sorry we took so long to call you, but I wanted to see if the diagnosis was correct, and if so, what could be done about it.

"I think it's best that I tell you all that I know about it, and then if you have any questions I'll try and answer them, okay?

"First of all, we're pretty sure now Michael has what is commonly called Reye's Syndrome. Though that's probably a new word for you, our logs show he just got over the flu and this particular illness usually occurs after a viral infection such as the flu or something of that nature. It was fairly prevalent in the late twentieth century and the first half of the twenty-first, but we've seen very few cases in recent times."

She paused, took in a deep breath, and then went on. "I guess I should mention right now, this affliction is about forty percent fatal, and he can sustain damage to his brain, liver, or other organs as well. I'm afraid he may already have some short-term memory loss, though whether this is from the accident when he stopped breathing or from his illness I can't tell until I run more tests. Furthermore, the accident rendered most of our safety equipment useless and he may have suffered some type of debilitating injury to the spine or his nervous system. That will need further tests as well.

"Right now, all I can say is that he hasn't been conscious for any extended length of time, he has a fever, and he's been experiencing periods of nausea and disorientation. There is no standard cure that we know of. I'm sorry. The only thing we can do is apply textbook treatments and hope he falls in the sixty percent survival area."

She stopped again and Paul was amazed at his difficulty in accepting the fact that the professional doctor who now stood before him had been the same smiling woman who had invited him to that Level Four party almost nine years ago. But the school of medicine, like so many other professional institutions, had given her a mask to wear, a mask that provided her with sharpness and complete control of her faculties in situations such as the present one, where an emotional doctor would be a definite hindrance rather than an informative help.

He became aware of Julie asking what Michael's chances were.

Laura pushed back a lock of her hair. "They're not too good," she warned. "The accident we've had has not only crippled our medical team, but it has probably worsened Michael's condition in any number of ways. Then again I might add that there have been many cases of complete recovery listed in the medical literature we possess."

Paul's appreciation of Laura's straight-forward honesty was darkly over-shadowed by what Sorian had said earlier about rescuing his son. "Do we need to worry about Sorian, too?" he asked.

Laura nodded. "I know, he already told me. It's not contagious, though, at least not in that way. We think several conditions have to be met before Reye's can be contracted. Still, there's already been another case reported, so this flu outbreak may be more serious than expected."

Julie took a couple steps to the bedside and slowly extended her hand until it touched the fingers of her son. Laura quietly excused herself, and as she moved off to another patient, Paul momentarily experienced the weight of Sorian's hand on his shoulder. Their eyes met, and a sympathetic understanding flashed between them and went deep into Paul's soul. Then the guard was gone and he moved to Julie's side and unknowingly joined her in a silent prayer for their son.

During the immediate days that followed, Paul spent many hours reading up on his son's illness. At first, he could not understand why, when it appeared Michael was making considerable progress toward full recovery, a relapse in his condition would occur. However, as he became more knowledgeable about the illness, he realized the recurring bouts with nausea, fever, convulsions, and behavioral hostilities were trademark symptoms of the syndrome. He could only marvel at the advancement in medical science technology that permitted the physicians aboard the *Stranahan* to successfully cope with the wide array of physical and mental ailments requiring corrective treatment.

When Michael's condition finally began to improve, the team of doctors overseeing his recovery suggested that Sammy Lassiter's daughter, Faye, should visit the boy daily to provide a level of companionship that would have proven therapeutic value. Paul knew that their selection of Faye had been no accident. A long-established friendship already existed between the two children, a direct result of the close working relationship of their parents. Faye, who was younger than Michael by about two years, enjoyed the opportunity to once again spend time with her friend. Both Sammy and Paul could see that she idolized Michael, at least in that way that children have of choosing role models as they begin to interact with one another.

As repairs to the *Stranahan* continued, Paul made frequent trips to see his son. He often took Faye along with him, especially when Michael, whose strength was improving, began to look forward to having someone with whom he could play games. By the time four months had passed, Paul and Julie discovered that their son's acceptance of the new constraints which life had placed on him was readily apparent. Although he'd had difficulty in remembering events immediately preceding the accident and had lost the use of most of his left arm, his boyish outlook on life remained healthy.

Paul knew, however, that he, as a father, had to also adapt to these changes. He knew, for example, that his career's work had not kept him from loving his son, but it had kept him from getting to really know Michael the way a father should know a son. The situation had not been made any easier, he realized, because he now had to somehow respond to the changes in his son's life. The distance that separated himself and Michael was more mental than physical, he knew, and it was a gap that he someday hoped to shorten.

As Paul continued to watch the *Stranahan* being rebuilt to a navigable condition, he developed a firm conviction that it was the computer-literate men and women who held the key to the star ship's eventual success or failure. Determined to ensure that Michael did not miss the opportunity to develop such skills, Paul placed a special order up to Sci-Tech for the services of a tutor and the installment of a top-of-the-line Personal User equipment package in Michael's room.

Although Michael's initial interest in the equipment and special lessons had been borderline at best, he suddenly developed a deeper, more passionate involvement in the opportunities being given him by the time the *Stranahan* was ready to continue its journey. Paul found that Michael began to rapidly absorb the material, even to the point of involving Faye in some of his computer programming experiments.

Despite the nerve damage that had resulted in the permanent loss of the use of his left arm, Michael soon developed a small following among the group of children with whom he regularly had classes. Many of the kids began to respect and envy the manner in which he was able to learn new concepts almost instantly. Paul knew that his son's computer analysis and programming skills would soon dwarf his own, but he humbly realized that the emotional distance between himself and Michael still remained.

Eventually, Michael entered his early teens, and he began to grow his sandy-brown hair longer — in the likeness of R.L. Dennings, whom he had read about in Sammy's journals. Paul did not provide much resistance to this change in image because he knew it was Michael's way of searching for his individuality and identity.

Michael's image became even more widely known, however, when he and Faye developed the first interactive computer program for many of the most frequently used Learning Discs. This development exponentially increased the value of the Discs, drawing back many people who had stopped using them out of boredom. The new program allowed users of the Learning Discs to create and run a seemingly endless array of simulation models based on the input of standard variables and intangible factors such as the level of learning difficulty or the relative availability of resources needed to complete a task or resolve a problem.

Captain Bill Enders took an interest in Michael by this time, and the young man was soon asked to enroll as a student in starship operations, to eventually serve as a ship officer trainee. Paul and Julie consented to the request. In time, Michael, whose shy and silent nature led many strangers into believing the young Torrden was completely unaware of his own gifts, began to quietly set new standards for the classes in which he was enrolled. He spent many hours under Sorian's tutelage, which resulted in an almost endless exploration of the *Stranahan's* inner hull.

Twelve years had elapsed since the *Stranahan's* accident and Michael's injury when Julie one day told Paul that their son was coming to visit. Michael, who was now 20, had just announced his engagement to Faye Lassiter. Paul was therefore not too surprised by Julie's news.

"That's good. We haven't seen him for a while."

"He wants to talk to you, Paul, not me."

Paul turned from his desk-load of papers to stare at his wife, who was sitting cross-legged on the bed. "Is that what he told you?" he asked.

"That's *all* he told me, Paul. I have no idea what he's up to now."

"Well, I'm glad he's getting married. Do you remember what it was like for us, at first?"

"All too well. I asked myself many times whether I was about to marry a man or an institution. I think in the end I got a little of both. Faye and Michael have a very promising future, though. I just hope this whole trip works out." Julie rose from the bed and approached her husband. She slowly placed her hands on his shoulders and drew Paul close to her.

Paul knew there were no words of consolation or assurance he could offer Julie. In fact, there was probably no one aboard the *Stranahan* who had not heard less than 50 different reasons within the past year for why the trip would succeed; everyone had tried to build his or her own empire of optimism.

They were still silently enmeshed in each other's arms when Paul heard the knock at the door.

"That's him now, Paul," Julie said, stepping back. "Be sure to give him the best advice you can. I'm going to exercise." She quickly grabbed an exercise suit and opened the door to let her son in. "Hi, honey, I was just going. You respect your father's words, now, okay?" She kissed him on the cheek and slithered past him.

Michael stood hesitantly at the door for a moment. The young man's smile reminded Paul of himself at an earlier age, before T.E.I.'s responsibilities had been thrust on him. His son's dark eyes also mirrored the shyness that Paul knew was deep within himself as well. Still, he knew Michael had found ways to overcome that shyness when necessary.

"The people about to get married aren't always the most nervous," he offered.

Michael, as if struck by a sudden realization, smiled and entered the room. Paul closed the door and offered his son one of the other chairs in the room. After a few moments of new silence, Paul sat back down. As he continued to admire his son, he realized that their eyes never strayed from one another. He knew that he'd rarely had the opportunity to comfortably stare into his son's eyes for such a long period of time.

Michael slowly leaned forward. "I can't deny that I got a lot to learn about that, dad, but I really came here to tell you that I've really appreciated all that you and mom have taught me about the snow leopards and what we're trying to achieve with them. I've also immersed myself in many other things, too, especially since the time...I was sick."

Paul nodded agreeably. "Remind me to nominate that for understatement of the year."

Michael smiled briefly, but his face quickly grew serious again. Paul knew that his son disliked recalling the days of his illness. Sometimes he had tried to imagine what it must have been like for Michael, but it was at those times that Paul's imagination knew no bounds.

"Sometimes I wish I knew what you really feel inside yourself about the leopards," Michael continued. "Then I could compare it with my feelings now. That way, maybe I would not feel so guilty."

Paul leaned forward, smiling, but only because he'd discovered the true nature of his son's visit. "In other words, you don't want to continue working with the T.E.I. studies, right?"

Michael's assent was a silent nod that stabbed at Paul's pride. He allowed the confirmation to sink in, debating it and turning it over in his mind. Thoughts came to his mind, and he carefully let go of the tradition that would never die. Pensively, he stated, "I'm content with your decision, Michael. I want you to feel proud about whatever you do. A man's faced with choices like these at some point in his life, and it's then that he's got to choose the right path to follow."

"You're sure you'll be able to carry out all the work without my being there when you need me? I know you've spent a lot of time trying to teach me everything you know and encouraging me to study the T.E.I. Learning Discs. Somehow, I have to imagine you had an implied purpose there."

Paul smiled again, revealing teeth that, despite the 60-year old body in which they were rooted, shown brightly in the artificial light of the room.

"I remember back when I was on Earth, fighting desperately to get on one of those New World Launches. I kept assuring the Space Flight Commission that there would be enough young, interested people to make the T.E.I. program worth its reservation on a ship. In no way did I know what it'd be like up here, but I haven't yet regretted making that statement. So, though I may be the guy calling the shots, and though you may be my son, I still feel that it is your choice to make. And no one's going to be in hot water as long as you make the right decision in your own eyes. By the way, can I ask what that may be?"

"I want to command a ship like this one someday," Michael said, returning Paul's smile.

After the dull shock had faded and Michael had left, Paul slowly allowed a big grin to spread across his face. Practically no one had made as much use of the ship's Learning Discs as Michael had in the past five years. In spite of his illness, Michael had proven that he was a quick learner, and the years of training he had in ship operations had given him invaluable hands-on experience. Paul was sure that experience would stay with him for a long time.

He was about to key on the Comm to find Julie when Annah appeared at the door, her eyes beaming out excitement that practically filled the room with electricity. She danced in and motioned for him to close the door behind her. Puzzled, he obeyed. She laid a stack of graphs she had been carrying on the table.

"Paul, remember all those tests I asked permission to do a long time ago, about the time of the accident?"

"You mean with the leopards? Sure," Paul acknowledged. "And I hope you finally have some good news." He knew that the behavior of the leopards had gotten progressively worse over the years and he was anxious to hear what his behaviorist had to say.

"Well, of all the tests I've run, the ones involving the monitoring of synaptic activity of nerve cells in the brain have proven to be the most intriguing. Just by chance, some of the monitoring we were doing just before we left Earth allowed us to identify several pairs of neurons which exhibited unexplained peaks in neuronal activity. Only now has the significance of those observations come into focus."

"Whoa, there. You've already lost me. Let's start from the beginning."

Annah's face became serious. "Yes, I must confess, the historical significance of these data has gotten the best of me! Okay, from the beginning — this much you do know: persistent changes in the efficiency of neuronal activity in the brain have long been thought to be related to the neural mechanisms of learning and memory. Indeed, your grandfather once predicted that the identification of specific neuron pairs known to be involved in a learning task was all that prevented us from perhaps proving this theory beyond a reasonable doubt."

Paul nodded his head. "You're right — this much I do know. It is part of the foundation for all the work that T.E.I. has done in its behavioral sciences research."

"Yes, so then you'll also know that another key tenet of this theory is that the observed clinical changes in synaptic activity that supposedly reflect learning processes — where neuro-transmitters are released by one nerve cell and cross over to another nerve cell — should occur in association with measurable learning experiences. This is where things get interesting, Paul. Here, take a look at these graphs from two leopards showing abnormal behavior in 2124, sometime prior to our leaving Earth." Annah handed Paul the graphs in question and picked up the remaining graphs that she had brought in. As she continued, her enthusiasm was impossible to miss. "Believe me, it took me years before I tried attacking this problem from this angle. Now, compare those graphs with control samples representing normal background levels. Note the difference in amplitude of the postsynaptic potential."

Paul noticed that the leopards examined just prior to leaving Earth had noticeably higher rates of neuronal activity and he said as much to the behaviorist.

"Good," she replied. "Now, here are the results of three leopards on which I took measurements about seven days after the accident. Notice again how the increase in postsynaptic activity is persistent and significantly greater than the control samples. And note also how closely these readings resemble the measurements of the two leopards examined in 2124."

"I think I'm beginning to get the picture now," Paul exclaimed. "You're correlating certain events with high brain activity levels, right?"

"In a way; but it's more specific than that. Here, I've tabulated the results of about twenty measurements I've taken since the accident. What do you notice that's unusual?"

Paul scrutinized the graph and compared it with the figures he had been given previously. Finally, he said, "There is not only persistence in heightened synaptic activity; but the increase appears to be specific to certain sets of neurons. Annah, why were these data not disclosed before?"

"Bear with me for a few more moments, Paul. You have a good eye for detail. Notice that these measurements leveled off about two Earth years ago. Brevin and I have been monitoring the leopards' behavior all along, and we're pretty sure that the abnormal behavior we've been seeing reached a peak about that time and has since maintained itself.

"Furthermore, these trends in nerve cell activity that I've been showing you closely adhere to the pattern you would observe in an animal undergoing certain learning processes, concluding, of course, with the arrival at a learned state."

Paul quickly glanced at the papers again before saying, "Okay, I follow you."

"Good. Because there's one thing peculiar about it all, the reason why we've not made the association until now: *every one* of these tests, without fail, were taken during periods when the leopards were not undergoing any training or conditioning."

"And you're asserting that the leopards are nonetheless undergoing learning processes, right?"

"Yes! It seems to be anticipatory in nature, but it still appears to be a type of learning process and it's significantly higher than normal background levels. It's just hard to visualize because it's never been scientifically described beyond what some might call the 'sixth sense.' Cognition and intelligence as we know it may be operating at completely different levels in animals. Those two leopards in 2124 had a way of learning that something was going to happen to them. They somehow attained that knowledge. I guess you could call that my hypothesis: these animals are learning in a way that is as yet undetermined. And the only other observable item of proof I have to back that statement is what you and I know as displacement behavior."

"Behavior patterns irrelevant to the situation," Paul interjected.

"Right!" Annah said approvingly, her outward excitement reaching a peak. "Arising out of conflict, too, don't forget. These animals *know* something, but there's usually nothing they can do about it — they're locked up on this ship with nowhere to go. They were in captivity on Earth, too. That's probably one area where Gregory went wrong, placing these animals in captivity. Ergo, the conflict, and the difficulty in ferreting out valid behavioral observations. You see, the problem of observing natural behavior under experimental conditions has plagued this field for almost two centuries. These animals' energies are thus redirected to another channel or outlet, and what we see as resultant behavior strikes us as abnormal.

"Anthropomorphically speaking, I could be wrong. But I think you'll agree that our snow leopards appear to be deviating too far from what we call 'normal behavior' for that to be the case. And what I've been getting at all along, Paul, is that what we may have here is what you once described to the Space Flight Commission as Gregory's alternate order of learning."

Paul was overwhelmed by the behaviorist's conclusion. Several moments passed before he was able to reply.

"After one hundred years of research, it is tempting to jump to conclusions, Annah. Which is not to say that I don't hold your argument in the highest regard. I do. But we're going to need more proof, if possible. I'm beginning to realize that the only advantage my grandfather had over the rest of us was his gut conviction that an alternate order of learning did exist. We, of course, have always had our doubts, and I'll be the first to admit that. Now what we have to do is make sure that what you have found is what T.E.I. has spent all this time searching for."

"I agree with you all the way, Paul. I don't think I'm ready to jump into stardom's lights yet. But there's something that still bothers me. We can no longer use the term that these animals *sense* something. They *know* something, Paul. Those two leopards in 2124 underwent a learning process that enabled them to acquire the knowledge that something significant was about to happen to them. Strictly speaking, we'll never be able to say exactly what went on in their minds other than that they somehow had an inkling of knowledge of their future. What's more, if we assume that the behavior we're observing now and the behavior we saw in those two leopards in 2124 is an infrequent occurrence —"

"Then these animals are able to see into the future at certain times," Paul concluded, a little hesitantly.

"Right, though I don't know if 'see' is the best word. Anthropomorphism catches all of us at some time or another. Rather, though I dislike the term because it's so general, I'd say that they sense into the future, that they have some type of knowledge, unknown to us, of the future. And what bothers me is that this behavioral phenomenon may be exerting itself when the future holds some type of potential physical harm to the animal in question."

"And anything dangerous to the leopards is potentially just as dangerous to us," Paul mused.

Annah nodded and began collecting the graphs she had shown to Paul. "In most cases that can be true. I'll look over all of these and see if I can't get any more additional data or proof. I admit, a lot of what we have been talking about here is conjectural and assumptive, but if we're right, there's something in the future that might change the lives of everyone on this ship."

"That could be," Paul commented, refusing to allow himself a reaction to Annah's statement. "In the meantime, I'm going to restrict anyone other than T.E.I. employees and ship officers from visiting the leopards. If their behavior gets any worse, I'd hate to be responsible for an accident. We've already had some complaints."

Annah agreed that was a good idea, and after she had left, Paul sat quietly for a while, reviewing their conversation in his mind. Was Annah right? Had they finally achieved Gregory Torrden's elusive goal? And if so, was this the end or just the beginning? Now that this pattern of learning had been possibly identified, how did one go about outlining the processes that were behind it and distinguishing it from instinct, or even from classical conditioning?

Paul now realized why Gregory had put into the original program so many training experiments that were designed to illustrate all the types of learning — habituation, conditioning, latent, insight, and imprinting — known at the time. Now the task of distinguishing these traditional types of learning from any new type of learning, indeed from the alternate order of learning T.E.I. was concerned with, might eventually be easier.

Yes, if Annah was right, she had taken what the common person calls a sixth sense, and what the scientific researcher continuously alludes to as that unknown sense in animals, and shown it to be a new mode of learning.

Which made this only the beginning, Paul silently concluded. Still, he sensed a difficulty that might hinder further research. How did one artificially induce animals to undergo this learning process? He was almost sure that certain environmental factors or stimuli had to be established first. That would be a fun chore: trying to find out what those factors were.

And something told him that Annah's fears were somehow justified; time was running short.

In the subsequent years, Annah's discovery, though accepted and regarded by most T.E.I. personnel as the evasive element of their century-old pursuit, spawned but a few serious research projects. This was due mostly to the *Stranahan*, that magnificent hunk of metal which most of its passengers were beginning to think was stricken with mechanical cancer.

Levels Nine and Ten, which had been hardest hit during what was now referred to as the Great Accident of '42, were the source of most of the recurring problems. The rest of the *Stranahan*, however, was in no way immune to the problems that faced the crew. Air leaks, reactor break-downs, power outages, mechanical malfunctions — the ship was riddled with these misfortunes on a continual basis. It was not until this late stage that the people began pulling together as Sorian had wanted them to do so many years earlier. Jobs were taken with enthusiasm, and the Learning Discs saw more use in a given day than they had in a month of years past.

The aging Paul Torrden observed all this with a bit of personal pride...and fear. He was still haunted by the occurrence of a final failure of the *Stranahan* which would leave all of them stranded in deep space for the rest of their lives.

However, at the same time, he was elated to see the number of his snow leopards constantly increase under the careful direction of Brevin Johnson and some of his younger aides, one of which was the medic man's own son, Jase.

Jase, who had married a woman of Irish descent from Level Seven, proved to be an able helper and quickly learned the skill and art of the veterinary trade from his father. His only child, Liraah, born in 2170, was to be immediately captivated and enchanted by the snow leopards once she was able to move about the ship.

Yet, Paul had an even greater joy to see, even though it was at the expense of a serious loss. In 2174, the *Stranahan* was stricken with a purely organic failure — that of Captain Bill Enders' heart. The melancholic atmosphere surrounding his death was not shared by everyone, but most of the passengers felt it was unfair that the Captain who they had come to know and love almost as one of their family should die before reaching his fiftieth year of service aboard the *Stranahan*. He had been one of the few remaining people of the star ship's original crew. Several crew members were immediately considered as worthy of succeeding in Enders' place. Among the younger of these candidates was Michael Torrden, who now had about 25 years of flight experience under his belt and had been one of the Captain's closest friends during the last two years of Enders' life. Although Michael was not ultimately chosen to succeed Bill Enders, Paul found that his son was honored by being placed in charge of the crews that would prepare and organize the *Stranahan* and its shuttles for arrival at the new planet.

Paul was proud to look upon Michael in his new position. He realized that his son's aspirations had finally become reality. He was also glad to see that Ian Torrden, born in 2169 to Michael and Faye, was a healthy child. Paul could only hope that his grandson would not experience any of the childhood ailments that Michael had been exposed to.

In stark contrast to these achievements, the *Stranahan's* 'mechanical cancer' continued its inexorable and sometimes frightening growth. Michael Torrden, however, met the metal monster's challenges time and time again. The shrewdness of many of the decisions and judgements he made regarding passenger anxiety and unrest, maintenance of machinery, and preparations for the upcoming end of the trip earned him much respect among the crew and passengers.

By the end of 2174, they began their final deceleration upon entering the binary system that they had set out for 50 years earlier. They soon adjusted their course to align the ship with a homing signal from the Tech Crews that had likely travelled this very same route nearly half a century before. The next four years were ones of endless anticipation and wonder. The *Stranahan,* as if borne only of a wish and a hope, moved its crippled and hobbled hulk ever so slowly towards the planet which was obviously capable of sustaining life despite its association with the stellar twins. There were two other planets as well, but no signals issued forth from these. Nonetheless, people flocked to the ports and viewing screens to catch a glimpse of the three celestial planets and their double progenitors. Some knew what was meant when they were told that the spectral types of the suns were almost identical, averaging between K_0 and K_5; and that the masses, likewise, were similar, each sun harboring slightly more than two-thirds the mass of Sol.

It was the last several hours of flight, however, that brought the strongest challenge to bear upon the *Stranahan's* crew. Michael Torrden had just broken communications with the Tech Crews of Refander, which is what the planet had been named, and had given orders for the final orbital approach and shuttle separation from Level Five. Two of the *Stranahan's* three surface to ship shuttles on Level Five were subsequently boarded by the space ship's crew and passengers amidst a great deal of confusion. The T.E.I. staff personnel and their families, as well as all of the caged animals, were assigned seating and cargo space aboard the lead shuttle, under the command of Michael Torrden. Transport operations were already six hours behind schedule when the shuttles finally departed the main hull of the *Stranahan.* A new course was plotted for arrival at Refander's Space Port. Navigational instruments aboard the two shuttles slowly, but gradually, reflected the crew's familiarization with the settings and controls that were used to maneuver the smaller ships. Radio contact between the planet's surface and the lead ship confirmed the new course heading. However, soon after entering Refander's atmosphere, the crew chief aboard the lead shuttle reported a malfunction of the equipment associated with the stabilizer gear.

Michael immediately consulted with the *Stranahan's* Captain on the other shuttle, his own flight personnel, and the Tech Crews on Refander. Atmospheric readings were taken and climatic predictions were quickly postulated. A scant 20 minutes later, Paul's son found himself the center of attention of his flight crew.

Michael had given the order to abort the landing attempt, but ongoing communication with Refander's Base Station and a review of basic training maneuvers quickly established that a return to the *Stranahan* with inoperable stabilizer gear was not possible. Refander space flight controllers did point out, however, that the shuttle may still have enough manual maneuverability to land even without full use of its stabilizers.

None of the crew objected when orders to resume the approach were given. The recommendations from the Refander controllers had been mere statements of fact. The shuttle thus resumed its ill-fated course, unabated. Lines of concentration, as if engraved in stone, were written across the flight team's faces. In theory, under the circumstances given, they should have been able to land the shuttle without any serious complications. But none of them had been on the original flight crew, and their inexperience at landing gave way to panic when a series of thermals along the Asinarian Mountains began to jostle the shuttle in the final minutes of flight.

Synchronization became chaos. Learning Discs and flight simulation trials were momentarily forgotten. Control of the ship became an elusive physical concept and, lacking the proper direction and speed to pull out of the approach, the crew was reluctantly forced to bring the shuttle down in an area of rocky and barren wasteland just northwest of Refander's Space Port.

The meeting of metal and earth that followed was like a flowering pillar of flame to some, a violent, personalized earthquake to others. Overcoming the initial shock that followed was difficult for many of the passengers because Refander was in the midst of its short but harsh winter. Several of the leopards were freed by the collision and, in the ensuing confusion, fatally attacked several of the shuttle's passengers before fleeing to the woods which lay far to the east.

The second shuttle arrived safely at the Space Port, but many hours passed before the last survivors from the lead ship were able to cast a final glance upon the scorched, scarred, and beaten hull of the damaged shuttle. Many of these individuals had experienced frostbite for their first time. However, rescue personnel from Refander's Base Station proved to be of invaluable help to all of the survivors, especially those who had been seriously wounded.

Jase Johnson, Brevin's son, had been the last to board the emergency shuttles arriving from the Base Station of Refander. Not only had he felt it his duty to release the rest of the snow leopards from the ship's cages (and put an end to the cats that had suffered irreparable damage), but he had been unable to find his eight year-old daughter, Liraah. Twice he had searched the shuttle, and three times he had closely examined every small body that had been retrieved from the crash site.

Finally, in response to the calls of the rescuing officers, and the bitter cold of the first winter he had ever experienced, Jase was forced to abandon his search.

In the end, he let a prayer out for his daughter ...

... and reluctantly boarded the packed shuttle that took him away from the scene that, for some, would forever be the 20th New World Launch's final resting place.

Part 3. (Date Subjective to Earth: July 2184)

The Rise and Fall of the Torrden Dynasty. So the history of this family can be likened to the Roman Empire. My memory of Gregory Torrden, the man responsible for the creation of T.E.I. and the controversial snow leopard research, admittedly lacks the clearness and vitality I would have preferred it to have. For I knew of him only by what others have told me and by what I have read.

Fate, however, granted me the opportunity to know his grandson, Paul. And I still remember the day when I, Sammy Lassiter, spoke up in defiance of Jerul Scalos' desire to not have the 20th New World Launch carry a cargo of snow leopards and T.E.I. personnel.

It was during those times that opposition, both public and private, to T.E.I.'s research was such an important and crucial factor. And when the opposing views finally changed direction, aboard the *Stranahan*, that magnificent generation star ship which brought us from Earth to Refander, life was made no easier for this family whose name still flows forth from the lips of many. A freak electrical accident and a damaging childhood illness almost vanquished the flame of determination and independence characteristic of the Torrdens. But the final plateau was reached when Michael was honorarily awarded a supervisory position on the *Stranahan's* navigation crew as we approached Refander.

However, the opposition has once again made itself known, for to this day, many feel that Michael made the wrong decision in choosing to proceed with the landing of the *Stranahan's* shuttle on Refander. Later examinations have shown that crucial landing equipment in addition to the stabilizers had been irreparably damaged (probably during the Great Accident of '42) and that there was no way the crew could have detected all of the malfunctions during the regular preventive maintenance inspections. However, even this evidence failed to affect the people's emotions.

The grim fatality of the landing, the memory of which I have attempted to avoid for six years, nevertheless still looms large in my mind...and upon my conscience. My wife, Annah, Paul, Julie, and Michael were among the more than 200 people who had their lives unfairly taken away from them. Unfairly because each of them spent more than 40 years of his or her life en route to this planet, and I constantly regret the fact that they will never witness the beauty and uniqueness of Refander. The sight of our two small suns moving gracefully across the sky would have simply amazed them. They would also have been equally as astonished at the brevity of our 35 day year.

The effects of that tragedy remain, however, and have been far-reaching. Even Jase Johnson, Brevin's son, was not spared. Three weeks after our arrival, a salvage crew discovered his daughter, Liraah, along the western edge of the Torrden Forests just east of the crash site. She had long been considered a casualty of the shuttle crash, but had obviously been overlooked by the rescue crews and had somehow survived in the wilderness during the intervening days. Although she had been able to reach the Forests on her own, it was a stroke of luck that the salvage team discovered her when they did. She was near death, and several fresh wounds on her face, arms, and legs indicated she had recently been attacked — perhaps by one of the snow leopards that was set free after the crash. Fresh leopard tracks were seen by the salvage team leading away from the clearing in which she was found. Liraah's miraculous story has never been told exactly the way it happened, however, because she has constructed a mental wall around herself that limits anyone's ability, including Jase's, to communicate with her. Our resident psychologists have told us that the mental trauma and shock resulting from the crash and her near death experience have caused her to block that part of her life from her memory and has limited her ability to freely associate with others.

Jase Johnson, motivated by his daughter's condition and the small demand for veterinary specialists, re-trained himself in the medical field. Though he had simply wanted to improve the quality of life for his daughter, his skill, experience, and knowledge have benefitted all of us on Refander, and have made this planet, at last, seem more like home.

Yes, the wonders of Refander never cease to interest me. Everyone, excepting the farmers (who remain in the productive lowlands year-round) lives at the Base Station Dome which the Tech Crews built when they first arrived. The atmosphere of Refander is breathable and appears to cause no serious or harmful effects other than several curable minor illnesses, and one documented case of a death of unknown origin. However, most people have elected to stay at the Station rather than attempt to make it on their own in a foreign environment. But I'm sure that in the near future the more individualistic constituents of our population will set off to colonize the nearby Torrden Forests, a wooded area of more than 11,000 square kilometers just north of the Base.

The Torrden Forests. Yes. So named because it was in that direction that Paul's snow leopards headed when last seen by human eyes. For some reason, I am unable to shirk the feeling that these hardwoods were named to spite the memory of Paul rather than to acknowledge it.

Accordingly, or so it would seem, Michael's son, Ian, has not found it easy to freely associate with many of the former passengers of the *Stranahan*. At the age of 15, he is more isolated than Paul or Michael ever were, and though Faye and myself have given him the most of our love and care, he talks constantly of leaving the Base Station, once he is old enough, with the intention of never returning.

For him, then, I have opened up this journal of memories on this day to finish what I began in the year 2124 of our ancestral Earth.

And for me — I think that it is only fair that I, in some way, let others know of the fate of Gregory Torrden's hypothesis. I remember when Annah told me she had discovered the alternate order of learning and how it was related to certain "feelings" of the future. And I remember the wave of emotion that swept through everyone when Captain Enders played the tape of the last transmission from Earth. And who can ever forget the Great Accident of '42?

These three seemingly unrelated memories are more important to me now than ever before, because just yesterday, Refander had its first visitor from afar. At first, our Weapons Detail had been alerted because we had been unable to make radio contact with the small ship as it approached our planet. When it became obvious that the vessel would attempt to land on Refander, our satellite defense systems were engaged and an attack was launched. The ship nearly penetrated our defenses, but one of our missiles ultimately scored a direct hit, causing the remains of the ship to fall harmlessly into the Vernonslaw Ocean.

But words can hardly describe what took place thereafter. Those parts of the ship that had not disintegrated upon entry into our atmosphere were retrieved and brought back to the Port. The largest fragments of material were eventually piled at the far end of the Port. All parts of the salvage material were of the same dark, obsidian-like color, and no one could identify the type of metal or alloy that they represented. As we began to examine the remains even further, it became abundantly clear that the ship we had destroyed was undoubtedly a smaller version of the same kind that had once been thoroughly studied by the crew of the Sixteenth New World Launch. These findings could only lead us to conclude that someone or, God forbid, some thing knows we are here.

This single event has caused Refander to slowly again become a planet of fear. And now I wonder if I, a layman, can step into the world of scientific postulation. *If* there is such a thing as an alternate order of learning, and *if* it does deal with significant future events, then could the snow leopards aboard the *Stranahan* have foreseen our close encounter with these aliens in '42, just before the Great Accident? Could they have somehow sensed the oncoming presence of whatever may have been aboard the ship that we destroyed yesterday?

We may never know the answers to these questions. Nevertheless, the bare facts remain. I fear. Everyone fears. And we continue to watch out for a sign of this perhaps inescapable threat.

Take care, Ian ...

Chapter 4

■■■■■■■■■■■■■■■■■■■ The Lortans
and
■■■■■■■■■■■■■■■■■■■■■ the Mandar

Part 1. Sren-Sol and Lar-Modi

Step *through* the universe now, and do not be appalled to discover that the prefix "uni-" does not always mean one. Appreciate the fact that you have traversed a surprisingly small amount of space, but be more impressed by knowing you have gone eons into the past. Eons ...

Into...

The...

Past...

Sren-Sol was a Lortan, a space warrior. For a Lortan, he was small, being only 1.4 lampars (2.3 m) tall. However, size is not important when one is a space warrior. To be able to perform and employ the Whertos tactics of interstellar battle was all that mattered.

The low hills that were scattered intermittently among the purple, rocky plains of Briedrin offered little resistance to Sren-Sol as he searched for his companion, Lar-Modi.

Lar-Modi had ignored his warnings and had gone off to an unknown destination to perform an unknown task. That was half a day ago. And now he, Sren-Sol, had to find him.

In Sren-Sol's mind, worry had taken the place of anger. If Lar-Modi were injured, the planet of Briedrin possessed many hazards that could mean a slow and sometimes painful death to a careless Lortan. Moreover, the toxic atmosphere of Briedrin, which was the fifth of six planets in the

Lortan solar system, forced every Lortan who visited the planet to wear a protective suit at all times; encumbered by such, Sren-Sol knew that time was plotting against his and Lar-Modi's lives.

Sren-Sol came to a stop. He put down the emergency kit he had been carrying. The thought of contacting Whertos to inform the Vahrsta of the situation occurred to him. However, realizing that Whertos, the third planet in the Lortan system, was far enough away from Briedrin to make any attempt at communication useless, he quickly dismissed the idea from his mind. He — no, he and Lar-Modi — had been assigned to guard the Brin-Loki Instrument, not to explore the surface of Briedrin. If Whertos Command learned of this unauthorized excursion, Lar-Modi and he would be suspended from the Whertos Warrior Fleet for an indefinite period of time. Frustrated, Sren-Sol took a deep breath. He knew that he had to make a decision and that the time to make it was now; the key was to make the correct decision.

Sren-Sol looked to his right and then to his left. He did not like what he saw: the purple landscape extended into a seemingly endless pattern until it met with the orange sky at the horizon. There was no way of telling exactly in which direction Lar-Modi had headed...unless...he had gone to the crater.

Easily visible from the air, the large geographic phenomenon was thought to be the entrance to an underground network of caves. Sren-Sol closed his eyes, lost in pensive thought. Logic did not tell him that Lar-Modi was at the crater, but logic did tell him that the crater, being one of the most distinguishable features of Briedrin within the immediate area, would be the best place to look.

Having made up his mind, Sren-Sol picked up his kit and started off toward his right, his sinewy, red limbs easily propelling his thick, luminous protective suit.

He quickened his pace; it was a long walk and there was little time. There was also an invisible string, the innate sense of a warrior never to leave his duty, that kept tugging at him, telling him not to leave the Brin-Loki Instrument. However, surprisingly, he ignored it, increasing his pace even more. *Besides,* he thought to himself, *no invaders have ever challenged the functioning of the Instrument yet.*

And so, this was the serious mistake Sren-Sol made, that of leaving the Brin-Loki Warning Instrument unguarded; a mistake he would never forget...and only briefly remember.

After travelling longer than he thought wise, Sren-Sol reached the crater. It was roughly circular with a diameter of sixty or more lampars.[1] It was bordered by jagged rocks, of which more could be found along its sloping walls. Sren-Sol stepped to the edge of the mammoth depression and peered downward. Recognition rushed through him like a blast of cold, Briedrin air: Lar-Modi lay motionless, halfway down the slope, directly below where he stood.

He hurried down the slope to the ledge where Lar-Modi had fallen. Upon a quick inspection, Sren-Sol found what he had guessed was true. Lar-Modi's suit had been punctured along his right leg, thus allowing the toxic atmosphere to slowly enter and play its deadly game.

Sren-Sol, acting on trained impulses, kneeled down on one knee and opened the emergency kit, a blue oblong box. He removed a red, glass-like object, oval in shape, and placed it on the upper portion of Lar-Modi's massive chest. Upon contact with the injured Lortan's protective suit, two dark narrow probes emerged from the instrument, slanting downward at an angle until they reached the luminous clothing. The light count which ebbed forth from within the instrument moments later was dull. There was little time left. The poisonous air had already rendered Lar-Modi unconscious and it was only a matter of time before it finally killed him.

Sren-Sol reached in the kit again and brought out a patch large enough to cover the tear. He peeled off the back cover, exposing a collection of a thick, pale substance. Pulling the two sides of Lar-Modi's torn suit together, Sren-Sol placed the patch over the rupture. The pale glue locked into place instantly.

The next thing to do was to pump oxygen into Lar-Modi's suit. To survive on alien and inhospitable planets, the Lortans had outfitted all of their protective suits with atmospheric regulation units. This was necessary as all Lortans were classic examples of a long evolved host-parasite interaction: they were participants in a symbiotic relationship involving three strains of red-hued bacteria that were embedded within the in-

---

[1] 0.6 lampars = 1 meter.

tegument of their skin and which absorbed over 90 percent of their metabolic ammonia wastes. Two bacterial strains oxidized the ammonia wastes to nitrite and then to nitrate; a third strain of bacteria broke down this excess nitrate and released atmospheric nitrogen to the air (the Lortan version of the human kidney was poorly developed as a result). Dead bacteria were lost when the dead outer layers of the epidermis were sloughed off. The regulation units functioned to remove the free nitrogen and other gaseous materials produced by these bacteria.

One tube ran from the regulation unit to the mouth of whomever wore the suit. This carried the oxygen. Sren-Sol would have to take his own tube and connect it to an opening in the back of Lar-Modi's suit to replenish his partner's supply of oxygen. But that would mean opening his visor, thus exposing himself to the poisonous gases of Briedrin. Sren-Sol's uneasiness over this next task came and went quickly, as he had been trained to ignore fear at an early age.

He knew that the absorbed concentration of Briedrin's atmospheric gases had to surpass a threshold level before becoming lethally toxic to Lortans. However, this threshold of tolerance varied between individuals, and if he exposed himself too long, an excess amount of gases would accumulate inside his suit and render his own unit useless.

Sren-Sol knew that it was impractical to waste any more time. He was a space warrior, and as a space warrior he knew he had to react quickly. He removed the red body-probe and turned Lar-Modi over to unscrew the cap on the injured Lortan's suit. He then raised his own visor and fitted his oxygen tube with a special attachment. After this, he connected the tubing to the small opening on his companion's unit. As he breathed his first breath of the officious smelling air, thoughts of Whertos Command raced through his mind once more. It was a disgrace to be out here, far away from his assigned duty, but it had to be done. The silence of Briedrin only served to magnify these thoughts.

The calmness of the planet's atmosphere was momentarily broken by a swirl of wind that wound its way circuitously through the crater. Time seemed to crawl before Sren-Sol finally heard a flutter of metallic clicks permeate the air. They had come from Lar-Modi's unit, signalling that the oxygen supply was almost replenished. Sren-Sol disconnected his tube from the opening and placed it back in his mouth; at the same time, he screwed the cap back on Lar-Modi's unit. He then pulled down his visor, glad to be rid of Briedrin's lurid smell.

Sren-Sol knew that it would be a while before Lar-Modi would hopefully expel all of the toxic elements in his system and regain consciousness. By that time, however, his own body would be at the mercy of Briedrin's poisons. The space warrior just hoped that he had not exposed himself too long, for that would mean certain death.

He inhaled deeply, almost attacking the oxygen that coursed through the air tube. Glancing skyward, he pondered at the best way to negotiate the slope leading out of the crater while carrying Lar-Modi. However, his concern over this task faded when he became dizzy a brief moment later. The next thing Sren-Sol knew was that the planet of Briedrin seemed to have increased its rotational velocity tenfold; the rocky circumference of the crater, mixed with the orange sky, spun around his head at ever increasing speeds. *Could this mean death?* he thought to himself.

Pain raced through his limbs and he would have screamed in agony had he not been a warrior.

Then the cold hand of blackness swirled down upon him. His last thought, as a space warrior's should be, was that of his duty.

And 1500 lampars away, the Brin-Loki Instrument had sounded its warning: an invader was approaching the Lortan solar system.

Part 2. The Mandar

Yet another race there was, in that ancient past, eons ago. They knew of the Lortans, knew of that race's pride in calling themselves space warriors; and they also knew of three races that faced near extinction as a direct result of doing battle with the mighty Lortans. They were ready to negotiate... They were the Mandar.

The Mandarian body, like the Lortans', was strikingly humanoid in shape, a result of the similar bio-cosmic conditions that had given rise to all three races. They differed from the Lortans by being slightly smaller and lacking the peculiar symbiotic relationship; and from humans by their smooth, bronze-colored skin and possession of certain internal skeletal and muscular structures. Both of these ancient races spoke languages completely different from those that were to evolve with the human race.

The Mandar had colonized several planets of nearby systems, leaving only a small and meager portion of their race on their native planet, Ekelon. As far as the Mandar of Ekelon knew, the Lortans and they were the last two intelligent races within the known realm of space that still maintained a sizable population. They also knew that, as a result, other members of the Mandar, on other planets closer to the Lortan system, would be trying to negotiate with the Lortans.

What fools! No one negotiates with Lortans. There were rumors that the malodorous red-bodied race was indomitable in battle; that certain members of their race had psycho-kinetic abilities which they used to control and manipulate their opponents. Yet, little did these Ekelonian natives realize that everything may have worked out peacefully had it not been for the ill-timed actions of Sren-Sol and Lar-Modi.

However, the Mandar of Ekelon had no time to be cynical over the intentions of other Mandar elsewhere; nor had they experienced a lack of scientific development because of their own small numbers.

And now, they thought they had the means to escape the inevitable conquest by the Lortans...Ever since history had been recorded, the scientific historians of Ekelon had noted that their planet experienced periods lasting from five to ten years during which it was subjected to irregular perturbations which, as many meticulous calculations showed, obviously did not result from the influence of the other planets or the two small suns that made up their solar system. Theories were put forth, and experiments were run. The data that were collected spawned the Era of Invention, regarded by many Mandar as the most significant cultural time period in Ekelonian history. The Mandar exponentially expanded their understanding and knowledge of energy and, with each generation, newer and better machines were built to model the latest theories on how Ekelon interacted with the known universe. Now, after 800 years of exercising one of the most highly developed technologies ever to exist, the colossal achievement, which they knew could grant them life as easily as it could grant them death, was almost complete. They hid this huge machine in a remote, mountain cave while they worked desperately to refine and construct the last, but necessary, components.

A minor setback was suffered when Elda, daughter of Brisb, one of the most respected scientists on Ekelon, refused to believe that an entire planet could stake its life on the hypothetical functioning of an untested scientific development. She took one of the large Medic Cruisers and headed for the Mandar Colonies in search of news regarding the negotiations between the Mandar and the Lortans.

Meanwhile, the experiments went on; and the Mandar knew that they were so close to the final answer!

Part 3. Decisions...

The Lortans had watched the approach of the Mandar ships with enormous suspicion. The Brin-Loki Instrument had been tested countless times in the past — why had it now failed to warn them of the approach of these ships? What had happened to Sren-Sol and Lar-Modi? These were the questions they had continually asked themselves.

As the Mandar ships drew nearer, the Lortans had questioned the occupants. Where had they come from? What was their mission?

In return, they had received answers: the ships had been of Mandar origin, their mission one of peaceful negotiations.

But the Lortans knew that the Mandar numbered more than enough to be considered a serious enemy. Could they trust them? The answer became apparent when, as they reluctantly allowed the Mandar ships to enter Whertos' inner atmosphere, they detected the presence of an enormous armada of radioactive weaponry aboard the approaching vessels.

A hurried discussion followed...Weapons aboard a negotiation ship? This was certainly unacceptable! The order had been given to destroy the ships, immediately, before they ever landed on Whertos.

And as the buttons were pushed, the Lortans lost any chance to realize that the Mandar had futilely tried to explain the presence of their illegal cargo only seconds before that dreaded massacre: they, the Mandar, had only wanted to exchange their extensive knowledge of weaponry for a promise that they would never be attacked by the superior space warriors...

And now ...

Four of the five members of the Main Vahrsta for the Whertos Warrior Force had gathered atop a mesa overlooking one of the larger cities of Whertos' eastern continent. They stood, facing one another, eagerly awaiting the arrival of the fifth member, the Vahrsta-Hd of Whertos. Behind them, their small transport vehicles glistened in the sunlight and the fierce Whertos winds.

The Lortan manner of speaking consisted of short, peaked phrases which expressed a basic idea or concept. The full meaning of each message was determined by the placement of one (or a combination of several) of the Fifteen Emotional Timbres in the tone of whoever spoke. Thus, Si-Worln, who presently stood facing the other three Lortans, was able to ask, by using the Querying Emotional Timbre, how much time was left. The question temporarily floated on the air, unanswered.

The tall stature of the Lortans' long, wily bodies became a dominant presence on the mesa top. Their skin was red, and their angular heads housed fire-blue eyes. Their hair, if one could call it that, was short and black and resembled dry tar.

Ri-Torn plucked the question from the air and his mind, almost absently, molded an answer from it. He told the others that Lon-Kyle would have all of the information when he arrived. Ri-Torn knew that the time that was left was approximately nine months[2] or less, but as second in command of the Vahrsta, he refused to digress into any affairs until Lon-Kyle joined them.

Ten-Shun and Leor-Kli, both of whom stood opposite Ri-Torn, began conversing with one another. After several nods of agreement, Leor-Kli turned to Ri-Torn. If the Mandar had destroyed the Brin-Loki Instrument and now threatened the entire Lortan race with extinction, she boldly asked, then did it not make sense to seek out these Mandar on their various worlds and destroy them?

Ri-Torn knew that Leor-Kli had brought up a new and unfamiliar topic, and he did not quite know how to handle it yet. In an attempt to suppress the rising emotions that he felt in the others, he clearly laid out what he saw as a fallacy in their thinking: certainly, the actions of the Mandar could not have been deliberate, committed solely as a catalyst for war. In fact, there had only been five ships that had approached Whertos — how could five ships have ever hoped to defeat the entire Whertos Warrior Force?

But now it was Ten-Shun's turn to step forward. The blue glow in his eyes seemed almost afire. The Mandar had defeated the Lortan race, he explained, but only if a counterattack was not mounted soon. It was certain that the Lortans would not live long if what they feared had happened were true. The only acceptable plan of action was to destroy the Mandar, now, while there was still time.

The Challenging Emotional Timbre in Ten-Shun's voice was not missed by Ri-Torn. As Ten-Shun stepped back, Ri-Torn contemplated what had been said. His attempt to change the subject of conversation had essentially failed and he realized, with a start, that the quick and unsound

---

[2] Nine Whertos months are equivalent to 12 Earth months.

decision to destroy the enemy crafts when they were so close to the planet had come back to haunt him once again. *Why? Why had it been done?*

Still, it was his responsibility to keep this meeting under control and he quickly reminded the other Lortans that no decision could be made in the absence of Lon-Kyle.

Si-Worln clasped his large, lengthy hands together and asked if other Mandar had attempted to approach Whertos, now that the Lortan planet was vulnerable?

Ri-Torn was about to answer when the sound of an approaching craft broke through the brisk winds. Lon-Kyle had finally arrived.

After landing the vehicle expertly beside the others, the Vahrsta-Hd quickly emerged from the transport craft. The other Vahrsta members could see he held an Information Cube in one hand and a voice recorder in the other. Ri-Torn now knew that the fears all of them had been harboring were about to come true: the voice recorders were only used by Vahrsta-Hds to record the evolving history of the Lortan's inexorable rise to power. There could be only one reason why Lon-Kyle had brought it with him to this meeting.

Lon-Kyle approached the group and took up a position beside Ri-Torn, carefully placing the machine at his feet. The recorder was capable of picking up most voice patterns, even in the worst Whertosian weather. The brisk winds that now plagued the five Lortans were considered a normal component of the average day on Whertos.

As Lon-Kyle looked up, the other four Lortans could see that anger resided in his face. When he spoke, the timbres in his voice were malevolently crossed back and forth, drawing their attention. Lon-Kyle began to tell the group about Sren-Sol and Lar-Modi. The reports on those two individuals had been assembled by a special Lortan reconnaissance team. From what had been learned, the reckless actions of those two Lortans on Briedrin may have cost all Lortans their lives unless a miracle now happened.

The Vahrsta-Hd's words slanted forth at hard angles as he continued to summarize what he knew. It appeared that Lar-Modi had gone to investigate the crater that was located near the landing base. He did not tell Sren-Sol, apparently believing that he would have been denied permission, which was true. It was believed that his purpose was to explore the caves that exist there to determine the feasibility of the Lortans establishing an underground defense base at Briedrin; he had more than once questioned his superiors on this matter in the past, in spite of the fact that the Brin-Loki Instrument is only stationed on Briedrin for two months out of the Lortan year. Regardless, on his way down into the crater, he apparently fell, tearing his suit and rendering himself unconscious.

When he did not return, Sren-Sol had apparently gone after him. Sren-Sol had obviously not contacted Whertos because he knew that his leaving the post would have resulted in his removal from the Force. When he finally found Lar-Modi, he must have realized that the only way to possibly save Lar-Modi's life would be to give him oxygen. This, of course, meant exposing himself to the atmosphere. Both Lortans had died from their exposure to Briedrin's toxic gases and, just by coincidence, it was at this time that the Mandar entered the Lortan system. In the end, the Brin-Loki Instrument gave ample warning of the Mandar ships, as the great Lortan scientist, Brin-Loki, had predicted, over eighty years ago; but neither Sren-Sol nor Lar-Modi had been present to take the appropriate action and to warn Whertos.

Leor-Kli, no longer able to contain herself, broke protocol and interrupted the Vahrsta-Hd. She repeated the question that Si-Worln had originally asked: how much time was left?

Ri-Torn stole a glance toward Lon-Kyle, knowing the importance of the upcoming answer. The Vahrsta-Hd responded by passing the Information Cube he still held to Leor-Kli. Ri-Torn knew that the Cube must hold the medical reports that contained the ultimate diagnosis for the Lortan race.

One by one, the Vahrsta members read the contents of the Cube. The destruction of the Mandar ships while they were so deep in Whertos' inner atmosphere and directly over the primary continent had caused the radioactive waste of the Mandar weaponry to quickly spread throughout Whertos. The planet's enormous winds had only enhanced this catastrophe. From what the medical experts had been able to conclude, the radioactive fallout had initiated a slow but irreversible mutation process within the Lortans' outer dermic bacteria. Although it was a slow process, it would increase exponentially with time. Already, only after ten days, the effects could be felt in many of the children. At best, it was expected that most Lortans had only nine months left before they all died. Their primitive organs would not be able to remove all of the toxic wastes their bodies would build up once their symbionts began dying. In short, they would poison themselves to a slow death.

A dark silence interposed itself between the Vahrsta members. They knew their entire population was not destined to die, but the meager few that would survive were sure to be massacred by other vengeful races.

Lon-Kyle now reached down and picked up the voice recorder. He then told the rest of the Vahrsta members that Lorn-Tator had already been summoned.

A look of surprise could be seen in all of the Lortans, but it was perhaps most apparent in Ri-Torn who had been on the Vahrsta longer than the others. If Lorn-Tator and his famed destroyer, the *Ralix*, had been summoned, then they were indeed once again at war. But a vote had not even been taken! At first, Ri-Torn felt cheated, but then he knew that even if Lon-Kyle had asked them to provide him with recommendations, the outcome would have been the same.

Lon-Kyle obviously knew they still had a great army — an army that could now destroy their last enemy. They had never lost an interstellar battle and there was no question in Ri-Torn's mind that they would obtain a victory one last time. Ri-Torn now watched Lon-Kyle as the Vahrsta-Hd observed the other Lortans who stood opposite him. One by one, an understanding seemed to flow between them all.

It was then that Ri-Torn knew that they would seek out these Mandar and destroy them, one world at a time. And it would be an act of vengeance that would perhaps never see its equal.

Part 4. Brisb

And light years away, the scientists of Ekelon carefully finished making calculations of the orbit of their planet. The time was almost right. Soon Ekelon would be at the best possible position to allow them to perform preliminary tests on their great machine.

But they still had to make the final parts. Brisb had said that the magnetic flux was not strong enough. How were they going to increase it? What were they doing that was wrong? And how many lives would need to be sacrificed to initiate the changeover? There had even been rumors that Brisb would sacrifice himself, if there were no other volunteers.

Others had raised the old arguments that, even if they succeeded in their venture, the new suns might be too close or too far away; and Ekelon itself might not survive the change. Could this be true?

They worked ever so frantically to find the answers. And though they had yet to hear the news regarding the catastrophe of the other Mandar at Whertos, they somehow sensed time was running short for them …

Part 5. Forj and Stahl

Two Mandar.

What has happened to them? This question was asked by Stahl, the junior Mandar officer.

The older officer, Forj, looked idly at his companion. *Probably the same that is about to happen to us,* he explained.

We have to keep hoping that they have succeeded in their mission, Stahl replied, in violent disagreement.

How does one succeed in taming the wrath of a mature korlawt? And how does one succeed in making a Lortan Warrior take pity on one's self? These are the questions that should have been asked to ensure this mission's success.

Why? Stahl insisted. *Look at how much knowledge we have. The Lortans would be fools to pass up the opportunity we offer them.*

Forj turned his back to the younger officer, a signal that he was not prepared to accept Stahl's suggestion as justification for the actions of the Mandar people. *But who is the real fool, the strong who refuse to acknowledge the weak, or the weak who offer the strong more technological aid? True, our technology may be far superior to theirs, but it was developed for totally different ends. The Lortans have travelled far and wide, spreading death and destruction everywhere they have been. Such was the case long before the potential of space flight was ever realized on Ekelon.*

And now you can only think that the same will happen to us?, Stahl persisted.

I have no other choice. Why should the Lortans change now? Only a few of our weapons could be considered a serious threat to them; and even then, we lack the skill and the experience to capitalize on that small advantage. Our people have rarely known anything other than peace. How do we fight a war now?

And such was the conversation of Forj and Stahl, two lonely Mandarian guards, stationed in a small patrol vessel at the outer edge of the Mandar territory.

Time passes slowly out here, in the bottomless pit of space. The limited confines of a ship only serve to intensify that eternity. Hence, although this assignment was a new experience for Stahl, he already was beginning to realize the futility and annoyance of the opposing views that he and his superior officer held. Forj's pessimism was almost over-whelming. Never before had he met someone whose arguments were so well thought out and seemingly irrefutable. He himself had always been proud of his race. Why couldn't Forj do likewise? But then, Forj also had twice as much experience as he; maybe that was the answer.

An exclamation from Forj made him shift his eyes back to the ship's instruments. Some as yet unseen objects had obviously been detected. He let his newly trained impulses take over and watched, with only a slight amazement, as his bronze-tanned hands fired up the patrol ship's engines. It was obvious that the incoming targets were approaching fast and would soon be in view.

Forj slowly rotated the ship in an arc so that the viewing screen would be directly in line with whatever was approaching them. As his partner was completing this task, Stahl turned the Communicating Translator on to the setting of the Lortan dialect. Forj had no sooner begun to protest this action when the tracer instruments confirmed Lortan presence.

Looking up, Stahl saw an approaching half circle of red ships. His cal-culating mind quickly saw that the Mandar vessel would soon be en-circled by the Lortan fleet. The spell in which such a fate held him and Forj was abruptly broken by a command to identify themselves. The slug-gishness of the Lortan's voice, as modified by the Translator, made it seem as if the command had been issued from the middle of a dense fog.

Forj hesitantly sent out the Mandar identity code, and when it was apparent that the Lortans had made the appropriate adjustments in their own communicating equipment, he reopened the channel.

"And I, in return, am Lon-Kyle," the foggy voice resonated, "Vahrsta-Hd of the Whertos Warrior Force."

The sharp, cliff-edged words of the Lortan were disturbing to Stahl, and he looked with envy upon Forj who, in response to Lon-Kyle's pro-fundity, assertively asked what the Lortan would request from them.

"That which you have forced upon yourselves, Mandar!"

Stahl pounded the panel in front of him, beginning to panic in spite of all his training.

Before returning an answer to the still approaching Lortan fleet, Forj quickly turned and grabbed his partner's arm. *Prepare the ship for evasive action. Set a maximum Cettor speed on an intercept course with our nearest battleship sector, and set the engines for immediate shut-down upon arrival.*

Stahl's eyes widened. The speed Forj had suggested would certainly prescribe their own deaths, if not the self-destruction of their ship.

Forj continued to stare at the junior officer. *We have to warn our people. Prepare the alert signal to engage when we are near enough to our battleships.* Forj then turned his attention back to the Lortans. Stahl passively watched him relay a response that, in effect, cleverly pleaded for an explanation of the Lortans' intentions.

In the pause that followed, Stahl realized that Forj had once again made the correct decision. And it was only common sense: their patrol vessel, though possessing six diser beam armaments, obviously was no match for the number of Lortan ships now approaching them. As he set the coordinates and prepared the patrol ship's engines for the high velocities they were soon to experience, Lon-Kyle's voice once again permeated the tense air.

The Lortan told them of the events which occurred at Whertos, beginning with the approach of the Mandarian fleet and the detection of its cargo; and ending with the unanimous decision of the Whertos Warrior Force's Main Vahrsta. It was short and brief, and included nothing about Sren-Sol and Lar-Modi, or the mutational calamity that now afflicted their own bodies. Lon-Kyle considered these facts irrelevant.

As the two Mandar listened, Stahl continued to watch Forj as he made the final preparation for their surprise action. They had almost finished adjusting their protective gear when they heard the Lortan's inevitable declaration of war upon their race, the Mandar.

Stahl felt another wave of mixed emotions as Forj glanced vindictively in his direction, but the younger officer needed no further prompting. His bronze-colored hands performed the necessary crucial functions as the invading Lortan fleet loomed ever closer. Then, accompanied by the painful discomfort of its two occupants, the Mandar patrol ship became a diminishing dot, hurtling through space.

Part 6. Elda

When Stahl awoke, the disorientation and sickness of undergoing maximum Cettor speed comprised the only reality of his mind. Slowly, and then more quickly, like an avalanche, the memory of the meeting with the Lortans came back to him.

He instinctively began to override the settings which he had set in the ship's engines but stopped. Upon the viewing screen was a sight more awesome than one of his own people being slain by a korlawt. At least five Mandar battleships lay ruined, long rigid cracks decorating their hulls. All of them had a seemingly frost-like appearance as they floated in the dark maelstrom of space. Intertwined amongst the holocaust was one Lortan ship that had obviously been ripped apart by an Ekelon diser beam. Its red, jagged edges starkly contrasted with the wreckage of the other Mandar vessels.

He hurriedly awakened Forj and silently watched as his older partner, after recovering from the effects of the Cettor velocity, registered the same astonishing disbelief he himself had felt.

Forj stared at the wake of the Lortan attack for only a few more seconds. Then he silently began setting the coordinates for the inner settlements. It was this action that made Stahl suddenly realize that the Lortans had not come this far without the intention of taking their attack elsewhere.

Motivated by his partner's actions, Stahl initiated a sweep with the tracer instruments. Both Mandar remained silent as the trace began to confirm what they had already seen. They had almost finished preparations for initiating travel to the inner settlements when a minor fluctuation in the trace caught Stahl's attention: one Mandar ship was still functioning.

Forj primed the engines and slowly rotated the ship until the moving vessel Stahl had spotted was centered on the screen. Stahl knew that caution was warranted, for they could not ignore the possibility that the Lortans had captured one of the Mandarian ships. But most of their fears were dispelled when, as the vessel in question drew nearer, they saw that it was a Medic Cruiser and therefore lacked any serious armament.

Stahl immediately disengaged the translator and after several moments they received a broadcast of the Mandar identity signal. Several minutes later, they heard it again, and Stahl realized that the Cruiser was only scouting about for survivors.

Forj, evidently having arrived at the same conclusion, sent back the standard Mandar code signal and a request for crew identification.

There is only Elda, daughter of Brisb, came the short reply. The Medic Cruiser had now oriented itself so that it was directly approaching the patrol ship.

Stahl was surprised by the mention of Brisb's name. Certainly the Lortans had not taken the attack to the mother planet, Ekelon, already!

Elda eventually explained that Ekelon was still intact, but she never-theless did not see how the remaining Mandar forces would prevent Ekelon from ultimately coming under attack by the invading Lortan fleet.

Stahl now knew that he and Forj had probably been spared destruc-tion because their own engines had been programmed to shut down immediately after deceleration. Forj's experience in these matters had been invaluable. But it was now time for all of them to serve their people and return to the war. He asked Elda to accompany them in seeking a vulnerable position in the Lortan fleet.

Elda's reply was simply a warning: *In any battle, one must know the enemy's strategy, strengths, and weaknesses.*

Forj and Stahl openly admitted that they lacked any previous battle experience with the Lortans. However, Elda shared with them an intelli-gence report she had compiled during her travels: the Lortans had easily nullified every strategic offense mounted by the Mandar. In addition, the rumors of their psychological powers had been no over-exaggeration. Because of the Medic Cruiser's limited defensive capabilities, she had been forced to flee this sector during the recent battle, but not before she had visually confirmed several occasions when Mandar ships had inex-plicably fired upon one another. Elda herself had even felt the influence of some external force compelling her to drive the Cruiser into the very heart of the battle. She did not know how it worked — whether it af-fected only certain individuals or whether it was limited in range — but it gave the Lortans an uncontested advantage whenever they chose to use it.

Yet, that was not all. The Lortan arsenal had been a complete surprise to the Mandar. Whereas the Ekelonian diser beam operated on the prin-ciple of intense adjustment and concentration of high radiation source particles, the Lortans seemed to have taken that process and somehow blended it with large quantities of a very unstable element that they had synthesized on Whertos. The result was devastating: battleships had been simply ripped apart by the simultaneous barrage of intense cross-fire.

This may only be the beginning, Elda warned. *The Lortans are indeed war-riors — and of very high calibre. Yet, I still do not know what has prompted their attack on our people.*

Quickly, Forj summarized for Elda that which Lon-Kyle had told them. When he was finished, there were several long moments of silence. At length, Elda responded: *The Lortans may have destroyed the Mandar messen-*

*ger ships before learning of the Treaty we were offering them. It is the only logical
explanation.*

That is possible, but it is now highly irrelevant, Forj replied.

His partner's obvious anger made Stahl remember their previous arguments. He was now beginning to realize that the Lortans were without
doubt naturally violent of mind — this had been an attack that would
have eventually taken place regardless of any circumstances the Mandar
could have fabricated to prevent it.

After additional discussion and a hurried strategic conference, Elda
and the two officers split up to check on the two nearest Mandar colonies, agreeing to meet once again at the third nearest colony.

When they conducted that meeting some time later, somewhat exhausted by the moderately high Cettor speeds they had subjected themselves to, it was only to share the news of death and annihilation. From all
indications, it was easy for Elda, Stahl, and Forj to see that the Lortans
were swiftly progressing, colony by colony, to the very center of the
Mandar territory. Realizing that such a situation now made it unwise to
approach the battle without additional reinforcements, the three Mandar
decided to risk even more time to search for survivors at some of the
other outer colonies and battleship sectors.

In the long run it appeared that this was a wise choice. Though they
lost much valuable time, they were able to organize a sizable fleet of 54
battleships, two patrol vessels, and an additional Medic Cruiser. Hastily,
they prepared a plan of surprise attack, and then set off once more to the
nucleus of the Mandar settlements.

The efforts of these Mandar, however, had long been in vain. Lon-Kyle
and the Lortans, spurred by a feeling of hatred their race had seldom
before experienced, had crushingly forced the Mandar into a continual
retreat. What had followed became a history which only a few Mandar
would ever get to study. The epitome of losing a barely understood war
became a shocking reality for the ill-fated Mandar. Their ships were dis-
membered by the dozens, and it was a rare sight indeed when a Lortan
ship fell prey to the diser beams.

Hostages were taken on the part of both sides. Information that was
gleaned from them was instrumental in the strategic tactics employed by
the warring factions.

Ekelon soon became the last key target. Both sides knew it, and the
Mandar defended it with all the wrath of a she korlawt protecting her

young. The battle continued in this direction, however, and when the Lortans had forced the Mandar back to within a couple light years of their native solar system, it was more than evident that, though they had fought a ferocious battle, the Mandar were no match for the superior tactics of the Lortan warriors.

Though the war had barely just begun, the Lortans sensed that their pulverization of the Mandar, whose inexperience at battle only served to aid the Lortan fleet, was to be their most monumental victory.

It was at this time that Forj, Stahl, Elda, and their armada of battleships burst forth from maximum Cettor speeds, assailing the flanks of the Lortan fleet.

The surprise was a fluent success, crippling many of the Lortan ships before the warriors could appropriately adjust their forces. The other Mandar had been hoping desperately for such an opportunity, and they began to take the offensive that had so long been denied them.

For several days the battle continued as such, the Lortans seemingly unable to thwart off the many Mandarian attacks which rained upon them. The Mandar, having learned from their Lortan prisoners of the mutational hazard which had afflicted their opponents, began to suspect that the bacterial infection would soon begin to take its toll on the Lortan fleet.

Lon-Kyle realized this too, and after a conference with the Main Vahrsta and Lorn-Tator, a plan to send the weaker of the forces back to the main base, Whertos, and to fortify the key strategic areas of the war with the healthiest members of their fleet, was established.

The full-scale changeover operation was performed quickly — as it should be for Lortan warriors — and the most severely afflicted warriors were soon making a slow retreat from the stronger side of the Lortan forces. This retreat gradually gained speed, as Lorn-Tator had carefully suggested, and the Mandar, their teeth still sunk in the hide of the beast of miraculous victory, swiftly and blindly gave chase.

The diversion, however, was what the Lortans had expected. Although only one-fourth of the defending fleet had vacated primary battle locations, the Mandar had thoughtlessly opened up gaping weak points in their own recently-attained solid defense.

Like a hunger-driven rattlesnake, the organism of the Lortan warrior fleet struck the Mandar, driving deep war fangs into the Ekelon defenders.

The Mandar, however, were not to be easily had. Sure that the final stages of the Lortans' radioactive catastrophe were fast approaching, they unsheathed their last weapon: the newly synthesized radioactive elements that had brought the slow hand of death to the Lortans almost a year before.

They intensely bombarded the Lortan battleships with the lethal products of their own research, relying heavily on the hope that the Lortans would become disorganized once more.

But the Mandar were never to regain control of the war again. As their forces were violently decimated by the hitherto unseen anger and wrath of the Whertos warriors, they constantly looked over their shoulders in the direction of Ekelon. Where were the reinforcements they had so long expected from the object of their defensive efforts? Why was Ekelon remaining passive? Why!?

As the number of the Mandarian forces grew increasingly smaller, panic began to eat away at what little was left of the solidarity which had surprisingly stayed with them throughout the course of the battle.

Main forces were separated from one another, and regiments were mercilessly broken up. Group by group, the Lortans quickly put an end to the lives of many Mandar.

Forj and Stahl, and Elda, in her Medic Cruiser, were able to see all too well the inevitable fate that awaited their race. They, with three other battleships, set out to their last stronghold — Ekelon. Yet, even this was denied them, as they were immediately set upon by two Lortan warships, one of which was Lorn-Tator's elite *Ralix*. The miniature war that ensued saw the tumultuous destruction of the three Mandar battleships as well as the one Lortan battleship.

Stahl, angrily confident in the one-to-one situation in which he now found himself with Lorn-Tator, maneuvered the patrol vessel with courageous finesse. Forj was able to score two direct hits on the *Ralix* before the two opposing ships collided with one another. Lorn-Tator, his experience aiding him in the end, got the better of this exchange, though the *Ralix* suffered significant damage. Nevertheless, as the Mandar patrol vessel spun helplessly away before exploding into oblivion, Lorn-Tator closed in on the Medic Cruiser.

Elda, now totally beset with fear, changed her course and, instead of heading for Ekelon, set off at a precarious maximum Cettor speed to the outer limits of the Mandar territory...and beyond.

Lorn-Tator, signalling back to the main Lortan fleet to inform Lon-Kyle of his frightened quarry, set out on the final flight of his life...

...while the rest of the Lortan fleet rapidly approached its final destination — the destruction of Ekelon.

Part 7. The Last War

She sat, unbelieving. Her eyes were focused ahead of her, scanning the near future, but she only saw the recent past — the recent, deadly past.

Elda was not whom she used to be. Once she had known the joys and experienced the pride of being a Mandar. She had learned and had taught others in return. Such had been the custom of her family, of Brisb especially, and of her race. And now, because of one fatal mission, she had become a being of loathing and anger. There was nothing to love, and only one thing to hate.

She remembered how she had left Ekelon to discover how the negotiations with the Lortans were proceeding. She remembered how she had met Forj and Stahl amidst one of the worst disasters she had ever seen. She remembered the several Mandar colonies they had then visited, and the expansive death they had resultantly found. The small fleet they had nevertheless been able to round up had temporarily thrown the Lortan war effort off stride, she recalled, but the Mandar had not been able to capitalize on that minuscule advantage. She remembered how she and several others had tried to escape to Ekelon, and how their mission had been quickly thwarted. Forj and Stahl had done good battle with the pursuing Lortan fleet, but in the end, even they had perished. And now, for what had already seemed an eternity, she had been pushing the Medic Cruiser to its limit in an attempt to escape Lorn-Tator, a Lortan who, by way of the various broadcasts she had heard through her Translator during the main course of the battle, was perhaps the best in ship-to-ship combat in present times.

So far, she had managed to match wits with the Lortan warrior, evading every trap and ambush that had been used against her. She had also noticed that her meager shields had repelled all of the destructive energy beams which the persistent destroyer had sent in her direction; and she could only assume that such was the case because Forj and Stahl had done more damage to the Lortan's ship than had initially been visible.

However, Elda could feel that her luck was running low. The Medic Cruiser, after having been through two major war areas and responding to almost constant demands for above normal Cettor speeds, was in need of major repairs, most of which she could not administer without the necessary tools and time.

All her mind could think about were the shocking remnants of the war; blasted vessels, dark ships floating in dark space...

She sat, unbelieving. Her eyes were focused ahead of her, scanning the near future, but she only saw the recent past — the recent, deadly past.

She looked down at her hands. The fluctuating lights of the Medic Cruiser formed slow, dark shadows that moved across her smooth but weary-torn face. To her, life — the very essence of it — was a disappointment. All that she had learned, and all that her race had learned, was threatened to be wasted. She knew three things — a meaningless feeling for the war, a vacant emptiness for those that she knew, and a horrid loathing toward the Lortans.

She raised her head again, slowly, and stared at the viewing screen, seeing the stars of deep space. And a subconscious clicking of gears took place; something had moved. She squinted her weary eyes, searching methodically to discover the source of the assumed movement. She was about to give up, thinking that her imagination had relayed a false message to her senses, when she saw it again. Far out in the distance. A...red...destroyer.

She could not understand it. Theoretically, maximum Cettor speeds could not be traced so accurately. Yet, ever since she had diverted her path from Ekelon to this immensely deep section of space, Lorn-Tator had never lost track of her. Maybe, she thought, maybe it was just a star, something that had momentarily caught her eye. Even as that hopeful thought crossed her mind, however, the object that had caught her attention only minutes before now loomed larger in her field of vision.

As if the action had become a part of her, her hand reached out to activate the map index. This time, though, she froze, her mind caught in the vortex of a last, desperate mental rally. The Stellar Index could provide many places to which she could flee, but she knew the outcome would always be the same: Lorn-Tator would find her, would never let her go.

Decisively, she allowed the *Ralix* to approach the Medic Cruiser, and as it did so, she purposely let her body feel every shred of hatred it had for the approaching Lortan. The monotony of this seemingly futile battle began to hit home, infuriating her to a level unreachable until now.

Again, her mind returned to the countless Mandar who had lost their lives in a battle that should never have been fought. She remembered Forj and Stahl, and though she had never really seen them, or touched them, she knew she was alive now because they had died to save the Medic Cruiser.

Her mind grasped that last fact: *they had died to save the Medic Cruiser.*

Her mind went over it again: *they had died to save the Medic Cruiser.*

And when the *Ralix* was almost upon her, her mind repeated it once more: *they had died to save the Medic Cruiser.*

Elda was never aware that she yelled out in anger as she shoved the Medic Cruiser into drive speed.

Lorn-Tator, apparently seeing the intention of the angry Mandar, aborted his approach. The two vessels eventually began to speed across the stellar void, their roles now reversed: the prey had become the predator.

Lorn-Tator had the smaller of the two ships and Elda knew if she could ram his ship with the Medic Cruiser, the latter might not be destroyed completely, thus allowing her to escape or at least administer lethal damage to the *Ralix*.

Across the star-ways they sped, Lortan and Mandar, wasting the endless measurements of time away in a death chase that defied all imagination. It was the same old tale: one could not die while the other lived. The chase might have lasted longer than it did had Lorn-Tator not entered the Legretti solar system, where only one planet was barely capable of sustaining life.

Elda, her mind working furiously with the new course of events, could only conclude that this Lortan was feeling the effects of the dreaded radioactive calamity that had struck Whertos. Her hypothesis was soon borne out as Lorn-Tator headed immediately for the single life-sustaining planet. Elda's concentration increased with her confidence, and she was certain that Lorn-Tator did not have much time left to live.

She knew the planet, too. It had been one of the first habitable planets discovered by the Mandar many ages ago. It had been rejected for colonization because the system's sun had been slowly losing its mass, due to some as yet unexplained and unique phenomenon. Scientists theorized that the reaction would cease within a reasonable geologic time period;

but by that time Siercurn, the only habitable planet in the system, would be a freezing sphere, with temperatures that would kill any organism that lacked adequate protection.

The history of Siercurn was of no consequence now, however, because Elda sensed that the end of this ordeal would not be resolved easily. She began decelerating, feeling the physical forces as they took their toll on the Medic Cruiser.

Lorn-Tator never deviated from his course, and as they approached Siercurn, Elda found herself wondering if indeed the Lortan was not throwing another carefully planned stratagem at her. Her keen mind examined the situation from more than 20 different vantage points, but she was unable to unsheathe any hidden dangers.

When they entered the atmosphere of Siercurn, the Medic Cruiser less than 3000 lampars behind the *Ralix*, Elda methodically began to take in the geography of what she knew would become yet another war zone.

As Elda neared the surface of the planet, she saw Lorn-Tator lead the tiny *Ralix* into a valley which was surrounded on all sides by snow-covered mountains and gently sloping hills. She landed the Cruiser nearby and was preparing to leave when she caught herself, her mind racing from the terror which had suddenly been made clear to her.

She was still playing his game — or so it seemed. It was originally he who had been trying to kill her, was it not? Still, she had followed him here! She quickly remembered the psychological powers of the Lortans, and she wondered how many of her recent actions had been solely her own. She knew her hatred was real, but was that enough to make her risk her life when she could freely depart this world without ever leaving the Cruiser?

Never before had an answer to a question eluded Elda as it did now. She knew she had the answer, but the turmoil within her mind refused to expose it to her. The obvious answer to so obvious a predicament, and all she could do was...

Glance at the atmospheric readings: they were as expected: slightly low accumulations of oxygen, nitrogen, carbon, and other foreign gases, but nonetheless breathable.

And check the temperature: cold enough to kill, if she exposed herself too long.

She calculated the distance from her landing site to the top of the hills overlooking the valley to be close enough to allow for a tolerable exposure time in the cold. The only other available apparel aboard the Medic Cruiser besides the uniform she had on now were the bulky space suits. Encumbered by such, she knew she'd be an easy kill for the Lortan. She was, therefore, restricted to only one mode of operation.

She turned toward the door. Above it hung the only diser gun aboard. She took it down and held it in her hands to feel the security it brought her. She then strapped the gun to her waist belt. She wished there were more, but the Medic Cruisers were generally not equipped for arduous combat of any kind. Moving with cautious grace, she opened the door and moved her body quickly through the frame. The blast of cold air that brutally met her strove to rip her exposed flesh to numbed shreds.

She almost turned back, but she thought of Lorn-Tator and once again anger drove her on. It was then that she began to question her actions once more. Never before had she, a member of the Mandar, known so much hatred. Never before had she felt so little control over her actions. However, to her slow surprise, she never turned back to the Cruiser.

Was this her? Or was this Lorn-Tator somehow forcing her to walk into a deathly ambush? She had no way of knowing, and the terror of that ignorance began to grow in her mind, assuming a significance that frightened her.

Her eyes scarcely took in the quiet serenity of Siercurn; blue trees, snow, and ice-covered plains and hills, and a red mist, probably some harmless gas approaching its freezing point, which floated wispily near the surface of the earth.

She had taken no more than a hundred steps from the Cruiser when her acute sense of danger was suddenly activated. She turned around (too late, she knew) and let instinctive reflexes take hold of her body. Leaping toward her was a black creature that somehow chillingly resembled the wild korlawt of Ekelon. Elda did not remember her hand aiming the diser gun at and killing the onrushing creature. She did, however, remember the pain as her left leg violently yielded to the solidly-packed mass of the animal which descended relentlessly upon her body, propelled by its own momentum.

The next several minutes were a painful study in semi-consciousness for Elda. The throbbing in her head grew into something as huge and oppressive as the very beast which had attacked her. Even as she waged her mental struggle with her own mind, she wondered if her leg had not turned into some evil beast as well: the pain it relayed to her neural centers was an endless and merciless torment.

Her mental processes, however, gave her hope as they detected the slightest perceptible progress in the involuntary repair mechanisms within her mind and body. It was not too long after this revelation that Elda was able to lift herself above the dangerously shocked state into which her body had been plunged. She realized then that the bitter cold had intensified the pain of the injury to her leg, making it seem worse than it really was. She knew, though, that it was not an injury she could leave immediately behind her. At the least, it would add a pretty noticeable limp to her gait.

She turned to take a closer look at the wild animal that had so nearly killed her.

Elda knew of only two times in her life when she had engaged in mental battle with a supreme master of the mind. One of those times was, without a doubt, represented by the lump sum of all her arguments with her father, Brisb, the famed Mandar scientist. The other time was now.

Lorn-Tator, a Lortan whom she had heard of all too often throughout the course of the Mandar-Lortan battle, had shown his superiority in too many areas for Elda to believe she was fighting just another Lortan warrior. She had, on occasion, been witness to the skill with which Lorn-Tator had dealt Mandar ships lethal blows with his deadly prowess. Even when the *Ralix* had been damaged, Lorn-Tator had not only been able to invariably follow her through every speed chasm into which she had fled; but he had also been able to keep his craft from suffering additional damage and at the same time had flawlessly out-thought her in a number of situations.

Now, as Elda stared ahead of her, she knew that Lorn-Tator had thrust deep with his last mental blow. She did not remember killing the animal because, of course, she never had: the diser gun was still strapped to her side! The thing that had resembled a wild korlawt had been nothing more than a fear in her mind, a fear that had been solidified into a horrifying force by way of Lorn-Tator's psychological warfare.

There was no dead korlawt-like animal in front of her. Her eyes simply fell on empty space. What frightened her most, however, was the pain in her leg. Theoretically, it should not be there either. How could a thought, a harmless image, cause such physical damage? She willed it to go away, told herself the pain had never existed, but she detected no change, no hope.

Had the creature been real? Had she actually killed it and, in the resultant confusion, re-harnessed the diser gun? Elda so wanted to believe that such was the case, but she knew she could never fall into such a mental pitfall. Picking herself up from the cold earth of Siercurn, she falteringly continued on her way. The going was slow, and she could feel the fear that raced through her mind as she desperately tried to justify the pain in her leg that should never have been.

As Elda continued on, she questioned her actions no more; she had gone through too much to stop now.

Lorn-Tator was having problems of his own, though. The radioactive decay of his body tissues had left him weak and with blurred and double vision. However, as a warrior, he was thoroughly engrossed in the thought of the upcoming battle and thinking of the various alternative strategies which he could use against his opponent from Ekelon. He had expected his pursuit of the Medic Cruiser to be a routine war maneuver that would end without too much expenditure of energy. However, the persistence, skill, and spirit of the Medic Cruiser's operator had challenged his own abilities to the point where, even when he realized he might not return to the main Lortan fleet in time to witness the actual destruction of Ekelon, he knew he could never voluntarily abandon his efforts to kill this one Mandar.

He, too, had only a uniform to wear, and that was where Elda had the advantage: a Mandar could tolerate more cold than a Lortan. However, Lorn-Tator was not overly concerned with this. He knew he was skilled in land battle, as all warriors were, and that fact alone told him that this she-Mandar who dared to challenge him had little hope of defeating him.

Lorn-Tator knew of the Mandarian's hatred of his very presence and his battle-oiled mind estimated that she was already on her way up one of the hillsides which would give her a good view of the area. He was also sure that his mind imprint of the korlawt, though intended to be only a temporary deterrent, had probably succeeded in instilling a measure of

confusion and fear in the mind of the Mandar challenger. With such
knowledge to boost his confidence, he stepped outside the *Ralix* and
began to employ the second phase of his attack plan.

Elda had almost reached the top of the hill when she stopped. She
tried to picture in her mind how the valley had looked from the overhead view she had so fleetingly seen, and where she would be in relation
to the Lortan's ship.

When she had figured out her position (allowing for some degree of
error), she knew that she still had some distance to travel along the rough,
uneven circumference of the valley to be in a position to attack the *Ralix*
from the rear.

Stooping low, she began a slow, labored trot, heading to her right. The
wispy, red mist was not present at this elevation, and somewhere in the
back of her mind she detected the absence of a gentle sweet smell. Such
an observation was of no importance to her now, however, as her mind
was racing on to more demanding matters.

As she ran, Elda began to take notice of her body: the diser gun was
still at her side, but her hands and arms had been numbed to the point of
non-feeling, hurting with an immensity that allowed them to respond
only to Elda's most concentrated physical exertions. Her wounded leg
was throbbing now, producing a blunt pain which became an antagonis-
tic force that fought against her forward motion. She could also feel the
ice that had formed on her face from her exhaled breath.

Elda became aware of these and other disadvantages which racked her
body; and in return she drew upon the bottomless pool of determination
that was welled up deep within her brain. She was a unique, self-sufficient
system, a generator and a battery that worked in an uncanny and yet
productive manner.

Amidst these thoughts, she soon reached her desired vantage point.
She crawled up to the top of the ridge and lay flat against the rocks,
managing with some difficulty to get the diser gun into her right hand.
She quickly glanced around, taking only slight notice of the wind-swept
and snow covered hillside that lay in back of her. Her senses tried to warn
her that something had been wrong there, that the accumulation of snow

and ice was unusually high; but her mind, dulled by the coldness of the air, and obsessed with her anger of the situation, failed to key in on the signal.

Swinging her concentration to what lay before her, on the other side of the ridge, she slowly elevated herself to her hands and knees. This was it, she told herself — if she did not kill the Lortan soon, her own body would cease to function and become a victim of Siercurn's coldness and her excessive determination.

She raised herself higher and was able to look down into the tree-clustered valley. For just an instant she was able to catch sight of a moving figure amidst the trees; and in that same instant she was able to spot the *Ralix*. But suddenly that instant was vanquished, obliterated by a violent wind which seemed to rise up from the valley floor itself.

Elda instinctively sank lower when the surprising gust of wind reached and blew past her. As she continued, without success, to locate the Lortan among the barely visible trees, she observed, with a heightened concern, the growing storm to which the wind had laid seed. The red mist which had gathered in the lower part of the valley quickly sprouted lengthy tendrils that jiggled repeatedly in the cold air before forming massive, swirling vortices that surreptitiously sped through the landscape. Then snow began to fall, and within an amazingly short period of time, a moving blanket of white flowed before Elda's eyes. It was then that she saw him! Lorn-Tator, so close that the shock of his presence temporarily submerged her into a state of paralysis. She fought to overcome this fear, and when she had succeeded, a crazy light gleamed in her eyes, and she felt her fatigued face break into a sly expression that reminded her of an old and wizened korlawt that had managed to elude every Mandarian hunter on Ekelon many years ago. She knew this was the opportunity she had been waiting for, because the Lortan was turned away from her. Raising her unwilling arms, she aimed and fired at the unwary Lorn-Tator. Nothing happened! Then she realized that her fingers would not move. She stared at her hands in a desperate attempt to will them to obey her. When she glanced up, she was dismayed to see that the swirling snow had begun to hide Lorn-Tator's form, enveloping him in a layer of white uncertainty. Gripping the gun harder, she practically shouted for her fingers to depress the trigger. They did, just barely, and the resultant beam shot forth into the cold white, penetrating everything in its path.

Elda stared nervously into the disturbing whiteness below her. She kept her diser gun at point, ready to fire again. Should she descend? Should she take the risk of moving just yet? Her mind teetered laboriously over the uncertainties of these questions until her roving eyes were attracted by a vague movement just to the left of where she had fired her gun. She could feel the loathing she possessed for Lorn-Tator well up inside her as she saw his figure dimly outlined in the snow once more.

She aimed her weapon and, after several long moments of intense anticipation, was able to once again activate the enormous energies of the diser gun. However, once more the snow converged to silently erase whatever results her actions had obtained.

Elda looked down at the ruins that had once been her hands and she began to worry that Lorn-Tator would outlast her in the harsh coldness that was, she now knew, the setting for the last battle she would ever fight. It had taken her far too long to engage the firing mechanism of the diser gun that last time, and she knew that the moment was not far away when she would not be able to use the weapon at all.

As these worries began to tax her mental strength, she spotted the figure of Lorn-Tator again, darkly outlined against the physical whiteness of the storm. Later, he appeared twice more, and each time Elda did her best to strike him down with the diser gun.

When she finally glanced down to see how much energy the diser gun had left, the shock of finding the meter almost on empty poured through her mind like liquid fire. Then she painfully realized how badly she had been fooled by the Lortan. Ever since that initial wind which had captivated her attention, her eyes had hardly left the scene of the valley below. The mystical quality of the wind and the snow now came back to her and she knew without a doubt that all her previous exertions had been useless, that she had given away her position to Lorn-Tator, and that everything — the storm, the wind, the snow — had all been a carefully calculated illusion put into her mind. She had never actually seen Lorn-Tator!

The anger of that humiliating conclusion sent her brain racing to new heights, and she found herself frantically concentrating the last of her mental efforts on just one thought: that everything imaginary would resolve into the nothingness it was supposed to be. She felt herself grow limp as the silent struggle drained her of her strength. Then there was a sudden tautness, a barrier which she had to surmount. It was huge and immediately attacked her as she drew nearer to it. Sharp stabs of pain emanated from the towering wall as Elda thrust her mental and, surprisingly, her physical self against it. Blazing white slivers caromed off of razor-edged points, seeking to blind the Mandarian's eyes. Elda, however, grew stronger as she slowly felt the pain in her left leg diminishing. She was winning! Her mental resources, aggregations of ethereal powers she had never before measured, were performing a task that even Brisb would have been proud to see.

At that moment there erupted a volley of quakes that rocked the massive wall to its very foundations. Elda could feel the mounting disaster that was inevitably approaching, and her mind marveled at the thought that this was all feeling — that none of this was taking place in the physical realm of Siercurn.

A horrendous, silent shriek then signalled the end of the psychological war in which Elda and Lorn-Tator had viciously participated. The wall was blasted away, and in its place there appeared to Elda the swirling snow of the storm. But that, too, blinked into oblivion, and left Elda with a sight she would never have been prepared for, even if she had her whole life to live over.

With the disappearance of the snow, Lorn-Tator, who had easily been able to pinpoint her exact location when she had senselessly fired at his images, now appeared as a crouching figure at the edge of the tree line. Elda's body, acting under the influence of the various stimulatory hormones in its system, literally pushed itself from where she lay. However, she was not quick enough; the Lortan's fire caromed off the rocks in front of her and struck her right leg. She flung her diser gun in the air as she recklessly grabbed her wounded limb in an attempt to quell the pain. Her weakened state did not help any, and as a bludgeon-like throbbing racked her body, she lost all sense of equilibrium. She felt herself pass through a confused state of orientation, and then she was dimly aware of her body falling into the pit that was behind her.

Elda had been to many planets, and each of them, so she had observed, had possessed its own variety of danger. Some of the dangers were scientifically unexplainable; others were easily anticipated. The danger in which Elda now found herself fell into the latter of these two categories. As she realized the importance of her present situation, she forgot all the pain that besieged her body. She now lay immersed in the aftermath of a small avalanche that her fall had triggered. Only her arms and head were free. As she assessed the situation, she was amazed at how calmly her mind accepted the inevitable conclusions: the weight of the snow and ice which lay above her, combined with her injured leg and numb body, restricted almost all of her movement and left little hope for escape. She was also afraid that any further struggling would only increase the chances of a second avalanche. She reached for a nearby area of melted snow, relieved to find her diser gun had fallen with her. It took almost all of her remaining strength to pick it up. Its energy output meter registered so close to empty that she found it difficult to determine if the meter could actually drop to a lower level of emptiness. Still, there was always a slim chance that enough was left just to be able to seriously harm or kill the Lortan — and she was sure she would have at least one last opportunity to perform that task.

However, as the pain in her body grew, she realized, slowly and quite bluntly, that she was dying...of the cold and exhaustion to which her body had relentlessly been exposed. Her legs were beyond any medical treatment, and she could feel herself sinking into the cold, white grave which threatened to cover her head before long. She hoped that Lorn-Tator would come before then, so that she would be granted that one last chance.

Lorn-Tator was almost dead. He was having convulsions almost continuously, and his head was being tormented by terrible flaming pains which mercilessly plagued it — the nitrogen-fixing bacteria were dying. He was being poisoned by his own body.

Because of his low endurance to the bitter cold, he could no longer walk; yet, he *had* to move. As a space warrior, he knew that if you can not see a dead enemy, then maybe the enemy is not dead. He would not die until he had verified that his mission had been achieved. Extending his arms before him, he slowly pulled himself up the valley side toward the ridge where he had last seen his quarry.

His pain was almost unbearable, but his long years of training had kept him alive so far, and he felt sure they would last him until his task was done. The she-Mandar had fallen so foolishly into his mind trap; he had to make sure he had not missed the opportunity for such an easy kill!

Extending his arms before him, he slowly pulled himself forward ...

Somehow, Elda's beleaguered mind informed her that night was slowly approaching. She was no longer sinking, and already an intolerable amount of time had passed. Logically, her body was no longer sufficiently warm to melt any of the surrounding snow and ice, and the frightening irony of such a situation gnawed away at the last remnants of her self-control. She knew that if she could only force her legs to move, she might stand a chance of freeing herself from the oppressively packed snow and ice which surrounded her. However, her limbs were no longer able to feel anything, and the pain that the rest of her body was subjected to as the air grew colder congregated into a voluminous source of suffering.

As she felt her consciousness ebbing away, she heard the muffled sounds of something breathing. She looked up at the spot whence she had fallen and saw the angled head of Lorn-Tator rise up over the ledge from the other side of the hill, his sparkling blue eyes sparkling no more.

Her mind started as she realized that the time had come. She raised her arms and attempted to aim the limply held diser gun at the Lortan.

Lorn-Tator, seeing her intention, gave one final exertion and succeeded in draping himself over the ledge. Several rocks were knocked loose by his movements and fell down toward Elda. One small stone glanced off her face, yet she appeared not to have felt it. With his hand weapon he took careful aim of the she-Mandar...only to discover that the cold which had rendered his opponent's arms useless had similarly affected his own hands. The silence of Siercurn increased tenfold as the two beings stared at each other, seeing the hatred in the other's eyes. This was it, the last war, and they knew it. And each one hated his-/herself for not being able to win it.

The sun was setting in the distance, taking away its minuscule amount of warmth as it went. Siercurn was headed for nighttime, its day almost spent. A slight wind picked up from across the valley, gathering snow as it went. It swirled the white fluff haphazardly through the air around the two combatants.

Then, as if their movements had been synchronized from the dawn of time, each one, Lortan and Mandar, gave that one final, climactic thrust, siphoning power from the last untapped recess in their souls. Elda raised her arms and fired, and the Lortan fired back.

Two birds with one stone; there was no victor. Elda, her body so weak and numbed with cold that it had hardly reacted to the energy ray which had lethally touched upon it, lay face up in the entombing snow and ice, her arms pointed forward, in the direction of the Lortan.

And Lorn-Tator, his huge body draped over the ridge, still held his hand weapon as his dead eyes stared unseeingly below him.

The last war had been fought, the destiny reached. Eons in the future, when Siercurn would become a planet submerged in an eternal deep-freeze, orbiting a distant sun, there would be a story for all to read.

Part 8. Vindication

Long before Elda and Lorn-Tator tampered with fate on Siercurn, there had occurred an incident in their universe which was to have a cosmic effect on the remaining Lortan fleet.

Lon-Kyle and Leor-Kli, the last two living members of the Vahrsta for the Whertos Warrior Force, organized their efforts for the final attack upon Ekelon. They brought together their strongest ships and their healthiest warriors to discuss their final battle plans.

The weaker warriors were dismissed, and to them the remaining ships were given. They were given the option of returning to Whertos or joining the forces for the final attack. Most chose the former, not because they feared to die while laying waste to Ekelon, but because they preferred to die on their home planet and knew that the contributions they might make to the assault on Ekelon in their weakened state could very well hinder Lon-Kyle's victorious plan.

They thus departed, leaving behind them a tragic waste the intensity of which was never to be equalled again in the galaxy. Thirty Lortan ships ultimately made it back to Whertos; all the rest failed on the way, accepting a destiny of drifting through the black void, their crews long dead.

However, even as these Lortans' lives were so quietly extinguished, Lon-Kyle was closing in on the Ekelonian solar system. Behind him rode a fleet of warriors which, though diminished greatly from its original size, was still powerful enough to easily destroy the small, passive population of Ekelon.

Lon-Kyle took pride in knowing that very few Mandar ships had escaped the scene of the last battle. With most of the initial opposition out of the way, he theorized that Ekelon would have to supply virtually all its defenses from its own resources.

It was not long before the marauding Lortan fleet reached the Mandar's native system. As they penetrated deeper and deeper they ran across an occasional enemy ship that still possessed the courage to defend the treasured planet of Ekelon. These the Lortans quickly destroyed, determined to allow none of the Mandar to escape their ruthless onslaught.

Lon-Kyle, however, was beginning to have his worries. None of the ships his fleet had so far encountered had borne an Ekelon insignia. Was the mother planet so ignorant of all that had been happening recently? Or could it be that Ekelon, the birthplace of the peaceful Mandar, was trying to win pity from them? Lon-Kyle managed to steer his mind away from thoughts of compromise — Ekelon would be destroyed regardless of the tactics it used.

When Ekelon was well within the range of the Lortans' remote sensing equipment, Lon-Kyle was once again forced to ask himself countless, worrisome questions. He was unable to spot any valiant defenders of the Mandarian sanctuary; nor did he see any patrols. The space surrounding the entire planet of Ekelon was...simply deserted.

Other Lortans had, by this time, been able to make the same observations as Lon-Kyle, who now found himself unable to answer the volley of questions which suddenly rained down upon him.

Leor-Kli hurriedly checked the star maps and consulted the Information Cubes. She performed this task three times before turning to Lon-Kyle and informing him that this was, indeed, the proper location for Ekelon.

For some reason her words rebuked Lon-Kyle. He had hoped to hear that they had miscalculated, that they had entered the wrong system by mistake. Instead, the affirmative answer only served to further darken his already worried mind. He transmitted Leor-Kli's findings to the other Lortans and instructed the members of the fleet to hold any additional questions until further notice.

The sweet taste of victory now turned into the bitter, reeking smell of suspense, and as Lon-Kyle and Leor-Kli entered the orbit of Ekelon, they immediately positioned themselves over their finely tuned instruments, sure that now the mystery would be solved. However, to their dismay, a problem of massive proportions emerged.

Leor-Kli was the first to ask the questions that Lon-Kyle was afraid to answer: How could this planet be completely void of life? Where were its people, its civilization? How could there be no evidence of the Mandar ever having existed here! Could they have somehow escaped the Lortans?

Lon-Kyle rechecked his own findings before turning to Leor-Kli. He had been surprised to hear the rarely used submissive voice in the timbres of his long-time partner as she spoke. However, he was beginning to share her concerns.

In the end, he offered her the only answer he had by reminding her that it had often been said by many that the Lortans were the most powerful race to have ever travelled the interstellar paths. The majority of them would now die here, surrounding this dead planet. Those that would survive, that somehow would remain untainted by the affliction which the Mandar brought upon their race, would be so few in number that their survival would be a painful, ironic death.

Lon-Kyle knew, with extreme humiliation, that the Lortans would perish without attaining their ultimate goal. They had always known Ekelon to be a populated planet, and they had heard of Brisb too many times to doubt that he had somehow arrived at a way to save his people from the superior Lortan forces. It was with these thoughts that he told Leor-Kli that they would at least die knowing that they were always feared by others.

Leor-Kli, somewhat stunned, watched as her commanding warrior checked his instruments once more. She knew he would have to make a similar speech to the other warriors; and she knew that he had to check his findings just one last time.

Leor-Kli shared his feelings. A planet's people can disappear, yes. She could be persuaded to believe that. But a planet's entire civilization! She knew what Lon-Kyle had never said. Sure, the Lortans would die knowing they had been feared...but they had also been defeated.

Part 9. When Equals Meet

The story of Brisb, who sacrificed himself to spare the lives of the other Mandar on Ekelon, was passed down from one generation to the next. In the beginning, the name of Brisb's daughter, Elda, was mentioned frequently in the stories. However, over time, the storytellers agreed that they could only speculate over what role she truly played in the ultimate success of Brisb's controversial theory. Eventually, some of the younger Mandar were never made aware that Brisb even had a daughter;

that fact became overshadowed by his other accomplishments which culminated in the loss of his life.

The escape from the Lortans marked the end of the Era of Invention for the Mandar. In time, this proud race turned inward upon itself, and sought a more simpler life than that which it had lived previously. By this time, the driving focus behind the lives of the Mandar was no longer measured by achievements in technology but by its cumulative understanding of divinity. The urge to seek out other planets to colonize was eventually lost, and the practice of retrospection became enshrined by many Mandar.

Several centuries passed as the Mandar civilization continued to embark upon this new path. However, not even Brisb could have predicted the next race that his people would encounter.

It was a windy, overcast day when the armada of black ships arrived from deep space. The Mandar initially greeted the race of gray beings which emerged from these ships with caution. However, the people of Ekelon quickly realized that their visitors sported an intellect the like of which they had never seen before, except within themselves. As they learned to communicate with one another, the Mandar relaxed the security measures they had initially established.

It wasn't until the first Mandar began reporting strange dreams that they suspected desperate times had once again returned. But by then, it was already too late...

Chapter 5

██████████████████████
██████████████████████

Refander

Part 1. (Date Subjective to Earth: September 2184)

Addendum: With my failing health, I sense that my time is near. Nevertheless, I have found the strength to put yet another entry into this journal of my life's thoughts and experiences. My time on Refander, though not as long as I would have wanted it to be, has allowed me to pursue fields of study that otherwise would have passed me by. Call it my investigative nature, my natural curiosity for the unfamiliar; perhaps that may explain why I chose the life of a cameraman.

For many years, I immersed myself into the world of Paul Torrden and his snow leopards. And before that, I covered many stories on Earth that required me to gain an intimate familiarity with the subject matter. Indeed, all of my life, I have chosen the path of the novice explorer, forging ahead through the bush with only a rudimentary map and a bare-bones survival kit.

And through it all, I have learned that to truly report a story, you must first experience it. In total. Uncensored. The snow leopards, the *Stranahan*, and even Refander — our new world. I have experienced it all through the eyes of a camera-man, from the point of view of a professional observer.

So, it is no wonder that I fail to find surprise in my latest interest — or should I say obsession — these last few months: the archaeological studies of our new world. While it is true that Refander's ancient hidden treasures have awed only a handful of the scientists on our planet, I believe that is merely because there are so few people involved in this line of work.

The first amazing discoveries of Refander's past were made during the construction of the Base Station Dome, not too long after the Tech Crews arrived. The most significant site, Wilson-6, was named after the Tech Crew explorer who discovered it. Located over 750 kilometers northwest of the Dome, Wilson-6 is still active. Although I have only made two visits to this area, I have monitored the new discoveries that are uncovered there and published in our weekly on-line data bank.

The field notes made by Wilson two days after his discovery sum it up best:

> *These ancient ruins may forever be a mystery to us mortal humans. But it is only fitting that we all bear witness to the testament that other, intelligent beings once walked this planet before us...[O]n Earth, whole centuries passed while scientists attempted to prove, or disprove, what we have discovered here today.*

Wilson, and the scientists that followed him, have painstakingly dug into the ruins of a civilization that once existed on Refander. Their discoveries were initially overshadowed by the intense desire to get the Base Station Dome built and operational, and then by the arrival of the *Stranahan*, and the catastrophe that followed.

However, science must march forward. What I find most intriguing, and refreshing, about our archaeologists is their attention to detail. They have postulated, based on the evidence available to them, that a race of beings once inhabited this planet and was even capable of space travel. However, the geologic time span that separates us from the previous tenants of Refander is mind-boggling. Unfortunately, much of what we want to know about this past civilization has been lost to the natural processes of time. Nevertheless, from skeletal and other remains, we have been able to theorize that this race, like us, walked upright, built structures not unlike our own, and perhaps had communities and cities, as well.

The latest revelation from Wilson-6 came today, when one of the researchers claimed he now believes the previous inhabitants of Refander had some form of electronic data storage, although as yet we have not been able to determine how it functioned. More startling, however, is the overwhelming evidence that these people met a most untimely fate at some point in the distant past. The scientists that have studied Wilson-6 and the other archaeological sites have reached near-unanimous conclusion that this race of people all died out at about the same time, perhaps of some natural (and as yet, unexplained) catastrophe. Prior to that time, there are no truly unexplained anomalies in the geologic record aside from a climatic shift to warmer temperatures that occurred about 1000 years before the demise of this culture. We have, as yet, been unable to explain why this culture, which was obviously at the height of its existence, suddenly died out. As we tried to explain the reasons why dinosaurs ceased to exist on old Earth, scientists on Refander are now postulating one theory after another that might account for the disappearance of this civilization. I have even heard one or two suggestions that we call our unknown predecessors "New Atlantisians", in tribute to the legendary continent that only the most faithful historians can remember.

If indeed there was an intelligent race of people that once walked Refander — and thus far, none of the available evidence would refute this — I would have welcomed the opportunity to have walked in their paths, lived their lives, and spoken their language. Uncensored. Perhaps one day we will uncover more recent evidence of this race's existence, some clue that will bridge the gap of information that exists between our two worlds. . .

Part 2. Ian Torrden

When Ian Torrden awoke, he knew that several darix were outside his cabin. He had sensed them in, and had even subconsciously made them a part of, his dreams; and now, every so often, his keen ears detected the quick, crackling sound a bit of vegetation made as it gave way beneath the pressure of a heavy paw. They were circling — typical behavior for darix when they were on the hunt.

He remained still for some time, savoring the warmth of his sleeping bag. He had made it himself several years ago, obtaining most of the material from the thick-furred hide of a sparth.

His mind drifted to the thoughts of the things he had planned to do this day. Farming had been foremost on his list. His fields of native-grown fruit were ready to be harvested. He realized, however, that as long as the darix remained in the area, his whole crop would have to be ignored — which essentially meant that it would all go to ruin. The short year of Refander was not something one could play games with, as the evolution of its peculiar annual flora so distinctly indicated. Practically all of the food crops on Refander were native in origin as the planet's short, cold year was too harsh for many Earth species.

Which meant that when the Tech Crews first arrived, they not only had to build a dome and adapt to a new way of life, but they also had to find an immediate source of food. It had been a risky process, but the fortunate part was that many poisonous plants had been quickly identified. Ian remembered all that from his days at the Base Station. But those times were over — and had been for some 188.5 years, Refander time. Yet, Ian had aged only 13 Earth years in that time and he sometimes found it hard to imagine what a 365-day year would be like.

However, he had little need to keep in touch with such old, nostalgic facts. Since he had left the Base Station, he'd had no contact with people except those he had passed on his way north through the Torrden Forests. After crossing the Crane River near its junction with the Patsteel and Rapibb Rivers, approximately 200 kilometers north of the Station, he had turned south for about 60 kilometers before building his cabin along a wide stream that fed into the Crane.

People on the west side of the river had warned him of the wild dogs, which was what they commonly called the darix. They had said that the darix on their side of the Crane had been less of a bother, but only because they had lethal weapons that could be used against the animals. Ian, however, had sensed a better and more challenging way of life.

The darix were probably one of the most ruthless predators humans had ever encountered, and the people of the Torrden Forests found it a constant job to protect themselves from the wild beasts. The darix never hesitated to attack a human, and there was never a shortage of stories of how someone had met such an untimely fate. Thus aware of the dangers of the wild darix, but also realizing that he enjoyed the peaceful tranquility that solitude offered, Ian crossed the river knowing that if he did not find a more effective way of dealing with the darix he would probably perish like many others had. No one had followed him across the Crane, and for all he knew, they probably considered him dead.

Ian knew he reminded many of the older folks at the Base Station of his grandparents, Paul and Julie. Sporting an athletic frame, he stood several inches above medium height. However, his rugged, bearded face and his rich, black hair combined to produce the contemplative, solitary essence which many people on the *Stranahan* had noticed in Julie.

Ian managed a half-smile as he recalled the Base Station. The farmlands were located northwest of the Base Station, and not too many people desired to be too far from either of those two communities or the services they offered. He speculated that very few people there spent more than a passing moment to think of Ian Torrden. As far as he knew, he was the only human east of the Crane, and that knowledge gave Ian a pleasant feeling of satisfaction. The chances that anyone would want to travel the excessive distance to reach this area of Refander were pretty slim, anyway.

A familiar, old chill came over Ian then, as he continued to contemplate his memory of the Base Station. For five generations, the Torrden name had been synonymous with controversy: Gregory Torrden had created T.E.I. despite objections from the public and private sectors. Later, both Gregory and Ian's great-grandfather, Carl Torrden, became active members of the GAP movement against the Pan-government, a decision which, according to the journals that Sammy Lassiter had kept, may have culminated in the mysterious trans-car accident that killed Carl Torrden in 2102. Then there was Paul, who continued the Torrden tradition by successfully lobbying for space aboard the 20th New World Launch despite fierce opposition from the Interplanetary Space Flight Commission. And Ian still remembered his father, Michael, whose last decision as an officer of the *Stranahan* forever branded him as the sole person responsible for the disastrous crash landing of the shuttle on Refander. Ian found it ironic that the animosity people had expressed towards him as a teen-ager and young adult was perhaps greater than anything his father or grandfather had ever experienced; and yet, of all the Torrdens, he was the only one who had never done anything to earn the reputation that would, inevitably, burden him for the rest of his life.

Ian reflected on these thoughts before stirring. As he crawled out of his sleeping bag, the cold air chillingly wrapped itself around his body. Rising, he was rendered off balance by a slight tremor which shook the cabin. Ian quickly ignored this event, however, as Refander had recently been subjected to several such quakes. He briskly walked over to his basin, washed, and put on a clean shirt. Then he laid out some additional thick garments, among them his large, hooded overcoat that had also been made from the productive hide of the sparth.

The fur from a sparth was the thickest to be found on any Refander animal. Ian knew a long journey was ahead of him, and winter was about to strike Refander once more. Under such conditions, the overcoat was unarguably a life-saving necessity. Though snow was not too common during the brief but bitter winter days, the high elevations of the Pascalian

Mountains, where he was planning to go, made snowfall a common, more frequent, and oftentimes more treacherous event.

After he had rounded up an adequate number of clothes and had set out his snowshoes, fur-lined boots, and mittens, he began stuffing his travel pack with large quantities of nutritious food. To this he added an adequate amount of sparth jerky and several small flasks filled with a juice he had made from two of the few edible fruits of the Refander hardwoods. He was thankful that subsistence farming was easy on Refander, enabling one to produce much more than was needed. The loss of this year's crop would hardly affect his stores at all.

When he finished packing, he laid his bow and arrows beside his coat and ate a quick meal consisting of juice and bread made from his own grain.

It was only after he had done all these chores that he went to the foremost of his cabin's two window openings, both of which consisted of five short, heavy wooden logs that were bound together. Ian swung the small door all the way up, thus providing himself with maximum viewing space through the rectangular aperture. He silently peered through the mesh he had placed across the outside of the opening as a protection from the small biting organisms which appeared in enormous numbers during the warmer parts of Refander's year-long cool weather.

His quick eyes roamed over the clearing in front of his cabin and after several seconds of observation he identified two dark shapes in the woods at the edge of his field. Going cautiously to the rear window, Ian let his eyes scan the thickets that lined the stream which meandered its way to the Crane. Again, after several moments of intense scrutiny, he was able to see three more darix moving slowly within the dense growth.

He slipped on his fur overcoat and took hold of the large, sharp-edged knife that was strapped on the inside of the garment. He'd had the long-bladed weapon since his days at the Dome and over the years there had been many occasions during which it had found use. Now, as he stealthily walked to the door, he knew it would inevitably find use again.

Slowly unbolting the door, he let it open slightly and after assuring himself that nothing lay in ambush just outside the entrance way, he swung it open, stepped outside, and closed it again, all in one quick motion. A silence seemed to steal over the clearing around his cabin and, as silently, Ian awaited the approach of the darix.

After his first two years of precarious and hazardous observation in the woods east of the Crane, Ian had discovered that darix repeatedly and relentlessly attack their prey. In response to this behavior, he had built his cabin so that the doorway formed a sloped-in recess, similar to a large cubbyhole. Nothing could approach him without sufficient advance warning, and the space was so designed that any defense he offered immediately became a vicious offense.

Slowly, Ian's heart beat rose. Three times before over the years he'd had to make this stand. Once, the darix had gotten to him and the only thing that had saved him was his determination to not allow the wild animals drag him out in the open. By keeping his back against the doorway, he had managed, though not without paying the price of several seething gashes, to ward off the pack of attackers.

The memory of that experience was still fresh in his mind when one of the darix he'd heard earlier in the morning exploded around the left side of his cabin and flung its muscle-toned, black-gray body towards Ian's neck. He let his blade fly, but one good strike was all he was able to land as the darix' body collided brutally with his. Fortunately, the power and depth of his blow had caused the magnificently huge teeth of the darix to close on empty air. Before the surprisingly nimble creature could strike again, Ian sunk his blade into the animal's lower chest, at the same time pushing the darix' body away from his own.

But even as the wounded darix pulled itself away from the flashing weapon that had so easily punctured its body, two more challengers came bounding toward Ian from his right side. Seeing them, he brought his knife around and crouched low, emptying his thrust into the belly of the lead darix' body and using it as a shield against the third attacker. He was knocked to one knee from the impact of the two large, twisting bodies and he cried out in anguish and anger as an armed paw raked the side of his face with spiked claws.

Sensing the ebbing life of the darix he had stabbed, Ian withdrew his knife, heaved the massive body to one side, and slashed at the third, unharmed darix. And though it had seemed he had moved so fast, Ian felt he was in limbo as he watched long, jagged teeth sink deeply into his right knee while his arm brought his treasured cutting edge down upon the animal's neck.

Twice more, as he writhed in pain, he struck the darix, and when the voracious predator finally retreated, Ian was alarmed to find himself several meters from his doorway. He scrambled back to the vantage point, assuming a standing position once more only after several painful attempts. The air was filled with dust and the smell of anxiety. He waited a whole half hour — during which time the wounded darix at his feet drew its last breath — before feeling safe that he had actually won this initial fight.

Turning, he hobbled back into his cabin and quickly cleansed and dressed his knee with a thick substance he had produced from the finely crushed roots of several species of the native hardwoods. Though it did not rank beside any advanced medical-technological discovery, the water-based salve at least served Ian's purpose in drawing out most infection-causing organisms from the wounds he had acquired over the years. After wrapping his knee with a makeshift brace, he quickly gathered his pack and weapons, cleaned his knife, and set off from the cabin at as fast a pace as possible.

The darix would continue attacking his cabin until they succeeded in breaking through his defenses, if he chose to stay. Knowing that meant he had only one logical choice left — and that was to lead the entire pack that had set seize upon his cabin far away from the area. He was sure that they would follow his trail, just as he was sure they were watching him right now. He knew, too, that he had only gained their respect and that he had instilled no fear into the pack by killing one of their members.

He was heading east along the stream that ran by his cabin after coming down from the northwestern arm of the Pascalian Mountains. He estimated his journey would take about 14 days, barring any serious interruptions.

Yet, Ian had not been foolish enough to think his travelling would be unimpeded by another attack. This had been the largest pack that had ever assailed him where he lived, and he was confident that there were more darix in the pack than the five he had been able to see.

Knowing that the pack was so large made him feel compelled to travel farther than he had ever gone in the past. The darix were merciless hunters and rarely abandoned the pursuit of their prey. They usually hunted sparth, and were occasionally known to pursue herds of the large herbivore for many days on end, if necessary. In the end, the darix were invariably successful, and the sparth herd typically numbered one less than it had before the hunt began.

After the first Tech Crews had arrived on Refander, it had not taken long for the first human-darix encounter to be documented. The relentless hunting behavior of the darix had immediately forced all humans living or travelling outside of the Base Station to always carry firearms capable of quickly killing the dark predators. Ian, however, had found a new and less destructive way of dealing with the darix, even though it meant placing himself into a more perilous situation. Nevertheless, he was content with what he was doing. He had voluntarily forsaken technology, and he enjoyed being without the weapons that practically everyone else on Refander depended upon for protection from the darix.

After hiking for some time, he stopped and opened up one of the flasks he had slung over his shoulder. He took a few sips of the liquid it contained. Already he had travelled several kilometers and just up ahead he could see the thick stand of trees that marked the sudden rise in elevation as one began ascending the western slope of the Pascalian Mountains. Ian knew the going would be rough for several days, as there were no trails through the harsh terrain and hardy vegetation.

Casting a half-conscious glance behind him, he shouldered his flask and set off once again, drawing his overcoat tight around his body. The not-too-distant trees would shield him sufficiently from the wind that had started to blow. However, as he got higher on the slope he knew he would not be able to depend on the trees to protect him from the drop in temperature he would no doubt encounter.

He trekked on for a straight six and a half hours before the approach of nightfall forced him to stop. He then searched for a large tree and, after five minutes, finally found one whose lowermost branches were spaced fairly close together. Ian began climbing the tree, stopping only when he had attained a height of about ten meters. Then, hanging his pack on the stump of an old, dead branch, he took hold of his bow and withdrew one of the 30 arrows he had brought with him.

There was still a half hour before darkness, and he was sure that at least one of the darix that had been following him would come within range of the tree in which he sat. Assuming a position as still as the tree itself, he patiently awaited the appearance of the large beasts.

Standing slightly less than a meter at the shoulder, the darix was an animal that immediately alarmed the fear centers in anyone's brain. Their coat of coarse, metallic black-gray fur enshrouded them with an air of steel and boldness. Many wildlife species native to Refander appeared to emanate a sense of helplessness when they found themselves under attack by a darix pack. Darix had powerful jaws but, except for their elongated canines, there was hardly any resemblance to the number and placement of the different kinds of teeth with respect to the carnivores of Earth. And their eyes, which were bright orange, never failed to cast forth a glow from the deep sockets of their dark faces.

Ian slowly filtered the image of the darix out of his mind, emptying his consciousness so as to allow room for more concentration. His eyes had become the only noticeable moving objects on his body, and as they once again swept across the forest floor below him, he felt a sudden tenseness race into his mind. Again, he let his eyes scan the area beneath him, and this time he discovered what was wrong: the lecki, small squirrel-like animals, the many species of which could be found in practically all of Refander's woodlands, had suddenly vanished. Ian remembered seeing several in the lower branches of the trees around him only minutes before. Their disappearance was what he had been waiting for.

Taking his right mitten off, he slowly fitted the notched end of the arrow into the taut string. Freezing in that position, he waited once more. This time, scarcely a minute passed before the object of his waiting came into view.

It was a lone darix, and even in the dim light Ian could tell from the two gashes on its neck and lower chest that this had been the first darix to attack him this morning. He raised his bow and began aiming it in the direction of the approaching darix. Suddenly, as if realizing that it had walked into a trap, the long-legged beast came to a stop. Ian quickly centered his bearing on the animal's flank and when all was set, he uttered a soft yell.

Even as the darix began to look up towards him, Ian released the arrow. The pointed projectile sank deep into the thick muscle of the animal's hind leg. The darix scrambled briefly in a tight circle before it began racing back along the trail it had been following.

Ian managed a smile to himself. Until his trip was over, he would frequently need to seek refuge in trees such as the one he was in now, and he could not afford to close his eyes with seven or eight darix waiting at the base of his 'bed,' watching for the moment he accidentally fell. He knew that the well-developed social organization amongst these predators would allow the wounded animal to warn the rest of the pack that their human prey was not yet safe to approach.

This task done, Ian hung his bow beside his pack and ate a little of the bread and meat which he had brought with him. Afterwards, he huddled up against the trunk of the tree and closed his eyes. Many times before he had slept like this, and his body had subconsciously trained itself to awake at the slightest change in equilibrium.

As the night progressed, he repeatedly flexed his hands inside his mittens, and every so often he would rub his feet to keep the blood circulating. Ian knew that this first night would not be as harsh as the ones which were to follow, but he always took such precautions against frostbite in cold weather.

He missed the warmth of a fire, but he was also aware of the fact that a fire was only good to someone if he slept inside an armed techno-tent, which was something that all Refander woodsmen first learned to do. However, Ian had even abandoned that technology. He knew the darix would gladly take a carelessly sleeping human whenever the chance presented itself, but he had trained himself well over the years and now knew how to avoid such danger.

The six hours of darkness soon passed, and as the nearest of Refander's two suns rose in the sky, Ian quickly ate a light breakfast before shouldering his packs and continuing his progression into the mountains. Like yesterday, the darix were nowhere to be seen, but he was sure they were once again following his trail.

The next two days, in fact, were in the same mold as the first, except that the severity of the cold weather began to increase dramatically. There had been one occasion, however, when he had glimpsed one of his trailing party not more than a stone's throw from his right side. He had been mad, and a little frightened, that he had allowed one of them to get so close, but no harm had come of it. The darix had evidently been trying to discover what other defenses he possessed. Though most packs of darix regularly ranged over an area exceeding 100 square kilometers, Ian guessed he was the first human this pack had ever seen.

Now as the night of the third day of his journey approached, Ian sat in what would probably be the last tree in which he would sleep for several days. The elevation he had reached was the upper limit for trees of sizeable height on Refander. In the coming days, he would see many of the small thickets and shrubs that populated the mountainsides at the higher elevations.

He had already decided to pass through the lower, central portion of the northwestern arm of the Pascalian range; that way, though he would be at an approximate height of 1900 meters above sea level, he would at least minimize the amount of time during which he would be dangerously susceptible to an attack.

However, at present, that was the least of his worries. The snow had started to fall, and he was not sure how long the storm would last. As the darkness overtook him, he could feel the thick sparth fur that he wore as it fought to keep his body warm. He shivered constantly, managing to get only a little sleep. The frustrating numbness in his fingers and toes had all but become a part of him, and everything he did was a study in clumsy dexterity. The wind had picked up again, and as it whipped past him, Ian could feel the small ice particles that had formed on his upper lip.

He buried his head in the space his folded arms formed as they rested upon his knees. This gave him a little relief by cutting down on the surface area of his body exposed to the wind, but he still found himself hard pressed to keep the numbness in his hands and feet from increasing. Every time he awoke during the night, he could feel the pitter-patter of the snow on his face and he knew his next encounter with the darix would be that much more dangerous with several centimeters of the winter's white product covering the ground.

The following morning, after he had eaten and started off once more, he saw that the storm had not lessened any since the night before. When he neared the edge of the forest line, he broke off a stout branch almost two meters long. He would use this as a probing stick when he reached the higher ranges of the mountainside where the snow oftentimes remained throughout the year.

He then continued on, acutely aware that he no longer had the lecki to warn him of the approach of the darix. He fought a rising feeling of apprehension as the snowfall gradually increased, diminishing his visibility.

His eyes, which could make out only the nearest land marks, now functioned primarily for the quick detection of any approaching danger. More and more, Ian began to rely on his delicate sense of direction and an old yet reliable compass to guide him through the snow.

When it reached mid-afternoon, Ian could feel his boots sinking deeper into the drifting snow. He knew that soon he would be forced to stop and put on his snowshoes. When there were about two hours of daylight left, he could feel the ice beginning to form a thick layer around his eyes and under his nose. Wiping this away, he began looking for a suitable resting location where he could safely spend the night. It was in the midst of this search when he saw the darix footprint in the snow directly in front of him. There was little doubt that it was fresh, and he barely had time to react to the growl he heard behind him.

Pivoting sharply on his right foot, he slung his pack off in the direction from which he guessed his attacker was approaching and rolled sharply into the snow. He ignored the pain as his knee protested against the sudden wrenching of his act.

His gloved right hand shot into his overcoat and whipped out the machete-like knife that he had used during the first encounter with this pack. Completing his roll, he came to a kneeling position, only to find himself facing three onrushing darix. He flashed his knife toward them and, as he had hoped, two of them hesitated, apparently remembering their first experience with that weapon; but the third came on, and Ian braced himself as he quickly slashed at, and sank his knife into, the huge, black body of the darix.

There was a shrieking cry of terror as the animal recoiled from Ian's vicious stab and staggered backward. Ian could see that he had struck the darix a fatal blow, and as the wrathful beast madly lunged forth once more, Ian rose to his full height and, with both hands, brought his long blade down upon the weakened darix' neck, almost decapitating it.

He quickly stepped away from the dying darix and turned to face the other two, but they had remained back, apparently unwilling to risk a direct confrontation at this time. Ian, however, did not wish to let the darix learn that which they had been on the verge of discovering: that by attacking simultaneously in numbers, they would eventually overcome the power of the blade which he held.

Knowing that he had gained a rare but temporary advantage over the darix, Ian stepped forward and raised his knife high above his head. The two would-be attackers stood their ground only for a few additional seconds before retreating, subtly blending into the swirling snow. Ian sheathed his knife and returned to his belongings, suddenly aware of how tired he was. The air was thinner up here, and exertions such as he had just put forth were bound to take their toll. When it came to his life, however, he would gladly fight the darix under these conditions again and again, if he had to.

After resting several moments, he picked up his pack, bow, arrows, and probing stick, and somehow managed to continue his search for a resting place. His knee was beginning to give him appreciable trouble when he found a suitable spot that would last him for the night. Limping slowly, he walked up to and entered a dense growth of thickets that lay snugly against the base of a steep outcropping of rock. Crawling, he managed to force his way through the growth to the wall itself. Here, he dug a hole in the snow and rested, his eyes keeping an alert watch as the last hour of daylight slowly gave way to the dimness of dusk.

The snow stopped falling just before dark, but Ian was sure that the storm had not spent itself. He could expect more snow tomorrow, but now he was more concerned with his well being during the course of the coming night. He was no longer protected by the height of a tree and as the darix could very easily approach him, he was now faced with the task of remaining alert and on guard throughout the night.

An hour after darkness conquered the mountainside, the wind picked up again and Ian found himself fighting his rising apprehensiveness once more. Despite his many years of experience with the darix, he was not confident that the pack would not risk attacking him in the close quarters of the surrounding brush. In theory, he was breaking new ground by spending the night under these conditions. But if his efforts proved to be successful, he knew that such knowledge would come in handy during future encounters with these beasts. These thoughts circled repeatedly through his mind over the next several hours.

Twice during the night he thought he heard darix approaching him, but his fear never became reality. When morning finally came, the fatigue that dominated his body was more emotional than physical. He also knew that he had barely escaped the gripping effects of hypothermia during the coldest part of the night. However, the worst was hopefully over, for today was the day he would attempt to terminate his current status as hunted prey of the darix and return to his cabin, alone. His entire plan, however, hinged on locating a sparth, a large, herbivorous species which inhabited some of the most inhospitable, high elevation terrain on Refander.

After yet another monotonous meal of bread, meat, and cold juice, he crawled cautiously out of the thicket and began hiking for the fifth straight day. He was now in the middle of the lowest portion of the northwestern arm of the Pascalian Mountains, and as he shielded his eyes against the glare of the snow, he could make out a ridge several kilometers in the distance. The ridge marked the first high spot he had come across in some time, and it was likely a travel corridor for a variety of wildlife species. He was sure the sparth would take advantage of the shrubs and plants that would most likely be found there, not yet covered by the snow.

When he was halfway to his destination, the storm started up again. Looking to the west, Ian could see a heavy bank of clouds slowly moving his way. In another hour, the storm would reach another peak, and Ian was unsure of how long it would last after that.

He continued on, determined to let this ritual play itself out like others had before it. When he got to the base of the ridge, he found he had to don his snowshoes before ascending the slope. Twenty minutes later, he reached the top of the slope, only to find that it was narrower than he had expected. However, he really was not bothered by that discovery as he continued to stare at the sparth trail that lay at his feet. The most recent tracks were headed in a southeasterly direction. With the wind out of the northwest, he was in a perfect position to lie in ambush within the thick snow that bordered the eastern side of the trail.

Placing his pack a good distance in back of him and removing his snowshoes, he lowered himself into the snow, the bow and arrows ready at his side. He placed his hands inside his garments to allow his body warmth prepare them for quick action. It was not easy killing a sparth, but he had done it enough in the past to quell any nervousness he might have experienced now.

Ian lay motionless for over an hour, watching the recharged storm approach the intensity it had reached the day before. As the snowfall thickened and the wind increased in velocity, Ian could tell that a good-sized blizzard was in the making. Nevertheless, he refused to move, choosing to ignore the common sense that told him to at least find a shelter to which he could go should the storm reach unendurable limits.

His mind's internal debate over his safety almost caused him to miss his opportunity. The awe of seeing a 350 kilogram sparth step majestically out of the swirling snow, its long, gray-white fur streaming in the wind, temporarily got the best of him.

He lost only a couple of seconds, however, and before the four-legged sparth got too close to him, Ian withdrew his hands and readied his bow. Less than ten seconds later, he carefully released his semi-numb fingers and the arrow, true to its mark, sank itself deep in the flesh surrounding the sparth's heart. Like a sprinter, Ian leaped from his hiding place and raced toward the confused sparth, his once again mittened right hand withdrawing the long knife from inside his coat.

> *The sparth are slow reacting animals, relying on the enormous power in their legs as a means of defense. After being hit by Ian's arrow, the sparth had experienced several moments of molasses-like panic, during which time one would have thought it was trying to make up its mind as to what it should do next. Only when Ian was almost upon it did it decide to escape this bringer of the immense pain that now racked its body.*

As the sparth turned to gallop up the path whence it had come, Ian flung himself over the lumbering back of the huge herbivore. Knowing that he would be able to hold his position for only a few scant seconds, he wrapped his left arm around the neck of the terrorized sparth and used it for leverage as he plunged his knife into the lower right side of the animal's neck. He tried to leap from the sparth's back as he had in years past, but the narrowness of the ridge caused the seriously wounded sparth to lose its balance and topple down the slope Ian had just recently climbed.

Ian felt the sudden change in equilibrium at the last moment, and his hands instinctively grabbed on to the thick fur that covered the shifting body beneath him. Together, he and the sparth hit the side of the slope and after rolling for several confusing and haphazard moments, they came to a stop against a thick bank of drifted snow. A miniature avalanche that followed in their wake temporarily covered Ian and the bleeding sparth.

Ian, slightly stunned by the fall, was brought back to total consciousness by the coldness of the blanket of snow that had fallen on his face. He thrashed wildly, sending snow in all directions, only to discover he had not been buried as deeply as he had feared. Resting, he cast his gaze upon the twitching legs of the dying sparth, realizing that the only thing that had saved his life had been the cushion of the snow; without it, he would have been literally crushed beneath the massive weight of the powerful animal.

However, his job was still not over and, after freeing himself from the snow that surrounded his legs, he crawled to the front of the sparth...where he sickly discovered that his knife was no longer embedded in the animal's neck. If there was ever a time that he needed that weapon it was now, for the darix were sure to attack with the smell of so much dead meat to raise their courage. The animals had been without a significant source of food for at least five days now, and there was no doubt that they were starved enough to engage in a full-fledged assault.

He quickly floundered over to the base of the slope, wildly looking for anything that glinted under the reflected light of the falling snow. After several moments of this fruitless effort, he stopped and tried to calm himself.

However, soon he was down on all fours again, plunging his probing and hopeful hands into the snow until the cold white layer met his shoulder. Again and again his hands returned, empty of everything save a fist full of snow. He had gone a quarter of the way up the slope when the hair on the back of his neck started to rise. Turning, he saw two darix at the outer perimeter of his visibility, five or so meters from the carcass of the sparth. As their orange eyes glared at Ian, time seemed to slow to an almost undetectable pace. Then, the darix faded from sight, as if a giant had stroked the place they had been with a gargantuan white paint brush. Ian remained still for several seconds, telling himself that he had seen them, and only after he had thus convinced himself of that reality did he return to his search.

The wind had become a fanged menace and Ian could detect a rising anxiety within himself as he grew aware of the fact that he was fighting a losing battle against time. Halfway up the slope, he felt the return of the feeling that he was being watched, and as he slowly turned into the wind, he could see five darix standing at the base of the slope.

A barbed feeling of failure began to eat at his innards as he sank into the snow, all strength seeming to leak out of his cold and sore muscles. Too late, he remembered his bow and arrow, and tried to clear himself on that count by thinking it would have been too awkward to handle those weapons in close combat.

A sixth darix stepped in from the swirling snow, and Ian, abruptly envisioning his body being strewn wickedly across the snow, raised himself and edged slowly up the slope. He would always remember, however, that fear had seized his body at that moment: as he moved, his eyes caught sight of a sliver-shaped red stain off to his right.

Cautiously sinking his fist into the snow under the red mark, his muscles suddenly tensed with the excitement of returning strength as he made contact with the knife. Ian now stood up, waving the blade in front of him. He could see the look of respect that appeared to enter the darix' countenances.

Half walking, half sliding, Ian returned to the bottom of the slope and assumed a defensive position over the dead sparth's body. He, the prey, had suddenly become a hunter of equal calibre to the darix; and his observations had long ago shown that certain behavior patterns of the darix followed a set of rigid and predictable rules. This highly aggressive species travelled in loose packs, establishing territories wherever food presented itself in ample abundance. However, when two darix packs encountered one another and competed for the same food resource, the outcome was always the same: the pack that exhibited the most aggressive behavior prevailed and took over the hunting grounds to show their dominance, leaving the weaker pack to search elsewhere for food. Such was the violent, deadly, and semi-nomadic nature of the darix.

Accordingly, Ian had planned to lose this fight. Three times before he had reached this stage, with other darix, in other areas of the Pascalians; and each time, he had put forth a convincing effort.

As two of his present adversaries swiftly advanced upon him, Ian knew that his role as a predator had to be realistic enough to make the darix interpret his behavior as if he were a competing pack of animals. Lunging forward with his knife, he sought to stab the foremost of the two onrushing darix. But his blade cleanly flew through unoccupied air as the two darix nimbly retreated, yielding to the rush of two others that approached Ian from opposite sides.

Seeing he was a victim of a sudden change in strategy, Ian rapidly turned to face the nearer of the two newest attackers. Just as the creature's body came within striking distance, Ian darted to one side, thrusting his knife upward; but again, it met with empty air as the darix met Ian's swiftness with a startling quickness of its own. It swerved in the opposite direction of Ian's initial lunge, and as Ian swung about to meet the second darix, he found he was too late to counteract the latter's charge.

Protecting himself from the powerful jaws that strove to sink their teeth into his body, he allowed himself to be bowed over into the snow. Landing on his back, he found himself in an almost hopeless situation; but the darix, in the deep snow, was momentarily helpless, also. Taking advantage of what little time he had, Ian utilized his lower position in the best possible way by brutally slashing the underside of the darix that towered over him. The hideous bellow that issued forth from the bowels of the wounded animal spurred Ian on, and he was able to rise to his knees before the darix struck him twice in the chest with its claw-sharpened paw. Grabbing hold of his knife with both hands, Ian slicingly swiped at his foe's neck, but the darix apparently had seen enough of the lethal blade for it lithely sidestepped the attack and allowed three of its companions to continue the assault.

Ian, however, knew that the time to relinquish the sparth kill to the darix was now. Holding his knife in front of him, perpendicular to his body, he swung it in an 180 degree arc while backing away from the sparth's carcass and moving toward the base of the slope. The darix, respecting the weapon he held before them, refused to renew the attack. Instead, they approached and surrounded the sparth that lay half submerged in the mounting snow.

Seeing that his job was done, Ian began climbing the slope once again. The going was slow without his snowshoes, but he was pushed forward by the knowledge that he had to soon be on his way. The darix, after feeding, would want to make sure their newly-won "territory" was solely their own; and Ian did not want to be anywhere near them when they set off to explore their hunting grounds.

Upon reaching the top of the ridge, he hurriedly re-strapped his snowshoes, shouldered his pack, gathered his bow and remaining arrows, and began his descent of the eastern slope. Though he was now in unfamiliar territory, the storm had gained little in intensity and severity over the last half hour. Ian figured that, with reasonable luck, he would still be able to find a suitable shelter.

His decision to not return the way he had come was partly influenced by the obstructing darix pack and partly by the hope that there could be less snowfall on the far eastern side of this arm of the Pascalian Mountains. About an hour before sundown, he came to a large ravine lined to the right with high cliffs and large rock outcrops, and to the left with a fairly long stretch of a deeply sloped hillside. Deciding that this was probably the only major canyon within several kilometers, Ian began to follow the stream channel, knowing that it would eventually lead him down from the high elevations he presently occupied.

However, as his first priority was to find a place to rest, he took advantage of the present narrowness of the partially frozen stream and crossed it to search the right bank for a suitable shelter.

Fifteen minutes later, protected from the wind and snow by a hollowed out cavity in the right bank of the ravine, Ian huddled his aching body against the wall of the recess. He spent the next several hours rubbing and applying friction to the seriously numbed parts of his hands and legs. After that, he applied some of his salve to the gouges the darix had made in his chest and re-bandaged his knee, which had, for the most part, improved despite the abuse he had thus far bestowed upon it. He did all this with amazing care and quickness; and when he was finished, he sat quietly and listened to the slow, quiet patter-falls of the snow flakes.

Eventually, he drifted off to a state of semi-sleep, which allowed him to replenish his reserves of stamina and energy. He returned to complete consciousness only when his cold extremities needed attention.

Thus he passed the night, only dimly aware of the moment when the wind began to die down. The snow also had stopped during the night, and as he looked out from his shelter the following morning, Ian could see that the worst of the winter was probably over. He knew that it would be a challenge to get back to his cabin before the squalls that marked the coming of spring began. The sudden changes in weather that characterized Refander's amazingly short year had become second nature to him.

After eating heartily, Ian forced his body forward once more, sure that the excitement of blazing a new trail over the next several days would keep him moving at a good pace. He paused at the mouth of the cavity in which he had spent the night to appreciate the view of the gully in the absence of a blinding snow storm. Deciding to take his chances on the more constant terrain on the left side of the stream, Ian began moving down toward the narrow path of water.

But his legs suddenly froze when, from out of his peripheral vision, he caught sight of a darix about 50 meters to his right. Inwardly, his mind began to ask why these animals were so relentless, and his hand slowly reached inside his coat to rest upon and grasp the knife that was strapped there.

He felt a sudden loathing come over his emotions as he removed the knife, and he found it odd and somewhat perplexing that he had never outright hated the darix before now. Up until this moment, they had just been an animal he could do without.

Slowly he turned to his right, fully prepared for the ensuing fight. However, the darix, instead of charging, suddenly leaped up and sprinted off in the opposite direction, following the stream bank. And that was when Ian almost dropped his knife — for what he was looking at was not a darix at all, but a snow leopard!

He remained rooted to the spot, watching the snow leopard until it was out of the range of his vision. Everyone had said they would never survive on Refander, that predator competition or climate severity would quickly deplete their numbers; but what Ian had seen now proved that those suppositions were no longer valid. Yet, he had to be sure. Twenty-one Earth years had passed since he had last seen a snow leopard, and that alone warranted his making an attempt to verify the sighting.

Approaching the spot where he had first spotted the leopard, Ian saw that it had recently made a kill. Upon closer examination of the prey's skull, he saw that it was that of a small herbivore he had never seen before. Bloodied piles of white fur were scattered around the kill. A feeling that he had stepped into a biological paradise began to take hold of his mind. Looking at the paw prints surrounding the kill, he found that they were not unlike those that his grandfather, Paul, had shown him when he was on the *Stranahan*.

Contentedly sure that he had indeed witnessed the first snow leopard in many years on Refander, the question of how many there were now goaded him on. He followed the tracks before him for the whole day, observing with a bit of suspicious surprise that his snow leopard never left the bank of the now widening stream.

To his right, several kilometers in the distance, he saw the jaggedly steep beginnings of the tremendous northeastern corner of the Pascalian Mountains, where some elevations were probably as high as 2,600 meters. It was here, so his little-remembered knowledge of the snow leopards told him, that he expected most of the remaining leopards to be. Yet, by following the stream drainage, he was being constantly led to lower elevations. However, just before nightfall, he found that the tracks led to his right — up towards an out-jutting finger of the northeastern Pascalians that almost extended to the stream itself.

Ahead of him and to the north, he could see the tree line in the distance that led to the Tartan River, and he knew that the beautiful virgin forest that lay beyond would just have to wait, no matter how many temptations it threw at him. Turning to his right, he quickly followed the tracks up onto a plateau that broke off into several adjoining ridges, each of which extended deeply into the main mountain range.

It was here that two things brought Ian to an abrupt and startling halt.

One was that the leopard tracks he had been following had suddenly joined countless others, from which Ian was able to distinguish at least three different patterns and sizes — could he have stumbled across the central territory of a pair of snow leopards?

But the second, and more astonishing, discovery was the fact that mixed amongst all the snow leopard traces were the tracks of a two-footed animal — of a man! And as if some unseen force had been waiting for him to make that realization, the smell of burning wood nonchalantly drifted upon him, borne aloft by the slight wind.

Ian's hand went for his knife, and as quickly he stopped it, silently cursing his instinctive responses. Starting forward, he followed what he decided were the more recent of the human footprints even though they appeared to be at least a day old. Darkness overtook him soon after that, but he was already within a couple hundred meters of his unexpected stranger. He could see the flickering glow of a fire up ahead of him.

Less than four minutes later, he found himself standing at the mouth of a small cave, his body greedily seeking the warmth of the crackling fire that lay before him.

Disregarding the caution that flickered and flashed in the back of his consciousness, he called out twice. Several moments passed and, when no one answered, he uneasily decided to wait just inside the cave until its occupant returned. Glancing around, he took one step towards the cave's mouth but instantly froze as a rush of adrenalin coursed through his body. Just in back of him, at the perimeter of the fire's light, he could now see not one, but two, snow leopards. Though they were lying flat against the snow, Ian could see that their bodies were enormously tense, almost as if they were waiting for the right moment to leap upon him. For some time, Ian was apprehensively transfixed by the uniqueness of the situation. However, when the leopards exhibited no additional movement, he regained his balance and took another step in the direction of the cave's entrance — only to freeze once again, this time in response to loud coughing and hissing sounds produced by the large cats.

Turning, Ian was alarmed to see that the leopards had now risen to a crouching stance, their ears flattened back upon their heads. They were breathing rapidly and deeply, and Ian was baffled by the protective behavior they appeared to be showing. Deciding it would be better to wait outside the cave until someone returned, he began removing his pack. However, he stopped once more upon hearing a faint noise from inside the cave.

He called out again but, surprisingly, still received no answer. This time he reached for his knife without pause, and after pulling it out he headed up into the cave. Never did the thought occur to his curious mind that he should leave the area for the sake of his safety. The two snow leopards coughed and hissed at him, but seemed reluctant to carry out the attack which they had so threateningly advertised; instead, the silver-gray cats nervously paced to-and-fro among the dancing shadows of the firelight.

Somewhat assured that he was no longer endangered by the snow leopards, Ian ducked his head and slowly entered the cave. The first objects his eyes came to rest upon were the small piles of fruit that lay at the back of the cave. Next to these lay the fur of a sparth. There were more unusual items scattered about, but Ian's eyes, which had begun to adapt to the dimness of the cave, suddenly warned him of a figure off to his right.

Lowering his knife until it rested at his side, he turned to face a huddled figure in the corner of the cave and the sharp-pointed lance which it held. Again, Ian was transfixed, but this time, he knew, the power of language was to his advantage.

"Hello. I mean you no harm. Who are you?"

There was no answer.

Stepping to his left so more firelight could enter the cave, Ian re-sheathed his knife and repeated his question.

Again, there was no answer, but Ian, aided by the additional light, could now make out the general facial and body features of the person in front of him and he felt the heaviness in his lips and tongue as he forced the word, "Liraah?" from his mouth.

At first, there was no discernible reaction, but suddenly the woman whom Ian thought to be Liraah rushed upon him with startling swiftness. Somehow, he managed to narrowly dodge the spear she thrust at him and he quickly wrapped his arms tightly around her body to prevent her from causing any serious harm. But, to his astonishment, the woman was now limp in his arms, and he could see that the only materials keeping her warm were the sparth furs she had wrapped around her body.

He carried her back to the large sparth fur that he had seen upon entering the cave, and laid her gently on this. Alongside the fur, he discovered some crudely made weapons, among them stone knives and two additional wooden lances. He stared at the woman on the fur. She had to be Liraah — but how had she made her way to this remote area of the Pascalians? Had she been part of a larger expedition? If so, where were the others? And how had she escaped an attack by the leopards just outside the cave?

Ian figured he might never know the answers to those questions, and as he continued to stare at her he realized, somewhat uneasily, that the woman's clothing, her tools, and the entire cave bore the signs of a long and extended occupancy. How had she lived all this time, and travelled this far, apparently on her own?

If he remembered correctly, she had been only eight years old when the *Stranahan's* shuttle trip ended in catastrophe. She had been discovered in the Torrden Forests three weeks later, having apparently fed upon the natural fruits of the Refander woodlands. Everyone had wondered how she had survived following her near fatal encounter with one of the leopards, but Liraah had never answered those questions or even acknowledged that she had a recollection of those events. Her schooling had been difficult, as she had been ostracized by many of her peers, not unlike Ian himself. And, more importantly, she had still been at the Base Station when he himself had left.

Ian looked around the cave once more. The place had obviously been occupied for several years. If Liraah had come here alone, how had she traversed the enormous distances between the Base Station and the Pascalians without succumbing to the dangers of Refander?

He gazed once more at the thin, black-haired woman before him, at the same time slightly touching her forehead. Though his hands were still too cold to detect anything, he could tell by the pale ashiness of her skin that she was running a fever. He wanted to wake her to determine if he could help her, but he was afraid that in her delirium she would only attempt to attack him again.

Quietly removing his pack, he let his eyes scan the rest of the small cave. In the far left corner, a glimmering caught his attention, and when he examined it closer, he saw that it was a hand-dug depression holding water that had probably been brought in as snow.

Ian was about to search the remainder of the cave but stopped when he saw the drops of blood by the water's edge. Smeared in places, they trailed back to the sleeping figure on the sparth fur. Ian remembered how he had avoided being stabbed when the woman rushed him...almost as if she had been unable to obtain the correct leverage for a lethal thrust.

Returning to the woman's side, Ian gently raised the sparth fur that was wrapped around her legs until it was up to her knees. He did not have to look any further, for the worst of his fears had been recognized: her right calf bore the signs of a vicious darix attack. How she had ever been able to stand on it just now, Ian could not say. However, he knew there was little time to dwell on the issue.

Using the few meager materials at his disposal, he began cleaning the wound. After this, he grabbed his pack and removed his flask of salve. This he applied in generous amounts on and about the infected area. Ian guessed the woman had been attacked not more than two days ago, which meant the wound was still fresh enough for his medical treatment to remove most of the infective agents that would have eventually killed her had he not found her.

He could also see that this had not been her first encounter with darix or the other dangers of the Refander woodlands. Her legs boldly bore the scars of many a wound. Lowering the fur on her legs again, Ian then moved to sit some distance away from her so that he would not overly frighten her when she awoke.

Twice during the night he added wood to the fire, and noticed, with a rising suspicion, that one of the snow leopards was still within sight of the mouth of the cave.

Sometime after that the darix were upon him again, and he found himself fighting the dreadful creatures with his bare hands. Repeatedly, like a tireless machine, they rushed in upon him, sinking their jagged teeth into his flesh wherever they could find a good hold. And when they had severely crippled his body, they disappeared, leaving only his eyes and his feelings. Soon, even his vision failed, and the only sense that remained was the feeling that something was watching him, forcing him to reopen his eyes.

And he did...to find his hostess staring warily at him. The weapons he had seen last night still lay at her side. However, the fear and shock that had produced the incident last night were gone, and in their place Ian could see the caution and restrained interest which her expression now showed.

Forcing an exaggerated smile across his face, Ian quietly asked again, "Liraah?"

For a second nothing happened, but then Liraah — and Ian was now sure that this was she — managed a weak smile in return and nodded her head twice.

Ian's elation over this initial success faded quickly, however, when Liraah unexplainably uttered a low, slow whistling sound. Startled by this behavior, Ian silently watched as Liraah looked toward the cave's mouth. Following her gaze, he was seized by a sudden chill that stole through his body as he watched the snow leopard that had remained at the border of the firelight all night slowly approach the inner thresholds of the small mountain cave. It hesitated for a few moments before moving quietly toward Liraah, snow falling like magic dust from its silver fur. The leopard emitted a soft puffing sound in response to Liraah's putting her arms around its neck. As Ian continued to stare in near disbelief at the leopard and Liraah, he briefly recalled his own childhood aboard the *Stranahan*. He knew that several of the leopards, especially those that had been hand-reared from birth, had been quite docile and essentially as tame as some of the domestic dogs that people had kept as pets aboard the star ship. Yet, when Liraah released the leopard from her gentle hold, Ian froze as the cat cautiously approached him. The snow leopard sniffed him thoroughly, frequently producing a soft, drone-like purr, before settling down in the middle of the cave, apparently satisfied that Ian was not a source of danger.

Gradually releasing his breath, Ian wrested his gaze from the snow leopard. When his eyes met Liraah's keen-eyed expression, an easy smile broke across the woman's face and she pointed to him and managed, with a little difficulty, to say, "Ian Torrden, yes?"

The story of how Ian Torrden encountered Liraah, the only child born to Jase Johnson and his wife, Mona (whom Jase had met on Level Seven of the now ancient *Stranahan*), would never spread quickly. Although Ian felt it was his obligation to learn why Liraah was here and to inform her parents of their daughter's condition, he was compelled by little, if any, urgency to complete that task. Instead, he found himself simply captivated by Liraah's presence. Everything about her seemed to set her apart from anyone he had ever known. He had not had many opportunities to interact with her at the Base Station, and he now found the many rumors that had once been spread about her highly eccentric behavior were mostly true. He had not even expected her to recognize him, but she had been surprising everyone who knew her all of her life.

At first, Liraah had very little to say to him. However, as her leg began the slow process of healing, he persisted in his attempts to engage her in conversation. Ian knew he had to be patient — Liraah's reluctance to willingly communicate with others was well known, even to him.

In time, she was able to tell him of how she had been mauled by the darix. She had been in the forested area near the Tartan River, collecting fruits for the winter, when she had sensed the dark predators were near. Ironically, as Ian discovered later, this had been the same day on which the three darix had attacked him in open country.

However, Liraah still had trees to protect her, and as she cautiously worked her way in the general direction of the cave, she climbed whatever suitable growth that was available when danger threatened. Once she began nearing the end of the tree line, however, there were frequent clearings that had to be crossed, and it was in one of these that the darix got to her.

Here she stopped, and it was only after Ian had sat through a couple minutes of silence that he realized Liraah might be withdrawing back into her shell.

"What happened next?" he prodded, doing so in a quiet, almost soothing voice.

Liraah sat in silence for several more minutes, her fingers running lithely through the fur of the snow leopard that lay beside her. When she finally said, "I...lost one of them," the softness of her voice subtly disguised any meanings her words may have had.

They were sitting on a flat ledge that lay along the plateau which led to Liraah's cave. Spring had arrived, but not without the annual rain and snow squalls that always accompanied it.

Ian was about to question her further when he was struck by the sudden realization that Liraah had referred to the snow leopards and not the darix. Liraah had apparently spent several years of her life in the presence of snow leopards, and he had quickly discovered that it was not unusual for her to speak of them in so casual a manner. Ian was still trying to determine the link that existed between this woman and the leopards that mysteriously stayed by her side. As he gazed at her, he found himself attracted to her removed, but attentive, state of being.

Several days after he had found her, he had concluded on his own that the two leopards he had seen on that first night were the only ones which frequented the area surrounding the cave. The others — if indeed there were other leopards; and Ian was confident that this was so — were probably living at the higher altitudes to the east.

Ian knelt down to Liraah's side, envying the look of love and affection hidden in the woman's face, yet knowing it was not for him but for the snow leopard upon which her hand presently rested. Thinking back to Liraah's last words, Ian now began to perceive the importance of what she had said. As he had discovered his own way of dealing with the darix, here was yet another method that worked equally as well. Liraah never had to worry about the darix mercilessly hunting her. As long as she remained in or near the company of these leopards, she would likely be protected from any pack of marauding darix.

Of course, there was always the price to pay, as evidenced by what she had just said, but nonetheless, it was a strange and exciting way of conquering the wilds of Refander, and Ian was intrigued by the uniqueness of it.

Yet...

"Liraah, how did you manage to travel so far from the Base Station? How long have you been with these leopards?"

Ian knew these things were a secret part of her past which she might choose never to disclose to him; but he could no longer ignore his need to know the answers to these questions.

He slowly extended his hands and lightly patted the back of the snow leopard beside Liraah. The woman remained silent for a time before speaking, and as Ian continued to stroke the leopard's fur, he wondered if he, too, were becoming attached to the animals. It had not taken him long to distinguish between the two leopards that were constantly in and around the cave, and he had given each of them a mental name of his own creation because Liraah had never given any indication that she herself had names for them.

The wind had started to blow again, and Ian watched a brown lecki dart in and out of a grove of thickets not too far away. The leopard stared nonchalantly at it, apparently bored of the small animal. Ian watched the hyperactive lecki until Liraah's crystal voice brought him back to attention.

"I was cold...I...remember waking up in snow and seeing a leopard. When I got to the ship, every one was gone. When it got warmer, I...followed where the leopards went. At first there were many, but then there were fewer, and only one stayed with me. I looked for people, but never found anyone. But I saw many new animals I had not seen before. I watched them — and ate the fruits I saw them eating. I got sick when I ate wrong things, but I found out what the good foods were.

"Then...the darix found me. I tried to run, but ..." Liraah stopped again, then, almost as an afterthought: "That's the day they found me."

Ian leaned forward. If Liraah's story were true...how could she have survived?

Liraah seemed to sense his question and, for the first time, volunteered more information. "I could never remember that day. Everyone said leopards had attacked me. For years, I accepted that — but I was 17 when I saw my first darix — and I suddenly knew that I had seen them before, after the crash."

Ian shook his head. "The darix would never have let you live."

"I know. Everyone told me that. Ian, I believe the leopard saved me — he didn't attack me."

"Did you tell your father that?"

Liraah looked away. "No...that's the day I left the Base Station. I...Everyone kept asking me the same questions, over and over. They confused me. I thought...I was scared...I thought I had done something very bad or wrong. I wanted to find the leopards again — I had to know."

Ian could clearly see that the shock of the *Stranahan's* shuttle crash had remained with Liraah, even to this day. Perhaps only now did she feel a close enough bond with someone to talk about it.

"So you headed north, to the Four Rivers?"

Liraah slowly nodded. "I was lucky — I saw only a few darix. I first went across the Patsteel River, then the Rapibb, and then the Tartan. I searched for weeks without luck. But when I made it here, I saw a pack of darix kill two snow leopards — their bite is like poison to the leopards. The darix left the area on the next day, and when I entered this cave I found two baby leopards. I tried to take care of them both, but only one lived. She was my first."

Ian's attention was once more drawn to the young leopard beside Liraah.

He reasoned that the leopard Liraah had originally saved must have eventually bred and had one or more litters. Perhaps now Liraah had found the answers to the questions which had plagued her as a child.

"Does your father know you're here?"

Liraah's eyes grew even more vacant, and it was some time before she slowly shook her head.

"I shall be leaving soon — I can tell them you are here."

When Liraah looked quickly at him he hastily added, "I won't if you wish me not to."

Liraah stopped caressing the leopard, and her hand momentarily rested on Ian's before she placed it upon her knee. Looking away again, over the expanse of the plateau, she asked, "You will return?"

Now it was Ian's turn to pause. He had not given any previous thought to Liraah's question, and the abruptness of it caught him off guard. He knew that if he looked at the situation in the right way, he could say he was attracted to Liraah; but he was not sure he could trust his judgement, or his feelings, just yet.

After a time, he said, "Yes," not knowing if he was being true to either himself or Liraah.

She offered no answer, and soon the wind blew away all evidence that there had been words spoken between the two of them. Ian refrained from asking any more questions, and sometime later Liraah took him to several places on the plateau he had not seen before. Here, the view of Refander's mountains and woodlands was perhaps the most magnificent he had ever seen.

Over the next few days, Ian was inspired to teach Liraah how to use his bow and arrows, and these he left with her when it came time for him to leave. He planned to head west, around the northwestern arm of the Pascalians, before turning south to his cabin. After resting there, he would return to the Dome and find Jase.

However, these things were still in his future, and as he shouldered his pack for the first time in almost 20 days, his mind was more preoccupied with thoughts of Liraah and the snow leopards. He had spent part of yesterday evening, his last full day with Liraah, watching two of the snow leopards hunt and kill a sparth. He had been very much impressed by the calculated ambush strategy the animals used and by the power of their forepaws, which they utilized to initially strike the large sparth. Though the leopards had not allowed him near their kill, Liraah had been able to approach them and, with the aid of his knife, section off a portion of sparth meat which they later cooked over an open fire.

Now, as the smaller of Refander's two suns began to scale the horizon, Ian felt Liraah's hand on his arm. She had silently approached him from behind as he stood at the mouth of the cave. Turning, Ian touched her cheek with his hand and, for the first time, lightly kissed her, letting his hand run along the smoothness of her face.

She accepted this with a smile and, after several moments of silence, moved to the rear of the cave as silently as she had approached him.

Ian, still troubled by his inner feelings, yet knowing that Liraah had only quietly bid him farewell in her own unique way, found himself wondering if she had wanted to say more when she clasped his arm. His mind worried over this for the next several hours, as he started back to his cabin; and it was only when he spotted a pack of darix in the distance that he was able to force the vexation from his conscious thoughts. He did not wish to experience another long, grueling trip, battling with canine forces that taxed him of all but his final reserves of strength.

Nevertheless, as Ian Torrden would soon discover, his wish would only be partially granted.

Part 2. The Arrival

Josef Riverst, Commander of Refander, stood at the Port end of the Main Transport Hall, the cool wind streaming across the exposed scalp of his balding head. As he continued to stare at the combat shuttle that had landed just moments before, he began to think of what would happen if his fighter pilots had not been successful. He knew that Refander's options were limited, and dwindling fast.

The last of the shuttle's engines was still powering down when Derek Gloid emerged from the small ship and began to approach the Commander, his silver flight helmet nearly concealed under his massive left arm. Riverst found himself wondering, as he had many times previously, how the nearly 300 pound pilot managed to crawl into and out of the small combat shuttles so effortlessly.

When the large pilot was face to face with Josef, he extended a hand. "Commander."

"Captain," Josef returned, shaking the other's hand. "Did we get them all?"

"All but one, sir. We were able to destroy two of the three ships that penetrated our satellite defenses, but the third one got through. We forced her down somewhere in the northern Asinarians — but we can't confirm a direct kill. We may still have some time, though, if we can act quickly."

Josef's eyes cautiously wandered again from the pilot in front of him to the combat shuttle. He then returned his attention to Gloid. "You knew there was no room for error."

"Yes, sir."

Josef took a deep breath. "So what is it you propose to do?"

Gloid smiled broadly. "This is still our ball game. We did enough damage to that ship that it's not likely anything survived. But if something did survive, then we need to hunt it down and kill it — now, before it does whatever it came here to do."

The Commander took a deep breath. "I hope you can move mountains, Captain. I certainly don't have to remind you that one of these things nearly wiped out Earth."

Gloid chuckled briefly, then said, "If you don't mind my saying so, I hope that wasn't your too-little-too-late speech."

Josef took in another breath to regain his composure. "I haven't the time to mince words, Captain. Come on, we better deliver the bad news."

Without waiting for an answer, Josef turned and reentered the Main Transport Hall. The large fighter pilot followed in his wake. Within several minutes, they arrived at the Dome. Two pair of guards approached them, but Josef waved them off with a smile. He knew he could not afford to have anyone else know about the failure of the clandestine operation that had just taken place above the skies of Refander.

As the two men neared a two-passenger Government Dome Car, Josef motioned for Gloid to take the passenger seat. He glanced around once more before climbing into the driver's seat and setting the car in motion. "I've set up a meeting in the Government Hall with Lieutenant Rielick, and your boss."

Gloid broke out another laugh. "Baronhart? How is that ol' bastard? He should get around to talk to us troops more often, you know. So, who else is going to be at this shindig?"

Josef stole another glance at the captain of the combat shuttle fleet. If Gloid were not such a good pilot, Josef knew, Baronhart would have replaced him a long time ago for his wise-cracking habits and tendency for insubordinate behavior.

Steering around a crowd of pedestrians, the Commander began to increase the speed of the Dome Car. "I've asked Paula Witkor to be there also. We may need to do some P.R. control before this is all over."

Gloid did nothing more than simply nod his head, indicating to Josef that the pilot probably harbored no ill feelings to his Economics and Public Relations Advisor. By now, they had left the Main Transport Hall and were entering the central portion of the Dome. Josef knew that Refander's security officers were closely monitoring his every move. He only hoped that he had thus far managed to portray an atmosphere of calm.

Several minutes later they reached the Government Hall, and Derek Gloid silently followed Josef into the building and up to the second floor Council Chambers. Josef let Gloid enter the room first, then he followed, making sure to close the doors securely behind him. Turning to face the table that was at the center of the room, he saw that everyone else was already in attendance: Lieutenant Rielick was dressed, as usual, in his military uniform; Baronhart Dietrich, a middle-aged man with a pock-marked face, sat to the left of Rielick; and Paula Witkor, whose crew cut hair style and large-rimmed glasses had spawned many stories and jokes throughout the Base Station, sat on the far end of the table.

Turning to his Second in Command, Josef said, "Lieutenant Rielick, I believe you've met Captain Derek Gloid once or twice before." The Commander motioned for Gloid to take a seat before continuing: "Baronhart, Paula — I'm glad you could make it. I've brought Captain Gloid here so that he can brief you on the outcome of the mission."

The three officials started, showing their surprise and astonishment simultaneously. Josef realized, too late, that his staff read him all too well.

"Why the hell is he in here, with us?" Rielick asked slowly, rising from the table. "If there's a war to be fought, then he should be —"

"Lieutenant," Josef declared, raising his hand. The Commander looked around the room and, when he had decided that the control of the meeting was once again his, he declared, "Let us begin this discussion. Please be seated."

Gloid positioned himself opposite the three other officials while Josef himself took a seat at the head of the table, next to Rielick. "You all should know," Josef continued, "that of the three alien ships that approached Refander this morning, two were destroyed before they ever entered our atmosphere. The third one was shot down, but was not completely destroyed before crashing into the northern Asinarian mountains. Nevertheless, the Captain is still optimistic over Refander's chances. Captain."

Gloid responded to Josef's introduction by placing his silver helmet on the table in front of himself. He first nodded to the Commander before focusing his eyes on the other three people in the room.

"What Commander Riverst said is essentially correct," he began. "Whatever it was that we were grappling with up there today, it took all of our fire power to knock them out of the skies. I might add, they're feisty little devils — shit, man, they took out five of our shuttles before we knew what was happening. If we ever have to take on the motherload, I'm afraid we won't stand a chance. We're still studying the fire power we ran into out there this morning — their weaponry systems can probably outgun us in every area. But we did an ol' razzle-dazzle on 'em and now, with a little luck I believe we can still pull this out."

Rielick shook his head. "If one of those things is already loose on Refander, and alive, then we're already history. Damn it, Baronhart, I thought you said your fleet could handle this!"

Baronhart Dietrich, Refander's Security and Weapons Chief, folded his hands and looked directly at Gloid. "If you have something to share, Captain, I think now would be a good time to get it on the table."

Gloid flashed another one of his hallmark smiles as he pushed his seat back from the table to allow himself to distribute his weight more comfortably in the small arm chair. "Certainly. I've been working for some time on a contingency plan just in case we ever found ourselves in this kind of situation. Me and my crew — we've studied all of the logs downloaded from the *Stranahan*, including the medical files that were originally transmitted from Earth near the end of the plague. Those ships we engaged this morning are definitely made of the same material and are similar in shape to the one that the Sixteenth New World Launch encountered. And, assuming that there are some kind of life forms aboard, then we can also conclude that whatever beings they are, they may be carrying some unknown virus or bacteria that we've never seen before. But frankly, I don't think that's what we have to be concerned about."

"Why is that?" Josef asked.

"Well, look what happened on the Sixteenth. They never made *physical* contact with the ship they found, yet they still brought some deadly thing back to Earth. No one ever found the evidence to support a viral or bacterial infection theory, but I think that's because they were looking in the wrong place.

"You see, this is what we know. The Sixteenth is flying out to the wild blue yonder, right? Then they see this weird ship and decide to investigate it. While there, nearly a dozen people have the exact same dream in which they experience feelings of being lost and of dying. Sometime later, the Captain of the ship experiences another, more intense dream, in which he says he actually sees these creatures — he calls them gray beings. And he also says that there is a feeling of being lost, and of dying. After that, there's no more dreams, so the Sixteenth continues on its merry way, but soon the Captain becomes sick and eventually dies. Is it just coincidence that he's the first one? We may never know, but I don't think it is.

"Now, the next thing we know, there's two more sick people aboard the Sixteenth, then eight, then a couple dozen. Hell, by the time they decide to turn their ship around and return to Earth, nearly fifty percent of their population is dead or dying. Only about five percent of the crew and passengers are left by the time they reach Earth and, despite the best quarantine standards in place at the time, they have an epidemic on the loose within days of flying the Sixteenth's crew and passengers back to the Alaska Port. No one ever finds evidence of a bacterial or viral infection on Earth, either, but something still nearly wipes out the entire planet's population."

"Where are you going with this, Captain," Baronhart Dietrich asked. "All of this is old news. Bottom line is, this thing is on Refander, and unless we nuke it now, which is what Earth failed to do, then we're going to make the same mistake they did."

"Not actually," Gloid said, shaking his head, "at least not just yet. You guys are all missing the point! The medical files we got from the *Stranahan*, the ones that were transmitted from Earth, remember? We know this thing eats away at the brain, and we know there was a report of some kind of telepathic communication between the derelict ship and the crew of the Sixteenth. Look, I know you guys think I'm just a showboat pilot, but you do pay me to do a job. We just don't drink beer with the think tank fellas from Sci Data just to satisfy our thirst.

"Okay, here's my theory: this ship, in space, that the Sixteenth encounters. Something that's alive on that ship transmits a thought, or a set of thoughts, to the Captain. Then, while the Captain is asleep and dreaming, he unknowingly transmits it to some of his crew and the other passengers, who in turn, give it to others in the same way."

Rielick stood up from the table. "This is crazy, Gloid. You're saying that everyone on Earth died of some...thoughts they got from an alien we haven't even seen? How do you expect me —"

"Sit down, Lieutenant," Gloid interrupted.

For the first time, Riverst could see that Gloid had no smile to show. The pilot and Rielick stared at one another for over 15 seconds before the latter slowly took his seat again. Then Gloid continued.

"Look, if you guys have a better theory — hell, if you guys have *any* theory, please speak up, okay? I know this is off the wall, but we're all alone out here. There's gonna be no one coming to our rescue like they said in the brochures that they put together to get everyone to come on these New World trips in the first place. Jesus, for all we know, we may be the last New World colony left intact, and we don't even know if Earth has been able to rebuild itself. So, what we do here today has got to count. My theory is going to be the best thing that's going to be said across this table over the next half hour, so may I continue?"

Josef raised his hand again. "Please continue, Captain. We're listening now." A knock at the door quickly followed the Commander's mediation and Josef, now slightly irritated, hoarsely cried, "Enter!"

The door opened and a junior officer quickly stuck his head through the opening. "Commander, you have a visitor. He says it's urgent."

For a second, Josef's pulse began to increase. *Could it have already started?* he found himself thinking. Then something told him that if it had already started, all hell would be breaking loose. "It's going to have to wait," he told the officer. "We may be another hour, and make sure we get no more interruptions."

"Yes, sir," the officer replied, slowly closing the doors as he left. Josef thought he had seen a look of intense curiosity and perhaps even fear in the officer's face, and he now began to wonder if he was actually handling this whole situation correctly. Lowering his hand, he again turned to Gloid. "Okay, Captain, let's cut to the chase."

Gloid this time managed a smirk before continuing. "Thanks. I'm not going to take all the credit for what I'm about to say, since much of it is beyond me, anyway. But what me and my colleagues over at Sci Data have worked out is this: we still have to look at this thing as if it is a virus."

"I thought you just said it's not a virus," Paula countered.

"Right. We don't think it is, at least not like any virus that we know of. Listen, basically, what a virus is amounts to some kind of small particle carrying DNA. Once it gets into a host cell, it uses its DNA or combines with the DNA of the host cell to generate the synthesis of additional virus particles. Then, in some cases, it kills the host cell and new viruses are released to infect other cells."

Paula persisted. "Right, but you said a moment ago we're not dealing with a virus."

"Perhaps not, Miss Witkor, but it certainly behaves like one. What if we assume that these beings, or whatever they are that's flying these strange ships around the galaxy, are actually telepathic? We can then liken their capability at telepathy to the virus particle, which serves to protect and transmit the genetic material of the virus from host to host. And in this case, the genetic material is a set of thoughts, almost like some kind of independent intelligence that, once it gets inside us humans, runs amok. We ourselves unknowingly feed this thing when we sleep, actually while we're dreaming, and in the end we become slightly telepathic ourselves, capable of transmitting this thing to others before we die."

"So, if we follow this one step further," Baronhart said, "I hope you're not about to tell us that all we have to do to beat this thing is to stay awake for the next century."

Gloid shook his head again. "I personally don't think it matters. We can't keep this thing form coming into our heads, whether we're awake or asleep. No, what we have to do is stay away from it, as far away from it as possible."

Rielick pounded his first on the table. "That thing came here for a reason! It's not going to conveniently set up permanent camp in the Asinarians. Eventually, it will seek us out. I'm with Baronhart, let's throw all we got in a twenty kilometer radius around where that thing went down."

Gloid laughed aloud. "I hope none of you get my job anytime soon. You're talking about killing something you've never seen. You don't even know if it's alive, what it looks like, how it moves about, or where it might be now. We could throw all the fire power we want to the entire range of the Asinarians, but unless we have an actual target, we're wasting our time and we'll never be sure."

"Then how do we make ourselves sure," Josef asked, for the first time beginning to think that Gloid might be on to something.

"We send somebody in. It's a one way ticket, well mostly. They track this thing down, and kill it. Chances are, they'll be infected. Either way, we'll know in three days. If they are, that's where I come in — we'll take him out from the air. The buck won't get passed any further than that."

This time it was Baronhart's turn to laugh. "How do you know one man's going to be able to take this thing on? And even if you do succeed, how will you keep him from infecting others?"

"I've already thought of that. We've rigged up a device, something like a non-removable necklace or collar. It's got a transmitter in it. Whoever goes in will wear it, around their neck, and we'll know his position at all times. If our gopher fails to find this being, or whatever may actually be loose in those mountains, then Refander may not have much of a future left. But if he succeeds in killing this thing, then we can at least rest assured that the danger is over."

Baronhart turned to face the Commander. "Somehow, I get the feeling Gloid actually thinks this plan is going to work. If we have to wait three or four days before we find out if we've succeeded, it may already be too late."

"True," the Commander mused. "But it may be the best option we have, and I'm inclined to believe the Captain may have a good plan here."

"Commander!" Paula exclaimed, "I don't think the odds are in our favor. We're talking about sending one person up against this thing. It's murder! And besides, nothing we could do would be able to defeat this thing in the long run. It conquered Earth, and Refander hasn't one twentieth the power Earth is rumored to have had at that time."

"She's right, Commander," Baronhart added. "And besides, I don't think you could send anyone into those mountains against their will — and it will be against their will once they know what the risks are. No one in their right mind would have enough pride in them to risk that."

"But what if pride is not a factor, Baronhart?"

"There's nothing else that even comes close to making someone want to go through with this. I say let's bombard the hell out of the area in and around the crash site now, before it's too late. Our logs from the *Stranahan* indicate that's the one thing that Earth could have done but didn't do. It's our only acceptable option."

Josef could see the confusion that surrounded everyone in the room. Glancing up, he slowly said, "All of you are overlooking the point the Captain made earlier: we have to be sure. But enough of that. Right now,

I need some damage control. Baronhart, you and the Captain know what you need to do to get the combat forces ready. And Paula, I need a P.R. strategy ASAP. The Lieutenant and I will continue to discuss Gloid's plan — we'll let you know of our decision within the hour."

Gloid chuckled softly. "If you don't mind my saying so, Commander, I wouldn't even wait that long. Every minute counts right now."

Josef was about to reply when the door opened and the officer who had entered the room only 10 minutes earlier stuck his head through the doorway once again. "Commander, your visitor is still here."

Josef, his concentration broken, started to admonish the officer for interrupting their conservation, but suddenly realized that such an action might only lead to more questions being asked about their meeting with Captain Gloid.

The officer, somehow sensing Riverst's momentary indecisiveness, offered some clarification. "Commander, his name is Ian Torrden, and he wishes to speak with Jase Johnson. I didn't tell him about Mona, sir."

"Send him in." Josef knew that Jase Johnson was down in a remote part of the farm lands, trying to wipe out a contagious flu-like epidemic that had suddenly broken out down there. If anyone managed to get in contact with him now, word of mouth would have everyone racing back to the Dome, which would only worsen things if infected people were present.

The man who now entered the Council Chambers, Josef knew, was not quite a living legend although he had supposedly lived where no other person on Refander dared to even visit. However, why this man wished to see Jase, Josef could not say. When the officer closed the door behind Ian, Josef said, "My time is short, Mr. Torrden. Mona Johnson died several years ago. And if you wish to personally speak with Jase, I'm afraid that he can't be reached at the moment. If you care to, I'll take the message and deliver it to him as soon as possible."

Ian stared back at the Commander. "I'm sorry, Commander Riverst, my news is for his ears only. If you could tell me where he is, that would be sufficient for my purposes."

Josef shook his head, keeping his eyes on Ian. The latter's clothes were probably more patched and rugged looking than anyone else's in the entire Base Station. "I'm afraid that information is beyond me at the present. Are you going to be here at the Station for any length of time? Maybe I can have him reach you when he returns?"

"I'm afraid we are talking past one another, Commander. I am not really welcome at the Station — you know that as well as I. My separation from the people of Refander is not solely of my own choosing. People hold grudges for a long time and I prefer not to cause any disturbances here. Instead, I'll continue moving — I think Jase's path and mine will cross soon enough."

But what if pride is not a factor?

"Ah, Mr. Torrden," Josef said, stopping Ian, who had started moving towards the door. "I know how you feel — but more importantly, I'm beginning to faintly understand the kind of person you are. I think you and I can talk to, rather than past, one another now. Have a seat."

Josef, with a little effort, ignored the startled gasp of Rielick, who sat beside him.

Part 3. The Encounter

As Ian restrapped the communication device onto his belt, he hoped that the location coordinates he had just transmitted to the Base Station would turn out to be the actual hiding place for whatever it was that he'd been tracking for the last two days. Now, as he stared at the mouth of the large cave just ahead, Ian wondered if the moment he'd both looked forward to and feared had finally come. He checked the laser rifle that rested under his right arm, making sure that it was fully charged and ready to perform the job he had come here to do.

He still remembered the briefing that Commander Riverst's staff had given him yesterday. By late afternoon, he'd found himself outfitted with an air shuttle, the laser gun he now carried, a two-way radio, and other necessities that he himself had asked for. It had not taken him long to locate the site where the alien ship had crash landed. He knew that he may have been the first human to ever approach one of these ships so closely, and as he looked through the remains of the wreckage he recalled the mixed feelings he'd felt when he saw the tracks leading away from the craft.

He had transmitted the exact coordinates of the crash site back to the Base Station before setting out on foot to follow the trail of tracks that had been left by whatever alien life form had emerged from the strange vessel. The tracks appeared to be only remotely similar in shape to a human's, but they at least suggested that this organism was a bipedal traveler. It had taken Ian well over one whole day to follow the traces that the alien had left, but he at least had kept his promise to Commander Riverst: not once had he lost the trail.

Now, as yet another day on Refander threatened to come to an end, Ian found himself staring into the maw of this large, Asinarian Mountain cave. Although the trail he'd been following clearly led into the cave, Ian knew that he still had to be sure that this was indeed his quarry's current location. Captain Derek Gloid would accept no less.

As Ian thought briefly of the Captain, he raised his hand and touched the metal collar that encircled his neck and continually transmitted a signal of his current location to Captain Gloid's fleet of combat shuttles. The device was uncomfortable, and made it hard to swallow; in effect, it was not that much different from a life sentence, which is what it felt like. Ian knew that if he did encounter the alien entity in this cave, he may be killed outright by it; or, he may somehow survive his encounter. If he survived, then he would hopefully have been successful and destroyed whatever it was that he had thus far followed to this site. And, assuming that he got that far, he knew that Captain Gloid and his crew were following his every move somewhere in the skies above Refander. If he made any attempt to return to the Base before 72 hours had elapsed, they would kill him, too, as if he were just another alien entity. Just to be sure.

Ian was about to step forward, when he stopped once more. In his mind, he could see Liraah's face, and he thought back to his meeting yesterday with Refander's government officials. All of them had told him this might very well be a one way ticket. Picking up the communicator from his belt again, Ian opened a channel to the Base.

"This is Base Station Dome, Ian, what do you got?"

Ian instantly recognized Lieutenant Rielick's voice. "Is the Commander there?" he asked.

"That he is," Rielick quickly returned.

Ian paused for a moment, then said, "Commander, if...something happens, and I don't return, please tell Jase, and no one else, that I have found his daughter and that she's still alive."

A few seconds passed before Ian heard Commander Riverst's voice. "What? Liraah? Is that why you wanted to find him?"

Ian smiled at the surprise he'd detected in the Commander's voice, and then he simply replied, "Yes."

And that was the last word the Base Station officials heard Ian utter before the grandson of Paul Torrden entered the cave in the northern Asinarian Mountain range.

Ian, took several steps forward. But he stopped once again. He knew that he'd volunteered to do this, but was he really up to it? Yesterday, Commander Riverst had stated the obvious: Ian was a natural, perhaps more qualified than anyone else on Refander to follow the tracks of a foreign life form through the rugged terrain of the Asinarian range. But there was more. Much more. Ian had thought more about his father and grandfather during the last 12 hours than he had at any other time in his life. Was he about to embark on the same, ill-fated path that previous Torrdens had taken? Or would his actions here today finally earn his family name the respect it had always deserved? Ian shook his head, suddenly frightened by the spirituality of his inner thoughts.

He glanced around at the nondescript, brownish walls of the cave's interior. Then he looked directly ahead, wondering how long the main passageway ahead of him extended into the mountainside. The black pit of the cave's main corridor appeared to beckon to him — sadistically, cryptically. After several more minutes, he turned on the flashlight he had brought with him and started forward once again.

Consciously, he slowed his pace to a cautious walk, and he briefly envisioned himself as a lone darix, stalking its prey. The fluctuating shadows given off by the flashlight generated strobe-like images of frightful expectation against the cave walls. He had spent about five minutes walking deeper and deeper into the cave when he stopped once more to allow his eyes to become more accustomed to the dimness within the cave. On the ground, in front of him, he could still see the tracks that had led him to this cave; they extended ahead of him, into the darkness. Ian knew that with each step he took, he must be getting closer and closer to the alien being. He tried to picture what he would find, but his thoughts only returned to the briefing he'd been given yesterday. He wondered if he would be able to locate and kill the creature before it used its telepathic powers on him. Suddenly, the impact of that thought shocked him. Would it be able to read his mind? Had it discovered his train of thought, why he had come here?

He sensed his body trembling and he tried to calm himself. *This is not for me,* he thought, as inner suspicions began to rise within him. And then he heard it: a sound, coming from every direction, surrounding him. He tensed, then an artificial sensation of blackness overcame him. It was beginning.

The sound was...he tried to find the words to describe it, but could not do so. Troubled, he listened some more.

It was...it was like...a scream...yet, a scream with music to it. It was dull, and yet piercing; it flowed and yet...it jumped. But it moved, and he moved with it. However, he seemed to be standing still, and he knew that this was the actual truth. He raised his right hand in front of his face, instinctively, to feel for anything that was ahead of him.

And that was when the horror of it came to him, for his hand was still at his side even though he had given the impulse to his arm for it to be raised. *This must be the first handicap I have to adjust to,* he thought. As he fought the panic that strove to overtake him, he tried to reason how his physical reflexes had apparently been slowed to a mere fraction of their normal speed. Yet, it was odd that his brain still functioned at the normal rate — or so it seemed. Then he felt a twinge, a quick throbbing in his head. Like something coming in, intruding, violating his inner thoughts. He knew then that his mind and all its associated thoughts had been...exposed...to something elusively foreign to him. He tried to identify with his mental interpretation of the event, and slowly, ever so slowly, he formed a hypothesis that his mind had been merged with another's thoughts. At once he tried to mentally shut down the doors and pathways in his brain, afraid of what the alien being might find lurking within his mind. Or was it just that he, Ian Torrden, was afraid of what was there? *Damn!* his mind yelled. Had he already failed in his mission? Would he die before he even got to see the alien entity he had followed to this cave?

Ian was dimly aware that his arm was extended at a 45 degree angle away from his body now, involved in fulfilling the impulse which he had given it two minutes ago.

However, at that moment, two things happened. In his left eye, a dull light appeared, as if from far away, calling him. He felt a compulsion to approach this light, to discover what it really was and resolve the mystery that surrounded it. Then he felt his legs moving forward, walking once again — but ever so slowly! It was like walking through a thick, dark swamp. And, damn! that light kept calling to him, telling him that it held more than what he saw; intriguing him; teasing him.

Then, in his right eye, he envisioned a land with a castle upon a cliff. No! with a castle that was built right into, and thus constituted, the cliff wall. It was majestically surrounded with trees, vines, and flowers, and the whole structure was enshrouded with fine mist. Men and women were moving about the castle and in the courtyards, and some appeared to be playing a type of musical instrument. Ian was on top of another cliff directly opposite the one at which he was looking. And then the irony struck him.

He was no longer looking at this; he was experiencing this, he was here! And yet —

"Hello, who are you?"

Ian wheeled around. Before him stood a woman with long, black hair and questioning eyes. Her beauty was enticing...and, at the same time, disturbing.

He was about to answer when the swiftness of his last action caught his attention. But the music — yes, he could still hear it, if he concentrated on doing so — it had slowed his movements when he had first heard it.

He was moving slowly — slowly toward the light in his left eye; or was the light ahead of him; and was he moving through a tunnel toward it? Was it the same kind of reality that now existed as he stood on this cliff top? As he stared at the woman, his arms were empty. Yet somewhere else, somehow, he could feel the cold metal of the laser rifle that he had carried into the cave. Was this the kind of waking dream the Captain aboard the Sixteenth New World Launch had first described so many years ago?

He could not quite be sure of anything, and the confusion of it twisted his worried mind. It was as if he were...in two different places at the same time. "Yes, yes, that is it!" Ian was not aware that he had spoken out loud, so engrossed was he in his thoughts. He temporarily forgot the woman ahead of him as he became involved with his elucidation: he was a man of two wills! His left eye, which he knew controlled the right side of his brain, was compelling him to move through a long tunnel — a journey which brought him closer (yet still so far away) to that ever-curious light. And it was this same compulsion which instinctively made him move forward, deeper and deeper into the cave.

And the left side of his brain — despite its experiencing what was happening on this land atop the cliffs — it also wanted to approach that light, even though it seemed more removed from that activity.

So...he was not actually a man of two wills. He had one will, one goal — to find that light. It was just that he was in two different places at the same time. Or was he just fantasizing, hallucinating in his mind? But everything seemed so real, so —

"*What* is it? Where are you from? You're definitely not one of them."

Ian turned his attention back to the woman. She was dressed in primitive clothes made from the skins of some animal, and her general appearance indicated that the forest had been a part of her life for quite some time.

"One of whom?" Ian asked.

After a moment's hesitation, she pointed across the valley to the far cliff, indicating the castle.

"Why would I be one of them?"

"I did not say that you were," the woman replied. "But I still want to know who you are and where you are from. They —" and she pointed at the castle again " — are the only people who live in this land. There's no one else within seven days of travel."

Ian started to answer, but stopped when he heard the music rising, forcing its way to the front of his mind. Only this time it was not moving him so much as it seemed to be talking to him, trying to tell him something. He shook his head and looked at the woman again.

"I'm Ian. Ian Torrden. And I...I'm from a place called Refander."

His words produced a wary expression upon her face. She eyed him closely, then said, "I am not familiar with that land, but you can tell me about that later. Where are you going, then?"

Ian laughed a little hesitantly. "I don't know if you will understand this, but I'm trying to find the end of a long, dark path; but that path does not exist in this land — or in this world, for that matter."

She smiled. "You are strange. And I like that. What you say is confusing, but you have no weapons on you, so come on and tell me about your long, dark journey." With that she turned and headed back to a line of trees whence she must have come.

Ian had no choice but to follow. But even as he took his first step, he heard the music inside his mind again — it was calling to him, telling him to do something; yet, he could not fathom what it was.

He shook his head a second time, then hurried to catch up with the woman, who was already well ahead of him.

When he was walking by her side, she glanced at him, grinning. "Call me Foleena, if you like." At that moment they entered the forest and he matched her agility as she deftly picked her way along a little worn trail.

"So, where am I, Foleena?" he said to her at length. "Maybe knowing that would help me."

Foleena looked back at him, frowning. "I thought you said your path could not be found here."

"I know, but I must be here for some reason."

"This place is not anything in particular," she answered. "It's the only land where I and those people of the castle have ever lived, that's all. You'll have to travel far before you will meet people other than our-selves."

Ian fell back into silence and continued to follow her. Five minutes later they came to a small clearing, in the center of which the remains of an old campfire lay. A somewhat large stone lay near the charred wood, and a fair amount of unburned twigs and sectioned branches was stacked on the opposite side of the clearing. Foleena pointed to these.

"The sun will be setting very soon. See if you can start a fire. There's some flint and steel with those twigs, okay? I'm going to get us some food."

She turned to leave as Ian, without thinking, said, "There are no darix here?"

Foleena paused, a frown crossing her face. She appeared to run the question silently through her mind a second time. Glancing confusedly at Ian, she attempted a smile and then disappeared into the brush.

Ian stared after her for a moment before he gathered together some of the twigs and laid them carefully over the remains of the old campfire. Apparently darix did not exist here, wherever 'here' was. After a few trials with the utensils she had left, he managed to get a good fire started. When it had been going for several minutes, Foleena returned. She observed the fire and then looked at him.

"Obviously not your first. You, too, know the woods pretty well. Here." She handed him several kinds of fruit; they were wet, and he guessed she had washed them in a stream or some other source of water. "They're nutritious, especially when meat is hard to get."

Foleena motioned for him to sit down against the small boulder.

"The wind usually blows from the north at night — that way you will be shielded."

She then sat down opposite him.

"What about you?" he asked.

"I've been here a long time in these forests," Foleena said. "Besides, my clothes are warmer than they look."

They sat in silence for a while, and by the way the firelight danced on Foleena's face, Ian became conscious of the fact that night was upon them. He pulled his shirt closer around his neck, wishing he had his sparth overcoat, and as he did so, he heard Foleena's voice.

"Now, tell me about your search, Ian. What are you trying to find?"

Ian looked at her and shrugged his shoulders. "I don't know that much about it myself. I'm here...and yet I'm not. And where I'm not, I'm trying to find that which awaits me at the end of what feels to be a long, dark path, as I've said before. I'm sure that doesn't help at all, huh?"

Foleena was silent, a troubled look coming into her face. But Ian did not take notice of her, for in his mind, the ever-present melodious sound was calling to him again. Suddenly, there was music all around him. The sweet notes were everywhere. As if in a trance, he looked at Foleena and said: "Can you play me some music? Will you play for me?"

He was dimly conscious of the music receding from his mind, its job apparently done. From far away, he heard Foleena utter a cry. As he focused his gaze on her, he was suddenly released from the dream world which had momentarily ensnared him, and he saw the worried look in her face.

"Foleena, I —"

"Please do not ask me to play music for you. I...I can not."

"I'm sorry. I don't know why I asked you that, Foleena. But —"

She leaned over and surprised him by taking his hands. "It's okay. This land is enchanted. Tomorrow, you and I shall go far away from this place — to where I live. You can relax there, and maybe you can find a way to get what you are searching for."

Ian looked at her for a few moments. Then, smiling, he said, "That sounds fine," though inwardly he felt he was fleeing from something which he should confront.

Foleena's eyes averted his for a second, and then she kissed him. As their lips touched, the light in the left eye of his other self fleetingly increased in its luminosity. Ian even felt he could see faint, wavy lines. But now they were gone, and the vision had vanished as if it had been suddenly afraid of Foleena.

He looked at her and at once discerned her questioning stare. At length, he asked, "Just where exactly do you live, Foleena?"

"In a place where harm is not always lurking around the corner, where we can enjoy being with each other and experience those things which give us pleasure."

"Do you go there often?"

She avoided his eyes for a moment before saying, "Too many questions, Ian. Tonight you need some sleep. It is getting dark."

Ian shrugged his shoulders, puzzled over her response. As he watched her, Foleena drew close to the fire, preparing herself for sleep. The disturbing feeling he had experienced when he first saw her came back to him now, and he forcibly turned his gaze away from her so that he could prepare himself for the cool night that promised to come. Then he stared into the fire, and as the flame reduced itself to dying embers, his eyelids dropped lower and lower...and then he was asleep. His dreams, fleeting glimpses of confusion, were of her.

When he awoke, his first reaction was one of astonishment; he had actually slept! He wondered if his real body had slept, too, or if it had continued its slow procession through the cave. He then tried concentrating on his left eye, but he only found that the mysterious light was just as far away as it had ever been.

Then he looked for Foleena, but she was nowhere to be found. His thoughts were then interrupted by a new voice.

"I see you met Foleena last night."

Ian turned to his left and before him stood yet another woman, somewhat smaller than Foleena. She had long, blonde hair that fell to her sides, and she had on a brown leather hat that was decorated with a wavy brim. She wore a poncho and jeans, and across her breast dangled an instrument which looked like a recorder, suspended by a chain that was looped around her neck.

"My name is Bliss. I come from the castle," she answered his inquisitive look.

"The castle?" Ian pointed at the instrument. "Is that what I saw everyone playing?"

Bliss touched the instrument. "This? Yes, everyone there knows how
to play one. It is called a yularra."

"It looks like a recorder."

Bliss smiled. "It is more than that. I'll play it for you some time and
you shall see."

"I take it Foleena does not have one of those? She said she could not
play when I asked her to do so last night. You do know her, don't you —
you look like you have been in these forests often."

"Yes, I know her," Bliss returned. "I live at the castle but, as you have
noted, I spend most of my time here.

"As for why you wanted her to play for you — this is a land of peace
and music. The land talks to its people, it yearns for music. In return, it
gives us knowledge about the universe and the beings which populate it,
and the factors which influence the lives of all. And that is what you
wanted to hear: music."

Ian got to his feet. "So where is Foleena now? Where has she gone?"

Bliss eyed him carefully. "She left when she knew I was near. What do
you think of her?"

"I — I like her...but she, or something about her, is strange. But, I'm
not too sure of anything right now."

"That is a good start, though. Come, let me play music for you. You
will understand more afterwards."

She turned and started off, heading neither in the direction of the
castle nor in the direction in which Foleena had been leading him.

"Don't worry about Foleena," she said, as if reading his mind. "You
can come back here afterwards, if you like."

Ian hesitated only a moment longer before following Bliss, his mind
blazing with questions.

"You appear to know a lot about what happened to me last night and
yet you do not even know who I am. My name is Ian Torrden."

"I only appear to know a lot because I know Foleena all too well. As
for you, you are still a stranger and I meant to ask why you are here. No
one other than the people of the castle have walked this land since I was
born."

Quickly, Ian told her what he had related to Foleena the night before
concerning his double existence problem. When he had finished, Bliss

turned and looked deeply into his eyes, almost as if she were fascinated by
what he had said.

"Can you help me?" he asked her.

"I believe I can," she said, mistily. Then she turned and was off again.
Two minutes later they arrived at a small stream, and here she sat down
on the trunk of a fallen tree and motioned for him to sit down in front of
her, on a flat stone. "Watch," she said, unclasping the yularra from the
chain. She raised it to her lips and began to blow into it. A melody came
forth that at once made Ian feel at ease. It was a sad song, but yet it had
meaning to it. Each note was like a gentle bubble bursting in the air. He
saw flowers of different shades of purple and green rising toward the sun,
rain lightly falling on the petals and sepals. On the horizon, a rainbow
formed, and from the rainbow's end, a delicately buzzing insect came and
gathered nectar from the flowers and then returned to the fabled pot of
gold.

Then Ian stared at Bliss' hands. Her fingers were a blur as they flowed
over the finger-holes of the slender bore. However, what held his attention the most was the apparent presence of two more bores over which
her fingers also managed to pass.

Then she removed the yularra from her mouth and looked at him.

"What did you see, Ian?"

He described the flowers and the rainbow. She nodded her head when
he was done. "Good."

"But — I saw two more bores on the yularra, didn't I?" He felt stupid
in asking because, as he looked at the instrument, it still consisted of a
single tube. Thus, he was surprised at her answer.

"Yes, you saw three bores altogether. One, the one you see now, is for
the music that you hear. Another is for the images that you see, and the
third is for the poems that you hear. You can not hear any words for your
ears are not trained to the yularra yet, and meaning is the hardest thing to
get out of music."

Ian nodded slowly, trying to comprehend Bliss' explanation. "But images and meaning are abstract and subjective, are they not?"

"In a sense. But listen again." Bliss put the instrument to her mouth
and began playing once more.

Even though Ian's eyes remained on her, he travelled to a far mountain
where, as they fell, the snowflakes danced and sang to him. Still, he could
not hear the words (and how he wished he could!). Above him, he saw

the snow-laden clouds soar by; and below him, a sparth stepped out from a thicket of trees. Ian then became one with the mountain and he experienced the lives and deaths of the many animals over the ages — the predators and the prey of a geologic lifetime; and he saw and felt the joy of this undisturbed, evolving equilibrium. And then he became a rock and he flowed viscously with the other rocks in the mountains, and he saw the tiniest atoms which collectively made up the crystals to which he owed his very existence. Then he grew and he became the mountain itself, and the mountain became a volcano and he experienced the plea-sure — never thinking that there could ever have been pleasure in it — of erupting and pouring himself out over the land, melting, flowing, and freezing back into rock to return to the earth and do it all over again.

And then he was back in front of Bliss and he realized she had stopped playing. She was looking at him now.

"I know what it is that you are looking for, and I will try to help you find it."

She paused, and as she did so, Ian discovered that the light in the left eye of his other self was closer; closer but still so far away. He could, however, almost distinguish the lines that he had seen previously. Bliss was indeed helping him.

"What is it?" he asked her anxiously.

"It's something that most people think they have; but they lack the ability to recognize it and that is why they are so confused when they lose their false conception of it — an imitation which they believe to be the real thing.

"I can not tell you what it is, for you must find that out yourself. I will, however, help with the yularra. Sit back and close your eyes. I'll play you one last song. It's the best that I can do."

Ian did as he was told, and soon he heard her notes. They pleaded; they questioned; they sought. And then they rose, coming faster, and he rose with them — through the trees, the air, the atmosphere, and into the limitless arena that was the realm of space. The stars twinkled and glit-tered and sang to him, and this time he understood what they said:

> *There lives a Rabbit, across the sea,*
> *and over the ocean of time and space*
> *it tries to tell us that you and me*
> *will be free of this darkness, such foul place.*

A Raven ever haunts us, screaming its call.
He flies and he soars, eyes piercing the night.
He beckons, shrieks — and it's clear to all
that ere the day's done, many shall take flight.

Some fight, some die, some cower in fear.
Some think precious thoughts and try to stay clear.
Some stay, yet turn 'way, bathed by a tear.
And some, to the sea, go tonight, when clear.

Fighting the oceans, climbing the hills,
a trip through time to a Rabbit so fair.
And in a mountain, to cure all ills,
we find what we seek, so tender and dear.

A blazing white light, yet so much more,
the Rabbit consigns to us all to keep.
And in the Springtime from us shall pour
tears for what we found, gladly shall we weep.

When the stars had stopped singing, Ian looked around and found Bliss at his side. They moved past moons and suns and other worlds. And they finally came to a land engulfed by a tremendous fog, and Bliss took him down. They floated just above the ground, still flying, she leading him by the hand.

Bliss showed him the Cosmos of all times and places, a being who was a god of the elements; and Ian felt hot and cold, and experienced a lifetime of pneumatic interactions between his body and the atmospheric influences.

Then, on through the fog, and Bliss brought him to two hideous black shapes which foreshadowed a distant moon and produced feelings of anger, cruelty, and pain in Ian. He screamed in his agony ...

...and Bliss whisked him through the fog again to a mythical unicorn standing in the sunlight; and from the gorgeous beast flowed many emotions that gently struck Ian, and he knew he had to find some way to understand them.

Then the sunlight faded and the fog returned once again. Through it they sped, Bliss and he, and they came upon a meadow, in the center of which stood a sagacious old man from whom emanated knowledge of the universe and the individual. Ian suddenly felt that he was in free fall, a harmless speck in the world's largest expanse of sky, as he tried to comprehend it all. Abruptly, he knew that this...this fantasy was more real than anything he had ever known.

And then he was back by the stream, sitting on the flat stone. In the left eye of his other self he could see a swirling mist enveloping the lines which appeared in the bright light; he knew that he was closer, and he could sense the calling of the light was stronger now. He wanted so much to reach the end of the pathway that led to this intriguing vision.

He looked at Bliss. She was staring at him, and she looked tired. "What do you see, Ian Torrden?"

Ian shook his head. "I'm close — so close that it seems to be only out of focus. Can you play me another song? I heard the words this time."

Bliss sighed as she turned her gaze to the yularra. "I can play you many more songs, but if that last one did not allow you to completely see what you search for, maybe no other song will. I have been told by my people that my version of that song is the strongest that has ever been played on the yularra in many generations."

"Your people?" queried Ian. "Why did Foleena not play for me last night — is she not one of your people, too?"

"Yes, she is. She is also very shallow — you would probably find that out if you spent some time with her. And it takes a deep understanding of people and one's self to play the yularra. She tried the yularra once, but was afraid of the images and feelings it produced inside of her. Because she could not play, she chose to isolate herself out here in the forest. Most of us still live in the castle.

"I myself spend a lot of time here because it brings me solitude when I need it. Come, I'll show you where I usually stay. It's farther up the stream."

Ian followed her, but his mind was still on the words that Bliss had spoken. He just could not quite believe what he had heard. In his eyes, Foleena had appeared to offer more than the simplicities Bliss had described. Maybe if he could see her again he could be sure? He knew he had felt something for Foleena. But he also knew he was beginning to like Bliss as well. Sometime he would have to make a choice, he realized — but who? Was it possible that his decision, when and if it was made, would play an important part in the outcome of this experience? He could sense a definite frustration growing within himself for not being able to focus the image that his left eye saw; and he knew that within that image lay the answer to his questions.

They soon arrived at the place of which Bliss had spoken. She led him through a hole in the face of a rock wall overlooking the stream. Once inside, Ian was not too surprised to see that it was exceptionally clean. There was some food, blankets, and several candles.

They ate some of the food, which consisted mostly of dry bread and fruit, and drank some water. Then Ian asked her, "Will you play me another song?" and she said, "Yes."

During the next two days, Ian explored the area immediately surrounding the tiny cave. In the evenings, they lit the candles and she played him many songs which took him to numerous, fantastically beautiful lands. He saw trees that sang, moons that rose and set with the sun, and snow that fell even on the hottest of worlds. And once, when she had played him a song about a woman who rode a silver creature through the forests of a crystal world, Ian asked her to give a repeat performance. She complied, and played him the song again; only this time, it seemed to grow in its realness and beauty. Afterwards, as if she had shared his feelings, she had whispered, "Love me, Ian."

He knew it was not a seduction or a perversion. The yularra had provided them with happiness, sadness, and so much more; and though their relationship had developed in a totally new way, their feelings were the same, and each of them was aware of the other's emotions at that moment. Amidst this awareness, Ian came to her and kissed her, and as he held her in his arms, he could feel the womanliness in her. He smelled the cool freshness of her hair. He touched her breasts, kissing her again. They slowly knelt to the floor, staring deeply into each other's eyes. Quietly laying their clothes to one side, the two of them slowly became one, taking a trip that was just as real as any they had taken with the yularra.

On the fourth day they took a walk down to the stream to the fallen tree where Bliss had first played the yularra for him. Here they stopped to lie in the sun. At length, Bliss said:

"I'll be leaving soon. It is a custom of our people. We live here so many years of our lives, and then we travel to many other lands and learn the

ways of many other people. When we return, we have a better understanding of the world, of people, and of ourselves.

"Do you want to come with me? My elders have said they have never
seen anyone play the yularra as fluently as I. Maybe I can yet make a song
that will help you find what you are searching for."

Ian was about to consent to her request when he thought of Foleena
again, his mind still relishing over that brief encounter. He was almost
sure he wanted to go with Bliss, but another feeling, seemingly somewhat stronger, kept questioning him: what about Foleena?

Maybe it was because Foleena had promised to take him to where she
lived — where, so she had said, he could probably solve the mystery that
so frustratingly plagued his left eye. Yet, Bliss had offered this as well.

He became aware of Bliss' hand on his arm.

"What's wrong, Ian?" Her eyes were large and there was a slight tone
of uneasiness in her voice.

"I...I don't know," he stammered, lost in his own confusion.

"Don't you want to go with me?"

He took her hand, holding it gently as he spoke to her. "I do, Bliss, but
there is something else, too."

"You mean Foleena?"

"Yes, but I don't know why, it's just that I feel as if it is something I
have to do."

For the first time since Ian had met her, Bliss seemed at a loss for
words. She slowly averted her gaze from Ian, and turned her face into the
soft wind that flowed along the stream bank. Ian's hand instinctively went
forward then, touching the wet streams on her cheek.

"What do you see in her?"

Ian shook his head. "I don't know. I feel as if I can't leave here without
at least looking at the things and places she promised to show me. That is
what is most important. Like you, she said she could help me. If that is
true —."

"Do you love her?"

Bliss' question took Ian by surprise, and he saw that there was no
honest answer he could give her.

"You believe that you will, do you not see that, Ian? You think you
know her, but you have not had the time to find out what she is really
like. She cherishes her own happiness so much that she's not able to
perceive those things that are deep and meaningful. Why do you think

she made all those promises to you only to leave you before you woke? Do you know where she lives, Ian? *Nowhere!* She has been looking for the place she described to you ever since she left the castle. She avoids anything that hurts her.

"I've shown you pain, Ian, and I've shown you why it must be. And when you bring pain to her, she will not know what to do with it. She is in her own little world and no one can bring her out of that."

A sudden tingling in the air momentarily stopped Ian from answering. He could feel the presence of...something; something he had felt once before. He looked at Bliss and as he spoke, he felt as if his words had been chosen for him.

"I don't know if I can believe that, Bliss. When I was with her she did not appear to be the person you claim she is. I have to find out why we see her as two different people. If I don't, I feel as if I would be more lost than I am now."

Bliss now turned to face the stream. "Maybe. Maybe that would be true. But, what you really want, what you are looking for — if only you could see it, Ian. I have tried my best to help you, I just wish I had succeeded.

"You are facing pressure right now, and it is blinding you, do you not know that? You are believing that good things can last without ever having pain, and that is wrong. I can not tell you why — you would not believe me. Only you can see that for yourself."

"Do you really believe that, Bliss? I'm not sure that there really is a right and wrong in all of this," Ian said, the presence in the air growing stronger. Then he realized what it was. He had previously felt it the last time he had been with Foleena. Could she be near them now?

Crying again, Bliss drew her hand out of his grasp. "I know what you are looking for, Ian, and I hope you find it." She looked down at the yularra, clasped to the chain. "I have shown you many things with this, but it does not change the fact that I am still a real woman in your eyes. Is that not the truth? The yularra only speaks my thoughts.

"I know what your problem is, Ian. I know you have many things to do. But will you do something for me? Will you bring your mind together? You have two parts, and they are drifting away from each other. Make them talk, let them see what you are searching for, Will you do that for me, please?"

Then she was gone, back up the stream, to her cave. In his mind Ian could still see the tears on her face, and he knew that she would wait for him, though for how long he could not say.

He spent the next couple hours staring into the stream, trying to decide what to do next. The disturbing presence gained strength, becoming oppressive, threatening to sap his inner will. He could feel what was happening to him, and though his inner self tried to take alarm, he slowly felt himself relinquishing his resistance to the force which was beginning to dominate everything around him. He saw his thoughts as the water, trickling effortlessly to all places, so simple yet so hard to catch. Could that have been what Bliss had meant? Could he bring his thoughts together, merge his two minds?

Closing his eyes, he concentrated on trying to put his thoughts in some sort of order. But they appeared to have no collective significance or, if they did, he could not find it.

Maybe he should just try to find Foleena, like he had told Bliss he had wanted to do. After all, he had gone through so much to do that already. Standing up, he began walking down the stream bank, back to where he had last seen Foleena, at the campfire. Then he stopped. Was he not being drawn by some force to do this? He could feel his inner will struggling to break free. He closed his eyes again, concentrating on his thoughts once more. He saw a temporary safety spot from all the pressure, and his mind raced toward it: logic. Logic told him that it had been almost five "days" since he had last seen Foleena. Chances were Foleena had gone far from here, and he had no clue as to where she might be now. He could spend days searching for her...unless...unless he knew what would happen if he found her...

He found Bliss in the rear of her cave, looking solemnly at the yularra which she held in her hand. When she saw him, a startled look came over her face and she ran forward to meet him. Ian raised his hand before she reached him, however.

"No, wait. I haven't yet been able to do what you wanted me to do, nor what I wanted to do. I've tried, but everything seems pointless. I need your help, but I don't want to use you — at least, I hope I will not use you.

"Bliss, I need to know what will happen if I go to Foleena. You've told me why I want to see her — even though I don't know if I can believe your reasons — but now I need to know what would happen should I do so. Can you play me a song and show me? Can the yularra do that?"

Bliss' eyes, so full of understanding, shone brightly from beneath the brim of her hat as she looked at him. Then her expression changed and took on a serious yet hopeful appearance.

"Yes, it is one of the powers of the yularra. But it has not been used by our people for a long time. When I was young, they told me how it was done, but I have never used the yularra for such a purpose. It is a very hard thing to do. Are you still willing to try?"

Ian nodded his head. "I have to know."

She took his hand. "Come to the back of the cave, then. Darkness makes it easier for you to see the images."

Ian followed her, and they sat down against the farthest wall. Bliss still had her yularra, and now she was staring at the instrument and running her fingers over it, almost, Ian thought, as if she were speaking to it. Then she looked back at him.

"Before I only gave you my thoughts, Ian. You could see them easily because they were complete in that they were built upon my feelings of past experiences.

"Now, even though my thoughts will still express my feelings, they will be even more abstract because they are telling about the future — things that have not yet happened. The images that you see will be your own this time, and I must ask that you concentrate hard on trying to see them. It will not be easy, Ian."

"I'm ready."

"Then close your eyes and I shall start. I have to reach out to you, I have to try to sense what is in your mind so that I can play the correct sequences of notes that will help you see your thoughts."

After that she spoke no more. Ian laid down with his back to the floor of the cave. He relaxed. He let the tensions trickle out of his body. He tried to cease all thinking processes, believing that his mind would be more receptive in such a state.

Then he heard it: a long, plaintive note that danced melodiously through the air. But it was a sad dance, a sad melody — all in one single note. Others then followed, crystal clear notes that rode the wind, yet were so delicate and fragile that Ian dared to breathe not a single breath. He felt himself rising, riding with the wind. It was a blue wind, and it streamed, running through his hair and body. It was this wind that carried him to a place that he would never know. And in that place the wind set him down and left him there: a place so black and still, that the very idea of life had yet to be conceived. Ian strained to see, but could not do so. His eyes roamed the blackness, feeling helpless and lost. Then he remembered Bliss' words: "...I must ask that you concentrate hard on trying to see them."

Ian allowed himself to sink deeper into the reality that the yularra was making for him. As he did so, he strained his mind, letting its claws reach out to cut away the wall of blackness which enclosed him. To his amazement, his mind developed long, sharp talons which attacked the wall with savage thrusts; and the blackness fell away in jagged edges, exposing a world that he had never seen. He drew closer to it and suddenly found himself flying over the land. He felt compelled to search for something, and so he let his eyes roam the forests, the mountains, and the streams.

He had examined a large portion of this world when he found what he was looking for: he found himself, walking with Foleena. They (he and Foleena) were talking and Ian strained to hear what they said. However, he found that he was yet once removed from this world. He tensed, fearing that he would never be able to hear what was being said between Foleena and himself. The tension only caused him to become more fretful, however, and the world began to fade, growing hazy and dim. In a last, desperate struggle, Ian fought the dimness in the only way that he knew how: he forced himself to relax — he put his mind and his thoughts at ease once more. The tensions and fears gushed out of him, seemingly afraid of his sudden calmness; and the world grew bright again.

Once more, he saw that other Ian Torrden on the world below him, still talking to Foleena. And though he still could not hear the words they spoke, he was no longer afraid of this inability. Instead, he calmly waited, carefully reaching his mind out even more, stretching it to the limit.

Soon, his efforts proved their worth, and he could faintly hear the world pulsing, singing to him in a rhythm that, though it moved with the lips of the two people he watched, had a musical uniqueness all its own.

The singing became louder, as if approaching from a far distant shore. Then it was upon him, and he listened to what it had to say:

Speak to me, tell me your secrets,
oh, mirror of mystery that reflects only form;
yet, is it true that you have none to say?

A life, turning away from its real meaning,
what became of the secrets I told to you?
Or could you not see the reality of which I spoke?

Wanted, is your ignorance, not consequence,
ever escaping the god of Pain, running
to unreal worlds where suns never set.

Another one is there like you, one who
can turn the sun into the moon and
reflect the images and thoughts of the deep.

Your knowledge of that, so
complete and yet so far removed,
has bonded you to mysterious innocence.

I go with you
and yet through it all, I see it is
a burning light never to be found.

Then the world stopped singing and everything went black again, but this time as if in anticipation. In that blackness that Ian saw, he began to remember, recalling the words that the world had just spoken to him.

What the world had shown him had been his thoughts, Ian knew, and now he could truthfully say that he had seen Foleena as she really was. Then he felt a guilt, a burning in his soul. To know that one woman had given him so much — music, happiness, pain, thoughts, and a touch of reality; and all he had given her in return was a wish to be free, a desire to go elsewhere. Suddenly, he experienced pain — the pain that Bliss must have felt when he had unfeelingly declined to accompany her on her journey. Then the reality of that pain became a pinpoint of light, and he felt his other self forcibly pushed through the tunnel; and in his left eye, the pinpoint of light grew larger and loomed in front of him, forcing the blackness away.

His left eye now dominated his senses, and he saw the swirling mists become an early morning dew, illuminated and lovingly pierced by the gentle rays of the sun; the lines became tall trees, reaching up for the sky, yearning to be free. Ian Torrden knew that he had left that other land in his right eye. Before him stood a forest so beautiful, so untouched, that he felt almost as an intruder. The light of the sun was glitteringly diffracted many glorious ways by the dew and the trees. And the wildlife — it walked unwarily at his feet, swung gracefully from the trees, and swam like an arrow through the streams. The air smelled of fruiting hardwoods in a light summer rain. Insects floated on the lofty wind, their wings singing an orchid-blooming song for those who cared to listen.

Ian sat down on the lush grass. He had found what he had been looking for all along...an expression, an emotion, a word that meant more to him now than it did to any other man. He had paid a price for this discovery, but the mere knowledge of what he had found was far superior to anything else he could ever experience.

Then, abruptly, everything stopped: the forest disappeared and the music ceased. For an instant, Ian became aware of his real self, in the Asinarian Mountain cave. He began to reflect on what he had so far encountered, but just as quickly he realized that a state or perpetual blackness still surrounded him. Why could he not see — somehow, he knew that the flashlight he carried was still projecting its light. But why was nothing visible to his eyes? For a moment, Ian wondered just how close he was to the alien entity, how close he was to his own death.

After this initial flurry of thoughts, Ian tried to calm himself. He breathed in deeply, and began to reflect once more on this experience. Slowly, he began to reason that the exposure of his mind to some type of stimuli had awakened some mechanism by which his own brain, mankind's brain, had reverted to its primal nature and had begun to function as two different, individual and independent parts.

But he had no sooner developed that thought than when the blanket of blackness surrounding him grew even more intense. From out of the middle of that blackness, and then from all around, came the music he'd heard before, that almost indescribable melody. He felt his movements involuntarily slow as the music, with all its unique, tonal qualities, abruptly riddled his mind once more. His body began to move, but in an awkward, haphazard manner, as if the movement had no destination. Seconds later he felt a disturbance of his thoughts, a gentle stabbing in his mind, and it was that impulse, that feeling of merging, which gave a sense of direction and a destination to his apparently moving body. With this added sense of direction, he became aware of his true self once again walking deeper into the Asinarian cave.

And then a world dawned upon him, so bright and so fast, that he found himself reeling in wonder and amazement. It was a world, like most, with rocks, earth, insects, and tall grasses. In the distance he could see rows and rows of large trees. He saw that he himself was standing on a long, unmoving plain. To his left was an area of barren soil, populated with too many rocks and stones to provide any space for grasses to grow. Ian looked to his right and...he saw Bliss. She smiled at him, and in that grin, like a thousand memories in a split second, he remembered all that had happened since Bliss had played him her last song — that song, then of the future, now of the past, but always to remain in his present.

Ian recalled how, after that last song, he had discovered he loved Bliss more than he had any other woman. He remembered his wanting to join her on her travels to the other parts of this world, away from the place where she lived. He remembered their journeys through other lands, meeting other peoples. And the fighting and the wars — he re-membered all of them, too. There had been poverty, and there had been killing, and there had been something else which people believed in and which poets wrote about; these people had called it love, and it was this false conception of a thing so mighty and beautiful that had so pained and disillusioned Bliss and himself. Ian recalled all of this. He remembered Bliss saying, "I must write a song about this. I know now that must have been my real purpose in coming here. Let us go to a place where no one will disturb us." And they had come here. Like a thousand memories in a split second, he remembered it all.

Ian now heard Bliss say, "Please sit down here at the edge of the grasses, and I will play you my song of all we have seen in these lands."

Ian looked at her with a slight touch of amazement. "I still don't see how you can write about such things. These people are so different from you and me that it hurts to even look at them."

Bliss shook her head. "We may be different, but you have already learned why we can not alienate ourselves, Ian. The yularra showed me that very fact many years ago. These things we must both accept and overcome, for too often people accept these things and are themselves overcome by them. You will understand more after you hear my song."

They sat down, but Bliss did not yet begin to play. She held the yularra in her hands and stared at the ground for several moments. Then she looked at Ian. "Your words are true — it does hurt to look at the people we have seen; and because of that, my song will also hurt. Please remember one thing for me, Ian. I love you."

Ian ran his fingers through her hair. Then, leaning over, he kissed her tenderly, and as their lips slowly parted, he whispered, "I will."

The way in which Bliss had spoken those last words would have frightened Ian earlier, but he knew Bliss now, and he was confident that he would benefit by learning what her song had to say. Ian saw that she now held the yularra in both hands. She glanced at him one last time, and he nodded for her to begin.

The first several notes were long and wily, spanning several octaves as they meandered through the air, weaving with the wind. After that, the notes began to descend spirally. And the geometry of that spiral was so clear, so real, that Ian could see the funnel that was formed by it. Then he became engulfed in that funnel, and he got a chance to see what the notes looked like from the inside. They had evil physiognomies that laughed like darix in the night. Their laughter stretched away into streams that became water, and Ian realized that he was no longer in a simple geometric funnel, but trapped inside a mammoth whirlpool. He began to resist, to fight, only to find himself stretching with the notes, stretching down to a molecular concoction of tumultuous confusion.

And that was when Ian lost touch of everything. His right eye, with which he had envisioned all that had happened between himself and Bliss, including the songs of the yularra, suddenly went blank, popping into nothingness with a harshness that frightened him. He then reached out his senses for his left eye, but it was blank as well, having been so since he had discovered the true nature of the curious light that had previously beckoned to him.

In the blackness that he now experienced, Ian felt a shifting of moods, feelings, and of self. Images fleetingly flitted through his mind, travelling so fast that he refused any attempt to grasp them, fearing his mind would be wrecked by their velocities.

But one image *grasped* him. It was that of a moon...hurtling toward a distant sun. To Ian, the sun, with all of its prodigious size and mass, seemed helpless against the minuscule moon — for the moon was angry! The furious silver-footed queen hit the sun like a blazing arrow, piercing the yellow orb, stabbing the very nipple of its existence.

Ian expected the moon to be harmlessly engulfed by the glowing inferno, but he was horrified when the sun screamed in a pain and agony untold! The universe leaped away, suddenly afraid of the wounded star. And the sun, with one last, hideous shriek, went supernova, and the brightness of it brought sight back to Ian's eyes.

In his right eye, he saw himself buried in the ground, many feet below the surface. He was digging at the earth above him, clawing in a frantic rage to be free. Something lay above him, something that he had to see; and the mystery of what ever it was that he wanted to see kept him scraping away at the dirt, cutting his hands into mauled shreds.

And yet there was another vision, this one in his left eye. It was a scene of a barren land which was devoid of all life. He felt this vision dominating his awareness, and he knew that this was a reversal of what he had known before, when it had been his right eye which had dominated his senses.

However, something was different here: he was moving faster now; he was afraid. Time seemed to be sweeping by, oblivious to who, or what, he was. Then he was plunged into the world his left eye had created and he felt and tasted the dryness of the land. Turning slowly around, he quickly became aware of the oppressive heat that was produced by this world's sun. However, the heat failed to remove the tenseness in the air, and the urgency which had recently manifested itself prompted Ian to send his senses in search of a clue. Clearing his mind, he opened himself up to his surroundings...and was rewarded with a far-off, plaintive series of notes — Bliss' notes. They were repeated several more times before Ian finally lost the thread of existence on which they had travelled.

He frowned. The notes — the very melody the yularra had produced just then — had spoken to him. *The wind*, the melody had said. The wind would show him a clue. Ian looked quickly over the barren landscape, becoming desperate in his attempts to find those things which were so easily eluding him. Why was he so afraid? What was wrong here?

Then he saw it, off to his left. A spiral of air was moving slowly toward the distant horizon, particles of disturbed sand clearly marking its trail. Ian headed toward it at a dead run only to be dismayed by the disappearance of the eddy at its present location. He doggedly continued, however, reaching the site as the last particles of sand which had been carried by the wind fell back to the ground, easily blending with the dull colors of the land. Ian's frustration reached a peak as he hopelessly knelt to the ground, the unrelenting sun needlessly emphasizing the stillness that surrounded him.

He lowered his head in despair. A spell of vertigo hit him as he felt the earth move underneath him. Extending his arms outward to steady himself, Ian suddenly realized the true nature of the movement: the land itself was motionless — yet the sand he had observed only moments before was now snaking its way rhythmically across the parched soil. Without hesitating, Ian scooped up the sand in his palm, letting loose with a cry as a jolt of pain shot through his body. Still, he held onto the life-like particles, his mind transfixed by the very energy they possessed. The pain racing through his body lessened, becoming a quavering wave of fear; which slowly gave way to a calling. Ian's eyes widened as he began to comprehend the patterns the sand was making on his palm. Bliss was in trouble, and she would soon die without his help.

The sand, as if realizing Ian's thoughts, altered its pattern of movement. A recognizable shape was formed before movement ceased altogether. Then, like the wind, the sand began to disappear, soon leaving Ian with his eyes trained upon an empty palm. However, now he had a clue — for the shape the sand had formed before it had disappeared had been an arrow, pointing north.

Quickly, Ian stood, only to be momentarily overcome by the pressing heat and his own body's fatigue. He was struck by a vision of his other self, in his right eye, still buried beneath the earth and digging with a ferocity unequalled by anything he knew.

Then he was back in that barren land, where he found himself briskly moving in the direction the sand-arrow had shown him. Somewhere at the end of his path, he knew, he would find Bliss. He strained his ears, trying to detect additional notes from the yularra, but the silence of the land would not relinquish its dominance.

Hours passed before Ian realized that the relative position of the sun in the sky had not changed. He had passed several hills and valleys, and now there extended before him a rolling, wind-swept plain. Glancing quickly at the sun once more, he continued his hurried pace across the open expanse of land. The yularra's powers were many and it was folly to try to understand how it worked. However, that very thought almost brought

Ian to a stop. If Bliss were in trouble, if she indeed were actually dying, how could she still be playing the song to which this world owed its very existence? Ian quickly dismissed this last question from his mind. He now realized that, to find an answer, one would have to separate illusion from reality, a task he felt he was no longer capable of doing.

Increasing his tireless pace, he moved boldly across the plain. Cuts and scratches soon covered his body, reflecting the denseness of the stout vegetation which occupied the area. Soon he began a steady descent and the environment gradually gave way to more mesic conditions. After passing several ponds he came to a major stream which blocked his path. He almost attempted to cross it, but he was suddenly compelled to turn west and follow the stream bank. The stream led him on a meandering path for a couple hours before he discovered a trail leading away from the stream in a southerly direction. Following his senses, he left the flowing water to pursue the new line of travel. He cast the sun another suspicious look, wondering if the yularra was not keeping it in the sky so that he would be able to find his way.

The thick vegetation associated with the stream bank and the surrounding woodlands soon disappeared as Ian continued his accelerated pace along the trail. Close to yet another hour had passed when he discovered the trail led onto a floating bog. The bog mat slowly undulated as he carefully stepped upon the sturdier, hummocky portions of the floating island of vegetation. He had taken no more than ten steps when he saw her, lying at the base of one of the small shrubs which the bog mat supported.

Gone was the radiant quality of her hair and face. If it were not for the slow rise and fall of her breasts, Ian would almost have concluded she was already dead. As he started forward, her eyes opened up — how dull they were! — and she appeared to try to warn him to stay away. Ian had almost reached her when he was abruptly grabbed and thrown back. He felt his feet break through the bog as he whirled around to meet his adversary. However, the shock of finding himself sinking quickly into the water was barely eclipsed by the surprise of finding no one behind him.

Extending his arms, he was able to grasp and hold onto the base of one of the shrubs while he carefully pulled himself out of the cold, clear water which lay under the mat. He looked toward Bliss again; she opened her mouth to tell him something, but her body was so drained of strength and energy that no words could be spoken. Ian wildly wondered what had happened to her and he started forward again, only to be brutally thrown on his back once more.

An invisible force? or foe? Ian's mind frantically skimmed over the possibilities as he angrily regained his footing. It was then that his eyes spied the yularra, much farther out on the bog, where open water began to disperse the floating vegetation. His recognition did not go unnoticed as Bliss' eyes reflected a faint surge of hope; but their concentration was broken by a blinding flash of sparkling light which appeared over her. Showers of solid light radiated outward from a bright point of whiteness suspended two meters above Bliss' body. Ian resisted a third attempt to approach Bliss, and as he watched, powerless, the brightness flashed into a narrow band of white energy, oriented perpendicular to the ground. To Ian's horror, the blinding phenomenon began to coalesce, and a silver sword emerged, the detail and sharpness of which grew as it fed upon the light that had created it.

Bliss now rose and Ian could read in her face the inner turmoil that presently occupied her as she tried to break free from the forces which obviously were controlling her, too. Nevertheless, she took hold of the sword, gazing at it only briefly before slowly turning it upon herself. Ian's eyes quickly sought the yularra again, and he darted forward in an attempt to retrieve it. Therein, so he thought, lay the power which would free him and Bliss from this evil place. His efforts, however, proved futile: the force which had prevented him from approaching Bliss earlier now grabbed him again.

Unseen hands violently forced Ian to his knees, and as he fought to free himself from his invisible adversary, his eyes fell upon Bliss. His attempt to reach the yularra had evidently inspired a last surge of resistance in her, but now there was no sign of recognition in her face. A new wave of desperate anger swept over Ian as the sword which she held touched the flesh on her neck. Crying out to her, he quickly shut his eyes to the sight of seeing her die. But a simultaneous echo of her spoken name startled him and his eyes flew open ...

... only to find that the vision in his right eye had assumed dominance. Time, too, he felt, had been altered, but he knew not how. He was crying here, beneath the ground; but the tears were those from crazed eyes, because he was only inches from the surface, from escaping this pseudo-grave that had somehow entrapped him.

With one final thrust, he pushed himself through to the surface of the earth, and his eyes frantically sought what it was he had wanted to see ever since he had become consciously aware of his underground imprisonment. As his vision cleared, Ian saw that he was in a deeply wooded forest. The nearby sound of trickling water was eclipsed by several black pits that gaped awesomely from the ground around him, lost caverns from many years past. Ian was afraid that the whole landscape would collapse, burying him once more beneath tons of earth. Then he heard the hooves of a tall, mystic stallion and he knew that Nighttime had come to take the sun away. He watched as a black horse galloped past him, its tall rider whirling a tremendous cord. The rope abruptly grew, reaching out to the sun. Nighttime rode his steed quickly through the forest and soon gained the top of a distant hill. The stallion's pace never faltered, and as they fell away, over the horizon, to circle the world in an eternal, furious crusade of blackness, the lasso caught hold of the sun and yanked it cruelly out of the sky! It had happened so fast, and yet it had taken hours.

Soon, the cold realization struck Ian. The sun which only the powers of Nighttime could overcome, the woods, the stream he had heard ...

He quickly gained his footing, and by the dark light cast by the world's tiny moon, he followed Nighttime's trail to the top of the hill. Below him, he saw where the stream made a major turn to flow in a northwesterly direction. As he had guessed, a trail leading to the south began at the base of the hill. He took the now familiar trail, and this time it took him only seconds to reach the bog. There he came to a jolting halt. He saw Bliss reaching out to grasp the sword which had just materialized above her. That he had expected to see, but the other two figures...he saw himself bolt forward to get the yularra, only to be struck down by a dark, hooded figure. How many times removed must he be from the real world to see his double? Only then was he able to fathom that the Ian before him was Ian Torrden of the Left Eye. He himself was Ian Torrden of the Right Eye, to whom the dark shape which had overpowered Bliss was not invisible.

As it was, he had almost lost the opportunity to save her as the sword was upon her neck once again. Calling out her name, he started forward across the bog. Upon seeing him, the dark figure released his other self, thus showing its fear of Ian Torrden of the Right Eye. It whirled and took the sword from Bliss' hands. Unharmed, she collapsed onto the resilient vegetation of the bog, weakened from her encounters with the mystic forces of the dark miscreant which now turned to face Ian Torrden of the Right Eye. The silver sword was thrust toward Ian and, over the glare of that weapon, Ian could see two tiny pinpoints of cold light within the hood of the dark figure. A shriek of laughter that was heard only by the chosen erupted forth from the deep cavern of the hood, and in that instant, Ian grabbed the hilt of the sparkling cold steel that had been offered him. All eyes, including those of Bliss and Ian Torrden of the Left Eye, were upon him.

Ian began to laugh, and to cry, and he knew not what he was doing. His hands, as Bliss' own hands had done, began to raise the dreadful sword; and as he slowly turned it upon himself, he could read approval in the dark pit of the hooded figure opposite him. It was then that he realized the identity of the dark one. His mind expanded with this knowledge, the outer fabric of his brain threatening to burst into irretrievable multitudes of shattered tissue. Something wanted to escape, to thrust itself free of his consciousness. Ian became painfully aware that he was witnessing the birth of...of something that had been unleashed by the fusion of the minds of two organisms; something that would lay him to waste unless ...

A blinding flash of light. Round, and around. A pit of nothingness — no motion. Silent. The gray beings were humanoid in shape — they talked to one another, but never spoke. Loneliness. Ceasing to think, ceasing to think. This is...death? Alongside the gray being is a man. Who are you? Leaving...Ceasing to think...Who are you?

Ian smiled at the gray being.

A blinding flash of light. Round, and around. A pit of nothingness — no motion. Silent. The gray beings are gone, we miss them. Our memories, our thoughts, our life! There must be others who will accept us; we must search for them. This will be death? Who were you? Leaving...Ceasing to think...Who were you?

Ian could hear the question, but somehow he knew it was not his to answer.

Others will come...to continue the search. This planet once again bears life. Save yourselves, as those before you once did, before our arrival.

Ian heard himself breathing heavily as he reached out to clasp onto the whirlwind of living thoughts that now moved away from him. An entire eon of memories...he could see them, almost touch them. He felt their life, their sorrow, their grief, and...their desire and longing, an intense, passionate urge. Looking down, Ian was startled to find the creature at his feet. He could see its wounds — it had probably been injured when its ship had crashed into the Asinarians. He reached out to touch the gray being...

...but he could no longer see it. The next thing he knew, he was once again standing at the entrance to the cave. Then, he felt as if his mind had fled down an ethereal staircase to escape an awful, impending doom. He tried to raise his conscious self to a normal level of functioning and feeling. His body became a winter world, thawing out with the onset of spring. And as the ice slowly fell away in layers of melted water, Ian's vision slowly focused upon the light of day. How long had he been here?

Voices. He heard voices. Without thinking, Ian plucked the radio from his belt and answered the Base Station. It was Commander Riverst.

"Ian! Did you find it? Is it dead?"

Ian slowly stared forth across the steep slope leading away from the cave.

He then looked down at the laser rifle. It was still at his side. Had he ever used it? He could not remember. Yet, he was clearly sure he had witnessed the death of the alien creature. He had even stood by its side. But he barely remembered what it had looked like.

"Ian, please answer! Can you read us? What did you find?"

The voices again. Ian saw an image of Commander Riverst flash across his wearied mind. He played the questions over again in his mind. This time he was sure. "Base Station," he finally answered, "it is dead."

Ian slowly let the radio fall out of his hands. He tried to lean against the side of the cave, but he stumbled forward, and the ground came up to meet him with startling quickness. He felt a pain against his cheek before he sensed his body, and his mind, slipping into a state of unconsciousness. Then somewhere, out in the distance, he heard the voices again: "I think he made it!" It had sounded like Josef (or could it have been Baronhart?)

He used his remaining strength to roll over on his back. As he stared up at the sky, he again asked himself how he had gotten back to the mouth of the cave. If he hadn't actually killed the thing — if he hadn't actually used the rifle — how was he so sure the alien entity was dead? It was daylight now. What day was this — how long had he been here? Should he warn the Base Station? Could he have been mistaken? He reached out blindly for the radio, but all of his strength was gone from his body now, and his arm listlessly moved a few pebbles as he lost his last remaining vestiges of consciousness.

"Do you have everything you need, Jase?"

Commander Riverst, heavily clothed in response to Refander's biting, pre-winter winds, stood approximately in the middle of the Base Station Port. Across from him the aging medical doctor, Jase Johnson, was busily checking the air shuttle he was about to fly, searching for any last minute trouble areas. The doctor now straightened up to his full height and turned to face the Commander. The lines on his tawny face and the whiteness in his hair did not go unnoticed by Riverst.

"Yes, I believe I do. I don't really plan to bring her back. Ian has advised me against doing that just yet. However, I've loaded the shuttle with supplies Ian and Liraah can use. I must say, I really want to see what she is like now, after all these years."

"That is probably a wise choice on your part. I guess you'll probably be back later on in the day, on towards night, perhaps?"

"I imagine," Jase returned. "Since I'll be leaving Ian off somewhere on the east side of the Crane, the shuttle will probably travel faster with one less man to carry."

As Jase spoke, Commander Riverst caught sight of Baronhart Dietrich and Lieutenant Rielick approaching from the Port end of the Main Transport Hall. He then turned his attention back to the medical doctor.

"Very well. I want to thank you for the excellent job you're doing down in the lower farmlands. If we can get that thing licked before too many people hear about it, it will be a great psychological advantage for us — people believe more readily that they can do whatever has to be done if they know that their government is sharp and on the ball."

"Yes, well, I have my folks working 'round the clock on it. We're close. But, to be honest, I think what we're doing down there is minor league compared to everything else you've just told me. What do you think everyone will say when you tell them we've only postponed the ultimate threat to Refander? From what you've told me so far, I get the feeling that Refander will not be left in peace for much longer. There is a race of beings out there that obviously knows where we are — and if we get another visit from them, we won't be able to throw a whole population of Ian Torrdens at them the next time."

"I've given all that considerable thought," Josef replied. "It's already been a couple days since Gloid and his crew have started patrolling the outer sectors surrounding Refander. We'll know soon enough of any kind of immediate danger approaching us. Maybe if we have enough time to attack this problem we can develop some sort of defense that would suit our needs.

"But before you tell me that my optimism has run errant, I think I'll let you go so you can get back before nightfall. We'll continue our conversation then, if you wish."

Jase, apparently satisfied that the shuttle bore no problems that needed immediate attention, began climbing the ladder leading to the overhead hatch door of the more or less spherically-shaped vehicle.

"Thank you, Commander. I'd like that very much. But, as you say, I must be going. Ian is probably already impatient to return to the solitude of his woodlands. And, of course, I guess I'm impatient as well."

Josef smiled. "And for obvious reasons. Liraah ran away from us so many years ago. No one would have guessed she'd still be alive. Give Mr. Torrden my regards, will you?"

The Commander then stepped back from the shuttle as Jase closed the hatch door. Scarcely two minutes later, the engines purring a sound that would have been sweet music to a mechanic's ears, the air shuttle took off, heading in a northeasterly direction. As the shuttle grew continuously smaller, Josef became aware of the presence of two other humans behind him. Turning, he saw that Baronhart and Lieutenant Rielick were also observing the now distant shuttle.

After a moment, Baronhart quietly said, "Never have I seen two men more important to our planet. How long do you think our luck will last, Commander?"

Josef, who had turned back to face the direction which the shuttle had taken, was barely conscious of the fact that he never answered his Security and Weapons specialist. Instead, the memory of how quietly Ian Torrden had just left the Base Station Dome to return to the Pascalian Mountains kept running through his mind. He, Josef Riverst, had been right after all — pride had not been a factor.

Josef shook his head as he recalled the events of the last several days. When it had become apparent that Ian had not contracted the alien contagion, they had flown an emergency shuttle in and evacuated him from the cave site. The clarity and vividness of Ian's recollection of his last remaining moments with the alien entity had surprised nearly everyone at the Base Station. During the debriefing, hundreds of questions had been asked. Josef knew that if it were not for the woodsman, some of Refander's most regarded think-tank personnel would have not been able to reconstruct the most likely chain of events precipitating the deadly pandemic that had swept across the Earth — and which had nearly engulfed Refander.

Based on the bizarre story that Ian had told, Josef and the rest of Refander's top officials now suspected that an alien entity capable of telepathic communication had transferred the equivalent of an engram of its thoughts or memories to the Captain of the Sixteenth New World Launch. This engram of thought functioned not unlike a virus within the human brain, where it quickly destroyed the cells associated with the corpus callosum — the bundle of nerve fibers that function to transmit information between the two hemispheres of the brain. It would then begin to multiply or expand in size, perhaps even combining with other memories, both real and imagined, of its host. At this point, the affected persons would fall into a deep sleep and, while dreaming, become slightly telepathic themselves. Under these conditions, such persons could unknowingly spread the engram to others.

Josef shivered as he once again thought of what Ian must have gone through. He knew that Ian Torrden was lucky to be alive. If these thoughts could be compared to a virus, then perhaps the thoughts of the being that Ian had found had been less virulent than the one the Sixteenth had encountered. In the end, it had merely shared a lifetime of sorrow, loneliness, and grief with Ian.

Josef suddenly found his thoughts once again dominated by the mysterious gray beings from another world. How had it all started? Perhaps this race had been like humans once, and had a culture not unlike those found on Refander or Earth. But somewhere in its evolutionary history, there may have been a spark — the first telepathic individual. But what does a telepathic being do when it dies? Could it pass on its knowledge, the essence of its life, to others? Could this race have somehow achieved, through this process, a condition of near-immortality for many eons? If such were the case, then it appeared that now, for reasons unknown, this race was alone — perhaps even dying out as a species. Could they have been responsible for the demise of Refander's previous tenants, just as Earth was ravaged by the virus from the Sixteenth? It appeared that in their last desperate struggles for survival, these gray beings probably knew what they were doing, but were powerless to stop themselves. Somewhere out here in the endless pits of space, they probably figured that they could find a new species, a suitable receptacle for its kind.

Regardless of what their motives were, however, Josef knew that Ian had been very specific about the last thing the gray being had told him: there would be more. Earth had perhaps been an accident. The outright attack on Refander, though, only meant that Refander was now on the map, or whatever the equivalent of a map was for these alien creatures.

Josef grimaced...and as he did so, Jase Johnson, satisfied that the shuttle was following the prescribed route, now focused his attention on Ian Torrden, his only passenger.

"I'm glad you waited for me, Ian, though I guess you had no choice. That encounter you had really did an awful number on you. As a matter of fact, I'm still having trouble trying to comprehend all that has happened here."

Ian shrugged his shoulders, still tired from his ordeal of several days ago. "Refander is a large planet that is made small by the lack of a significantly huge population. I'd like to think events of such cosmic importance are not suitable for a planet like ours.

"You know, Commander Riverst and his staff briefed me quickly before I went after that thing, but I've practically forgotten much of what they told me; and to be honest, I only vaguely remember being forced to learn all of those details."

"I guess I could imagine why. They said you were on another level of awareness throughout most of your debriefing. But, tell me, what exactly did you see — or experience — when you were out there in the Asinarians? So far, everyone I've talked to says you have pretty much refused to speak of that, but I know from the medical files how quickly this thing overtook the people on the Sixteenth New World Launch. Somehow, I get the feeling that the same thing almost happened to you."

"I haven't openly spoken of it except to Josef and his team, of course," Ian said, after some thought, "because most people would have trouble trying to understand how what I went through mentally could produce the unstable condition which I was in when they got me out of there. I'd hazard a guess that what one sees at the moment of contact are manifestations of his own thoughts. But I also met another intelligence in there,

Jase. An intelligence that was crying out to me as well as trying to warn me. I guess I could say that it's terribly awesome when you are given an opportunity to see just how complex your mind can be in its thoughts and emotions, but beyond that I would rather not offer any comment, even to you, an old friend from the days of the *Stranahan*."

"I guess I have to respect you on that, Ian. Though I can't grasp how someone could see his own thoughts the way you have more or less described it, you nonetheless have your own privacy. So, I guess if we were to change the subject, it would almost naturally be to Liraah, right?"

Ian offered a meager grin. "I was wondering when you would ask about her. We'll be there soon, if your shuttles are as fast now as they were when I used to ride them a lot. Then you can see with your own eyes how well she has done for herself. How long has she really been out there, Jase?"

"Years. As I recall, it was not too long after you yourself left for the Crane River. We had no idea why she did it, or even where she had gone. She just ran away one day, without warning. We searched for days and days on end. By now, most people who knew her would tell you she's been dead a long time. I tried to never give up hope."

"You'll probably recognize her quicker than I did at first. And, of course, with no one else around to hear us, I guess I can safely say that she has a tremendous surprise which I will let you discover yourself."

Jase threw a quick glance at Ian. "Oh, good or bad? Or shouldn't I ask?"

Ian waved it off. "No, that's okay. That I can answer. It's damn good, Jase, damn good."

The two men reminisced over old times, temporarily dismissing the subjects of Liraah and Ian's experience in the Asinarian Mountains. When they crossed the Crane River, Ian pointed out the location of his cabin to Jase.

For both men, however, the northern reaches of the Pascalians approached too soon, and Jase was once more manually operating the shuttle. He intently followed Ian's directions.

Soon the plateau was in sight, and Jase expertly landed the shuttle on a small, level abutment of land that marked the beginning of the ridges which broke off from the flat expanse of rock.

"Ready for a brisk walk?" Ian asked, donning his fur overcoat, which he had taken all the way to the Base Station.

Jase grinned, and motioned for Ian to lead the way. "Never will be more prepared — I've got a reason to walk all day if I have to. Let's go."

They started off at a fast pace, the going made easy by the fact that the first snowfall of the season had yet to hit this remote area. Ian smiled as he watched the older man take in the beautiful mountain scenery that only two other people before him had experienced.

The ten minutes it took to reach the base of Liraah's cave passed rapidly. Neither of the two men spoke during that interval but now Ian turned to Jase and declared, "This is it. This is where I found her." He then faced the cave and, raising his voice, he called, "Liraah!"

The thin, black-haired woman who then appeared at the cave entrance was, oddly enough, seen by both men for the first time: Ian somehow could not shake the feeling that he now looked upon Liraah in a different light, as if the confusion that had momentarily touched him when he'd been with her before was now gone.

As for Jase, Liraah was the culmination of a maturation process which he had never been fortunate enough to observe.

Liraah looked from Ian to Jase and back to Ian again before slowly descending the worn trail leading up to her cave. She reached Ian's side and glanced at Jase again.

"Liraah," Ian began, "I hope you don't mind that I brought your father here."

A mistiness invaded Liraah's countenance before she slowly shook her head.

Jase, close to tears, asked, "Liraah, how—. Why did you do this?"

Liraah edged closer toward Ian. At first she refused to look at Jase, but finally she did turn toward him. Her eyes were unmoving as she said, "I was alone."

"You were alone?" Jase cried. "You came all the way out here because you were alone?" Then, as if he remembered something from long ago, Jase calmed himself. At length, he soothingly stated, "Liraah, I'm ready to listen."

After a moment of nervous hesitation, he finally succeeded in approaching Liraah with his arms outstretched. Liraah accepted this without any outward signs of resistance.

Ian, satisfied that the reunion was proceeding as well as could be expected, silently made his way up to the mouth of the cave. It was light enough for him to see inside and quickly find what he was looking for:

two snow leopards lay against the back wall, alertly watching his every move. They laid their ears back when Ian stood in the mouth of the cave, but he mindfully sank to a kneeling position and silently waited for the leopards' keen sense of smell to remind them of who he was. When the sound of a soft purr reached his ears he knew it was safe to approach them. They allowed him to caress their soft, silver-white fur, and he quietly knelt down between them, pleased that these last remnants of the Earth he had never seen were so beautiful. He talked softly with them for several minutes, noting that they appeared to respond with recognition to the tone of his voice. He then returned to the cave's opening. Below him, Ian saw that Jase was emphatically conversing with his daughter, trying to make up in a matter of minutes what many years had taken away.

Hoping she had not yet spoiled his surprise, Ian called to Liraah and, when he got her attention, he said, "Call them out."

He sidled down the slope until he was once again at Jase's side. Liraah now made the same sound she had made on that first day when she had called the snow leopard into the cave, after he had found her.

Jase looked quizzically at Liraah, then at Ian; and when movement at the cave's entrance caught his attention, he finally looked up there.

For a full two minutes, the older man continued to stare at the snow leopards, his eyes slowly measuring every magnificent hair on their bodies. It was as if he knew he would be the only human on Refander other than Liraah and Ian who would have an opportunity of such a sight for many years to come. Crying once more, he managed to say, "Ian, will you never cease to perform miracles? This I would never have believed, even if you had taken a picture of it and showed it to me."

Ian shook his head. "Jase, I lay no claim on this miracle, as you call it. This is all Liraah's doing. I found them here when I found her. As a matter of fact, I was trailing one of them, and it led me to this cave. And from what she's told me, Jase, I really don't think Liraah would be alive today if it were not for these snow leopards."

"What? You really mean that, Ian?"

This must be what it's like to be old and feel young again, Ian thought to himself as he watched Jase's expression of near disbelief.

"This is something I wish my father and your grandfather could have seen, Ian. These animals have adapted to a world that has made a failure out of practically all of our attempts to introduce vegetative Earth species. It's likely that not many other animals would have survived here, either, based on what we now know of Refander. Where are the rest of them, or are these the only two?"

"There must be more, Jase — at the higher elevations," Ian replied. "Perhaps even a small, self-sustaining wild population. From what Liraah has shared with me, I have concluded that they maintain a shared but separate existence with the darix — these leopards are obviously big and strong enough to handle any darix that might come along, but the bite of the darix is like snake venom to the snow leopard. In a prolonged fight, the darix don't stand a chance; but if they inflict enough injuries onto the leopards, neither does the snow leopard. It's too bad no one's been able to study this in more detail. But I don't think anyone has ever gone that high into the northeastern arm of the range."

A barely perceptible nod from Liraah seemed to confirm Ian's statement.

"I wish you could also see them hunting, Jase," Ian continued. "These leopards have made a real art out of it. I know you don't get too many sparth down your way, but you at least have an idea of how big they are, right? Well, the last time I was here, Liraah and I watched two of these snow leopards hunt and kill one."

Jase could only shake his head in astonishment. "This is simply astounding, Ian! What else is here that I have not seen?"

"Well, Liraah could show you around the plateau; she's as good a guide as any. I'll wait here and take a little R and R."

Liraah, who had been listening alertly to the entire conversation, remained motionless until her father signalled for her to lead the way down one of the worn trails leading away from the cave.

When they had gone, Ian sat down on one of the large, cold rocks that lay at the base of the cave's entrance. The two snow leopards casually settled down near the mouth of the cave. Ian knew from his last visit here that the cats were most active at dawn and dusk, preferring to spend much of the mid-day at rest.

As he stared at the leopards he could not help but feel that a lot of things had changed since he had left here. It was mostly just a feeling inside of himself, but he was glad it was at least a feeling he was comfortable with. He laid back on the rock and closed his eyes, finding himself intrigued by the burnt orange of his eyelids as the sunlight tried to fight its way through them. In the distance, he heard the high, shrill call of a lecki, and his thoughts returned to his most recent ordeal with the darix. This rugged land east of the Crane was what he enjoyed the most, and he knew he was glad to be back.

He figured he dozed off soon after that, because his next conscious action was that of opening his eyes in response to the returning voices of Jase and Liraah. Sitting up, he saw that the snow leopards were still stretched out where he had last seen them. Then Liraah and Jase were in front of him.

"Ian, I'm afraid it's time for me to be starting back to the Base. But before I do, I'd like to have a word or two with you." Jase knelt down in front of Ian, glancing briefly at the two snow leopards who were now watching both of the men. He then looked back at Ian. "I still can't believe that both of you can live off the land the way you do. But I can't completely convince Liraah to return with me to the Base Station. Being out here, in this wilderness; do you still think this is the right thing to do?"

"Yes," Ian said. "Like I told you this morning, this is a way of life we both chose independently. Who knows — perhaps in time one or both of us will want to eventually return to the Base."

"Yes. Well, will you be in this area of the mountains this winter?"

Ian shrugged. "I can be. Is there any particular reason why?"

"Yes, there are several. First off, Commander Riverst, I'm sure, never told you why you were not able to contact me when you first arrived. Though only top officials are supposed to know about this, I'm telling you because I know it won't go beyond your mouth and also because it is for your own safety.

"I was sent down to the lower farmlands to work on some newly discovered disease down there which has reached epidemic proportions. Though I've made progress, everything is still in the experimental stage. It will be a while until I actually discover if I've found the correct cure." Jase paused long enough to reach into his pocket and pull out what appeared to Ian to be a small communication device. "So, until then, I'm going to leave this transmitter here with you. It's a direct link to someone you can trust. It only sends out a homing signal — you can't relay any message on this thing. The directions are self-explanatory.

"Next, and you may not realize it, but living up here does put you at a slight technological disadvantage. Over the past couple years, we have had several good quakes, and the tech people at the Data Terminal Building have recorded many minor tremors over that same period of time. And these haven't been the first time this has happened on Refander, either. So, just in case of an emergency, accident, or something of that nature, I feel obligated to leave this with you. You may choose to do with it as you please.

"Finally, I've loaded the rear of the shuttle with supplies: a techno-tent, back packs, sleeping bags, clothes, and a supply of food. I'd like to leave whatever you need here for you and Liraah."

Ian leaned forward and gently took the communication instrument from Jase's palm. "Don't worry, I accept this gratefully. None of us is invincible, I guess, and we can always use another's help, right? Come on, Liraah and I will walk you back to the shuttle and help you unload the rest of those items."

He laid the instrument down on the rock, and together the three of them headed off in the direction of the shuttle.

One hour of daylight was all that was left when Jase finally kissed his daughter on the forehead and started climbing the ladder leading to the hatch door on the small shuttle. He then turned to Ian and Liraah one last time. "By the way, as long as no one happens to chance upon this area of land, we will be the only three who will know of the continued survival of the snow leopard, for now, agreed?"

Ian grinned. "Agreed."

Later, when the shuttle was barely visible against the slightly darkening sky: "You are staying?"

He looked at Liraah. "Yes, for a while, anyway. You handled that pretty well — I didn't know if he and you would be comfortable together. You never really told me whether you wanted to see him or not."

Liraah glanced in the direction the shuttle had taken. "Yes. I am happy to see him. He talked of mother."

Liraah hesitantly lowered her gaze to the ground, where the soft colors of the rocks dully reflected the waning sunlight.

Ian gently placed his hands on her shoulders. "What's wrong?"

"They found something."

"You mean the leopards? What did they find?"

Liraah started walking back in the direction of the cave, her hair streaming behind her as the wind began to increase with the change in temperature.

"They left, after you left. That way —" and she pointed eastward "— into the mountains. They were gone for several days. They found something up there, and now they want to return. I have to go, too. Soon."

Ian stopped walking and lightly grabbed hold of her elbow. "Liraah, how do you know all that? How do you know you must go, or even that these snow leopards will go there?"

She looked at him and Ian could see she had no answer he would understand.

"An impulse? Something that you feel?" he queried.

"No, more. It will happen."

Ian shook his head. "It may be a while before I comprehend all this. But until that time comes, I made a promise to Jase not to leave your side."

Liraah smiled at him. "Yes. You must go, too."

And that reply only served to heighten Ian's state of perplexity.

Chapter 6

The Secret

Part 1. Healing

"It's hard to believe that this is it, Josef," Jase said as he maneuvered the air shuttle in for a landing. The two men watched the house below them steadily grow larger and larger as they neared the ground.

"I'm sure that it won't stop here," Riverst replied, at length. "There will be other cases elsewhere to conquer. But at least it's good to know we got this thing under control before it got a chance to go too far."

Jase's old hands gently guided the shuttle to a smooth set-down about 35 meters from the house. As the engines calmly died down, Jase pulled the release lever for the overhead hatch door. "What you say may well be true, but now that we have a cure we can handle any future outbreaks without worrying about any uncontrollable panic or mass hysteria."

"Yeah, but we couldn't have done it without you. There will be a time when everyone on Refander will be able to read about your work on the history discs. And yet, I'll probably never be able to understand how someone can work so efficiently with microorganisms that can't even be seen by the naked eye. I myself, I would have probably been so scared that I'd catch the disease and die before I found a cure to treat the damn thing that I would not have been able to make any progress at all."

Jase allowed himself a leisurely grin. "Believe me, we all feel a little frightened now and then. And please, don't give me all the credit here. I've had three well-trained assistants helping me all along. In fact, if you're going to give credit to anyone, give it to Liraah — after seeing her, I was able to come back here and look at this whole situation from a completely different perspective. I guess I don't have to tell you what it's like to suddenly have a limitless source of motivational energy."

"No, I guess not. I've had that feeling many times myself. But I think it's time we start getting to work — looks like we got company."

Josef began climbing out of the hatch door to meet the man and woman who were approaching the shuttle. This was the last family he and Jase were scheduled to treat for the disease Jase had been working on for so long.

Jase had found the cure two days after he had returned from his visit with Liraah. In the six days following that monumental discovery, he and several crews of medical personnel had administered the medicine to every person in every household of the lower farmlands. Josef had come down himself only two days ago to see what progress his ace medical doctor was making. Now they were hopefully at the residence of the last three humans which had to be treated in this remote part of the farmlands.

"Good day! The Nicholiasons, am I correct?" Josef asked, extending a hand.

A large, red-bearded farmer returned Josef's gesture, his huge hand easily engulfing that of the Commander's. "Yes, we're glad you're here. Our daughter has worsened considerably since our last communication. I hope it is not too late."

Jase apparently heard this last exchange of words, and as he climbed out of the air shuttle, he said, "Well, let's go in and have a look at her, then. Could be that she's only exhibiting the more visible symptoms of the second stage of the sickness — in which case I'd say any real complications are still a long way off."

At these words, Josef noticed a slight look of relief temporarily spread across the faces of the red-bearded man and his wife. The couple turned and began leading the way back to their small, solidly built house. When they entered, it was not hard for Josef to find the object of concern: she was a tiny figure in the corner, floating amidst a sea of blankets. The room was well lighted and provided sufficient heat to turn away the chill of yet another Refander winter.

"Her name is Leonora," Josef heard Nicholiason's wife say. He glanced over, actually noticing her for the first time. Lines of worry crisscrossed her face and any beauty she might have had was hidden by her concern for her only child. She was moderately built, but not stocky; and her medium length black hair was unkempt and hung in streams about her shoulders. A gentle elation began to stir inside Josef as he realized that within four days this woman would no longer have to worry about the health of her daughter.

His attention then swung back to Jase and he saw that the older man was already at work. The doctor knelt down beside Leonora and was now examining her quite meticulously. At length, he said, "Yes, all the classic signs, Mr. Nicholiason: elevated temperature, partial loss of hair, blurred vision, and difficulty in breathing. I'd say that within three to four days you will be able to see a marked improvement in her condition."

"Are you sure this medicine is safe for her?" the woman asked, moving forward until she stood beside Jase.

Josef quietly found a seat as Jase began pulling his medical instruments out of the supply kit he had brought with him. The whole process would take a while — that Josef knew from what he had seen in other houses since he had started travelling with Jase just two days ago. There would be the preliminary tests to make sure the child was not sensitive to any of the chemical treatments that would be administered. Then Jase would have to apply the Wrist-dermic Pad — a medical bandage which osmotically transfused the appropriate serums at prescribed rates into the patient's circulatory system.

As Jase went on about his business, Josef let his attention roam about the house in which he was sitting. The chair he was in, as well as the large, polished table which was no more than three meters away, were an obvious product of the Refander hardwood forests. Josef could see that Nicholiason was quite a carpenter. His eyes roamed to the walls where, not too surprisingly, they landed upon several wooden carvings of the lower farmland lecki. The detail was amazingly graphic, from the long, curled tail to the plushiness of the richly-furred, roundish face. The paint job was yet another work of art, the drab black, gray, and brown colors of the lecki being exactly reproduced by the artist.

In the middle of the wall there hung a sparth fur. As the large animal was more typical of higher elevations, Josef began to wonder when the farmer had been able to kill the beast. Even as his mind began to turn this question over, a clay-fired mug was thrust in front of him, and he looked up to see the tall, red-bearded farmer gazing down at him.

"Here, Commander. Some home-brewed beer — probably the best to be found down here. In comparison to you guys up at the dome, we have lots of spare time down here when the crops are in and growing. I like to spend my time on beer and woodwork. Those lecki you were looking at are probably the best work I've done in several years."

Josef sipped at the beer that had been handed to him, finding himself quite impressed by the quality of the cold liquid. "Your beer, like your art work, Mr. Nicholiason, is A one stuff."

The farmer hardly grinned as he extended his hand, saying, "Call me Jakob, Commander."

They shook hands for a second time and then Jakob moved over to the table. "Pull up your chair, Commander, let's talk."

Josef did as he was asked, and when Jakob sat down opposite him, he could see the cool intelligence in the farmer's eyes that had somehow gone undetected until now. Then he tuned into what Jakob was saying, "Commander, I first want to thank you for all the work you've done to help all of us out down here. We're all pretty tight in this country, if you know what I mean, and when friends start dying on you, it's like losing a part of your family."

Josef chuckled. "Seems like everyone's getting credit today when it's not due. Don't thank me, thank Jase over there. And when you do, he'll deny it and tell you to thank his staff."

Jakob's eyes lit up as he appeared to perceive the humor of the situation, but soon his face was once again hidden behind the lustrous red growth which covered it. "I see what you mean — but still, everything that's been done is greatly appreciated. Now let me ask you this. Refander is a large planet. There's a lot of land left to be taken yet and it's getting near the time that people are getting that independent spirit, you know? Well, what I want to know is if you're willing to provide me with any information on whatever you've found out about other suitable places on this world."

"Oh, I'd be more than willing to do that. After all, I really can not say that someone can not go to place 'X' or 'Y' if that's what he has a mind to do. The least I can do is tell him what he might expect to find there."

"I was mainly interested in something across the Vernonslaw Ocean, Commander," the farmer continued. "Specifically, can we expect to find the same agricultural opportunities as we have here; and, perhaps more importantly, what precautions would you be willing to take to handle epidemics or any kind of serious illnesses like the one we've just had here?"

"Our surveying has been rather limited in scope, and for obvious reasons," Josef returned. "But from what information we do have, I'd say it would be pretty easy for you to find productive land. Of course, if you want specific localities, I can give that information to you, too. However, the thing is, Refander is a slowly developing world, as I'm sure you are well aware. When the Tech Crews first arrived here they found that many of their expectations were shattered and that practically everything they had planned to do had to be revised to meet the strange and almost inhospitable conditions that Refander threw at them. Everyone stuck together more out of fear than anything else. A lot of people that came here had never seen a real world before — they had been born in space and that's all they were used to. Of course, it did not help any when they found out what a group of darix could do to a careless person. Hell, people did not start moving out to the Torrden Forests until just recently.

"What I'm trying to get at here, Jakob, is that the government has never really been that far ahead of the people. We've concentrated most of our efforts around the Base Station, these farmlands, and the Torrden Forests because that's where our future success lies: by providing for the people until they become reasonably self-sufficient, we assured ourselves of a continuously growing population.

"I'm not saying that you shouldn't go across the Vernonslaw because we don't know that much about what is over there. As a matter of fact, our geological expeditions have turned up many locations both here and across the ocean that tend to support evidence of past intelligent life on this planet in an earlier geologic period. We've only just begun to investigate some of those areas. However, it's my feeling that any farmer travelling across the Vernonslaw will be a lonely pioneer for quite a long while. Not too many people may follow in your footsteps for some time yet — at least not until they have a pretty good idea of what to expect from over there."

Jakob took a slow, long drink, draining his mug of beer. Then he smiled wryly at Josef. "Now, Commander, do you really expect me to buy that? I know that you know people better than that. The urge is here, and I'm not the only one who may want to move on. But what if I were to ask you whether you'd think it would really be wise for our population to be expanding to new areas of Refander at this particular point in time? What would you say then?"

"I promise you," Josef began, "Jase's medicine will do the job. If you—."

"Commander, let's lay our cards on the table. I was about ten Earth years old when the *Stranahan* finally made it to Refander. My father was killed in that accident. He had been one of the guards on the *Stranahan* and had been a close friend of Sorian's at the time of the crash.

"Sorian, as you know, more or less adopted me after that. He always had pretty interesting things to say and one of the last times I talked to him, before I moved here to begin farming the land, he asked me to make a special agreement with him."

"Which was what?" Josef inquired, his curiosity now aroused.

Jase, who was finished explaining to Nicholiason's wife how the Wrist-dermic Pad should be removed when Leonora had recovered, now moved over to join the other two men at the table. The woman, as if she already knew what was about to be said, calmly refilled the two glasses with beer and prepared a third mug for Jase.

"Just this, Commander. He always wanted someone outside of the government to be acutely aware of what was going on. I was his choice for that someone.

"Now, from what I can see, you and Paula Witkor did a pretty fair job of convincing the masses that all those missiles and explosions in the sky we've had lately were nothing more than Captain Gloid and his crew learning new reconnaissance skills. And you got Ian into and out of the Asinarians without anyone even taking notice. But the —"

"That's privileged information, Jakob. I think you better hurry and explain how you came to learn of all this."

Nicholiason slowly raised his mug to his lips, and as he drank the beer his wife came to stand in back of him, placing her hands on his large shoulders. After several moments of silence, the mug was returned to its former position on the table.

"I have nothing I was planning to hide from you, Commander. I've been aware of practically everything that's gone on at the Base Station since I moved down here to farm."

"You're saying, then, that you have a source?"

"Yes, Commander, and a pretty qualified one at that. No names, let's keep it clean, okay?"

"I take it that this was Sorian's arrangement with you?"

"Yes," Nicholiason answered. "And to make sure you understand a little more about the whole deal, I think you will be pleased to hear that the information generally does not go beyond me.

"Now, to return to my original question — about the land across the Vernonslaw. I personally have no true desire to go anywhere other than this land I've been farming for the past ten Earth years. However, my argument is still valid — people are talking of moving on, and some do want to go across the Vernonslaw. What you said a while back — that you really can not tell people where they can and can not go — is more important than what you may believe. As far as I'm concerned, people are going to start disappearing on you right and left, and I'm sure a lot of them will not even consult with you before they do so."

"And you think you're doing me a favor by telling me all this now?" Josef asked.

"Not quite, Commander. What I really wanted to do was determine how and when you were planning to disseminate the news of our recent visitors. I think so far you have handled the situation well: no panic here on Refander, and we actually made it through the first round of adversity. But, now you have to tell the people, everyone, about what's going down. They deserve to know — they have a right to prepare themselves for when more of them come. I admit that, if what you all have pieced together about this race is true, we may stand no chance of defeating them. But at least if the people of Refander know about this, they can at least prepare themselves for the time when the going gets rough; who knows, many of them may even wish to do whatever they can to help the government defend itself against these things. I think you can see why, morally speaking, it's just not right to keep everyone in ignorance over this whole matter."

This time it was Josef's turn to take a slow, long drink from his mug. Looking up from the table, he noticed Jase's quiet, attentive expression. He then refocused his concentration back toward Nicholiason.

"Quite impressive, Jakob. It's obvious you've given this whole thing a lot of thought. But I think the real battle will be won or lost above the skies of Refander, not on its surface."

The farmer's eyes grew large. "You mean you are willing to pursue these secretive operations? Don't you see any advantage to letting others know about what's going on?"

Josef shrugged. "Hate to say it, but it doesn't really matter if they do or not. It's not like we can just go hop over to the nearest New World planet for help, you know. Besides, for all we know, there may be no other New World planets left to run to if what happened to Earth and almost happened here is more widespread than we believe.

"Basically, what we have to do is figure out some way of preventing these alien beings from ever reaching the surface of Refander again. Ultimately, I do propose to inform everyone about what has happened before asking them to blindly support whatever plan we develop. But there's a proper time and a place for everything. For example, this epidemic in these farmlands — it's important to ensure we have that under control before we release news that's likely to cause a widespread panic."

Nicholiason nodded his head in an almost approving manner. "So I judged you wrong. You were planning to inform everyone after all, right?"

"Quite true. Let's just say that you forced my hand a little early today. Up to now, I've discussed my plans with no one, which explains why you were uninformed about this. You have, however, alerted me to something I should have been aware of — that people have been planning to explore Refander. Regardless of how we ultimately plan on responding to another invasion attempt, my goal is to leave the ultimate decision to the people. And whatever we do, we must have a strong, united front."

"You surprise me by being so open now, Commander," Nicholiason stated.

Josef chuckled hesitantly. "I did it for the same reason you revealed your secret to me earlier."

In the thoughtful silence that followed, Jase drained the mug of beer that sat before him. Then, clearing his throat, he said, "Josef, I hate to break in, but we have to be back before dark and I still have to give them their vaccination shots."

"That's quite all right," Nicholiason blurted. "I think the Commander and I have come to a good end of a successful talk. You ready, Pietra?"

Nicholiason's wife nodded her head, and as Jase once again reached into his medical sack, Josef let his attention gradually return to the ornaments of the farmer's home. The pride that Nicholiason took in his carving was not too uncommon on Refander; rather, it was the skill which the man obviously had that was outstanding.

Josef was really beginning to admire the farmer. Here was a man who knew practically as much as he did about the political, economic, and social features of Refander and yet had remained quiet about it all until now. That made Josef think: Nicholiason had a virtually unbiased opinion of Refander and the way the world had been run. If there was anybody whose advice could be heavily depended on, it was his.

Josef continued to marvel at the interior of Nicholiason's home until it was time to leave. There were many handshakes, and after a promise that they would keep in touch, Josef Riverst and Jakob Nicholiason parted company.

Several minutes later, Jase and Josef were in the shuttle again, cruising at a moderate speed toward the Base Station.

"I know there's no need for me to say it, but that sure was a surprise visit," Jase said, glancing at the Commander.

Josef just nodded slowly.

"Who do you think the source is?" the doctor asked.

"Now that's a good question. I think I can pretty much rule out Paula. Which leaves Rielick and Dietrich or someone immediately below them.

"As I think about it, though, I guess it really does not matter. As far as this whole affair is concerned, Nicholiason had the potential to severely disrupt the orderly flow of things on Refander. The fact that he kept his mouth shut despite everything he knew makes me really respect him."

"I agree there, but why did his source go so far as to tell him about our alien friends in the first place? If I were in that person's shoes, I would have said, 'Sorry, Jakob, not this time.'"

"I thought about that, too," Josef answered. "And I think it keeps coming down to one thing. Sorian. You knew him as well as I. And if we're to believe what Jakob said about Sorian arranging the whole deal, well, then I'm not too surprised about our friend Jakob learning of all this. Sorian would not have picked idiots to do this. He probably knew he needed someone he could trust — almost as much as he could trust himself. I'm beginning to think that Jakob is one such person."

"And whoever is telling Jakob all his information is another?"

The Commander nodded again.

"I'd go for Rielick, then," Jase said. "He's always been a quiet type, you know. Almost as if he's always thinking."

After that the two men rode in comparative silence. They arrived at the Base Station shortly before the onset of Refander's brief night. Jase guided the shuttle slowly into the Port. Both men climbed out and leisurely walked to the Main Transport Hall. Josef noticed how tired they appeared at that moment. He was mildly surprised at all the work they had done in so short a period.

Upon reaching the Hall, they entered one of the Government Dome Cars that had been reserved for them and Josef began driving toward the far side of the Dome. He dropped Jase off first, thanking him again for a job well done, before heading to his own apartment complex.

Several minutes later, soft quiet music emanated from the digital disc console in the Commander's room. Josef Riverst sat on his bed and ran his hands through the hair on the side of his head. He took in several deep breaths, exhaling slowly. In an almost half-conscious state, he leaned back, allowing his head to hit the pillow. Almost instantly, he began to experience his first period of sleep in almost two days.

The Commander was to discover, however, that Jakob Nicholiason's words were more truthful than Josef, or even Jakob himself, had imagined. About an hour before he usually awoke to prepare for work, Josef's Comm began to ring. At first, the ringing became a part of his dream, subtly working its way into his mind's fabrication as the voice of birds, Earth animals which he had read about but which had no true counterpart on Refander. Slowly, the vision of a winged animal transformed itself into a living telephone which hovered errantly around his head. The oddity of such a situation brought Josef to a state of semiconsciousness, and he recognized the ringing sound for what it really was. His hand shot out from the plush blankets and stabbed at the Comm panel on the wall above the bed.

"This is Riverst."

It was Rielick. He was talking quite rapidly and Josef was not sure he caught everything his Second in Command was saying. However, what he did catch was enough: two of Refander's off-planet scout ships were missing. No warning signals had been received from the missing pilots, and all communication attempts had been useless.

Josef, now fully awake, gave orders for a search party to be organized. After a few more words, the conversation was over and, though it was still early, Josef began making preparations for the day.

He allowed himself a leisurely breakfast, but still arrived at his office in the Government Building 20 minutes earlier than usual. Baronhart Dietrich was already there.

"Morning, Josef," Baronhart uttered when Riverst was close enough to hear.

"I take it you got some news for me?"

Baronhart nodded. "Yeah, I do. Rielick already got a hold of you? Good. Should we go in?"

Josef grunted an answer and opened the door to his office. Once they were inside, Baronhart spoke up quickly.

"We've been aware of the missing scout ships for a little over five hours, now. Both were last reported on the outer fringes of our patrol area — in the K and L Sector Series to be exact. Taylor and Roberts are the pilots; both have appreciable years of experience. The fact that they've disappeared from adjacent Sectors essentially rules out coincidence. Following your orders, a five ship search party was outfitted. We drew some ships from duty in the M and N Sector Series to do that. They've been reporting in every thirty minutes."

"Anything yet?"

Baronhart shook his head. "The K and L Sectors are a long ways out — over six days using maximum travel speeds. There's a lot of space in between here and there, and those missing ships could turn up anywhere."

"I think we better call our other scout ships in closer to Refander. I've a feeling —."

Riverst stopped, noticing the blinking lights of an incoming call on the Comm panel. He hit the panel with a flick of his wrist, his eyes returning to look at Baronhart.

"Yes?"

Rielick's voice blared forth: "Commander, we've found them. Both ships have been physically disabled. The search party requests permission to look for survivors. Reports also indicate the presence of an unidentified squadron of ships, not yet within critical proximity but approaching the outer reaches of the L Sector Series."

Riverst contemplated for a few moments, his mind anxiously scanning over all the details that had just been given him. At length, he said, "Lieutenant, permission granted to board scout ships, but make it pronto. Also, instruct them to attempt to identify approaching ships without putting themselves in harm's way. And make sure they understand that — they're not to endanger themselves. One more thing, inform all other scout ships that patrol duty is to be restricted to the B Sector Series only, effective immediately. They are to start evacuation of all outer Sectors now."

As Rielick acknowledged his receipt of the message, Riverst threw a questioning stare at Baronhart. The Weapons Official, as if he recognized the cue, said, "We have a small, but reliable battle fleet, Josef. Captain Gloid can have all of the ships outfitted and airborne within twenty minutes of your command."

Riverst grunted again, slowly nodding his head. "I think we better head over to the Data Terminal Building and find out what's happening out there."

Baronhart followed him out the door, and both men quickly boarded the nearest elevator. Upon reaching the ground level they initiated a brisk walk towards the adjacent building.

As they approached the main entrance, Dietrich walked past Riverst and opened the door. The tense silence between them was suddenly broken by the sounds of conversing scientists and computer printers. The two men entered the Flight Control Room and Riverst let his eyes fleetingly search through the confusing array of paper, people, and machinery until they found Rielick. The Lieutenant was at the communications panel and was apparently listening to another incoming message from space. Riverst hurried over to him, arriving just as Rielick handed the headphones back to the Sergeant from whom he had borrowed them.

"Ah, Commander. We just got the reports in on the scout ships. Both pilots died an instantaneous death. None of their defensive weaponry had been activated — looks like it was a sudden attack at high speeds. Our guys probably never saw what hit them."

The officer with the headset turned from the communications panel to face the three men. "Commander, the search party has attained a positive identification on the —." He stopped as Riverst raised his hand.

"Tell them to get the hell out of there, Sergeant. Their mission is complete."

Riverst hardly heard the Sergeant's acknowledging reply. Everyone, including himself, had seen through his euphemistic order to "identify" the approaching ships. Practically speaking, there was only one fleet of vessels that the Refander scout ships could positively identify. And the fact that they had done just that gave Josef a very sick feeling.

Riverst saw the women and men around him in the room expectantly staring at him. He came out of his reverie and turned to face Baronhart, "Have every available defense ship armed and ready for takeoff three days from now."

Baronhart looked somewhat surprised. "You know what they want, don't you — you know why they're coming here?" he asked incredulously.

"I know," Josef said quietly. "They're at least four days out, assuming they take a direct approach. The least we can do is carefully plan our strategy."

"That's not what I meant," Dietrich argued. "Why don't we launch our defensive posture now? Once everyone on Refander finds out what's going on, they won't elect to sit by and wait. The least we can do is give them a valiant fight."

Rielick made a motion with his arms, but before he could speak, he was suddenly thrown off balance and his body bounced off the Comm panel in front of him. Josef was equally surprised to find himself and Baronhart lurch forward as a deep rumble echoed throughout the building. Out of the corner of his eye Josef saw a huge, splintering crack manifest itself in the wall behind the panel. The sound of broken glass meandered through his ears and then all was abruptly still. The noise of restarting machinery and computers made a conversation with itself for several moments before the Sergeant removed the headset from over his ears and announced: "Earthquake. The guys downstairs say this one's like all the rest — no known origin or cause, and it did not appear to have been limited to any one fault line."

Josef was not the only one to breath a sigh of relief as he shakily raised himself from the floor. Momentary visions of a surprise attack faded from his mind.

"We've certainly had enough of those lately," Rielick said, straightening his clothes.

Slowly, the sound of human voices joined the constant chatter of the computers as people got back to work. Josef, however, had the feeling that everyone was periodically glancing over at him. Never before had the feeling of superiority and responsibility been so strong in him. To many of the women and men in the room, the news of a threat to Refander was unexpected. His recent conservation with the red-headed farmer now took on a stark and chilling irony.

Five or six people still stood around him, waiting for his next move. He glanced at the large break in the wall behind the panel, and then down to the panel itself, where a red light began blinking on and off. "Sergeant," he said, and pointed to the panel. He idly watched the officer place the headset over his head as he said, "Baronhart, find Paula for me.

Tell her to meet me in my office in two hours. I expect you and you, too, Lieutenant, to be there."

"Okay, Commander," Dietrich said, this time not dissenting. As the weapons official ambled off, Josef turned to the other men and women around him and blurted, "In the meantime, I expect everyone else to be doing their job."

When only Rielick was left standing next to him, Josef turned to the Sergeant, who had once again removed his headset. "Yes?"

"That was the search party, Commander. They have begun their return and report that the approaching fleet is still headed toward Refander. E.T.A. for target ships is sixty-one hours and twenty-five minutes."

"Very well, Sergeant. Keep me informed on what's happening. I will be in my office."

"Yes, Commander."

"Lieutenant, in two hours?"

"I'll be there," Rielick replied.

Josef nodded approvingly at Rielick, then turned and left. His mind was heavy with thoughts. In 61 hours the end of Refander would begin; and, as Jakob Nicholiason had suggested, he owed it to the people of Refander to tell them what was going on. He would have to begin working on his speech right away. The people of Refander would want to defend their planet with all they had. Combat shuttles would have to leave at least 50 hours from now. It would be a futile battle, Josef knew, but then no one on Refander was a coward.

If there was ever any doubt in Josef Riverst's mind that he had guessed wrong about what was to happen, they were erased when he got back to his office: the Comm panel message light was indicating yet another incoming message. Sergeant Peters, at the main communications desk, was on the other end of the line. Josef listened as the Sergeant spelled it out to him: several of the alien ships had changed course and had begun pursuing the five ship search party. At present, the search party was under attack.

"Keep me posted," Josef ordered.

Five minutes later, the Sergeant called back. "Commander, all five ships have been targeted by the invading fleet! We're receiving no signals from them at all. The entire fleet has returned to its original course. E.T.A., sixty hours, fifty-seven minutes."

Josef quietly acknowledged the message. He then leaned back in his chair. A sickly feeling invaded his stomach and he felt himself losing control of his bladder. Anyone would pay much to see into the future; it suddenly seemed cruelly unfair that one could not sell his future to someone else when he came across his own inevitable death.

Part 2. Liraah

True winter appeared in a fury two days after Jase left to return to the Base Station Dome. The snow, though unusually late, began piling up outside the entrance to the cave. On the night of the second day, Liraah once again brought up the subject of travelling to the higher elevations of the northeastern Pascalians. Ian had questioned her thoroughly, but had not been able to determine why she was so intent on making the trip nor how she had obtained the notion that it had to be done. In the end, Ian had conceded to going with Liraah even though in the back of his mind he was still asking many questions.

They spent the third day preparing for their journey. Ian slipped on his snowshoes, which he had left at the cave only a scant year before, and trekked down to the timberline where he cut some wood to make a pair of snowshoes for Liraah. Snowshoes had been something Jase had overlooked when he had given them supplies. However, Jase had left them a supply of twine and a couple of hand axes; and with the leather straps from an article of clothing Jase had given him, Ian was sure he could fabricate some makeshift snowshoes. It did not take him long to get the wood cut, and he spent most of the rest of the day in the cave. By late afternoon, the snowshoes were finished. Because he'd been rushed, he knew the quality of his work would not endure more than a couple of Refander winters. It was his hope that the shoes would not even be needed at all.

Liraah had watched in concerned fascination as he fastened the snowshoes to her feet and showed her how much easier it was to walk in deep snow with them. They spent the latter part of the day getting the rest of the supplies packed. Ian was grateful now of Jase's thoughtfulness. Without the doctor's gift of supplies, Ian would have been forced to tell Liraah there was no way he would go into the northeastern Pascalians in mid-winter. If he had to make a similar trip by himself, or if there had been an emergency necessitating the execution of such a trip, it would have been a different matter. However, he would never have agreed to accept the broadened responsibility of making this journey with anyone other than himself without at least having the proper supplies.

By combining the food Jase had left with Liraah's own accumulation of edible goods, they were able to come up with a well-rounded food supply for the trip. By the time everything was loaded the backpacks had become somewhat heavy, but this did not cause Ian much worry as he was sure that Liraah's experience in this mountainous country had made her hardy enough to be able to do almost anything that he himself could do.

On the morning of the fourth day the snow stopped falling and they left the cave. The two snow leopards accompanied them, but only superficially; the animals spent most of the time ranging far and wide, only periodically returning to find Ian and Liraah's trail. Ian could not keep from admiring the sleek and graceful way the silver-gray cats moved about in the snow.

However, it was Liraah who occupied most of his attention. At times, she behaved as if in a trance, seeming almost to be in constant silent communication with the two large animals. Yet, when he was alone with her, she became more talkative. She had been really excited about wearing some of the clothes Jase had given her: insulated pants and boots, shirts, and a thick coat. Ian could understand why, knowing that this was the first time in many years that she had worn clothes not made by herself.

They had travelled for most of the day, finding the going difficult at times because of the snow. With the onset of evening, they pitched the techno-tent Jase had given them. Ian had been hesitant at first about even bringing the tent along. Regular tents were something most people of Refander never used, for they only invited surprise attacks by the darix. In the upper Pascalians, however, there were no trees to rest in at night. A techno-tent, consisting of an inner, insulated living space and an outer shell that armed itself with a sub-lethal dose of contact-induced electrical charges, was modern man's invention to keep in touch with the outdoors. The tent came equipped with a tracking device that detected approaching objects and triggered the outer shell to a "state of readiness," according to the directions.

The techno-tents had been the answer to many problems on Refander, but when Ian got inside it, he could feel claustrophobic sensations begin to stir within himself. After he and Liraah had gotten into the tent there was no room left for even just one of the leopards. For this reason, Ian deactivated the tracking device so that no harm would come to the animals. His actions had been unnecessary, however, as the cats had already taken an immediate dislike of the tent and regarded it with extreme wariness.

Ian had no way of knowing if the cats stayed nearby, and he knew that without their presence darix could quite possibly approach the tent unnoticed. These thoughts were still in his mind when, as he finally crawled into his sleeping bag, he laid his large knife within easy grasping range.

It was then that Liraah casually told him that he somehow appeared different to her. At first, Ian had felt the statement to be somewhat ironic because he felt the same way towards her. However, everything they had done in the past several days had precluded much talk about recent events at the Base Station and in the Asinarian Mountains.

He began talking, hesitantly at first, finding it hard to break down the mental barriers he had built to keep from thinking about the experience. Once he got started, however, he discovered it took his mind off thoughts of the threat of darix, and he began to relive the experience more freely, stopping only when Liraah asked that something be explained in more detail.

Over an hour later, as they lay side by side in silence, Ian had an opportunity to really think about what had happened. After having heard himself tell of the ordeal, he found it hard to believe that all of it had actually happened. At length, she asked, "Will they return?"

"I'm afraid that they will, Liraah. I'm sure they are capable of breaking through our defenses. The only reason why they failed the last time is that only one of them actually made it to the surface. But I'm sure they will be back. The power that they have is tremendous. I still remember when it...when it entered my mind when I was in that cave. It's a scary feeling."

Ian wondered if she understood everything he had said. Talking to someone in the dark was not always easy. However, with Liraah it was even more difficult because she always seemed to mull over anything that was spoken to her.

In the end, he assumed she had grasped the gist of his answer because she suddenly said, "You will go when they return?" There was a touch of cool concern in her voice which bothered Ian. She had asked the question in a somewhat mystical manner, reminiscent of her behavior when she appeared to be in communion with the leopards. Nevertheless, Ian did not have to give the question much thought. He turned his head in her direction, more out of habit than anything else. His eyes sought out her face in the darkness.

"No. There is nothing I would be able to do. Josef Riverst was able to buy some time, but he won't know what to do with it. Refander's defenses are just too meager to be able to withstand any outright attack, especially an attack from a race of beings whose powers and capabilities we probably never will be able to fully understand.

"Besides, this is where I like to be. I, like you, am more at home in these mountains than anywhere else. I got a feeling that in the not too distant future, Refander will undergo a drastic change and there won't be much any one can do to prevent it. I'd rather be here when that change comes."

Again, Ian sat in silent anticipation, wondering if Liraah had comprehended everything he'd said. Only this time, he never was offered a clue. Ian waited several minutes more, the silence in the tent beginning to bring back thoughts of approaching darix. He knew that Liraah was still awake and, slowly, he fathomed that she had understood everything. He had learned that it was in her nature to ask about those things which confused her.

He thought back to when he had kissed her, just before leaving on his trip to the Base Station. She had accepted it, and almost seemed to know why he had done it. Which only confused Ian more because even as he lay next to her now, he was still not sure of what his feelings had actually been trying to tell him on that day. If he ever had been physically attracted to her, and he guessed that such had been the case at one time, he knew that he was not now. The reasons for his change of feelings toward her eluded him, only confusing matters worse.

He knew it was nothing physical. Liraah was actually a very attractive woman. Her firm, medium-sized breasts and dark, shiny hair gave her a noticeable bloom. No, it was something else — something in the way she unconsciously made him think about her. He remembered the day he had returned to her cave with Jase — that had been when he had first noticed that his attitudes toward her had shifted. She had somehow become a different person, worthy of more respect than Ian had given her previously. His subconsciousness had somehow silently told him that Liraah was not so much a woman to be loved as she was a woman to be understood; a woman to be followed. The reason why this was so, Ian did not know. It just was.

It was with these troubled thoughts that he slowly drifted off to sleep. At some time during the night he awoke to what sounded like the hissing or snarling of one of the snow leopards. He lay awake for several minutes, but did not hear it again. Consequently, he turned over in the sleeping bag — which was almost as warm as his sparth sleeping bag that still lay in his cabin — and resumed his dreams.

The next morning, Ian was awakened by Liraah. Outside he could hear a slight wind blowing. Some of the sunlight was able to make its way through the tent's synthetic material, and in the dim light Ian could see her face. He smiled at her and, momentarily, she returned his grin.

Then she spoke: "We must go."

Ian nodded his head, suddenly beginning to feel captivated by Liraah; no longer questioning the things she wanted to do. They breakfasted well, eating dried meat and several fruits of the Refander hardwoods.

As they began packing their belongings, Ian asked her what she thought of the sleeping bag.

"It is warm," Liraah had simply answered.

They took the tent down last, folding it somewhat quickly in spite of the cold temperature. They continued heading northeast, Ian following the trail Liraah unerringly made. Her motivation continued to puzzle him, and he was reasonably sure she had not been in this part of the Pascalians before.

They had camped at the base of a steep slope leading up to a ridge. Now, as they were about to reach the top of the slope, a quick flash of movement caught Ian's eye. From underneath a small shrub some 15 meters to his right, a short-legged, white-furred animal burst forth. The animal's fur was long, like that of a sparth, but was more of a silky nature; and it had no discernable tail. At first, Ian could not identify the animal, but then he abruptly realized that this must have been the same species on which the first snow leopard he had seen — the one which had led him to Liraah's cave — had been feeding.

As if to erase any doubt that may have still been in his mind, Ian instantly found the reason for the animal's sudden burst from cover: one of the leopards was chasing it up the hill. The white-furred animal and Ian reached the top of the ridge almost at the same time. The chase was beginning to interest him because it appeared the leopard would not be able to keep pace with its prey. However, just as the animal reached the ridge top and began putting on extra speed, the second of the two leopards leaped up from a rock-steady crouching position it had been holding and intercepted the animal with a quick swipe of its huge and powerful paw and, less than a second later, a ferocious snap of the jaws. The first snow leopard arrived at the site of the kill while the second leopard began tearing into the carcass. The large cats sat on their haunches — their typical feeding position so Ian had observed — and began to feed.

Liraah arrived at his side while he was still marvelling at what he had witnessed. Though the darix might pursue prey in a cooperative fashion, they never used a drive-the-prey-to-the-ambush technique that the leopards had just employed. This behavior had to be, Ian thought, one of the keys to the leopards' success on Refander. Moreover, he guessed that the animal they had killed was more common than he originally thought because it was undoubtedly one of the few sources of prey for the other snow leopards which more than likely were living at these higher altitudes.

Ian observed the snow leopards for a few seconds more. From his observations of over a year ago, he knew that the leopards were characteristically slow eaters. It would be a while before they completely finished off the last of their freshly killed prey.

He turned to Liraah, expecting to find her ready to forge ahead once more, but instead he found her eyes fixed to the ground to her left. He followed her gaze downward until he, too, saw it. In an instant, he remembered the snarling of the snow leopards the night before. That had probably been no illusion, and he now had a good idea of what had caused it. Not more than two steps away from where Liraah stood there were four sets of paw prints scattered in the snow; and each of them bore the signature of a darix.

Ian quickly glanced up at Liraah, only to see her already looking at him. He had expected to see anxiety, or at least a little indecisiveness in her eyes, but instead a steel-blue determination seemed to emanate from her expression.

Ian shook his head. "Liraah, it is dangerous to continue. I think they've already set their minds on pursuing us. Last night the leopards —."

"We will go on." she said, interrupting him.

It was not an order; nor was it a command. Rather, it had been a statement, like any other. Ian pensively considered her choice, weighing the chances and the alternatives. The snowy silence of the Pascalians swept over him, and for a moment he was tempted to continue his argument against Liraah's plans. However, the sounds of bones cracking sharply drew his attention to the snow leopards, both of which were still feeding off of their prey. Would they be able to offer the protection he and Liraah needed? Certainly, they had provided Liraah with similar protection all these years, but there were only two leopards; and from what the tracks to Liraah's left indicated, there were at least four darix.

Ian's hand instinctively felt for his knife. It was still there, sheathed underneath his thick sparth overcoat. Memories of fighting off darix with that deadly weapon flashed erratically through his mind. He knew he could do it again, if necessary, but he did not look forward to it. Yet, in an eerie sense, he enjoyed fighting the darix with his knife, arrows, and wit. It was what separated him from everyone else on Refander; he lived with the darix, matching the dark animals' cold sagacity with a cunning wisdom of his own.

Yes, it separated him from everyone else — everyone except Liraah, who had managed to do the same, only with the aid of snow leopards. He turned his attention back to Liraah. After several additional moments of indecisiveness, he nodded at her to continue.

After all, he mused, four darix probably did not pose that great a threat.

They continued higher into the Pascalians, reaching one of the range's highest elevations by mid-day. The Pascalians were, for the most part, a huge yet somewhat subtle mountain range, and it was this characteristically gently sloping nature that made them more susceptible to climbing by humans than ranges of more violent origins. However, the northwestern and easternmost faces of the Pascalians, which were exposed to the Tartan River and to the Vernonslaw Ocean, were much steeper, and Ian and Liraah found they had to choose their steps with greater care.

Ian knew from maps he had studied that the Tartan River was less than 50 kilometers distant, and he began wondering if Liraah was going to attempt to cross it. He was also not sure if the leopards would follow them into the steep canyon. Eventually, he was forced to ask, "How much farther do you think we'll be going?"

Liraah, hardly checking her stride, glanced at him briefly. "They will know," she answered at length.

Which did not do much to answer Ian's questions. *They*, of course, meant the leopards. Ian could still not understand how the leopards knew so much; how they knew Liraah had to travel to this part of the Pascalians; how they would know when it was time to stop travelling.

Or, Ian surmised, maybe they really did not know. Maybe Liraah was just hard pressed to find a better descriptive word than "know." Would it be possible, he asked himself, that the leopards were merely *sensing* things, and that Liraah was actually interpreting the leopards' behavior? He tried to recall the passages that Sammy Lassiter had written about the leopards and his grandfather's research. But the mystery behind the chain of events which had led him to this spot remained.

"Do you think it's close," Ian queried, hoping for anything. Only about two hours of daylight remained, and he wanted to start making plans for the next day.

"Yes."

Ian remained silent, pondering over Liraah's unexpected yet sudden certainty that their destination was near. Then he began to scan the horizon. Out along the not too distant landscape, he could see some rock outcrops that jutted forth conspicuously from under the deep snow cover.

As they neared the geological formation, Ian became aware of the serenity of the area, and of the silence that seemed to be magnified by the view. It was then that he abruptly halted his forward progress, his ears registering the sound of approaching animals. Ian almost had to smile to himself as he realized Liraah had come to a halt at the exact same instant as he. Together, Ian thought, Liraah and himself probably represented the two people on Refander most adapted to the wilds of the planet. Most men and women would not have detected the sounds he and Liraah had heard almost thirty seconds ago.

Behind them, over a huge mound of snow, the silvery figures of the snow leopards appeared. Outlined against the sunlight, the leopards held their pose for only an instant before descending the slope to join Ian and Liraah.

Ian playfully petted the head of one of the cats as he began walking forward once again, but his left arm was suddenly grasped by Liraah.

"No!"

Ian wheeled around, only to discover Liraah staring at him, her eyes large and excited. He looked from her to the leopards and then back to her again. And then he felt it, too. Whether or not it was because her hand was still tightly clasped to his arm, he suddenly knew what was happening.

As he eased out of her grasp and began shucking his backpack, the two leopards surrounded him and Liraah and began opening their mouths and drawing their lips back. Primal expressions of snarling and hissing issued forth from the leopards as they became increasingly agitated. Ian's hand darted deftly into his coat and he withdrew the knife which, like the ancient hawks of Earth, had been roosting there, awaiting action.

Up on the same mound of snow the leopards had occupied earlier, as if it had suddenly sprouted from a seed, there appeared a darix. It was a lanky animal, but its metallic fur and shimmering orange eyes somehow told Ian that this darix was wiser than most. It spat what most surely was a nasty challenge to the two leopards.

Then, like a shattered dream, it was gone. Ian, remembering the outcrops he had just seen, turned back around, his mind racing over the odds of trying to make it there. But those thoughts were brutally pushed from his mind by the sight of three additional darix. Strung out in a line with more than forty meters between each animal, they were approaching at a slow, calculated rate.

Ian silently admired these black predators: they had very neatly cut Liraah and himself off from the nearest site at which they could have mounted a sound defensive stand. As it was, he, Liraah, and the leopards were stranded at the base of a medium-sized snow drift which overlooked a stretch of about 180 meters of level land. They had evidently entered the hunting territory of a pack of darix, and the darix, responding to an age-old biological stimulus, were doing the only thing they knew how to do in such a situation.

Ian's grip on his knife increased as the darix drew nearer. He took two steps forward, placing himself in front of Liraah, whose weapons had been left at the cave. The snow leopards, their anger completely riled by now, paced swiftly to-and-fro at Ian's side.

The three darix had come closer now, and when they were but 20 meters away, the lead animal broke into a series of leaps which propelled it directly toward Ian. Ian went down to one knee and braced himself, his armored arm already cocked back in striking position. At the same time a volley of harsh snarls issued forth from the leopards at his side. Instead of remaining by him, however, the leopards turned and darted in the opposite direction. Too late, Ian remembered the first darix which had appeared over the mound of snow. As he flung his arm forward and rolled with the onslaught of the attacking darix, Ian could simultaneously hear the sound of clashing fangs as the leopards engaged the first darix which had no doubt attempted to attack Liraah from the rear.

After that, Ian's brain had no time to ponder. Only lightning swift thoughts were all his and Liraah's lives could afford now. The darix he was presently grappling with had deflected the first plunge of his knife with its shoulder, but as it strove to find a vulnerable spot in Ian's defenses, Ian struck again, quickly and deadly. It was two powerfully swift jabs: in and out of the throat, and slicingly up the midsection. The darix bellowed forth a hideous cry of pain, but even before the bright orange of its eyes began to fade Ian heaved the body aside to meet the other two darix.

One of the black beasts rushed directly at him, but the other made a determined rush toward Liraah. With perfect timing, Ian feigned his concentration on the darix before him only to leap aside, at the last possible instant, to fling himself at Liraah's attacker. Later, Ian would realize that what saved Liraah's life at that very instant was the fact that she had used her own backpack as a shield against the vicious teeth and claws that sought to gore her. The darix, momentarily frustrated by its victim's protective reaction, allowed its guard to fall. Ian took two quick stabs, in and out at the base of the skull, and a vehement, forceful plunge into the animal's side; the steel of his arm wreaked havoc everywhere it struck. The black Refander nightmare struggled to retain its balance, but only managed to utter a stifled howl of anguish as its nervous system failed to respond and its innards rushed out onto the snow.

Saving Liraah's life did not come without a price, however, and before Ian could turn to face the last darix, a piercing pain raced up his left side as he felt several dagger-like teeth sink their way into his left leg. Like a snapped twig, Ian crumpled to the ground, flinging errantly with his knife at his dark oppressor. In an instant the darix gained full advantage and lunged itself at Ian's throat. Liraah's cry, somehow as loud as that of one of the darix, made its way to Ian's ears. And then Ian Torrden saw what he had so wished to see. As he tried to gather the strength to make one last swipe at the snarling, orange-red jaws which bore down upon him, and as he realized that this would be one time when he would not be swift enough, the sound of a spitting cough erupted to his right and a silvery-haired bludgeon came forth and struck the darix broadside with a tremendous blow.

Ian's savior, one of Liraah's snow leopards, followed through with its attack and leaped upon the darix it had struck down with its mighty paws. There followed a flurry of gleaming, red-stained teeth and steel-toned, muscular movements that marked the sign of two animals that were expertly fitted for the cold environment of the high Pascalians. The darix was no match for the tremendously powerful jaws of the leopard, and with each crushing bite the latter took, the former suffered injurious fractures within its black body. Thirty seconds later, the darix was a twitching pile of snarls and black-red fur that would soon be prey for whatever animal was adapted to scavenging in Refander's Pascalians.

As Liraah knelt down beside him, Ian continued to marvel at the immense power the snow leopard had shown. Then he let his gaze wander to where the other leopard was standing weakly in the snow, beside the largest darix Ian had ever seen. With a quick look, Ian could tell that this leopard was not going to live much longer. It was favoring what appeared to be a broken left foreleg, and over a dozen jagged gashes and wounds scarred its body a bright scarlet red. The multitude and severity of these wounds, although tolerable on Earth, were like a death sentence for leopards on Refander, where the snow leopard was still trying to adapt to the diseases carried by the darix.

Liraah and the other snow leopard slowly moved toward the wounded animal and together, the three of them participated in what Ian guessed to be a silent farewell. Liraah put her arms around the once beautiful and majestic animal only to reluctantly let go 15 seconds later.

The wounded leopard, still able to somehow move with the dignity and aloofness it had always possessed, turned and limped away from the scene of the recent battle. After a moment's hesitation, its healthy companion followed. Liraah, still on her knees, watched them for a full five minutes until they were no longer visible. When she returned to Ian, he saw for the first time that she had been crying.

"I'm sorry, Liraah."

She threw a quick glance of understanding at him, but offered no more than that. She then swung her attention to where the darix had bit him and he directed her to help him to the backpack. She removed his old flask of salve and applied this liberally to the wound which was still bleeding and throbbing painfully in the cold weather. When this chore was done, Ian struggled to his feet and they re-hoisted their backpacks. Ian re-sheathed his knife and together they made their way through the snow toward the rock outcrops they had seen over an hour earlier. The going was slow, as Ian found it somewhat painful to travel on his freshly injured leg; but the pain was bearable.

As they neared the rocks, Ian began to speculate on the unique geologic processes which had given rise to the outcrops. At one time, the Tartan River had probably been a large mountain stream with tremendous erosive potential. Over the eons, it had somehow slowly etched its way down through the substance of the northern Pascalians, creating its own steep canyon. The rock formation for which they were headed more or less marked the imaginary line where this canyon began. Beyond the rocks, Ian could see that the slope of the terrain increased precipitously.

They finally reached the geological landmark, and in the fading daylight, Ian and Liraah both took in the magnificent beauty of the vast, spacious, and violently white canyon. The wind had begun to pick up from the northeast, and it spread its chill silently around the two humans.

Liraah pointed to their right, at some large overhanging rocks facing to the southeast. They began making their way to this place when Ian's attention was suddenly drawn to the ground all around them. The canyon had been so immense and beautiful that they had failed to realize the presence of two sets of paw prints in the snow at their feet. Not only were these tracks made by snow leopards, but Ian could see that each set bore a signature that was different from Liraah's snow leopards. Paul Torrden's snow leopards had been able to make it on their own in the harshest environment on Refander! Ian wondered if the stretch of land they had just crossed had marked the boundary line between the territories of the pack of darix and this pair of snow leopards.

As he looked at Liraah he could see a charge of silent gratification spread throughout her face. They marvelled at this discovery only slightly longer before crawling into the cavity produced by the overhanging rocks.

Deciding there was not enough space to put up the tent, they simply spread their sleeping bags parallel to one another on one side of the recess. Ian broke out some dry lecki meat and they ravenously ate the spicy sustenance before crawling into the almost instant warmth of the sleeping bags. Ian spread his sparth overcoat over the two of them to provide added shelter. Exhausted from the day's ordeal, they fell to sleep without hardly another word.

It was in the late hours of the short night when Ian was awakened by Liraah getting out of her sleeping bag. As his senses became more alert, he could detect a soft puffing sound and he realized that Liraah's remaining snow leopard must have followed their trail here.

Ian remained in the warmth of his sleeping bag, his eyes open, barely gathering in the ultra-dim lightness of Refander's more distant sun as it climbed its way toward dawn and the inevitable sunrise. As he silently took in the sounds of Liraah's fingers moving coarsely through the leopard's fur, Ian began to sense an uneasiness in the air. Liraah and the leopard had already moved to the far side of the cavity, and as he strained to listen, Ian could almost touch the excitement that surrounded him. He thought to himself: could this be what Liraah felt when she seemed so lost in self-concentration, so far removed from reality?

As if to answer that question, the woman was suddenly at his side. "Ian," she cried, "this is it."

Then she was gone, back to the far side of the recess in the canyon wall. Ian then thought he saw the outline of the leopard as it left the cavity, probably to go hunting, but his attention was quickly drawn back in Liraah's direction by the sound of rocks being pushed and moved around. Then the meaning of her words hit him: they were at their destination — the very place, supposedly, that they had left Liraah's cave almost six days ago to find. How Liraah or the leopard knew that this was so, Ian could not tell. However, he was sure about one thing: his nerves had never been on the edge like this before. There was something in the air that sparked tiny packets of energy with each breath he took.

He glanced again in Liraah's direction and, to his dismay, could no longer see her outline in the dim light. He listened, but there was nothing. Deftly slipping out of his sleeping bag, Ian pulled on his overcoat and grabbed his knife. He moved over to where he had last seen Liraah and in the gloom of the morning he could make out some scratch marks, presumably made by the leopard; some large rocks, which he had undoubtedly just heard Liraah moving; and a large hole in the rear wall. Had the leopard shown her this, or had she found it herself? He guessed he would never know the answer to this question.

Throwing some of his caution to the wind, he began to slowly crawl into the hole. It was a narrow squeeze, but two minutes later he suddenly found himself tumbling into a spacious hollow. A rustling sound to his side made him increase his grip on the knife, but Liraah called out his name, preventing any action he might have taken.

"Liraah, how did you —" But he stopped short, overwhelmed by the feelings his nerves were relaying through his body. A feeling of paranoia rose within his inner self and he instantly felt very much oppressed by...by something he could not touch. Or see. He could not put his finger on it, but there was...something, some presence, that was here in this cave with him and Liraah.

He flinched when he heard her voice.

"Ian, I am scared. There is..." Her voice trailed off, seemingly lost.

Ian placed his hands on her shoulders. "You feel it too?"

"There is a power. We must find it."

And then she turned away from him, leaving Ian standing alone. Outside, the sun had climbed above the horizon, and its rays, deflected particle by deflected particle, added a murky dimness to the darkness around them. The meager light allowed Ian to make a vague outline of his surroundings. He moved with careful steps to the nearest wall and let his hands run over the surface. It was rough and sharp in places, smooth in others. This hollow was a natural formation, he guessed, probably formed by water erosion some many eons ago. However, that thought did little to smother the fear he was beginning to have for this place. The feeling of oppression he had experienced earlier continued to increase, and he felt a sudden urge to leave this place, to return to the harshness of the snow-covered mountain tops of the Pascalians.

It was at that moment that a surge of fright impaled him from all sides. Simultaneously, Liraah screamed his name loudly several times, her voice forming a picture of untold horror in Ian's mind. Where there had once been an immense amount of energy in the air, there suddenly appeared a feeling of leakage.

Ian spun around. His legs hardly supported his weight as he staggered to the side of the screaming woman. In the murkiness he could see that her hands were on the wall in front of her, but this only confused him more because he could not determine the cause of her anguished cries.

It was only when he touched her shoulder to calm her that Ian was introduced to the turmoil that beleaguered the woman beside him. An orgasmic rush flowed through him, and as he felt all support go out of his legs, his hand gripped Liraah's shoulder tighter. He did not fall; instead, his body became violently and uncontrollably tense, and he felt a prodigious force drain his muscles of their strength. Oblivion suddenly became a very big word to Ian, and just as his senses began to experience a paralysis of feeling, he somehow wrenched his arm from Liraah's shoulder. Stumbling backward, he fell in a mangled heap of flesh and bones, and he found himself wondering if he would ever be able to regain control of his reflexes.

Liraah continued to scream, but her voice eventually weakened to a whisper. Then it suddenly quit altogether. The light was about as good as it was ever going to get, but Ian would always swear that what happened at that instant was definitely the result of a force acting *upon*, and not from within, Liraah's body. She was brutally pushed back from the wall and, like himself, fell like a stringless marionette, completely incapacitated. It was over an hour before Ian's muscles allowed him to move. He crawled clumsily to Liraah's side, and was bitterly pained by what he saw.

Her eyes still open, her lungs still breathing air, Liraah appeared almost as a whisper, a plume of gentle fog, as she stared back at him. Ian fumbled with his overcoat, finally managing to remove it. He placed it over her and then supported her head in his arms. He leaned against the opposite wall, holding her, talking to her, praying for her.

But as the minutes rolled by, he could somehow sense that what was left of the life energies within her body were slowly dying.

An hour passed.

And another.

A sound.

The snow leopard crawled into the tiny hollow. It approached Liraah and made sounds that only snow leopards can make; and which only Liraah seemed to understand.

Another hour.

And then: Liraah stirred. Ian looked down at her, staring deeply into her eyes. Her lips moved, a whisper. He placed his head closer and she spoke again: "It is done."

Ian turned her words over in his mind and then asked, "What is?"

But she spoke only one more word. She whispered, "Go."

Then her muscles relaxed and Ian could feel the coldness that neared her. Yet, contrary to her wish, he did not go. He stayed with her, hoping that somehow, some way, a miracle would be granted. There was nothing he could do, for he did not understand yet what had happened here in this cavern.

Holding her, Ian was able to tell when death was almost upon her. He lowered his head to her's and gently kissed her. Still barely conscious, Liraah's eyes acknowledged his touch. Five minutes later, her eyes closed for good.

In a state of confusion, Ian stared into the dimly lit darkness ahead of him. He held this position for he knew not how long. He was barely aware of the snow leopard, which had laid at Liraah's side all this time, until the animal rose and gently placed his jaws around Ian's arms.

The leopard slowly brought Ian back to reality. As Ian began to rise, the cat released its grip and stepped back towards the far wall. Ian carefully laid Liraah's body on the floor of the hollow before putting his overcoat on his own cold and aching body. He picked up his knife and cautiously approached the far wall. What he had not seen before, in the excitement, was now readily visible. Liraah, in her search for what she had called the "power," had stumbled across this. Curious, she had probably reached out and touched it. Ian would never forget what it had done to her — and almost had done to him. The energy that had once been so omnipresent before was still near at hand, but it seemed to be...moving away from him now.

He extended his hand toward the object in the wall: a shiny metal plate made of a material Ian had never seen before. His heart was pounding fast when he finally touched it.

However, nothing happened. He let his hand rest there. And waited. The sound of the distant wind brought Liraah's words back to him: "It is done."

"*What* have we done, Liraah?" he asked her, only to begin crying at the silence that answered. He sheathed his knife and moved toward the hole in the opposite wall by which he had entered. Once there, he stopped and glanced toward Liraah. Twice he had kissed her before he had left her side. He wished relentlessly for many more chances to kiss her, but he knew that there would never be another opportunity.

Quietly, he asked the darkness once again, "*What* have we done, Liraah?"

Then, crawling toward the Tartan River canyon, the lone snow leopard following him, Ian left Liraah for the final time.

If he had known what they — he and Liraah — had done, he would never have believed it.

The distortion of the cosmos had once again been set in motion.

Part 3. Many Worlds

In the most primitive time, before time itself even existed, there was no space at all. Matter failed to exist as well, for there was no place in which it could occur. There was no waiting: expectations were inconceivable; observers were nonexistent.

The formation of the primeval gas and dust which was to become the precursor of the first stellar objects, coupled with the instantaneous presence of the omnipotent observer, created both the universe as we know it as well as the first and most important bifurcation that exists to date. At the time of this massive eruption, space itself was created; and an infinite quantity of matter was condensed to an infinite density while taking up the whole realm of space. Time itself had begun.

As the swirling clouds of gas and dust began to contract, time was on its way to completing its first eon. And it had already been proven long ago that the prefix "uni-" does not always mean one.

The universe was the system. It was a wave function representing the superposition of many possibilities. An observation was made, and a bifurcation was born. The remaining possibilities did not become a part of the void, however; rather they became absolute realities the presence of which is almost impossible to detect. Even the omnipotent one, as a result of having made the initial observation, is split into a myriad of mutually equivalent selves, one for each absolute reality.

A pencil is dropped today. The wave function representing the universe points out that the table on which it falls may or may not be there. A bifurcation is born.

A ten solar mass star in a distant galaxy goes supernova, leaving behind a core which is two point five solar masses. The wave function representing the universe points out that the neutron degenerative pressure necessary to support the collapsing core may or may not be present; both a neutron star or a black hole are capable of forming. A bifurcation is born.

At the beginning of time the universe split, producing a cosmic separation of realms. Perpetual splitting on either side of the major bifurcation continued for eons, resulting in a multitude of universes, each separated by the fabric of the wave function.

On a distant binary star, in one of these many universes, there arose a race — the Mandar. Inhabiting a planet called Ekelon, the Mandar grew to become a peaceful and wise race whose knowledge eventually enabled its peoples to colonize

other planets. The scientific historians of Ekelon, however, generation after genera-
tion, were baffled by the mysterious perturbations to which their planet was sub-
jected.

The day arrived when Brisb developed a theory. What if the universe as the
Mandar knew it was not the only one? What if, at the beginning of time, a major
separation of possibilities had occurred? Could it be that some other universe,
except for that initial bifurcation, had paralleled their own universe in its develop-
ment? If this were possible, Brisb theorized, the juxtaposition of two binary star
systems, each in its own universe, would create a localization of instability in the
fabric of the wave function. Were the Mandar, with all their technological capabili-
ties, able to create a device which could overload this gravitational instability? If
done at the right time, Brisb calculated, a local overloading of the gravitational
system could produce fantastic results. When the Lortans threatened, the Mandar's
intellectual interest in Brisb's theory became a life saving desire.

Part 4. Rebirth

"Why does he insist on living all the way out here?"

The quiet drone of the air shuttle's engines filled the silence following these words. Josef Riverst glanced quickly at Lieutenant Kowlper, his newly assigned Second in Command. Lieutenant Sherry Kowlper was a stockily built woman whose sturdy figure, short-cut hair, and sharply defined facial anatomy discouraged anyone from trying to take advantage of her. Josef allowed a brief smile to cross his face.

"You're young, Sherry," he said. "To understand a man like Ian Torrden would require a thorough understanding of the events preceding, surrounding, and immediately following the arrival of the *Stranahan*. It's one thing to read about it in the history tapes and discs, but it is another thing to have actually been old enough to live through and comprehend all that actually happened at that time. For the moment let that suffice as an explanation. After you meet him you can make your own conclusions."

"Perhaps. I should think I will really enjoy meeting him."

Josef smiled a second time. "I think it's only fair to warn you, however, that you should not get your hopes up too high. For a man with as much notoriety as his, he's actually a pretty low key fella." The Commander then let his eyes shift to the third passenger of the shuttle, the pilot. "Why all the silence, Jase? You've hardly said a word since we left the Base Station."

Jase idly touched the controls for a few seconds, not actually changing them. His face showed the lines of an old man who was pushing himself excessively hard to do the tasks that would normally take two men to accomplish. Jase was still regarded as the most learned man in the field of medicine and he always felt obligated to personally administer the majority of medical services which were of significant importance. He glanced at Josef, aware that he had let the Commander's question go unanswered for too long and had thus disclosed his growing uneasiness.

"I've been working for ten days, now, as you yourself have been doing, Josef. Trying to put this planet back together is hard on everyone, no exceptions. One day, though, all of us are going to have to sit back and ask ourselves what actually happened. That question scares me more than the present reality of having hundreds of injured persons to take care of.

"When you think about it, you and I are lucky to still be alive. I wish I could say the same for Lieutenant Rielick and a lot of others. I just hope Ian and Liraah were just as lucky."

"What makes you think they wouldn't be?" Lieutenant Kowlper interjected.

Jase scowled. He felt more like thinking than talking right now, but he knew he could not be rude to his companions.

"Mostly because when I saw them last, I gave Ian a transmitter which he could use to contact me in the event something went wrong. I still have not received any signals from him."

"So, maybe he is okay," Josef offered. "He would probably have had better chances than most of us."

"There's also more than one way to look at this situation, Josef," Jase said, refusing to abandon his fears. He began to slow the shuttle down, as they were approaching the Crane River. "Start looking for a fairly large stream coming in on the east side of the river," he directed his passengers. "His cabin should be along here somewhere."

Ten seconds of silence were followed by Lieutenant Kowlper's exclamation, "Would that be it over there?" Her arm pointed to a large break in the trees through which crystal clear water cascaded luminously down toward the fast-flowing Crane.

"Yeah, that should be the one," Jase said as he adjusted the controls to slow the shuttle down even more. In his nervousness he pushed one of the break levers in too far and the shuttle faltered several times before he made a correction. Ignoring the casual glances of the other two occupants, Jase guided the shuttle towards Ian's cabin, which was located on the north side of the stream. He found himself surprised by the size of Ian's agricultural fields, a facet of this place that he had missed on his first flight over the area the year before.

When the shuttle made contact with the ground the three of them stepped out. Lieutenant Kowlper was immediately fascinated by the fields. "Maybe it's not so bad living up here, after all," she proclaimed. "Why, in one season, he could probably grow enough crops to last him two years."

"And with an occasional sparth, you're well on your way to self-sufficiency," Josef added. "But just remember, it's the darix that make these parts of the country so inhospitable."

"Believe me, Commander, I know. A couple of my friends are not with me today because of those animals."

Jase halfheartedly listened to this conversation before proceeding to the door of Ian's cabin. His main reason for even coming on this trip (he knew that he was more than 14 hours overdue for a good period of sleep) had been to see Liraah. The fact that he had gotten no signal from Ian had disturbed him greatly. As it had been the Commander's idea to check in on Ian, Jase had decided to take advantage of the situation and find out for himself if his fears had any justification. He knew and trusted Ian Torrden more than any other man on Refander; he would not have left Liraah out here in the mountains with anyone else but Ian. In spite of all that, however, his fears would not let his consciousness rest.

He had come to this cabin first more because of a promise to keep a secret than for anything else; proceeding directly to the northern arm of the Pascalians would have meant having to run the risk of explaining away the presence of the snow leopards. Actually, he realized, he hoped Ian had not returned to the cabin because something told him that, barring any difficulties, Ian would have elected to remain in the Pascalians with Liraah for a much longer time. His presence here would only mean...what?

As he knocked on the door of the cabin, the magnitude of his fears began to escalate as his eyes locked on to the dirt path leading to and from the door. The freshly made footprints he observed in the path glaringly spoke of the presence of only one pair of feet. He knocked several more times without getting any answer and almost felt that he had been vindicated when, from behind him, he heard Lieutenant Kowlper cry out, "Oh, that must be him now."

Jase turned around to see a man approaching them along the trail which paralleled the stream. Though still some 50 meters distant, Jase immediately knew the gait and stature of Ian Torrden. As Ian drew closer, Jase recognized the ever present knife swinging smoothly from Ian's left arm while the bodies of five or six lecki were clutched in the grasp of his right hand; evidence of a good morning's work with the trap lines Ian evidently had set up somewhere. When he was within hearing distance, Josef voiced a hello.

Ian eventually came to a stop in front of the Commander.

"Ian, this is Lieutenant Sherry Kowlper, my new Second in Command. Lieutenant, Ian Torrden."

Ian sheathed his knife and briefly shook hands with the woman, at the same time casting a quick glance at Jase. His eyes, however, quickly returned to rest upon Josef as the latter continued talking.

"Thought I'd pay you a visit to see how things were coming along. I'm trying to check in on most of the people living out in the rural areas to make sure the quakes did not do too much damage. Many died back at the Base, as I'm sure you've already guessed.

"Looks like you've had a fine morning — I hear some of these northern lecki are really good eating."

"Thank you for your concern, Commander. I was on my way back from the Pascalians —" and he stole another quick glance at Jase " — when everything happened. I was fortunate enough to have my sparth coat with me — it was slow going in the snow drifts in the mountain valleys. Most of my damage was to my cabin here, but I've got almost all of that taken care of already."

Jase, who had remained by the door, now joined the other three individuals. "Looks like you are going to have a good crop this year, Ian." he said, looking over the three fields which were collectively about one and a half hectares in size. He then let his pleading eyes come to rest on Ian again.

Ian nodded slowly, placing the lecki down at his feet. "Yes, I think it has potential. Maybe you all might want to take a closer look at the fields — most of the plants are native and I just may have some undiscovered strain in there."

Lieutenant Kowlper did not need an invitation and she immediately began approaching the orderly rows of trees. Jase perceived that, although Josef followed her without hesitation, the Commander had nonetheless seen through Ian's ploy.

Ian and Jase made motions to follow but soon came to a stop. Jase waited until the other two were out of earshot before speaking. He continued to stare out across the openness of the fields as he asked, "Liraah?"

"I'm sorry, Jase. She died last winter."

"Was there anything I could have done."

A pause. Then: "No. It was...under very unusual circumstances. That's why I was unable to contact you — I'm still trying to figure out what happened myself."

Jase took his eyes off the fields and looked at Ian. "What do you mean?"

"Right after you left us, she began telling me she had to go higher into the Pascalians. For what, she would not say. At first I thought she wanted to find some of the wild leopards, but I realize now that, at that time, even she did not know what the trip was for. And that's where I begin to lose my understanding of it — although the more I read of Sammy Lassiter's account of the research my grandfather was doing, the more I'm able to comprehend the peripheral events surrounding what finally happened to Liraah and myself.

"Jase, I know you'll think this is quite impossible, but I'm ninety-nine percent sure Liraah had some way of communicating, albeit in a primitive way, with those leopards. According to her, it was the leopards who had told her she had to go into the Pascalians; what's more, she did not lead the way — the leopards did; and the leopards told us — well, Liraah — when we had reached our destination. Standing in your shoes, I can sympathize with any disbelief you might have; but I was there. At first I was skeptical of all that was happening, but now I'm not so sure that it actually wasn't happening the way Liraah said it was."

Ian then described, in great detail, the events leading up to, and surrounding, Liraah's death. Jase was surprised at how well he took Ian's news. The tears which had begun to well up in his eyes slowly dissipated, leaving a dry, lonely feeling of sorrow. When Ian had finished, he asked, "And you never figured out what this metal plate was?"

Ian shook his head. "No. I guess I could have — maybe even should have — stayed longer, but at the time I was not thinking with one hundred percent efficiency. Whatever it is, it's one mystery I do not mind leaving unsolved. If that thing ever gets the power again to do what it did to Liraah — and almost did to me — I know for sure I'm not going near it. That's snow leopard country up there, anyway, Jase. Let that cavern be their secret."

Jase shrugged his shoulders. "Perhaps you're right. I guess there's no harm done in having the two of us know what we know and not be able to come up with any practical explanation. And by the way," and Jase pointed toward Josef and Lieutenant Kowlper, who were walking along the far side of the nearest field, "what came of the last snow leopard that was with you when all this happened. Did it follow you back here?"

"She followed me for five days. It was the last day of winter and I was on the western slope of the northern arm."

"The last day of winter — that's when the big quakes hit," Jase interjected.

Ian nodded his head. "I've never felt anything so powerful before in my life. I must have lost one hundred meters in elevation before I was able to latch onto something to keep me from rolling down the mountainside any further. There were several avalanches, but I was fortunate enough to escape any serious injury. That was the last day I saw the snow leopard. She was with me in the morning, but within a half hour after I started walking, she was gone. She was getting pretty nervous, anyway, because there had been several large tremors during the three days before the big one. I never saw her after that. That evening, as you know, was when everything was turned upside down. Have you figured out what caused it yet? I've read about earthquakes before, when I was growing up at the Base Station, but whatever happened to Refander on that day seemed more powerful than anything I have ever read about."

"I really can not say, Ian. That was just ten days ago and, needless to say, the majority of our equipment was put out of working order for some time. We're just starting to get back on line again."

"At first, I thought we were under attack again," Ian offered. "But when I did not hear any ships passing over, I knew it had to be something else."

"Well, according to Josef, we may not even have to worry about that again."

"Why do you say that? Based on what we know about them I don't think there will be any way we can avoid another confrontation."

"I don't doubt you there, Ian. As a matter of fact, twelve days ago, we had actually sighted more of those strange ships. They had reinforcements and had destroyed two scout ships and a five crew search party. We tracked them in all the way up to the time the big quakes began. Then they disappeared. It was estimated that they would have arrived at Refander by the first day of spring. But we have not seen or heard anything from them since."

"You mean they just disappeared without a trace?" Ian exclaimed.

Jase chuckled. "Looks like you and I have traded fantastic-but-true stories this afternoon."

"Are you sure it is not a trick?"

"Positive. They killed the crew of that search party without mercy — a style they were doubtlessly planning to use on Refander to ensure we offered little resistance. Don't worry, though. Once we get Refander cleaned up, we can shift more personnel to the Data Terminal Building. Maybe then we'll find an answer. There were a lot of casualties, you see. We're still trying to recover from that."

This time Ian was silent and Jase could see that the woodsman was lost in deep thought. He placed his old hand on the young man's shoulder. "Don't worry about it or let it bother you. Just so long as Captain Gloid never has to lead his combat shuttles on another defensive mission, I'll accept any answer the guys at the Base Station come up with. Now, let's have a look at those lecki you caught."

The two men walked over to where the pile of freshly killed meat lay. Ian removed the knife from its sheath on his belt and carried the animals over to the front of his cabin, where he promptly began cleaning them. He worked with a speed and dexterity that Jase could only equal on an operating table. He was busy with his third one when Josef and Lieutenant Kowlper returned.

Jase looked on and smiled as Josef and Lieutenant Kowlper complemented Ian on his agricultural prowess. Ian shyly nodded and continued working on the lecki. The swiftness with which he worked quickly attracted the attention of Riverst and his Second in Command.

Lieutenant Kowlper finally said, "You must really enjoy living out here. Before I met you I had fears for your sanity — but now I have to admit I envy you in a way."

At this the entire group burst out in a laugh, and after a few more lively comments, Commander Riverst announced that he still had other places to visit and offered to drive the shuttle to his next appointment. Everyone slowly followed the trail back to the shuttle. Lieutenant Kowlper climbed up the ladder to the overhead hatch door first, Commander Riverst close behind her.

Jase had just placed his left foot on the ladder when he felt a dull pain cross his right arm.

"Jase!"

He turned to find he was in Ian's grasp.

"Jase!" Ian insistently whispered.

Jase stepped down. "What?"

Ian released his grip. "I've been thinking about what all you just told me. What if Liraah's death and the disappearance of those alien ships were related? I never thought of it before, but that metal plate she found in the cavern could have been built by —."

"Built?" Jase queried.

"Yes, yes. By some other civilization."

Jase began to shake his head but Ian continued.

"Archaeology's a much ignored field on Refander, Jase. Besides, only four or five days separated the two events. Remember the tremors during the days preceding the big quake? Well, this may sound a little disconnected, but this winter, during the eclipse, get out of the Base Station. Look up at the constellations at night. I've got a feeling the stars will be different. You may not see it at first, but look closely. I'm sure something will be different up there."

This time it was Jase's turn to be silent. Then, as the meaning of Ian's words dawned upon him, he nodded his understanding at the younger man. As he climbed the ladder to the hatch door he found that he believed the stars would be slightly different this winter. After all, he could not believe in all that he had seen and read about the snow leopards and not believe in what Ian had just told him. Liraah — he wished he had known her better. She must have been someone special to have been able to see into the world of the snow leopards and their secret.

THE END

Glossary

Asinarians
Mountain range on Refander.

Briedrin
Inhospitable planet in the Lortan solar system. It is the fifth of six planets, and occasionally the Brin-Loki Device is stationed here.

Brin-Loki Warning Instrument
An instrument invented by the Lortans which gives them advance warning of non-Lortan space ships that approach the Lortan system.

Camera Pack
A tiny device used by modern reporters to telecast and record news breaking events. It has a direct link to the optic nerves of the reporter who uses it.

Camera-person
A reporter who has been surgically outfitted with the equipment used to allow his or her eyes serve as the "camera lenses" that record news breaking events. Sammy Lassiter, for example, is a camera-man.

Cettor
The Mandar's official measurement of faster-than-light velocity. Travelling at maximum Cettor speed presents many risks to Mandar ships and their passengers

Comm
Communication network aboard the *Stranahan* and on Refander.

Communicating Translator
Universal speech translator employed by the Mandar and Lortans to allow them to understand the languages spoken by intelligent races in their galaxy.

279

Crane River

A river on Refander.

Darix

A vicious carnivore-like animal native to Refander. They hunt in packs and ruthlessly pursue their prey. They may range over an area exceeding 100 square kilometers. Although nomadic, they have a diagnostic behavior involving the establishment and subsequent defense of hunting territories, especially when territories can be usurped from weaker packs of darix.

Diser

A type of laser invented by the Mandar which results from the intense adjustment and concentration of high radiation source particles. The Mandar employ this weapon on their patrol ships and in their hand weapons.

Earth Wildlife Alliance (E.W.A.)

A worldwide wildlife conservation agency established on earth in the 21st century.

Ekelon

Ekelon is located in the Mandar solar system and is the Mandar people's planet of origin.

Four Rivers

The junction of the Patsteel, Rapibb, and Tartan Rivers on Refander; these three rivers meet and form the Crane River which eventually empties out into the Vernonslaw Ocean.

GAP

Group Against the Pan-government; an underground, anti-government organization that was formed soon after the establishment of the Pan-government.

Hoverplane

A small, maneuverable, and economically efficient aerial transport machine operated on Earth in the 22nd century.

Hyper Leap

The process of achieving temporary hyper space-like travel. Allows generation starships to reach destination planets in 40-60 years.

Information Cube

Data storage and retrieval device used by the Lortans.

Interplanetary Space Flight Commission
A branch of the Pan-government responsible for overseeing the New World Launch Program. It is chaired by two officials appointed by the Thirty-five Consulting Members.

Korlawt
A much-feared four-footed predator native to the planet of Ekelon. It is not unlike the darix in shape, color, and habits.

Lampar
Unit of measurement used by the Lortans. One lampar is equivalent to 1.67 meters.

Lecki
A small, squirrel-like animal native to the forests on Refander. There are many different species of lecki on the planet.

Lortan
Lortans are the beings that originated on the planet, Whertos. They are a supreme, warrior-like race that takes pride in conquering other life forms.

Lower Farmlands
The bottomlands farmed by the colonists on Refander. The farmlands are located west of the Asinarian Mountain range and northwest of the Base Station Dome.

Mandar
The Mandar are the beings who originated on the planet, Ekelon. They represent the supreme culmination of intellect and peaceful existence; they've expanded to many outer worlds, leaving a small, declining population on their native planet, Ekelon.

Medic Cruiser
A large medical class ship constructed by the Mandar.

Micro-vision Film Clip
Short film clips shown in trans-cars for the enjoyment of passengers.

Neural Electro-sensor
An instrument that has been surgically implanted into the cranium of a reporter.

New World Flight/Launch
A program involving generation starships that fly selected indi-

viduals from Earth to predetermined planets that have high prob-
abilities of sustaining human life.

Nightside

A drinking establishment located on Level Ten of the starship,
Stranahan.

Old Alaska Port

A space port on Earth located along the coast of what was once
known as western Alaska.

Pan-government

The world-wide centralized government existing on Earth. It originated circa 2070, and included a governing body called a Triship; a
consulting body consisting of 35 representatives; the International
World Police; the International Space Flight Commission; the Economics and Transport Commission; the Sci-Tech Research Commission; and other lower offices.

Pascalians

A mountain range adjacent to the Vernonslaw Ocean on Refander.

Patsteel River

A river on Refander.

Priority Clearance (P.C.)

A high rate of speed achieved by trans-cars, approaching 400 m.p.h.
Must be requested by special authorization, and all passengers must
wear protective suits.

Ralix

Destroyer vessel piloted by the famed Lortan, Lorn-Tator.

Rapibb River

A river on Refander.

Refander

Destination planet for the 20th New World Launch. It is part of a
binary star system and has a mass 0.87 times that of Earth. The
Refander year lasts but 35 days (14.5 Refander years are the equivalent of one Earth year).

Sector Series

Outer space transportation network established around the planet
of Refander.

Siercurn

The only life-sustaining planet of the Legretti solar system. Originally discovered by the Mandar.

Sparth

A large, herbivorous animal native to Refander. Its fur has high merchantable value.

Stranahan

The generation starship that leaves Earth as the 20th New World Launch.

Surface to ship shuttle

Space craft used to shuttle passengers, crew members, and cargo between the surface of a planet and a generation starship.

Tartan River

A river on Refander.

Tech Crews

The pioneer crews that fly to target destination planets and prepare the planets for subsequent occupation by the passengers that would arrive via the generation star ships under the New World Launch program.

Techno-tent

A camping tent used on alien planets that is capable of repelling many forms of dangerous species indigenous to such planets.

Thirty-five Consulting Members

A branch of the Pan-government on Earth that acts as a check and balance against the operations of the Triship. Its membership consists of 35 representatives from various countries across the globe; these 35 representatives are also responsible for appointing the members of the Triship.

Torrden Enterprises Incorporated (T.E.I.)

A controversial research institution founded in 2051 by Gregory Torrden. It also supports a small privately-operated university.

Torrden Forests

A large, expansive area of forestland on Refander north and east of the Base Station Dome.

Trans-car
A dual-rail mode of transportation used in North America in the 22nd century.

Triship
The governing body of Earth's Pan-government. Its actions are checked by the Thirty-five Consulting Members.

Uprisings
The riots occurring on a global scale in the 22nd century on Earth. The riots are a result of the failed attempt to implement a centrally-controlled world government.

Vahrsta
The Lortan ruling council of the Whertos Warrior Force.

Vahrsta-Hd
The highest ranking member of the Vahrsta.

Vernonslaw Ocean
An ocean located on Refander, adjacent to the Base Station Dome.

Voice Recorder
A portable recording device used by the Lortans to document the details of important meetings.

Whertos
The native planet of the Lortan beings. It is the third of six planets in the Lortan solar system.

Yularra
A magical musical instrument, capable of providing the listener with words, music, and visions.

Other Available
Titles from Lost Coast Press

Fiction

God's Mafia
Alfred Fortino
An ethical and intelligent courtroom drama.
Paper • 240 pages • 6" x 9" • ISBN: 1-882897-09-9 • $23.95

Sepharad: The Embezzled Land
Salamon Eskinazi
A historical novel that follows a family of Sephardic Jews.
Paper • 610 pp. • 5½" x 8½" • ISBN: 1-882897-17-X • $29.95

Time and the Maiden
Matthew R. Piepenburg
A tender love story spanning 70 years and two world wars.
Paper • 248 pp. • 5½" x 8½" • ISBN: 1-882897-15-3 • $15.95

Malmond
Ivan Laszlo
Intrigue and sexual politics in a parallel universe.
Paper • 208 pp. • 5½" x 8½" • ISBN: 1-882897-00-5 • $12.95

The Kid from Custer
Richard Clason
A young cowboy searches for the man who killed his father.
Paper • 208 pp. • 5½" x 8½" • ISBN: 1-882897-05-6 • $12.95

Zalacain the Adventurer
Pio Baroja
Translated from the Spanish by James P. Diendl
A comic novel of the Carlist wars by a 19th Century Spanish novelist, beautifully translated by an American scholar.
Paper • 192 pp, • 5½" x 8½" • ISBN: 1-882897-13-7 • $16.95

History & Philosophy

Olompali: In the Beginning
June Ericson Gardner
A brief history of the Coast Miwoks in Northern California.
Paperback • 64 pages • 6" x 9" • ISBN: 1-882897-02-1 • $7.50

The Spiritual Gyre:
The Recurring Phases of Western History
Richard Sellin
A cyclical view of history for the new millennium.
Paper • 208 pp. • 5½" x 8½" • ISBN: 1-882897-19-6 • $14.00

Memoirs & Travel

Belo Horizonte: Around the World in 80 Years
Richard Abbott
High finance and hijinx on the high seas.
Paper • 248 pp. • 5½" x 8½" • ISBN: 1-882897-01-3 • $14.95

Tonderai: Studying Abroad in Zimbabwe
Perrin Elkind
"A remarkable first book about a young woman's immersion in a foreign culture."
— Kim Chernin, author of *My Life as a Boy*
Paper • 208 pages • 6" x 9" • ISBN: 1-882897-20-X • $16.95

To Live in Paradise
Renee Roosevelt Denis
A delightful travel memoir.
Recommended by *National Geographic Traveler*
Paper • 352 pp. • 5½" x 8½" • ISBN: 1-882897-07-2 • $15.95

Out of Darkness—Ramela's Story
Ramela Martin
Memoirs of a survivor of the Armenian Holocaust.
Casebound • 152 pp • 6" x 9" • ISBN: 1-882897-12-9 • $16.95

Business & Finance

Money & You—A Woman's Financial Guide
Holly Nicholson
How to protect your assets and provide for your future.
Casebound • 160 pp • 6" x 9" • ISBN: 1-882897-14-5 • $24.95

Education

Drama in the Classroom:
Creative Activities for Teachers, Parents and Friends
Polly Erion
Educational fun and games for gradeschool children.
Paper • 192 pages • 8½" x 11" • ISBN: 1-882897-04-8 • $24.95

Barbara and Fred—Grownups Now
Living Fully with Developmental Disabilities
Lotte Moise
An activist mother teaches her daughter and the nation
how to overcome life's barriers.
Paper • 212 pp. • 5½" x 8½" • ISBN: 1-882897-08-0 • $16.95

Dear Substitute Teacher
Margaret Sigel
Restoring discipline and responsibility in the classroom.
Paper • 80 pages • 5½" x 8½" • ISBN: 1-882897-10-2 • $9.95

On Wings Like Eagles
Lamar Dodson
Instilling moral precepts in elementary school children.
Paper • 160 pp. • 5½"x 8½" • ISBN: 1-882897-16-1 • $12.95

Animal Welfare

Greyhound Tales: Stories of Rescue, Compassion and Love
edited by Nora Star
How abused racing dogs are saved and raised.
Paper • 128 pp. • 5½" x 8½" • ISBN: 1-882897-18-8 • $15.95

Drama & Poetry

Trilogy
Allan Carson
Three one-act plays after Irish, Greek and Japanese classics.
Paper • 100 pages • 5½" x 8½" • ISBN: 1-882897-06-4 • $9.95

Conversations with Keith
Adams
Accessible poetry celebrating life.
Paper • 84 pages • 5½" x 8½" • ISBN: 1-882897-11-0 • $9.95

To order books, or to receive a complete catalog
Contact **Lost Coast Press** at
1-800-773-7782 *or* (707) 964-9520
Fax (707) (964-7531
e-mail: lostcoast@cypresshouse.com
http://www.cypresshouse.com